RINGS ON HER FINGERS

RINGS ON
HER FINGERS

Pamela Constance

VANTAGE PRESS
New York

In the interest of protecting the privacy of individuals, whose real identities are not central to the true story told here, certain names and other descriptive details have been altered in several instances.

Copyright © 1991 by Pamela Constance

Published by Vantage Press, Inc.
516 West 34th Street, New York, New York 10001

Manufactured in the United States of America
ISBN: 0-533-09148-9

Library of Congress Catalog Card No.: 90-90169
1234567890

To my father and mother

I wish to acknowledge special thanks to Morgan Grant, my mentor, and express my gratitude to Doris Jean Keller, my friend and mentor

Also, I am grateful for the loving support and patience of my husband, Theodore von Hunnius

Contents

Foreword

The author, Pamela Constance, through the many years I have known her, has been a gifted storyteller who cleverly charms her audience with a patchwork of fact and fiction, weaving her characters through a maze of love and hate, brilliance and stupidity, bringing them from the depths into a realm of spiritual beauty.

This novel, *Rings on Her Fingers*, has been the thread of divine brilliance that has dominated the author's life for several years. Through times of severe mental depression and physical frailty and destruction, Pam has clung to the belief that someday this story would become a reality—a best-seller.

Pam's novel will entertain but it also has something important to tell the reader about life and about surviving the inward battles between love and hate and about finally loving ourselves. Through my observations, life has been a struggle for Pamela, and I have prayed for her through her times of stagnation and rejoiced for her in her revelation that true love, divine love, does create . . . it never destroys.

Doris Jean Keller,
Friend and mentor

[Doris Jean Keller is managing partner of a real estate company and long-time child advocate. She is founder of an Illinois statewide child advocacy organization that helps support children who are abused and neglected and dependent on public policy for their well-being.]

Rings on Her Fingers

Prologue

Thea and Luke were stranded in a small town somewhere in Indiana. They stopped by the only hotel on Main Street and Luke stalked into the bar. Thea followed him. The bartender asked, "What's your pleasure?"

Luke replied, "Well, it's not a drink we want. It's a job for the two of us. We're strangers in town."

"Have you ever tended bar before?"

Luke smiled. "Plenty of times, but she hasn't any experience."

"Okay, I'll take you on at three dollars an hour, and throw her in for free, in return for your rooms here. You get one dinner each at six o'clock in the evening. Take it or leave it."

"We'll take it. Thanks buddy."

Luke winked at Thea as though he had achieved wonders. She had never waited tables in her life. She looked around at the disheveled characters in the dimly lit lounge. Luke handed her a tray with orders for a table close by. The beer bottles clattered and the glasses shook as she nervously set them on the table. In the pocket of her brief apron, she carried her twenty dollar float. Well! She dropped the change, the dollar bills scattered to the floor and she spilled beer in the lap of a hostile character. She could see the rage on Luke's face as he came toward her. He held here by the arm and took her outside.

"You can't do anything right. Just go up to the room and stay there until I earn us some money, woman!"

They had been given a room on the fifth floor. Thea flopped down on the shaky double bed and wept hard. She was hungry and exhausted.

"What the hell am I doing in this dump anyway?" she asked herself.

She got up, washed her face, and headed down the back stairs. She took the side entrance out to the street, so Luke wouldn't see here. She stood there awhile, in indecision, as she stared down the unfamiliar streets. Ahead of her stood the Western Union cable office. Her immediate thought was *Help Mummy, Help!* She entered the tiny room and stepped into the telephone booth, picked up the phone and dialed the operator. As she looked at her wristwatch, she thought of the imposition of the time difference. Mother would be asleep, as London was six hours ahead of the United States. Too bad. This was urgent. The phone rang a couple of times before her mother's anxious voice answered.

"Hello . . . Thea! Do you know what time it is child?"

"Mum, I'm sorry. I'm stranded in Anderson, Indiana. Please cable me a couple of hundred to this Western Union office. I'll wait here until it arrives. Don't ask questions now. I'll write immediately. Send it soon, okay? Bye, I love you."

Thea wearily returned to her room and must have fallen asleep. She was awakened by the door opening. Luke put the light on impatiently as he muttered to himself, "He who travels alone travels fastest."

Thea turned around in bed and faced him.

"You remember that. When I do get my money, you go your way, I'll go mine," she said.

"Hah! Where the hell are you getting any money? You can't even serve a glass of beer."

She was in no mood for arguments in a confined room. He threw his clothes on the floor and got into bed in the nude. Within seconds he was asleep. Thea couldn't get back to sleep. Not long after, she noticed some smoke creeping into their room. She got out of bed and gently opened the door, proceeding down the hallway in her bare feet. There wasn't anyone in sight, so she continued to the floor above, and up to the top floor. Thick smoke blurred her vision.

"My God! This building is on fire."

She banged on doors all the way down the corridor. People rushed out in panic, some half clad. They screamed and pushed their way toward the only elevator in the building. She headed down the stairs as fast as she could to awaken Luke.

"Luke! Luke! Wake up! The hotel is burning down. We have to move fast!"

He looked at here with blurry eyes as though he were having a bad dream.

"Come on, get dressed. We have to get out of here!" she said. He fumbled for his glasses on the dresser, put on his trousers, and keeled backwards on the bed. He couldn't find his socks.

"God dammit. I can't dress you and pack the suitcase and dress my-self at the same time!" Thea said.

The main lobby was in a state of confusion. People hurled toward them, driving them in different directions. They got separated. Thea's main concern was to get herself out of the building. She hurriedly passed a doorway, in front of which a baby cried for its mommy. She reached for the toddler who clung to her rag doll with fear, placed her under her free arm, and continued down the stairs two at a time. Finally, they were out on the sidewalk as they coughed and sputtered. The hotel behind them was now an inferno. Fire engines had arrived on the scene, but the water force wasn't powerful enough. The hotel crumbled in a blaze to the ground. Thea ran with the child as fast and as far as her legs would carry her. She finally stopped to catch her breath.

"Mommy, Mommy," the baby cried as she reached for her mother, who at first looked at Thea as though she were an abductor. Then she gratefully thanked Thea for having rescued her baby.

Where the hell was Luke? Thea sat herself down on the suitcase and watched the building slowly disintegrate. Suddenly, he was beside her.

"Where did you get to?" she asked.

"I didn't lose sight of you for a minute," he replied.

"Come on, pick up the bag. It's time you carried the bloody thing," she said.

"Where are you going in such haste?" he asked.

"To the Western Union office, right over there."

"What for?"

"A crock of gold," she answered.

"More like a crock of shit," he said.

She walked into the office and asked if they had received money for her from London, England.

"Not yet, Ma'am."

Luke searched her face questioningly. Then he walked across the street to the coffee shop.

"Get me a cuppa tea while you're there," she called to him.

She sat on her suitcase with a scratch pad and pen on her lap. She composed sentences that formed her immediate feelings, interests, and intuitions, past and present. She shielded her face with the other hand from the sunshine in her eyes. The radio announced the news of the burned down hotel. Then there was music that inspired her as she wrote. Luke returned with her tea.

"What are you doing now?" he asked.

"Doodling," she replied.

"That sounds just like you. Here we are stranded, and you're doodling."

She looked up at this insensitive male to whom she had entrusted her life as though he were a complete stranger. She felt like some kind of vagabond, always on the run. Time was of no significance as her pen flew rapidly across the paper. Luke circled around her like an anxious hound.

"Still doodling?"

"Yes."

He made several trips to the Western Union office. Finally he yelled, "It's arrived! Come here and sign for it!"

She looked at him wearily. "Wait a minute, I'll be there presently."

"Woman, are you crazy? Or have you just gotten attached to the sidewalk?"

She folded her papers carefully, went into the office, and collected the money.

"Now what do we do?" she asked.

"Now we wait for the next bus out of this hick town."

It was dusk as the long awaited Greyhound bus came around the corner toward them. She paid for two tickets to Chicago and got seated.

"Boy! I could sure go for a cold beer right now," said Luke.

"That's all you ever have on your mind."

"Well, all you have is your pen and paper and that stupid transistor radio."

She brought out her notes again, paying him no heed.

"What the hell are you writing? A book?"

"Could be. Yes I think I am. I have enough material for one."

"Well, when you get through, call it, *She Shall Have Music Wherever She Goes.*"

"That's the first sensible thing you have said. I think I will. I like that!"

4

Part 1

Thea's Early Years

Chapter One

It was just another one of those sweltering monsoon days. They eagerly awaited the rains to break, to cool down the atmosphere.

Thea lay on her crumpled white cotton sheets, awaiting Patti the registered nurse. The clock by her bedside ticked away the minutes moving toward 8:00 A.M. She heard a voice beyond the curtain by her bedroom door.

"Here she is. How is my little patient this morning? Come come, it couldn't be all that bad. You look so much better today."

Patti was pretty, tall and slim, with blue eyes and blond hair. She wore rimless glasses, and was dressed in a white starched uniform, with a cap on her head. She had a wonderful disposition. She had attended to Thea's father's coronary attacks a couple of years before this. She was no stranger to the family.

She now held Thea's wrist to take her pulse, and with the other hand she placed the thermometer in her mouth. She smiled as she did so. How well she knew this child. After all she had worked on this private case for a year now. Previously Thea had developed a minute ear infection, and the family doctor had suggested a holiday of recovery by the ocean. Mother's preference had been the mountains, rather than the ocean, so for the first time ever Patti had been called upon to accompany Thea to the fashionable resort the Palm Beach Hotel, which was situated at Gopalpur-on-Sea by the Bay of Bengal.

Thea was extremely excited to leave home on her first seaside holiday, away from her mother's watchful eyes. She didn't even know how to swim, but that thought hadn't crossed her mind as yet. So Patti and Thea set off on their overnight train ride to a marvelous adventure.

Theodora Martin was nine years old, skinny, olive skinned with a freckled face and an abundance of black curly hair. Her enormous expressive dark brown eyes and thick lashes resembled those of her mother. She had her father's gregarious, extroverted personality and was doted on by both her parents. She was what one could have called a spoiled brat.

The hotel limousine met them at the station and they proceeded to drive along the miles of white sandy beach and magnificent ocean.

"Patti, Patti, isn't this glorious? I've never seen anything so beautiful before."

After they had been shown to their rooms, Thea and Patti changed into their swimsuits, and they took a leisurely walk on the beach. Thea impetuously ran ahead leaving her nurse in the distance. She pranced toward the high swelling waves that beckoned her. It was too late to retrace her steps now, and she got tossed by an incoming breaker that repeatedly buffeted her frail body. With blurred vision and a belly full of ocean, she was finally tossed onto the beach like a corpse. She reacted with astonishing composure as Patti's bewildered face looked down on her.

"Child, are you crazy? You could have drowned. Why didn't you wait for me?"

They were informed that the best of swimmers would not have attempted the rough ocean unattended by the native fishermen who were paid to escort women and children.

The first three weeks flew rapidly, and Thea kept a close surveillance on her nurse, almost to the point of possessiveness. One night at the dinner table she noticed Patti's interest in a shy American army officer who sat at a table across from them. Thea instantly felt resentment, and she told Patti so.

"I'm surprised at you. I may be your nurse and companion, but I am a grown woman and not here to be criticized by a child," Patti stated.

"Well, you don't spend enough time with me since he came along. I don't like him; so there!"

Patti would smile at him every chance she got, and after she got her little patient to bed, she and the American would chat outside the rooms on the veranda. Thea stayed awake as long as she could, intensely listening to their conversation, until she finally gave in to sleep. In the morning she would question Patti.

"Did you kiss him? Did he kiss you? When I get home, I'll tell Mummy you neglected me and fell in love with an American soldier."

"You won't have to, I'll tell your mother myself."

"Don't scream at me Patti, you're making my ear hurt."

"Why must you feel left out? We could all be friends. You have several friends your age here; I must have mine also."

"My friends have their parents with them. I only have you."

So in anger Thea took a long walk alone to a prohibited area on the beach, unknown to her nurse or her friends. Her footsteps led her to a stagnant backwater lagoon infested with malarial mosquitos. Mother had instilled fright into her about typhoid fever, but as long as she didn't consume the dirty water, she thought she could still wade in it. She breaststroked through the green slime pretending that she was in the deep jungles as she swam deeper into the unknown. Nobody would ever find her in this remote area. When she returned at dusk to the hotel, Patti was a nervous wreck. She had the police in Gopalpur in search of her.

"Where have you been?" Patti's blue eyes were enraged, as she shook the child severely.

Thea replied smugly, "I have found a secret hideaway where nobody could find me."

"You are truly an exasperating child, and I'll be thankful to get you back to your mother. You have ruined this holiday for both of us."

Thea frowned as she boldly watched her disturbed nurse scolding her. The remainder of the holiday was not as joyful as it had started out. So after a month they returned home to Calcutta.

Patti now removed the thermometer from Thea's mouth.

"Do you think I can have a cup of tea with your mum before I start my day with you?"

"I suppose so, but don't be long, you know I'm sick and before too long I'll worsen."

Thea was totally familiar with this infectious disease. On one occasion she had momentarily gotten out of her physical suffering, and the anxiety of Mother, and Patti fussing over her condition. The fever elevated deliriously, as she experienced herself out of the body that designated an astral dimension, beyond normal human perception. This indescribable spiritual enlightenment attracted her to a bright light energy force. In the distance she heard voices.

"More ice! Bring more ice. The fever has broken. Her temperature is receding."

Thea's eyes wearily opened to consciousness. She never attempted to explain her fantastic experience.

Weeks turned into months as Thea became a skeleton. She hadn't attended school for over a year now; her mother tutored her from time to time. The highlight of her day was when she'd hear her father's car drive into the compound, and she eagerly listened to his footsteps on the winding staircase. He called out in excitement as he approached her sickbed.

"I'm here Mickey Mouse. Daddy has a present for his princess!"

"Daddy, Daddy, what did you bring me today?"

She would hug her father weakly as their eyes beheld each other with affection.

"Oh Daddy another pen and pencil set. I have so many already."

"Tomorrow I'll bring you something nicer."

Father wasn't living at home permanently. However when he did visit the family gratefully accepted his presence. The children never dared to question their parents' differences. The head member of this family did not conform to specifications. He was a businessman. He'd graciously kiss Mother on the cheek and acknowledge anybody else's presence in the house. Father believed in "live and let live." He lived for the moment, not for a minute planning a future. To quote him, "Life was kismet." By that he meant your destiny was predetermined.

Father was vibrantly handsome, of medium build, with black wavy hair parted in the middle. He was fair complected with a distinctive freckled face. Thea thought he resembled Cary Grant. He was a tremendous flirt, and his promiscuousness had been no secret. The women loved him, and his generosity complemented his good looks. He was an orphan of Armenian heredity, and as a youth he'd lived in Northern India. He had a sparse education, but was blessed with an acute business ability. He came to Calcutta during the early twenties, where he cultivated his trade, which was jute. In the eighteenth century, jute was woven on hand looms, which were in common use in the Bengal villages. Not until the nineteenth century was it introduced to England. The city of Bombay is built upon cotton. Calcutta is built on jute. The hemp is grown in the delta of Bengal and refined in mills. Father was a jute engineer. It was a lucrative business, which enabled him his affordable life-style. His dream was completed when he met and married Mother in 1925. Mother was a stunning brunette who was born in Calcutta of middle-class German parents. She was a lady in the truest sense of the word. She was educated, with a Cambridge degree, honorable, refined, and most Victorian and conventional. She was of a nervous temperament and was never prepared for her husband's exuberance, and enthusiasm. Yet she was instantly taken with him. He was an adventurer from day one. Mother's parents had passed on by the time she was nineteen, so she relied on Father for her newfound life. Father admired her refinement and guidance, and she in return appreciated his ingenuity. They complemented each other. From this dynamic amalgamation were produced their two daughters, Lydia and Thea.

For as far back as Thea could recall of her incredible youth, Mother's exceptional fascination and love for Britain's royal family generated extreme interest in her over the years. Mother made no secret of her prevalent desire where it concerned her two daughters. Throughout their childhood and into their teen years the girls were dressed alike, and they virtually grew up in the image of Princess Elizabeth and Margaret Rose.

When Thea was six years old, she was devilish enough to amuse and intimidate her older sister. By the time she was thirteen, she had an amazing self-assurance about her. Lydia, six years her senior, was studious, shy, and grave. She loved her younger sister in her own way, but she was quick to scoff at her sister's zest for life. Lydia spent a lifetime battling with Thea and hoping she would outgrow her flightiness. But alas! Thea wasn't in the least conventional. She was an authentic free spirit.

Their lives would have been far less complicated if Lydia had been a sister, instead of a mother image. Sorrowful as it appeared, Mother became intimidated by her older daughter. The lack of Father's presence in the family household seemed to give Lydia the domination over all concerned. She was the matriarch of this family. Through the years Thea had little choice when it came to this accepted fact. The sisters persevered until their teen years when it became a catastrophic relationship.

In the early days living in the jute mill area of Cossipore, some miles on the outskirts of Calcutta, was wholly different from any other child's environment. Thea was a frail child, and both sisters constantly ailed with tonsillitis. The girls were driven daily by the family chauffeur, Ramnareese, to the Catholic convent in the city. At four years of age, Thea returned home from school to her mother and said, "My hands are too small to write." Her development was slow. It wasn't that she didn't comprehend the nuns; she was petrified of their black and white habits.

Her most beautiful recollection of the convent was the day she made her first holy communion. Catholics as a rule prepared for this solemn event at age seven. Because of Thea's fear of the sisters, she received the sacrament at age nine. She was extremely nervous as she entered the vast church with a dozen or so of her classmates and even more so when the girl in front of her fainted. All their parents were present for the communion breakfast. Eggs and bacon had never tasted so delightful. It was the only time Father graced them with his presence within the convent walls. It was the highlight of Thea's year.

Chapter Two

In their early years, Mother and Father were a dynamic couple and a joy to their friends and children. Thea felt truly secure. Living was such an adventure. They were constantly on the go. They traveled to distant places, and their parents gave to them with abundance. Thea never felt threatened though she had a life of discipline.

At home parties Mother would play her Bechstein piano and sing beautifully. Poor Father couldn't carry a note. Thea would turn the music sheets to their repertoire of Nelson Eddy's and Jeanette MacDonald's "Ah! Sweet Mystery of Life" while friends accompanied them. Both the sisters at an early age took piano and dancing lessons. Thea's preference was the latter.

As Father became financially prosperous over the years, Mother had decisive plans for her girls. Because her husband's work was on the outskirts of town didn't mean they should be restrained. Her daughters were growing up and required exposure. Their school and friends were in the city. So they moved to an exclusive area of Calcutta called Park Street. After the mills, it was certainly a fairyland.

As one approached the long pebbled driveway toward the mansion, one drove through the impressive main gates, passing the formal garden, which was a burst of color, with beds of huge dahlias, snapdragons, marigolds and astors. Along the high wall that surrounded the house, thick vines of brilliant bougainvillaea intertwined abundantly. The entrance to the house, with its winding stairway, was decked on either side with shiny brass jardiniere implanted with tall green palms. The spacious marble floored rooms boasted lofty ceilings, from which hung electric fans. The children ran from room to room, up and down the stairs. The wall curved, step by step and sported splendid photographs of Father's eternal hobby; race horses, spanning years of the family winners and cup presentations. Father referred to racing as the sport of kings. He was a true gambler, however his passion became his downfall, for which he paid dearly over the years. There are three types of gamblers: social, compulsive, and professional. He was a bit of all three.

It was a pretty turf with a golf course in the center where daily enthusiasts played their game totally unconcerned with the horse racing. The prosperous clubhouse, sheltered beneath vast trees, was a meeting place for members, owners, and their guests. The bearers softly glided around the manicured lawns with trays of iced coffee or tea. At teatime guests took a break and had hot tea and finger sandwiches and assorted cakes, hot buttered scones and marmalade at individual tables set with white linen cloths on the lawn.

Thea held the binoculars to her eyes as she followed the race with intensity. Her field glasses centered on each and every thoroughbred until the last furlong. Now she could capture the jockey in her father's familiar red and gold silks and the distance from the winning post. Her heart would race as fast as the horses' hoofs thundered past the finish.

It became even more exciting when she owned her own horse at the Gymkhana races at the age of eleven. Her father had given her her first filly, Theodora. Her passionate enthusiasm for horses was inbred in her from the time she could walk, and would find her way to the stables situated behind their mansion. Each morning she would attend the track trials accompanied by her father. He would talk business with his trainer and jockey while Thea inspected the gee-gees (horses) after their morning trials. After having breakfast at the clubhouse and completing their final discussions for the Saturday main event, father and daughter would adjourn for the day. The sun shone above them as they got into the Chevrolet and headed for the noise and bustle of the city.

"Bye, Daddy. See you in the morning. Same place, same time."

Father, after leaving Thea by the front gate with a kiss on the cheek, drove around the compound, and headed for the mills in Cossipore.

She'd hurriedly dress in her school uniform. As Ayah carried her books and beckoned her against time, they would rush in the direction of the convent, which was three blocks from her home. Thea's mind was far from her days activities in the classroom. She would take leave of Ayah at the school entrance, and walk toward the assembly hall, where all classes gathered for daily prayers. The girls then proceeded to their various rooms. The juniors were on the first level, the seniors on the second. Lydia and Ayah would meet her at lunch, but soon Lydia was to be sent to boarding school, and Thea would be alone.

As the six-week summer holiday approached, the monsoons would break, and it would rain for several weeks. With it came along the swarms of insects and flies. The humidity would get intolerable and they would be on their way to the hills, leaving behind the rains and the stench of the city.

Lydia attended boarding school at an early age at the Loreto convent in Darjeeling. She returned to Calcutta for the three winter months, which included the Christmas holidays. Thea attended Loreto in the city. She was the baby and never out of Mother's sight. However she did visit the convent in the hills at vacation.

As the train dragged out of Sealdah station, referred to as the *chota* station of Calcutta, meaning small, the cool evening breeze covered everything in the compartment in smut from the engine. Summer vacation, Thea was accompanied by her faithful Ayah Phoolmia and the nuns, regretfully leaving Mum and Dad behind on the station platform. No sooner had they settled in for the night on their bunks, both Ayah and the child stared, awed and dismayed, as the nuns disrobed. Thea was scared silly of their black and white clothing. The sisters would pray as they clutched their big black rosary beads before going to sleep. Thea thought it must be difficult living the life of a nun.

In the morning the big train arrived at Silliguri station. Here everybody changed over to what was referred to as the toy train, to journey the hills on a narrow meter gauge, looping and winding around until they finally approached the foothills of the Himalayas. After six hours they got to the village of Goom, before arriving at Darjeeling, which lies over the first range of hills, and covers the slope facing northwest toward the gorge to the Ranjit River and the eternal snows. The plains were left behind in another world.

Darjeeling is a famous hill station known for its large tea estates, but also for its large schools established under various Christian religious denominations to which children were sent as boarders. It became customary for families to go up to the hills in the hot weather and stay at boarding houses, or as Thea's parents did, at the famous Mt. Everest Hotel, which stood like a giant amongst the hills. Mothers and children whiled away the summer whilst husbands bore the heat and burden of the plains below.

The boy's school, which was another landmark, was St. Pauls, founded in 1863. As you walked a few minutes uphill you found yourself at the Chowrasta, the mall and crossroads of the town. Another road led into the little town of Jalaphar, where the schoolchildren went for leisurely pony rides. Thea and Phoolmia would spend most of their days there. The familiar shed of the small ponies stood by as they were given their preference. Eventually the Bhutias, tribespeople of Tibet, got to know you and your choice of pony, and automatically you were seated in the saddle for a two- or three-hour ride around the hillside.

Sunday was the highlight of Thea's week, when she'd look forward to her participation in the convent procession. Dressed in their spruce navy and white tunic, blue blazer and black patent leather shoes, the girls would be led by two senior students that carried the huge banner that depicted the Loreto emblem. The nuns chaperoned the four hundred students with their orderly discipline in and around the mountains. After their sinuous path of course was completed, the Loreto girls, who were recognized for their distinctively haughty and reputable snobbery, assembled at the famous Pleavers restaurant for afternoon tea. Some Sundays they would enjoy a picnic at Tiger Hill.

Loreto Convent, the oldest establishment in Darjeeling, was founded in 1846. The parents of the English and Asian pupils accepted the school's religion for the sake of the superior education it offered.

Thea was now comfortable when Phoolmia would take her for walks in the morning. Hand in hand they would walk around the endless invocation of the prayer wheels, which were carried around by an old woman of Lasha. They believed that prayer need not be uttered to be heard. Tibetans write chants on paper strips and coil them inside a cylinder spun with the aid of a weight. The devotions can thus be uttered over and over. Use of prayer wheels, once found everywhere, dwindled during Chinese rule.

A visit to the miniature pony track at Lebong was informal in comparison to the big track back home, but nonetheless, gambling was a serious business.

In Thea's tenth year she had been sent to boarding school with Lydia. Her intentions were good, but by her eleventh birthday in March she had not been able to conform to the convent discipline, so her parents were asked to remove her from her studies. However, this didn't hinder her yearly vacations at the convent. Lydia attended to her sister as much as was humanly possible, but Thea was uncooperative and unwilling to conform to house rules. She had been restricted to sleep in the junior dormitory with others her age. The sounds of the night frightened her. The jackals would howl all night long at the bottom of the hillside, and she had visions of them carrying her away while she slept. So she'd rush down the dimly lit corridor from her side of the building clear across to where her sister slept in the senior dormitory. She'd jump into Lydia's bed and awaken her sister from sleep. No sooner had she gotten warm as she snuggled close to Lydia, she would wet the bed, not caring for an instant that she had done so. Lydia catered to her pranks as though she hadn't left home, but to be deprived of her rest was more than she could tolerate. Finally the time drew near for their parents to visit, and Thea got more rambunctious. The girls were sent for by Mother Superior in the parlor for their weekend permission with their parents. Thea was all packed up in order not to return for the duration of the school year. But poor Lydia would have to go back after her sister's birthday celebration.

Mother and Father had their reservations at the Mt. Everest Hotel as usual. The beautiful spacious and gracious Tudor building with its richly adorned tapestries and thick carpet, and the huge fireplace that graced the main hallway as they entered the revolving doors was exquisite. The birthday party was held in the main dining room. Thea's traditional cake was a buttered yellow sponge with fresh cream filling and pink icing. It was moulded in the shape of a horseshoe and was decorated with chocolate horses heads.

Umm! Just like home, she thought. She said, "Mummy you know I can't live anyplace but home, so why do you even try to send me away? It won't work, I tell you."

Chapter Three

Before the second world war threatened the boundaries of Calcutta, Mother desired to take a holiday in Malaya. She and her daughters sailed on the British Indian Steam Navigation Company ship the "Khendalah," which stopped at Rangoon, Penang, Kuala-Lampur, Singapore, and Port Sweatnum.

Thea's recollection of this holiday was sparse, though some incidents did come to mind. It was her first ship voyage and the one time she proved to be a good sailor. There was gala entertainment each evening, as the orchestra reveled in the music of Gershwin. They enjoyed fine living at the majestic Strand Hotel in Rangoon, which was bombed soon after their visit. She took her first ride in the funicular tram of Penang's Craig Hotel on a mountaintop. She saw enormous statues and shrines of Buddha in Rangoon. For a little girl, tripping through these exotic cities was awesome.

Most impressive to Thea was their summer of '42. The three of them made a tedious journey by train from Calcutta to Madras in Southern India. From there they boarded a four-seater airplane for a turbulent flight that only Amelia Earhart or Pancho Barnes would have appreciated. They were all wretchedly sick. After refueling at Trichinopoly, relief was in sight at Ratmalana airport, situated on the outskirts of its capital city, Colombo, Ceylon.

Here they were received by their gracious friend and host, Sir Oliver Goonetilleke, who later became governor of the island.

They rode in his state limousine festooned with pennants on either side. After their flight over the Indian Ocean and the brown plains, this sudden vivid, fecund beauty was breathtaking. Alongside the limo at the start of their ride, the watchful eyes of elephants close by padded the road ahead urged by *mahouts* (elephant drivers). Colombo's palm lined avenues, the flamboyant trees and bougainvillaea were reminiscent of Calcutta. Green hedges and orderly beds of cannas were familiar flowers introduced by British gardeners. Upon their arrival at Sir Oliver's home, his family assembled on the front steps to greet them. The Singhalese were a proud people who extended extreme warmth and hospitality. After they were taken on a tour of the splendid gardens and house, they were directed to the guest quarters. This was to be their home for the next three months. A banquet awaited them in the large dining hall. Singhalese cuisine, similar to Indian, was highly palatable. They did not kill the taste buds with chili-heat, as was the case in India. The bearers brought vast platters of gastronomical variations that continued to please their hearty appetites. Thea objected to the overindulgence of the coconut in all the courses, so the cook was requested to omit it from her meals.

The weeks followed with a planned itinerary that covered the island from end to end, to places large and small, each exhibiting its colorful heritage.

They began in Kandy. The main attraction here for the visitor was the "Temple of the Tooth." The story goes that in 1560 a Portuguese military mission captured this sacred tooth. From the time of its arrival in Ceylon hidden in the hair of a Princess from Orissa in Northern India in A.D. 313 to the annual August *"Perahera,"* a procession in honor of the tooth relic, it has been a unifying force for the Singhalese. Thea was amazed at the huge tusked elephant belonging to the temple, which had the honor of carrying the relic during the regal ceremony. The elephant's symbolism was predominant in these parts. He was emblematic king of the jungle, a fine carving in ivory or wood, and a way of transportation.

They visited Newara-Eliya, which was a tea estate that reminded them of Darjeeling. Once again they were traveling on a narrow gauge railroad, except these trains were far more luxurious. The compartments were of highly polished teakwood, the beds were made with clean starched monogrammed linen, and the waiters handed you a marvelous menu in the dining car. The platforms were devoid of the filth of India, with its vendors selling food not fit for consumption and the squatters begging for alms. The train silently circled the spectacular range of mountains through deep gorges and tunnels, into the dark jungles, until they reached the snowcapped mountain resort at the top. This part of the journey stood out vividly in Thea's memory.

During their weeks in Colombo, they attended three official weddings, each more elaborate than the last. Marriage, the most important of all social events, is taken seriously for all concerned. It involved caste, finance, and a sealed contract. Young people in love did not defy parental authority. Horoscopes were cast and often arranged by brokers who were paid. Then the dowry was settled by the bride's family. Another unique custom was the wedding cake. It was packaged in small silver and white cardboard boxes with the inscription of husband and wife's name, placed on silver trays, and served by the bearers to the guests. All of these weddings were in the form of garden parties under a big tent.

Thea and her family attended their first government ball in Colombo at the Galle Face Hotel on the Strand. That indeed was a regal affair. But, then, she was accustomed to this type of protocol. If racing be the sport of kings, then it was an accepted fact that she mingled with its society.

She socialized with the families of maharajas and maharanees. Bia Cooch Behar was a close friend of her father's. The Begum (high ranking Muslim lady) of Dacca was a daily visitor at their home. There were ruling princes of major states usually present at family functions. For that matter Father frequently sought the wisdom and companionship of Mahatma Gandhi and would refer to him as "Bapu" in conversation.

Thea's lifelong struggle toward the cultures of the East, which differed from those of the West, presented a separation of belonging as she got older. Because of her British heritage and family programming, she leaned toward the mother country, but in all sincerity, where were her roots? She hadn't any. She wasn't prepared for the nomadic course she was already destined for.

The ladies of Sir Oliver's home took great pleasure in the ceremony of dressing Mother and Lydia in their beautiful, rich saris. Before departure from the island, Mother was presented with several of these costly garments, which were woven with threads of real gold and silver. At a later date Mother handed the fabrics to the family jeweler, who in turn melted the precious ore from the garments, designing such items as cigarette cases and compacts. These made for desirable gifts.

Their holiday would have been incomplete without the regal occasion of a couple of visits to the Colombo racetrack.

Sir Oliver, the enthusiastic horse owner and dear friend, and the man who had made this holiday possible, was to remain in Thea's mind forever.

Chapter Four

Each year returning back to the strict discipline of Loreto was a tedious readjustment for Thea. She remained in her classroom just long enough to be upgraded to the next, or sometimes demoted. The nuns made it awkward for her, and she in turn did the same for them.

On the evening of December 7, 1941, Mother and Thea were sitting on their veranda in Park Street. As usual the native paperboy was making his rounds on the street. First he yelled the headlines in Hindi, then in English. He yelled at the top of his voice, "Star of India. Today Japanese bomb Pearl Harbor. America joined in the war!" Mother jumped out of her chair and beckoned the *durwan,* the servant that stood guard at the front gate, to purchase the paper immediately! Thea switched on the radio for the All India news commentator. They were both in a state of shock.

In a matter of days the American troops flooded the city. The popular CBI (China Burma India) Air Force flew from Calcutta over the well known "hump" into Burma. Swarms of British troops, some of whom were already stationed in the city, commandeered public hotels and restaurants. Everything was up for grabs by the men in uniform. Calcutta would never be the same. In the weeks that followed, several new English girls had been evacuated from the tea estates of Burma and Asam to Loreto. There was complete chaos all around. Ugly sandbags were stacked high around the convent walls, and in front of department store windows and public offices. Inflatable silver barrage balloons covered the sky above against the awaited enemy. The unfamiliar blasting of air raid sirens deafened their ears for the first time. Calcutta was in preparation for its first air raid. In all this turmoil Mother had planned their next holiday within the boundaries of India. She termed it as an evacuation from the city, which would definitely be a target, as it was headquarters for both British and American troops. Father never left the city or his business; he stayed no matter what the circumstances. Lydia was hastily returned from the convent during midterm and Mother and her girls departed on their next sojourn. The chosen destination was Kashmir, truly the most picturesque part of India.

They traveled first by train to Lahore, Pakistan. This was before partition, so it was still considered India. Mother visited her only sister who lived there with her husband and two daughters. Thea and Lydia met their cousins for the first time. Lahore was a pretty city and rather countryish in comparison to Calcutta. After residing at the Metro Hotel for a month, they set off by car to Srinagar, the capital of Kashmir. There wasn't any form of air transportation then, and Thea was about to experience the most horrendous motoring of her life.

The hazardous journey along primitive winding roads began at dawn. This time Lydia fared pretty well. Thea and her mother threw up each time the car shifted in and out of gear. As they twisted and turned they were constantly conscious of the steep range of mountains on one side, and the onrush of the wicked pitted whirlpool Jhelum River on the other, as it tenaciously followed its rough course. This continued all day until finally all three of them had succumbed to the most dreadful car sickness. As dusk fell they were forced to break journey for the night at a hotel in Murray Rawlpindi. This was "Pindi," the British name for this garrison post. It was a cold miserable night, and the three of them passed out with fatigue in front of a huge fireplace in the bedroom.

Unfortunately, this had only been a third of their journey. After a hearty breakfast, which didn't adhere to them for long, they continued where they had left off the previous evening. By the time they reached the outskirts of Srinigar, they were exhausted, although the beautiful poplar-lined avenue momentarily took their minds off their discomfort as they approached the city center.

Here was a picturesque city intertwined with lakes. Most tourists rented houseboats on the lake, but because of their mother's obsessional fear of typhoid fever and water pollution, they refrained from living on one. Instead they checked into a beautiful hotel. As noted, a fair proportion of the population resided in houseboats on the lakes and paddled small gondola-shaped boats called *shikara*, which were richly covered with bright canopies and blinds of rich brocade and silk in dazzling hues. These were used to ferry people to and from the shore. From the houseboats you captured the ambiance of the town on the "bund" or main shopping esplanade.

The natives of Kashmir were fair of face, with fine chiseled features.

The rare mountain air was beneficial to their general health and well-being.

On Thea's first day on the lake, her attention was drawn to a large houseboat moored to the quay bearing the improbable name of "Suffering Moses" on a sign over the entrance. As she and here mother and Lydia entered this floating store, chock-full of local artifacts and handcrafted goods, the Kashmiris sat crosslegged on the floor. They industriously embroidered the most beautiful rugs, known as *numdars,* with birds, lotus buds, and flowers in a profusion of gaily colored wools of fleecy black and white backcloths. The wood carvings and papier mâche objects d'art were primitive in design, abounding with flowers and pomegranates and birds such as the kingfisher and woodpecker, the emblem birds of the state. The natives were extremely keen copiers. Mother had trays and cigarette boxes and gifts galore made, to perfection, of walnut wood.

Lydia and Thea both took turns with the heart-shaped paddles as they glided smoothly and noiselessly in the *shikara* over the mirrored surface of the lakes. Sometimes the boatman in livery and ornate turban helped them along. Dal Lake was the largest of them all. There were several shoots off the Dal Lake like the Nagim Bagh. These were gardens splendidly laid out, with fountains, waterfalls, and pavilions fashioned in the distinctive architecture of the Moghul dynasty. The most famous were the Shalimar Gardens, doubtless the source of inspiration for the famous ballad Kashmiri song, "Pale Hands I Love beside the Shalimar, Where Are You Now?" run the words. But not even the immortal bard could have captured in prose or poem the peerless beauty of those famous gardens, built in a bygone age by a monarch with absolute power. The flowers and foliage were dazzling. Tulips of red and gold and black held up their heads to meet the benign warmth of the sun, against the lush background of herbaceous borders, fragrant with the scent of oleander, franjipani and jasmine.

The bright dart of birds of exotic plumage among the majestic frieze, the tinkling of fountains and waterfalls as they splashed joyously over the marble mosaic, and granite beds in which twinkled coins tossed in for good luck by throngs of suppliant visitors, all contributed to the lush beauty.

Another form of transport on land here was the horse and buggy, called the tonga. Once again both girls took turns driving around the town. Like the shikara, these were richly patterned with painted wood panels and had leather seats in red and gold with deep button back supports.

Srinagar was truly a hidden city. In the 1940s it had not been exploited like others in India, probably because people had no reason to travel so far north. The population lived mostly on cottage industries and on the produce of the market gardens and orchards that flourished along the terraced slopes away from the hubbub, turmoil, and heat that is characteristic of the dry plains of India. The citizens either were not aware or simply did not care that there was a war going on.

Their first pony trek took them to Gulmarg, the winter sporting resort. This was farthest north, and could only be reached on horseback, there being no other feasible means of scaling the heights.

In the summer it was rather bleak with nothing much to see, but the eternal snows on the summit were inspiring. After their three-month visit in this beautiful part of the country, they didn't look forward to the dreadful car ride back to the plains. However, Mother had contemplated a continuation of this magnificent holiday to another hill station, Mussoorie, which was situated in the United Provinces of India. It took two days and nights traveling by train. . . . How would one describe the magic of Mussoorie?

It was a latter-day Camelot, but probably a lot nicer. Here was a resort visited by the British and American forces to convalesce from the rigors of jungle warfare in Burma. It became a veritable haven to which they returned time and time again. Mother and her two girls would spend nine months in this glorious mountain atmosphere, at the renowned Hakman's Grand Hotel, owned and operated by a Viennese widow from the old country.

Thea was now greatly aware of her sophisticated surroundings and of the glamour of the luxurious suite of rooms reserved for her and her family each year. She observed guests coming and going, but she had become a permanent fixture.

Here in the obscurity of the hills, was the culture of Europe, plus the splendor of Las Vegas, topped off by an elegant dining room with gourmet menus. How was it possible to conform to a daily routine? She had always had an exciting life that couldn't be termed average. However disciplined she may have been, she had little chance of following through in this environment.

Mother permitted a certain amount of leisure time while readjusting to hotel life. Thea wouldn't dare be contrary when it came to her mother's command. Mother, always overprotective, permitted her to attend the daily entertainment which was from 6:00 to 8:00 P.M. It was referred to as the tea dance. This was the era of the big band. The Glenn Miller sound, the Dorsey Brothers, Harry James, Duke Ellington, and all the other marvelous music that flourished during the time of the Second World War. The orchestra and cabaret attracted droves through the doors of Hakman's splendid ballroom. Each evening Thea would take her place as she sat behind the piano player on stage. She would tap her feet and watch the grown-ups jitterbug until showtime came around. The cabaret extravaganza was based on the great Ziegfeld routines. After each performance she would hastily follow the cabaret artists to their dressing rooms. Here she watched them eagerly, with her big brown eyes, as the artists changed into their colorful costumes and makeup. She was absolutely fascinated by the rich assortment of people. Chinese, Russian, Hawaiian, Spanish, Italian, people from all over the globe assembled here. She made friends with them all and they didn't mind her intrusion. In fact her newly acquired Hawaiian boyfriend, not much more than sixteen, and one of the top paid artists, was her constant companion.

"Where is Thea? Where is she? I must find her before I go on," he'd say.

Mother's watchful eyes followed her and would remind her of her curfew time. How could any child sleep, or even shut her eyes when all this distraction was so close to her suite of rooms? Impossible!

Miss Hetty, Thea's governess would await her appearance in the room with her supper tray. She was back in harness again in the childish routine. Mother and Lydia would be getting dressed in their finery, bedecked with jewels, feathers, and sequins, so they could partake of all that fine devilment that awaited them in the evening's entertainment.

She would sit in her bath, taking her time getting into bed.

"Miss Hetty, I wish I was grown up like them. It's not fair, is it?"

"My sweet child, you had a couple hours of fun, now didn't you?"

"It wasn't enough. Now is when the real show begins, and I have to go to sleep!"

She would lie in the darkness of her room as Miss Hetty sat reading close by, however the woman's eyes would soon close in sleep. Thea would eagerly listen as one song ended and another tune would begin. She had familiarized herself with the routine by now. When the first few bars of the "bolero" began, she couldn't resist much longer. Making sure Miss Hetty was fast asleep she would creep out of the back door to a corridor leading to the back of the hotel. In her nightie and bare feet she would swiftly run until she reached the door to the kitchen, which led to the dining room, and finally through to the ballroom. Here she would crouch in her hiding place, where she would never be discovered, except by an old waiter or bearer who would be too busy to take a second look at her. From here she got a full view of the spectacular late show. The performances changed as rapidly on stage as that of Radio City Music Hall, each more colorful and exciting.

The devastating mob of servicemen in jungle and regular uniform, both British and American GIs and officers of all ranks, would shout the house down with applause. This to Thea appeared as a unique conglomeration of the Hollywood Canteen, and the MGM Grand Hotel in Vegas, only to be experienced at Hakman's Grand Hotel in Mussoorie. In the audience were the wealthy maharajahs with their Indian and European wives and also their girlfriends. They were adorned to the hilt in glittering jewels and opulent saris. Many of them were familiar to Thea from the racetrack and restaurants of Calcutta.

The final cabaret ended with a grand finale that represented the flags of all nations. The showgirls patriotically circled the ballroom to the tune of "Boom Why Does My Heart Go Boom?" Thea would mime the words from her hiding place, as she had watched them at rehearsals. She now held her breath, overwhelmed at such glorious razzmatazz. Unless one has partaken of such an opulent extravaganza, nobody would associate this culture with India.

Now Thea had to quit while she was ahead! She couldn't risk her mother's reaction if discovered. After all there was always tomorrow. She swiftly retraced her steps toward her room.

Miss Hetty still asleep. Thea jumped into bed and covered her head as she listened to the final strains of "Goodnight, Sweet Dreams."

"Ladies and Gentlemen, we hope you had an enjoyable evening at the one and only Hakman's and will return to us for more. For those of you that are less fortunate, we leave you with 'For All We Know We May Never Meet Again'." The song ended, "Tomorrow was made for some, tomorrow may never come for all we know." How true! Many hesitant dancers with their eyes closed were in the arms of their loved ones, not knowing if they would be in combat on land or sea, or flying over unfamiliar enemy territory toward the unknown.

Thea would shut her eyes tightly as Mother and Lydia rustled in in their gowns. They would discuss their marvelous evening as they undressed in the dark, for fear of waking the child and nanny. This is one time Thea felt like Cinderella.

In the morning she informed her nanny, "Hetty, I'm going for my pony ride this morning before my studies, so if you should be here, please inform my mother where I am."

"Miss Thea, leave her a note as you do most times."

"No, I'll probably return before they awaken, and I'll join them at the breakfast table as usual."

Thea's horse awaited her outside the hotel entrance. The servant helped her get saddled and she took leave of him, waving her crop in the air saying, "I'll see you back here in a couple of hours."

It was beautifully tranquil as she rode in the early morning mist on her mare, Mandy, as they headed for the camel backroad, away from the town center. There were several enthusiastic riders out in the early hours of the morning. Thea would trot along as she waved to them. The blue hills in the distance were obscure until the sun shone through the pine trees, then the acute serenity of nature helped her come in touch with herself. That's more than she could say about her three-hour study period that awaited her upon her return.

"Good morning, Mrs. Harrison. I'm sorry I'm a wee bit late. You haven't been waiting long I hope?"

She'd smile. "Well where did we leave off yesterday? English Literature. Let's take the subject you like best first."

"I think we should take arithmetic, the one I loathe with a passion. We'll get it over with while I'm still fresh and maybe able to concentrate."

Toward the last hour Mrs. Harrison's eyes would be drowsy. Thea couldn't figure whether she was bored, or she suffered from a low tolerance. Thea would startle her and say, "Well! That's it for today; it's already lunchtime." Thea would run up the stairs toward the main ballroom, where the orchestra played classical music for the lunch period. She'd scramble toward the dining room, where her mother and sister silently ate enjoying the ambiance, until Thea disturbed them by her presence.

"Well! What's good on the menu today? I think I'll take a look for something tasty in the kitchen. They always have something tucked away there, we don't know about."

"Honestly child, why must you be different? You're just like your father, never satisfied! Thea, I wish to talk to you first," said her mother authoritatively.

"Mum, I'm hungry. Can't it wait?"

"Sit down immediately child! How long were you with Mrs. Harrison today?"

"The usual; ten to one o'clock. Why?"

"Because I wish to help you with your lessons today."

"Oh, Mum, not again. I can't study all damn day!"

"I'll see you in our suite at three o'clock before tea time. You'd better be there."

Occasionally Thea would attend the 3:00 P.M. movie downstairs in the hotel. Hakman's had a change of film twice a week. She would sneak in, in the middle of a show for free, and sit through it repeatedly. Abbott and Costello and the Wolfman were her favorites. She had enjoyed "Orchestra Wives" eight times, and "How Green Was My Valley" six. She would get so enraptured in the scenes. She thought, *It's a pity her family didn't accept the fact they had an actress in their midst.*

When Mother helped her with her homework, she meant business! Thea didn't show fear anytime, except now. Mrs. Harrison, an inconspicuous little English schoolmarm was treated indifferently by her pupil. Mother would throw the book at her daughter, until Thea proved herself in her estimation. That was more than presumptuous. But it was only with her mother's tutoring that she passed her final exams. Mother could have saved herself a bundle with the private tutors, both on the plains and in the hills.

"Now may I go to the confectionary and get some cakes for tea?"

The Swiss bakery at the entrance of the hotel gave Thea carte blanche to the fresh baked goods stored in glass cases. She'd choose a dozen of the assorted cakes of her choice and rush back to the rooms to share them with Lydia and their new found seasonal friends that lived in the hotel.

"Thea! Thea! I want to talk to you now. I have some exciting news you must hear about," said Lani, her Hawaiian boyfriend.

"What is it?" she asked.

"As you know, the hotel holds amateur night once a month. My mother thought she could instruct you in a dance routine, so you could perform for the tea dance audience. You'd like that I know. You're a good little dancer, so it will be easy for you; that is with your mummy's permission."

"Oh, Lani! Yes! Yes! I'd love that. You come with me and ask my mum, would you?"

Thea's dance lessons over the years hadn't been in vain after all.

Mother agreed, and Iris, Lani's mother, began the rehearsals the next day. They didn't have long, and a costume had to be made by the local tailor. Thea's pièce de resistance was a rumba to the melody of *"Amapola."* At last, she thought, *this was to be the evening when she would perform with the lights on her, and the audience would be hers.*

Iris was so proud of her little pupil, as she fussed over her costume of red and white polka dots, flouncing it every which way as Thea stood in the wings ready for her exciting debut. She listened to the introduction of the big band for her cue, as Iris pushed her toward the crowds. Helen O'Connel had nothing on Mademoiselle Thea!

Until now Thea had no concept as to how vast the dance floor was. Sam, the piano player, her buddy, smiled, and his profound professionalism gave her confidence to begin singing in front of the microphone. After the first couple of bars of music began and she heard the sound of her voice magnifying across the ballroom, she was exhilarated. *I sound good,* she thought. *They like me out there. This is wonderful!* The bright lights focused on her as the masses of troops whistled and applauded. After the song, she danced, and as the big band accompanied her along, she got even more enthusiastic. This wasn't work, this was fun! After she finished and threw the crowd a kiss, she sang some more. They wouldn't let her go. She watched her mother's face close by glow with pride at her antics. After her final bow, she ran toward Mother, Lydia, and Iris. They hugged and kissed her with excitement. She ran backstage in search of Lani. He picked her up off the floor and whirled her around.

"You were precious! I knew you would be. I told Mother you should be out there, you've watched us all for weeks. Today it was your turn."

"Oh, Lani, it was because of you I did it. You gave me the courage."

"No, little one. It was you who did it. You danced for yourself, and to bring joy to others, because that's you. Don't you see?"

"Next time I want to tap dance, Lani. You must show me a routine, you're the best, anything you do is wonderful!"

"Okay, you're on. I'll show you a nice little number to your song 'Maybe.' That will be a good song and dance. We'll begin in the morning."

And from then on, there were more costumes and more arrangements until the end of the season. Alas! All good things had to come to an end. Her fantasy of show business shattered. She would dream of being a runaway with the troupe, to live like a gypsy out of a suitcase. It was like the big circus come to town. Little did Thea realize the heartache connected with the business, traveling from city to city, different hotels, all over the world. The glamour and glitter would carry her imagination to faraway places.

Oh well, they would all return back to Hakman's the following year. In the meantime, she'd keep in touch with Lani and his mother and father, until they performed the winter season at the Grand Hotel in Calcutta.

Hakman's was the center of attraction and a wonderful memory for those who have partaken of its happier days. For Thea, it was one more added experience to chalk up with the rest of them.

With the hills behind them, Thea and her family were on the train back to Calcutta. While still in the United Provinces, referred to as the U.P., the weather was still exhilarating. Now in their second day they neared the Province of Bengal, where there was a whisper of warmth.

Traveling on a train anywhere in India in those days was a performance. To enable absolute privacy, it was necessary to purchase tickets for a six-berth compartment. Periodically the train was air-conditioned, or the alternative was a ton of ice placed in a tin tub in the center of the compartment. The ceiling fans were directed upon the ice, and this cooled the atmosphere. All Britishers and wealthy Indians traveled first class. Second had less amenities, and third was definitely steerage. Here the poor folks huddled together on the floor and the bunk beds. There were no toilet facilities, so they matter of factly relieved themselves from the compartment door, whilst the train was in motion. The frequent stops at villages and towns enabled the passengers to stretch their limbs and stroll around the platform. The natives tumbled out of their confinement, toward the public latrines. Some urinated against the wall or squatted to do their toilet beside the train track.

Thea never questioned this primitive behavior, during her first nineteen years of residence in this country.

Frequently the train was furnished with a dining car, or else the train stopped at the British Railways restaurants. These were obtainable at the larger towns where the food was moderate and clean. While traveling anywhere in the country, Mother never permitted the intake of water or milk, for fear of typhoid fever and cholera.

The train stopped several times, in the course of the day, and Thea would observe the miscellaneous traffic from her compartment window. Vendors rushed toward her with huge brass or metal trays of watermelon, cakes, Indian sweets, and jugs of lemonade, all of which were infested with flies, and not fit for consumption.

The Indians made a practice of haggling, and if you listened to their conversation long enough, its reference was inevitably directed to money. The women would yell, the babies would cry, and the men spoke in several dialects. It was like watching a movie from the window. Lydia stood guard by the door, so as not to let strangers in, while Mother fanned herself.

After the crossing of the Ganges River and the holy city of Benars, one became aware of the overpopulation of refugees and the poverty prevailing more so in the Province of Bengal than any other part of the country. The skeletal cows and water buffalo sorrowfully grazed on the dry parched land as the train rushed full speed ahead. At last they approached Calcutta, and its shimmering Howrah Bridge in the distance. It wasn't long before the train slowed to a crawl as it circled into the huge busy station. Here was tremendous chaos, as they alighted from the train. The coolies stampeded toward them to carry the baggage. Lydia as usual directed traffic, while Mother and Thea followed her, until finally they were met by their father, and the chauffeur. Mother gave a sigh of relief as they stepped into their Rolls Royce and departed from the hubbub.

It seemed strange to be back in Calcutta after the beautiful mountains. Although it was home to Thea, she lived long spells away from it, and upon return she felt that much more removed.

Chapter Five

As they reached the family residence, the *durwan* (guard at gate) gave a welcome salute at the main gate and they proceeded up the driveway to the porch. The girls rushed up the winding stairway, toward their respective rooms. It was good to be home. Nothing had changed, it was all as lovely as when they had left, nine months ago.

Popeye, their English bull terrier, welcomed them, as he sought recognition. He wasn't the ferocious dog depicted of his breed. On the contrary, he was a lovable friend to everybody. He was white with a black eye, and the only pet the family had owned for thirteen years.

Home once more the family readjusted to their old schedule. Kitchens and servants quarters lay separately in the compound, behind the mansion. Life was pleasant with an average of twenty servants. Mother proceeded with her monthly payroll. As they filed past her desk she would take an individual thumb impression and spread it over a payment stamp in the logbook, as few could read or write. They were furnished with uniforms and personal clothing for the winter season. The cook and Thea's Ayah were the most privileged. Phoolmia got her vacation to her homeland in Nepal when the family was away during the summer months. She had returned with her husband and grandchild, Nepti, who lived on the premises. Thea and Nepti were companions, and they met joyfully after many months apart. Nepti sat on the floor with her slant eyes, flat nose, and pigtails, mouth open, fascinated by Thea's adventure stories, told in Hindi, as Nepti didn't speak English.

The familiar aroma of mothballs in the huge trunk signaled the unpacking of the girls' winter school uniforms.

Thea never grew rapidly, so her sister's clothes could not be handed down to her, as there was six years' difference in their ages. Summer uniforms were white pique with light blue ties, winter's were navy serge skirts, white wool shirts, and navy tie, accompanied by a navy blazer with the school emblem on the left pocket. In those days a school beret was compulsory.

Thea dreaded her first day back at the convent. Although she had had private tutoring with Mrs. Harrison, it was not acceptable by the nuns. Last but not least, the girls would resentfully eyeball her in the classroom.

The walk from the main gate to the assembly hall seemed like forever, and Thea felt as though she had lead in her shoes. Finally she took her place in line, and faced all of them. There were a lot of new faces amongst them, and she felt like one of them. So far she had avoided the sermon on the mount at Mother Superior's office. However, she was now face to face with the sister in charge with whom there had never been any love lost.

"Well Thea Martin, it is you isn't it? You've been away an awfully long time."

"Yes, sister, I have, but I always am away each year."

You could have heard a pin drop in the silence. Nobody had greeted her upon return, which hadn't helped her disposition. In the classroom her desk was occupied by another, but this didn't discourage Thea, as she promptly removed the other girl's books from inside the desk. The nun's eyes focused on both girls as they tenaciously clung to what each thought belonged to them.

"Well, Thea! What seems to be the problem?"

"Sister, this is my desk, and she says it's hers."

"Well yes, it's been Jean's all semester, and rightly it still is. But I suppose you are behind in your work as usual, so you had better sit up front."

Finally the ice had broken, and the girls began to giggle, and Jean had little choice but to find another place in the classroom.

At eleven thirty, the bell rang for tiffin. Everybody in the building emerged from the classrooms, in the general direction of the refectory downstairs. The dining hall buzzed with voices, until the bell rang again for silence. Some students brought box lunches, others had their servants deliver home lunches in an aluminum tiffin carrier that kept the food hot. Phoolmia, usually first in line, would set Thea's place setting in front of her as she served her with various courses. Patricia, Thea's closest friend, was completely alarmed by this catering. Most times she shared Thea's lunch, as there was enough for two. She exclaimed she had never eaten such good food in her life. Thea agreed, as her cook had worked for her parents ever since they got married, and over the years even the top restauranteurs of Calcutta had tried to bribe him for their epicurism.

Lunch completed, Thea and her classmates dashed out to the playground for a game or two of basketball. Thea excelled in sports and art, and the nuns were aware of her negligent attitude in the classroom. She was thirteen and was requested to go to the Mother Superior's office with her parents. She instantly felt that it meant trouble.

Father had never interfered with domestic affairs. Mother asked Thea the reason for the summons? She said she had no idea, other than her general behaviour disturbed the nuns. Thea stood diminutively in front of Mother Superior's vast desk. Peering over the rimless glasses on the bridge of her big nose, the nun's fixated stare was on the culprit, as she began. . . .

"Well, Thea, you know, of course, why you are here."

The child's eyes scanned the ceiling, looked around the office, and traveled down to her shiny black patent shoes. Her eyes then fixed on the nun's expression. Sure she knew why they were both here.

"I'm afraid we have to expel you. Firstly, for your lack of attending the full term, and secondly because you are constantly out of line. You seem to relish uncalled for attention from the children. In class and on the playground you are bossy. You are always the center of attraction, with your fantastic stories of places you visit. You have the girls in a complete tizzy, and you make them late for class. You are a problem to all the sisters. The pupils would rather listen to you than the sister in charge. You argued with Sister Theresa that she was teaching an outdated text. We cannot tolerate such insubordination in our school."

Thea was completely flabbergasted at this outburst. For once she was at a loss for words.

"Well what do you have to say, child?"

Mother's perplexity didn't help any. Thea could have compromised with each individually, but the two together, that was even beyond her. Mother asked to be excused, and she led her daughter by the arm outside of the office.

"Do you know what this means? To be expelled—the disgrace you bring on your family and friends. How do you think I am to explain this? You had better apologize immediately to Mother Superior."

"I will do no such thing. I am not in the wrong, they are. You call this one of the finest schools. It's a prison. So there!"

Mother felt humiliated, as she returned alone to the office. Thea listened to their conversation from outside.

"Mother Superior, Thea's withdrawal from school at midterm is

34

hardly her fault. My husband and I feel our daughter's education is not jeopardized as she is privately tutored and is properly prepared for her final exams upon her returning here. Thea is an expressive girl, and I know she doesn't mean to be irrational.''

"I'm sorry. You were an excellent student, and so is Lydia. However Thea is impossible. Maybe she would do better in a non-Catholic convent. She truly is a handful, and we cannot cope.''

So with a grand finale, mother and daughter walked toward the main entrance. The case was reopened at home.

"Shut up you brute! You are always in trouble. Well let me tell you, your lessons will triple at home. You're not getting off easily.''

Father returned home on a rare occasion for dinner, and the subject was rehashed. His answer to Mother was, "I don't blame Mickey Mouse one bit. I couldn't take those nuns either. They are not in the least sympathetic.''

"It's all your damn fault,'' Mother said. "You've spoiled this child, filling her head with gibberish, racetrack outings, and leading in horses, when she should be in school. She has no fear.''

"I thought the nuns were supposedly a good influence. We certainly haven't brought our girls up with fear.''

"I've never had problems with Lydia. Why must this child be so contrary?''

"Mickey Mouse is a leader; she will never follow like a sheep. You can't call her spoilt for that. She's expressive.''

"If you stayed home long enough to watch her antics, you might understand a whole lot more.''

As Thea watched her parents quarrel over her, she got the shakes and was put to bed. Mother took her temperature, and sure enough, she had a fever. Thea lay emotionless on her bed, as her mother nervously fluttered around her.

"Mum, maybe you and Lydia understand the rigid discipline of the nuns in their cloistered order. But I seemed to get in trouble sitting down. The times I've covered for Patricia Nolan, when she's reprimanded in the classroom. She said to me, 'Thea, your mum and dad don't vent their anger on you for a bad report card as mine do. I can't go home if I don't make it. I'm told over and over that this is an expensive school, and I had better live up to its expectations. I'm frightened, whereas you are not.' ''

Thea had never enjoyed school. It wasn't the fear of her studies, or the lack of knowledge. She felt both at school, and at home, be it her teachers, or her parents, nobody took the time to answer her questions or question her answers. She was forever being told to shut up or to leave the room. She didn't know why. Hence she reacted in the manner in which she did.

The weeks turned into months, and her absence from school did affect her, though the private tutor and her mother assisted her with her studies. She missed her arts classes and sports activities tremendously. Her school friends were not permitted to visit an expelled scholar.

In the mid forties her father's jute business virtually came to a halt. He was forced to find another means of livelihood. Gambler that he was, he was certain his new venture would prosper. Mother thought he had truly lost his mind when he informed her of his latest scheme.

"Are you crazy!" she exclaimed.

"No, my dear. If you wish to live the life-style you are accustomed to, the jute mills are inadequate."

Mother, at this period in her life, had taken a private course in dressmaking, and she was the owner of an exclusive dress salon, to which she devoted most of her time, until the war was on their threshold.

"You're asking me to invest my hard earned money, on some hare-brained scheme. No! I can't possibly agree to such foolishness."

Father was on the brink of an inconceivable project. It was comprised of acres of land upon which he was to build a pig farm and slaughterhouse. It wasn't too far from the jute mill area, in a town called Sodepore. By the time his plan had materialized, the American army was already in-stated in Calcutta, and they were given the assignment of the development, and in the year that followed, Father's International Farm & Cold Storage was built. Father's new title was military contractor. It was indeed the only farm of its kind in the country. His premonition was that the British and American Allied Forces, which would eventually dominate the city, would have an acute shortage of food if his pigs didn't go to market.

At first, friends and associates condemned the idea of the unclean animal, the pig, being lucrative in a Hindu-Moslem country. But at the right price the required staff worked the farm and the machinery. Imports became scarce, and father's produce became a household word in Cal-cutta. The military was his main objective, but the large stores and restaurants were also provided with the finest ham, bacon, sausages, pork chops, and suckling pigs. All far surpassed any imports.

Father may have had a sketchy education and humble background.

But this didn't prevent him holding his own with British governors, viceroys, and commanders of both American and British forces. In the market square he opened his Allied Restaurant for the troops. Here they could eat for a pittance. Last but not least, there was his generosity toward poor people. Periodically, truckloads of pork were delivered to the sisters and fathers of the poor. Even the nuns in the convent that expelled his daughter were bountifully provided for.

Mother was now active in volunteer work at the canteen on the *maidan* (park) called the Rondelshay Hut. She also drove a Red Cross ambulance to and fro from the station. Thea escorted her twice a week for an eight-hour day, and sometimes for an evening. She helped her mother, and other British ladies with the cause. During this time she'd pour hundreds of cups of tea and lemonade, and serve many dozens of sandwiches. Father had donated the ham for this, along with three hundred folding chairs, and tables for the canteen. Thea's feet would ache standing behind the counter, as she'd come in contact with masses of youths and older men, far from the shores of Britain, in this strange territory partaking of her hospitality. Most of them had already experienced jungle warfare, and others were on their way.

Thea, always sympathetically inclined, would converse with them individually, as she handed them refreshments. Sometimes she would encourage a sing-along playing the piano in the corner, accompanying the boys on the war songs such as "The White Cliffs of Dover," and "Till We Meet Again."

Lydia was a brunette sophisticate who, at the age of nineteen, had completed her Cambridge exams, and had a top-secret position with the British army. She was not as volatile as her sister, and this probably explained the bone of their contention in the years to follow.

Calcutta, renowned for its public squalor and private splendor, confronted them everywhere. The girls had never been exposed to or permitted in the back streets of the city. They kept within the residential neighborhoods, more so now that the military had commandeered the city. Chowringhee Road, Calcutta's most dignified thoroughfare and shopping center, Firpo's, the exclusive Italian restaurant which was frequented by the family on weekends for dinner and dancing, the Grand Hotel, an established place to be seen, were all situated alongside each other. Around the corner was the new market, where one could purchase articles from a fur coat to a bird cage, jewelry, imported fabrics, silver and brassware, delicious Indian sweetmeats and nuts, piled high in a delectable pyramid. This colossal indoor bazaar was uniquely fascinating with its changing paraphernalia.

One of Thea's preferred visits was with her dad to Fort William. The entrance to the fort was below street level and heavily guarded around the clock. Upon entering, father presented his ID for business purposes.

In 1696 a fort was built in Hastings, not far from the Strand on the river Hooghley. It was named after King William, and flourished until 1756, when it was attacked by Siraj-ud-Daula, Nawab of Bengal. A number of the British who had not fled, but surrendered, were imprisoned and locked in a stifling cell in the black hole. After the battle of Plassey, the following year, a bigger and better Fort William was built. It grew doubling and redoubling the British Indian permanent headquarters. Here lay a self-contained city, within a city for the army and their families. After her father got through with his business, he and Thea, would drive toward the beautiful marble Victoria Memorial, at which Queen Victoria herself was present for her inaugural ceremony. This was Curzon's magnificent monument to the British Empire. The acres of manicured green turf, with red gravel paths intertwined by canals with floating lotus and surrounded with flower beds of tall red and yellow canna, was one of the few gardens left untouched by the city squalor. Thea had spent much of her youth on these grounds, which reminded her of the history attached to this once great city, the second largest in the British Empire. Little did she know as she sat with her beloved daddy, that in a few years she would be courting with her husband to be, on these very grounds, and the surrounding *maidan* (green park), where on the tree-lined streets, monkeys outnumbered human beings.

Saturdays at the racetrack Thea created considerable excitement as she stepped out of her father's silver Rolls Royce. It was certainly the only one of its kind in the city. The magnificent silver body of the car shone in the glistening sunshine, or it shimmered with nobility in the evening, when the family was chauffeured through the main thoroughfares. All heads would turn as the chauffeur proudly maneuvered the great length of this fine piece of machinery toward the members' enclosure at the racetrack. The crowds gawked and envied, as the family alighted from its splendor for a day at the races. Once they got seated in their private enclosure, tea would be served by the bearers. Lydia and Mother studied the day's events on their race forms, and Thea joined her dad in the paddock with the trainer and jockey. The horses walked around them. The family raced and owned some forty thoroughbreds between the Calcutta turf and the Tollygunge Gymkhanna tracks. Father and Mother jointly owned Mr. Peabody, a costly gray stallion. Over the years, Mother had won three beautiful huge silver trophies with her three best horses. After major events they celebrated with champagne at their residence.

Racehorse owners in India retained their jockeys from England and Australia for a season or more. Some of these jockeys had never left their native shores, and were extremely unpretentious, but it didn't take them long to get the lay of the land. Most successful jockeys were retained for more than one season. Others could neither accept nor cope with the extravagant life in India. The jockeys that returned became prosperous along with the owners and trainers, who would make it worth their while. One such jockey had his moment of triumph when he rode Thea's father's horses to victory. He returned to England to ride for his Majesty the King, never to return to Calcutta.

During the 1940s prosperity seemed to reach its peak and then dwindle. What better example could there be than the ephemeral world of gambling? Racing could be a capricious and treacherous game. Friends and owners would smile at you when in reality some would like to cut your throat.

There was no man like Thea's father, and there never would be. He was a man out of his time, a man who lived to the utmost and did what he wanted. You just went along with him or dropped out. He wasn't a man of convention; whether he won or lost, either way he made headlines in the newspaper. He was a true sport, and he was known to place bets for friends and employees out of his own pocket. However, his generosity and acute superstition would be his downfall.

On a cold winter day, he would request Mother to wear her white sharkskin suit because it had brought her luck on a certain occasion. Of course she wore it, and her horse did win. If it was his wish, she knew better than to argue with him. When the crescent new moon appeared, he would beckon his Mickey Mouse to show her face, and then he would take out the silver change from his pocket and kiss her, saying, "Now your daddy will have good luck."

Father was constantly in touch with his fortune-teller. This man pretty much dominated Father's life. He exercised tremendous power, casting a hypnotic effect. Father had succumbed to his mystic spell, which had to take its toll in due course.

Each year Father's picnic was magic to Thea. It took place in late summer, on a river launch, to which all their friends were invited: trainers, jockeys, wives, and children. Early in the morning, a hundred or more would assemble by the riverside jetty. The excitement grew as servants got on board with huge blocks of ice, crates of beer, lemonade, and a truckful of assorted food. The suckling pigs got started on pits, vast platters of rice pilaf were prepared in huge kettles. The old fashioned wooden ice-cream machine was churned constantly by a bearer. Long tables were set with china plates and silverware. Father directed traffic until he was generally satisfied with the outcome. Finally the launch was cut adrift from land, and they cast away down the river Hooghly. The picnic continued to the beautiful botanical gardens, or to the small town of Chandernagore, held by the French for nearly three hundred years until 1951.

Their pleasurable entertainment was enhanced by a dance band that played to the wonderful melodies of the forties. Toward sunset, couples danced romantically into the evening beneath a galaxy of stars, as the boat gently glided up the river. The natives nearby watched with curiosity from their fishing boats, and barges. The band ended to the tune of ''When Day Is Done.'' A fun time was had by all, big and small. . . .

Chapter Six

In November of 1946, Lydia became engaged to an American in the Armed Forces, and her mother and sister were to accompany her to the States for the wedding. To obtain a visitor's visa in those days, one had to have a substantial reason.

Thea had temporarily been accepted back to the convent, so as to have a clean slate (in their eyes). She informed the nuns and the girls in school that she would never be returning to India. This of course was a false statement on her part, but she thought it sounded ravingly exciting. She reveled at their reaction to her exaggeration.

"All the way to America," they gasped!

On a cool November evening, mother and her two daughters boarded the ten thousand ton, British cargo vessel "Empress of India." Lydia had literally transported most of the personal belongings from her parents' mansion in Calcutta to her future home in Michigan.

They were three of the thirty-six passengers that departed from the Kidderpore docks in Calcutta. The anticipation of forty-two days on the ocean on a cargo boat confounded them, and Thea was most excited over this adventure. Father was the last visitor to leave the vessel. He had consumed many a scotch and soda with the ship's captain in his quarters. Now fully assured of his family's welfare and safety during the long voyage ahead, he kissed his wife and daughters farewell. Thea cried with despair, and she had mixed feelings as to when and if she would see her beloved daddy again.

As the huge rusty anchor churned its way up out of the muddy river, and the hum of the engines indicated their departure, the vessel slowly slipped away from the pier. Thea waved to her father until his image was just a miniature on the jetty. The familiar sight of the Strand, where they had taken their evening drives, was now behind her. The beautiful sunset on the horizon beckoned them into the unknown. Thea moved slowly away from the ship's rails and walked toward the ship's bow. The heavy odor of engine oil penetrated and overpowered her senses, as she watched the deck hands reassemble the cargo drawn down in heavy nets to the bowels of the hold below. The crew was English, and the first sitting for dinner had been announced by a gong.

At early dawn the Empress was out of the Sunderbunds, which indicated the demarcation of where the river ended and the ocean began. They entered the Bay of Bengal, and were aware of the turbulent ocean as the boat started to rock. Their first night at sea, had been very unrestful, because of the constant noise of the metal crane, and the chains lifting and moving the cargo in place. Unlike luxury liners, the decks were narrow, and the cabins small.

Thea ran up to the captain's bridge and took a deep breath of fresh air, as she marveled at the expansive ocean ahead of her. It was a beautiful morning, and she was hungry. The first passenger down for breakfast, she entered the small dining room, but she wasn't alone. The smartly dressed crew in their starched white uniforms sat at a long table, and bid her a good morning.

"Oh! It's a beautiful morning," she replied.

Thea felt very much at home her first day at sea. After a hearty breakfast, she went up on deck with her gramophone and began to wind it, as she placed a record on. She heard a quiet voice behind her.

"Look Roger, that girl has a gramophone."

She smiled at the two boys as they approached her.

"I'm Roger Parker and this is my brother Neal. We are on our way to Toronto, Canada. Where are you going?"

"My name is Thea Martin, and I'm going to New York City with my mum and sister. Would you care to choose a record while I wind this?" The boys were both shy. Neal left it to Roger to choose.

"That's my favorite, Tommy Dorsey's Boogie Woogie," he said.

The boys chuckled as they sat by her side.

"I bet you're the only one with a gramophone on this ship," Roger said.

"I don't know, but I take it wherever I go. Do you like to dance, Roger?"

He smiled shyly.

"Some. I'm not good, but I do like to."

"Come on, this is a happy tune, let's give it a try."

Thea was instantly attracted to Roger. He was all of sixteen, English with blue eyes, and slick brown hair. She thought him very handsome. Neal was twelve, an extrovert, who didn't stop talking. The three of them were the only children on board ship. As the days followed they explored the ship fore and aft, until they were familiar with all of the vessel, from the engine room to the captain's bridge. Thea looked forward to the boys' company for their six weeks at sea, and was glad to be able to share their adventures together at various ports of call. In the evenings they were occupied watching the ship glide through the phosphorescence on the tip of the waves, the masses of silver fish flying through the air—the wonderment of ocean life.

Now in their second week they were in the Indian Ocean, and there was still no land in sight. Lydia had introduced herself to the passengers in the lounge as the ship's entertainment organizer. She took it upon herself to plan daily activities and amusements. The captain and officers on board were also included.

"Ladies and gentleman, tonight we are going to play a fun game. I hope you all will participate. It's called sardines. Each of you will leave this room in pairs, to find a hiding place on the ship. We allow each couple fifteen minutes, when the next couple will go in search of the previous ones, until this smokeroom is empty. The idea is we must all be together by the time the three children who will be the last to leave here to find the rest of us. Please don't make it difficult, until we get familiar with the game. The purpose, of course, is that it is time consuming, and a lot of fun. So let's begin." Time consuming it was, but also hilarious.

Thea and the boys were always the first to be on deck in the morning. She didn't want to miss the glorious sunrise as it crept onto the horizon, and the activity of the seaworld as it surfaced. There were many porpoises around both sides of the ship. They were humorous in their mannerisms. While she watched, she felt a cool hand upon her neck.

"You always beat me to it don't you?"

"Hi Roger! I wouldn't miss this time of day to sleep it away in my stuffy cabin. Look, look! I see land at last. Do you see it in the distance?"

"Yes, I think that's Ceylon."

"Silly, we passed that a long time ago. You know I lived there with the governor when we visited some years ago."

"Sure, tell me another," said Roger.

Their first port of call was Cochin, a former native state of Southwest India, which in 1949 merged with Travancore, now part of the State of

Kerala, which is on the Malabar Coast. Trivandrum is the capital. It's a very serene mystical area.

By now the passengers were anxious to get on land, so after custom's clearance, they had been granted permission to board the motor boats provided to take them across. Thea and the boys scurried down the ship's ladder, while the captain ushered Mother, Lydia, and Roger's parents not far behind. After being at sea for such a long time, they felt their legs expand like rubber bands, before they got seated in cycle rickshaws for a tour of the town ending at the Malabar Hotel for lunch and a swim. It was a tropical island where the ship was to unload cargo for three days. On the third day, Thea and her family and friends remained on deck as they watched the unloading of tea, nuts, and oil, from the hold onto the dock. The captain had previously warned them that as the cargo was disposed of at various ports, the ship would get lighter in tonnage, and this might cause a rough voyage.

The Empress now plunged through the Arabian Sea toward the British protectorate and colony of Aden situated in Southwest Arabia on the gulf of Aden.

"Come on Roger and Neal, we are going shopping at the duty free port at Steamer Point with the captain, and after that to visit the reservoir tanks that date back to Cleopatra."

"Says who? Thea you are such a storyteller."

"I swear, I read about it. There isn't much to see here other than these that are situated in a crater."

"Oh does this harbor have a pungent stench of oil and petrol."

"Of course, silly, this is where all the liners en route to India, Australia, and Great Britain refuel," replied Thea.

After a full day spent in this British colony, they returned to their ship in the late evening, exhausted.

"Roger, isn't this a glorious breathtaking sight? Ships of various sizes, all with their national flags and in the background that rustic sunset, bidding us farewell. The seagulls are swooping one more time for the refuse thrown from the ship's galley before nightfall."

"Yes! All in a day's activity in this harbor."

They moved away from the rails, and headed toward the captain's bridge so as to get a fuller view. Thea closed her eyes, as the winds soothed her.

"Roger, I feel this moment has happened before. I have been here before, or I'm returning here again. Is it déjà vu? I don't know."

"I think you're crazy, that's what I think. Come on let's go. We are moving away from the pier."

"Let's stay awake all night as we pass through the Suez Canal," Thea said.

Soon after the dinner hour, all the passengers on deck watched the ships file through the canal, which joined the Mediterranean and the Gulf of Suez. It was a hundred and seven miles long. This brought them to Port Said. Here the captain was their guide once more. He collected his group of passengers and ushered them to the tourist department store, Simon Artz. Mother, like many of the others, purchased leather hassocks, camel seats, and trinkets made of scarabs. Scarabs are a dark green shelled beetle, which are supposedly a sacred stone worn by ancient Egyptians. They varied in price from cheap to expensive.

When they had returned to their ship in the late afternoon, the Egyptian magicians were on board with their slight of hand tricks, and the native boys with red hennaed hair were diving from the pier, whilst passengers threw in coins that they captured with glee, until the ship's departure in the late evening.

Now having left the Red Sea, their voyage was in jeopardy as the ship plunged into the Mediterranean with vengeance. The passengers were confined to their cabins, and the lounge and dining chairs were chained to the floor. Thea, Roger, and Neal, were the only ones in attendance in the dining room. Anticipation grew as stewards and deck-hands prepared for the worst to come. From the smokeroom, Thea and Roger fearfully watched the horrific height of the waves as they lashed across the decks, and beat against the sealed portholes blurring their vision. All main doors had been double bolted, as the crew worked in their mackintosh raincoats, against the fierce storm.

Mother fared the worst. The washbasin in her cabin had dislodged itself from the panel, and she and Lydia were frightfully sick.

"My goodness Roger, this all looks like a movie. But it's for real."

"You better believe it is. Suppose we don't come through it."

"Remember the Titanic disaster. That was supposedly unsinkable. This little tub could splinter to pieces."

"Oh, we'll be okay; this is a regular occurrence for them."

"What's that funny sound? Do you hear it?"

"That's the fog horn. It's to warn other ships in the area that we are here."

They finally gave in to sleep on cushions in the smokeroom.

45

As the gale grew, so did the mood of apprehension.

By dawn the storm had ceased, but the swelling ocean still persisted. Thea couldn't even play her gramophone, because she would have ruined her records. She crept toward her cabin, to find both her mother and Lydia lying silently exhausted in their respective bunks. The ship's doctor regularly visited them as well as Roger's parents and other passengers.

After the storm, came the calm. It lasted just long enough to have Thanksgiving dinner. All the passengers came out of obscurity, thankful to be alive. The captain prayed at the turkey dinner, praising their bravery and cooperation during the hazardous storm.

The worst was yet to come when they reached the Bay of Biscay. Their thirty-eighth day at sea, they literally bobbed along like a cork at the mercy of Mother Nature. To add to the confusion, all the passengers were requested as a precaution, to take part in a boat drill during this fierce winter storm. The strong doors were unbolted and the rain scattered toward them as they clung to each other. They were attended by reassuring crew members who urged them not to be afraid. With tight fists and clenched teeth, they moved toward their assigned lifeboats. Thea wasn't truly afraid as much as she was exhausted. The ocean was on a level with the main deck. Some passengers panicked, and Mother was constantly seasick. The drill was over in minutes, and they were ushered back to the smokeroom.

Their fortieth day they were in the cold, bleak gulfstream of the Atlantic. The fog was so heavy, one couldn't decipher night from day. Johnny, the chief steward, eased the discomfort of this endless journey, by serving chicken sandwiches and hot chocolate. By their forty-second day, icicles had formed on the decks, as the ship pushed its way through a dense fog into Boston's Albany docks. The Empress and its passengers, all of who survived the worst six week crossing on the British freighter with its prospective brides of war veterans, students, and immigrants, were now swarmed by newspapermen and women with photographs in the main lounge.

After the warmth of the Indian ocean and the Mediterranean, they had arrived in a freezing Boston. Thea in her light wool red overcoat, through which the sharp wintery winds penetrated to her bones, kissed Roger good-bye with tears in her eyes. She clasped him round his neck as they both promised to keep in touch. The American customs held Thea's family the longest of everyone. If not for the captain's reassurance that all their baggage was personal, they would have spent the night there.

The captain handed Mother a printed plaque as a souvenir of her voyage. It said ''Don't Worry It May Not Happen.'' She smiled as it was so appropriate.

Chapter Seven

Lydia's fiancé stood some distance away on the desolate pier. She walked toward the unfamiliar, handsome, shy, blue-eyed civilian. They apprehensively embraced each other, and seemed the two least likely candidates for betrothal. Thea at that moment was sure the romance had definitely terminated. At any event, now wasn't the time to rationalize her sister's immediate feelings. It was too cold to think, and Thea missed Roger dreadfully, and felt very alone.

After six weeks at sea, Captain Jonathan Fortesque diligently persevered to chaperone the family to whom he had gotten attached. Mother was quite confused in her strange surroundings, Lydia for once wasn't directing traffic, and Thea clung to the captain's coat sleeve, as they were ushered to a taxi. They checked into their respective rooms at the Lenox Hotel on Bolyston Street. They dined at the George Washington dining room, and after a long day, retired. The next few days they toured what little they could with the captain by their side. Boston was aglow with the Christmas spirit, and they experienced their first subway ride to the beautiful stores. They ate at various restaurants, and then continued by train to New York City, arriving at Grand Central on Christmas Eve.

For Thea, New York was comprised of skyscrapers, Forty-second Street, Macy's, Gimbel's, Sak's Fifth Avenue, and the movie *A Miracle on Thirty-fourth Street*. But never in her wildest dreams did she imagine she'd be in the midst of it all. As the train pulled into Grand Central, she didn't seem too impressed. It was all too fast moving and strange. But when they got to Times Square and the holiday crowds, "Wow!" was all she could say. The five of them huddled together in amazement at the huge Camel cigarette billboard, which was the length of a city block, and the smoke rings traveled clear across Times Square.

The Christmas music from the penny arcade held fascination for Thea, as she stepped into a booth to record her voice.

"Look Mum, a plastic record with me singing."

Later that night, the grown-ups snuck her into Jack Dempsey's bar for a nightcap, before they retired to their hotel on West Seventieth Street, which in those days was an Irish neighbourhood. The captain then took leave of the family as he had to return to his ship, which was bound for South America.

Mother and her daughters escorted by Lydia's fiancé took a train to Detroit, where they checked into the Book Cadillac Hotel for a couple of days, after which they continued to Royal Oak, Michigan, to meet with Lydia's intended in-laws.

It was a true wintry day, like one of those scenes on a Christmas card. The soft fresh snow was falling as they approached a pretty cottage. The door opened to a roaring wood fire, and the wholesome aroma of hot biscuits, bacon and eggs and white gravy. The family's hospitality overwhelmed their guests from India, who were delighted to meet with their first newfound American friends. After breakfast, they all took a sleighride through the fresh fallen snow, to a nearby lake where men were gigging.

"Just like the movies huh! Lydia?"

But alas! Lydia had a change of matrimonial plans. She and her fiancé parted good friends, and Mother and her girls returned to New York, after having spent Christmas in Michigan.

Upon returning to New York, Lydia had a problem regarding her visa. Now that she wasn't to be married, she was considered by law to be illegally in the country. Mother assured immigration that they were not beholden to the state or destitute, and had the sufficient funds to remain on in the country for a year. After a tremendous ordeal with the authorities, they were granted permission to stay.

Thea attended the Catholic school across the street from the hotel, and Lydia took a course in beauty culture.

Mother awaited her daughters daily. She had never attempted to cook in all of her life, so they ate at various restaurants in the neighborhood.

"Mummy, I don't know much about this school you have chosen for me, for the sake of convenience. If the convent back home couldn't tolerate me, then this is a joke. The kids have little or no respect for the sisters in charge, and the boys throw spitballs, and stick chewing gum in my hat, and trip me down the stairs. I don't like it at all."

"I don't understand," said Mother. "It's a Catholic school."

"Because it's Catholic doesn't mean the education is wonderful. It's not a convent, and there's no discipline at all."

"I'll see the sister in charge tomorrow, and ask her more."

"No! Don't do that. They assume I'm not able to speak English. In fact they are rather backward in world geography. I find it rather amusing, so let me get used to their customs." After a couple of weeks, Thea ignored their pettiness as she faced this ordeal the best she knew how.

"Here she comes. The movie star that lives at the hotel. Richard the doorman has to carry her books across the street. La de da."

Thea let their jibes roll off her back. She knew full well they wouldn't get away with it for long. Not if it were left to her they wouldn't!

A short time later she was sitting on a bench in the gymnasium, observing a basketball game, when she felt a hand on her shoulder from behind. A sweet, shy, freckle-faced boy handed her a piece of paper.

"I didn't think you wanted this pinned to your back, so I took it off," he said.

Thea read the paper. "What does 'Kilroy was here' mean?"

"Ehh, it's just a joke. Don't pay attention to them. They give all new kids a hard time."

"Do you know which of these smart ones did this?"

"I have some idea, one of the girls. She's the instigator in our class."

"You just point her out to me, this minute."

"No way, I ain't getting in the middle. You'll find out in due course."

The game was over, and there was a general rush for the front door. Thea was deliberately pushed and tripped. She lost her balance but grabbed the handle bar of the door. She quickly turned around and their eyes met on contact. Thea had super reflexes as she promptly reacted. . . . She had the girl flat on her face on the sidewalk, and she pulled at her carefully arranged coif as she pounced on her, saying, "Melissa Hamilton, when I get through with you, even your own mom won't recognize you. Don't you ever touch me again, you trollop!"

Thea picked her books up from the gutter, as she heard her mother's voice clearly beckon her upstairs. Mother had watched the fight from the hotel room window on the eighth floor. As Thea got in the elevator, she noticed the freckle-faced boy follow her.

"You forgot your jacket. It needs a wash."

"Hey! Mike Duffy, why are you so considerate of me?"

"Because I wouldn't like being a new kid on the block. Specially one from Injia."

"What do you know about Injia, as you call it?"

"Nothin' much, except you have sacred cows walking the streets, and the folks there are poor."

"Come on up with me, and meet my mom and sister. I need moral support. Hi, Mum! Meet Michael; he's in my class. Ask him how it all began. I'm sure he'll tell you the whole truth."

"Are you aiming to get expelled from this school now?"

"Don't talk that way in front of my new friend. He won't understand you."

"It wasn't her fault, Ma'am. She's new, and the kids give all new kids the same treatment. You know—a test of endurance."

Thea and Mike walked out the door in the hallway as she pressed the button for the elevator.

"Thanks Mike. It was nice of you to explain circumstances to my mum."

"She's a real nice lady. I like her. She dresses pretty and speaks real English. I never met anyone as nice as her before."

Thea smiled and walked him to his building at the end of their street.

"Would you care to take supper with my family? My mom will like you, because I do. Please say you'll come."

From then on Thea had found herself a new boyfriend. His mom expected her every day for supper, and Mike helped her with her homework. The elevator in Mike's building was old and forever on the blink. Most times they'd get stuck between floors for lengthy periods of time. This induced amorous kissing and petting, but that's as far as they went. Mike had always been a loner, and the girls didn't have time for him, until Thea chose him to be her steady beau. He started to take interest in himself, and he dressed spiffily. On Sundays he wore a suit and tie when he escorted her to church. Thea's family liked him and felt he was a good influence on her. His cousin, Kate, lived with him and his parents, as she didn't have any. She became Thea's best girlfriend, and the three of them spent the summer at Rockaway Beach with Kate's cousins and aunts. Each weekend Mother and Lydia would take a trip downtown for Chinese lunch and a Broadway show with personal appearances of the big bands or a movie star on stage, and the three children would accompany them.

In the forties the magnificent theaters, such as the Roxy, Paramount, and Capitol, were still in existence, and of course the famous Rockettes at Radio City Music Hall. Although Michael and Katie were New Yorkers, they had not been accustomed to the luxuries of downtown entertainment, and had never eaten Chinese food. Mother insisted on them joining Thea each weekend, which they looked forward to.

Late that summer Mother and her girls visited the nation's capital, Washington, D.C., where they resided at the Ambassador Hotel. From here they took in the sights to Maryland and Virginia, and finally spent a month in Toronto, Canada to stay with Roger and his family. The experience of Niagara Falls and the Canadian country was most enjoyable, but they had to return to their duties in New York City.

After a life-style such as this, Thea couldn't imagine reestablishing herself ever again in Calcutta. Unfortunately, their year had drawn to its close. Central Park in the fall was glorious, and her visits with Mike to Staten Island, the Yankee Stadium, and the Bronx Zoo, had now drawn to their end. Michael was especially saddened.

"I can't imagine life here without you," he said.

Each night before retiring, Lydia and Thea would gaze out of their hotel room window, across Broadway at the Hudson river, where the ocean liners were docked. Among them were the extensively lit funnels of the R.M.S. *Queen Mary*, which was to take the family to Southampton, England. Mother and Lydia were anxious to leave New York, as they had never got accustomed to the city's chaos, whereas Thea was saddened over her departure. She had many friends, and she even enjoyed school. She had experienced melancholy moments several times in the past, because of circumstances that had deprived her of living and growing in a community. She seemed to be constantly traveling and explaining her life to transient acquaintances. Mike and Kate would graduate, get jobs, and marry, and probably never leave New York, so how could they seriously envy Thea in her wanderings. But they often spoke of it to her.

"How lucky you are to be living in the best of hotels, and seeing all these places, having servants wait on you, and parents that share in this colorful life. We are so ordinary."

Thea hugged and kissed Katie, and a few of her schoolmates that had come to see her off on the Queen Mary. Finally she held Michael in a strong bear hug. They both tried to keep the tears back, but to no avail. Mike slipped a gift-wrapped package in her hands, as he turned away and walked down the gangplank. Thea waved to them as the tugboats escorted the huge liner out of the harbor. The impressive lady with the lamp stood on Bedloe Island, and Thea watched her from the main deck.

"Someday I'll return, Lady Liberty. I don't know when, but I will, of this you can be sure."

With tears streaming down her cheeks, she opened the package from Mike. It was a tan leather bound five-year diary, with her name inscribed on the cover in gold. Inside it read, "Come back to me in five years. I love you, Mike."

Thea moved away from the railing and went in search of her mother and sister. Amid the assorted faces on this luxury liner, she felt terribly alienated. If only Michael were by her side, it could have been adventurous, instead of just another Atlantic crossing. Mother and Lydia were dressed for dinner, and the events of the evening. Thea looked around at the spacious cabin with two portholes, furnished decoratively in all its English splendor.

"Well! This is truly first class isn't it?" Thea said.

"I gave your pink dress to the cabin steward to be pressed. He should be back with it presently," said Mother. "We'll see you in the main lounge. Hurry up and get dressed."

Hurry up, is all she was ever told. She was always out of the cabin before they were. She didn't care if they hurried, or missed the second sitting in the dining room. They would probably both be sick before the trip was over.

Dinner was as stately and stuffy as the passengers that were carefully browsing over their vast menus. The haute cuisine was served by English stewards, who identified with the stately ship.

Thea's footsteps followed the strains of a strict tempo ballroom orchestra playing in the lounge. She watched the piano player; he seemed as bored as she felt.

"Hi! Would you play me a request?" she asked.

"Sure, what's it to be?" He seemed pleased that someone in the audience was even listening.

" 'Till the End of Time.' "

"You really like it?"

"Yes, it's been on the hit parade for weeks, and Perry Como sang it to me on the stage."

"Is that a fact little girl?"

"I'm not as little as you think, I'm old enough to be in love, and sentimental enough to appreciate a love song."

His eyes rested on Thea's ankle socks and black patent leather shoes. "My mother persists in dressing me like a child. This gives her the right to pay half price for my ticket."

He laughed! "Enjoy it while you can, the years go by soon enough, young lady," he said.

Thea looked at her wristwatch and thought about Michael. It was about the time he would call her each night to tune the radio to the "Fat Man." Tears ran down her cheeks once more. This was not where she wanted to be. She was so terribly lonesome. The four evenings on board ship, Thea attended four movies. She hadn't met anybody her age during this voyage, but at least she was able to say she'd traveled on the Queen Mary.

Chapter Eight

The Queen landed on a foggy morning at Southampton pier. Thea detested her destination on sight. The weather was as dismal as the aftermath of war that had left its traces in this country. After their baggage clearance, which was an all day affair, they proceeded toward the boat train, to Waterloo station.

Mother's purpose for this trip to England was to visit with her friends from Calcutta who had immigrated here, also to satisfy her curiosity as to whether, at a later date, she might do likewise.

The first weeks of readjustment to the austerity of their new surroundings, after New York, were horrendous for Thea. Mother had the ghastly thought of leaving Thea here to complete her neglected education.

"Don't you leave me at a school here for three years. I'll run away," she protested. "A day school will do just fine, until you decide to leave here."

Even Lydia didn't argue. If anything she agreed with her sister.

They resided in a country hotel in Walton-on-Thames in Surrey. Thea attended an all-girl day school with the discipline of Loreto. She chummed up with Linda from Flatbush, New York. Her parents were with the foreign service in London. After the first weeks of initiation, she made more friends and discovered that many hadn't indulged in a candy bar or ice cream in their young adult lives. Thea felt compassion toward her fellow mates, as they spoke constantly of food rationing and the unfortunate circumstances they lived in. Thea wrote Michael regularly of her life in the English countryside, and her visits to London.

"Today I and my class visited the tannery in Guilford Surrey. Here we watched the process of hides and beautiful leathers made into various articles. We also took a trip to London, to the Houses of Parliament, and Westminster Abbey. It took me back to my days of English Literature, and of Poet's corner. I never thought my English text would come to life, and I would stand amongst the great poets and statesman of this country. This country is graced with ancient history and protocol. Now

I can relate to the Englishmen's pomposity in India. I guess you must have watched the royal wedding on your TV. We visited St. James Palace to see the exhibition of gifts received from all over the world. The display included the full bridal attire, jewels, and period furniture. There were costly gifts from royalty all over the Commonwealth, and an incredible stamp collection, which attracted me most of all. There wasn't a trace of austerity there. I wish we could have shared this together. I'll write soon again. Miss you dreadfully.''

Thea's closest friends were Ann, and her brother, Tom Jenkins. They lived in a nearby town, Weybridge. Tom was a motorbike enthusiast, and attended college, a perfect gentleman. Thea invariably spent most of her evenings with Ann and her parents. Their home cooking was a lot more desirable than the hotel food. The cook at the hotel wasn't in the least creative with the allocated ration books. When Tom was home on holiday, he escorted Thea to the cinema, and local dances, but she refused to ride on his motorbike, which was a blow to his ego.

"I'll never ride those wretched contraptions. If you can't drive me, we'll take the bus," Thea said. Tom was handsome. He had dark brown hair and dark eyes, and he had a terrific, dry sense of humor. He never showed temper, or got into altercations of any kind. He even played the piano and sang, "We'll Gather Lilacs in the Spring Again." He was a gentleman in comparison to Michael, who was just a lad. They were different ages and types, but both had been compliant to Thea's needs. The first time Tom kissed Thea, she withdrew on impulse. She had been so true to Michael, that she felt terribly guilty of her desire for another. She consoled herself by thinking Mike probably had a girl by now, and it had been a year since they parted. Mother had entrusted Thea to Tom's care. He would never take advantage of her. Thea hadn't implied any knowledge on the birds and the bees, it was the furthest subject from her mind. Tom wasn't focused on sexual desires as yet, he had many other interests such as motorbikes, fishing, school, and the arts. He hadn't gone steady, he said he couldn't find the time for that sort of stuff. He did have a gleam in his eye for Thea, and his sister, Ann, would embarrass him at times over her. His face would flush as he'd look askance at her teasing. She enjoyed every minute of it.

Christmas brought a lot of excitement to their simple lives. In school Thea baked her first fruitcake. Neither she nor Ann questioned where they would come by the ingredients to bake a six-pound cake. Mother's and Lydia's friends from Australia, who resided at the hotel, miraculously provided Thea with the fruits and nuts from their gift package from Sydney. Other friends in the country came up with fresh eggs, butter, and flour. The outcome was successful, and Thea brought her cake for the guests in the hotel. The hotel chef came through with the first turkey they had tasted in a year, and a diplomat from the foreign office in residence provided a baked ham. No Christmas would have been complete without plum pudding and mince pies, which they made. Lydia and Thea, with the help of other guests, decorated the dining room with balloons and paper festoons. The dinner was one they would remember, as they had beaten the calamitous ration books. Everybody had a gift-wrapped package under the tree in the corner, and they sang yuletide songs and danced the hokey-pokey with great merriment. The following day, Thea continued her holiday at Ann and Tom's home. They attended candlelight service at the local church and sang carols from house to house. Ann's mother didn't seem to have a problem with her promised turkey dinner. Their home was brimful of relatives, and friends, and gaiety.

Thea's final day in school was marked by a supper dance in the auditorium. She said farewell to all the girls and the school principal, and her class teacher presented her with a leather writing case. London had had its first snowfall, and Tom and Thea had a rip roaring snowball fight along the country roads. He hugged her tightly and kissed her full on the mouth. She backed away laughing hard, but it was so good, she thought to herself.

New Year's Eve was celebrated amongst friends at the hotel. Their stay was drawing to a close once again, as Thea felt the same old feelings of having to depart one more time. Each time it seemed to get harder. Somehow she felt she hadn't seen the last of these shores either. She never sensed a finality in her travels. She became so much a part of other people's lives, and they in hers. But it was inevitable that she and her family had to return to their homeland. After all her father was still awaiting his family, even though they had been away over two long years.

Mother had made reservations on the P & O liner, the Strathmore, which sailed from Tilbury to Bombay.

When Mother purchased their tickets, she hadn't been informed that the Strathmore had served as a troopship during World War Two, and was never converted for passenger use. There had been little choice. They had to take it or leave it. The ship's final destination was Sydney, Australia. Mother and her two daughters were to share a cabin with six other women. Women and children were separated from the men in their cabins.

Thea stood by the rail on the main deck, as she watched the passengers embark the big ship. A young Scottish gent stood alongside of her. In his cheery brogue he said, "How far are you traveling lass?"

Thea turned to his handsome face, smilingly.

"As far as Bombay," she said.

"Ay! So are we. My mum and dad, and little sister. My dad is a civil engineer, and we are to be situated in a town called Asansol, not too far from Calcutta. He's going to build a bridge there. We are from Edinburgh. Where do you come from?"

"I come from Calcutta, but I haven't spent much time there."

He gave her his hand in a shake. "My name is Kirk Stewart."

"Mine is Thea Martin. I'm traveling with my mum and big sister."

"Ah! That's nice. I hope we will be friends for the two weeks on board. My Dad and I are in a cabin with six other men. I don't much fancy that. But that was all that's available. How about you?"

"The same, we are with six missionaries, on their way to India."

"Sounds like we're off. The engines have started and we are moving away from the pier. Well, I had better go and search for my parents. Are you first or second sitting in the dining room?"

"Second," Thea replied.

"So are we. See you later," he said.

The dining room was empty of passengers, as the ship plunged through the rough Atlantic. *Was it always so turbulent?* Thea thought, remembering her last crossing on this ocean. Once again her mother and Lydia were confined to their bunks. Thea wouldn't stay in hers, on principle. To watch folks throw up wasn't in the least pleasant. So she forced herself topside, to get the fresh air on deck.

Kirk and his sister Jenny joined her. Their parents were also the worse off, and confined to their cabins.

"There's a picture show on tonight, shall we see it?" he asked.

"Sure, might as well."

"The ship is creaking, brother, maybe the cinema will be canceled," Jenny remarked.

"Well I'm sure it won't. There are some folks around."

After the picture show, Jenny went to bed, and Kirk and Thea played checkers in the lounge. Neither of them wished to retire for the night, so they strolled around the deck. Some passengers were covered in blankets on deck chairs, and others stood by the rails watching the ship plunge to and fro. Thea and Kirk sat on deck chairs.

"Do you think we'll like India?" Kirk asked. "We have heard so many stories about the country."

"Well! I don't think I could answer that the way you want me to, as I grew up there and understand its people. You must overlook the wretched poverty that surrounds you, and get on with living there, as in any other place."

"Oh, but that sounds dreadful. How can one overlook the begging and starvation that surrounds one?"

"Because any place you go in the East, be it India, the Far East, or Middle East, there is poverty. What's more if you try to intervene, they wouldn't thank you for it. You must leave them with their customs and theories, which are older than history itself."

"Is that why the British go out there on a tour of three to four years, and then return home to the U.K. for a six-month home leave? I suppose they have to take a rest from the depression."

"Could be, I never thought of it. My dad never leaves Calcutta. He makes his living there, so his family can travel extensively. He wouldn't want it any other way. India is his home."

Once again the ship passed through Suez, and Port Said, and the passengers shopped at Simon Artz, and Thea reminisced about the last time she was in these waters with Roger. This time she was Kirk's guide. He was fascinated by the camels and mules on the streets, and the performance of the Arab magicians on board the ship. In Aden, they drove to the parched tanks, and shopped at Steamer Point. Along the Red Sea, and into the Indian Ocean, the weather had got warmer. Though it was winter, it wasn't bleak and cloudy like the shores of Britain. Thea and Kirk enjoyed each other's company, and she sat with him and his family at meals.

Their last night on board, all the passengers were preparing themselves for the final gala dinner dance. Thea was ironing the ruffles of her gown in the utility room. As she completed the final touch, and was happily humming to the radio, she was interrupted by a news flash.

"We interrupt this program to bring you the latest news. Mahatma Gandhi has just been assassinated!"

"Oh my God!" she exclaimed. Did she hear correctly? She dropped the iron, and rushed toward the cabin to disclose the news to her family. Mother gasped!

"It's true I just heard it over the radio."

In minutes passengers gathered in clusters, as all radios on board gave the details of Gandhi's final moments. The dance was immediately canceled, and the diners ate in gloom, as a hush came over everybody. Here they were sailing in the Indian waters, only hours from their destination.

How was it possible? This slight gnomelike figure, bareheaded, and bare chested, clad in white dhoti, a saint savior, or rabble rouser. The humility of his self-elected poverty. He traveled third class on railways, dressed like a peasant, ate little, yet was arrogant enough to assume the role of mentor and conscience of millions of people. His devotion to nonviolence was itself expressed in fighting terms, such as the struggle for independence. The quit India campaign of 1942 had been a bloodbath of violence, so there were more casualties than in the Second World War. Well now he had reached his heaven for sure.

Thea and her family were uneasy and anxious in regard to Father's welfare, and the unrest of the country. Father hadn't corresponded much, other than sending Mother their living allowance, and a cable from time to time. He had never mentioned the political unrest.

At early dawn, Thea caught a glimpse of the Gateway of India, the magnificent archway that stood at the entrance of the harbor and seaport of Bombay. The ship got closer, as passengers assembled on deck. The ghostly city was devoid of activity, as coolies sat prostrate on the pier, unconcerned about the harbor traffic.

Chapter Nine

The passengers didn't disembark upon arrival. The captain informed them that he required authorization and customs clearance. Thea and her family, Kirk and his family—all anxiously awaited the outcome. They didn't sleep that night, for fear of the unexpected. Finally, the next morning, the passengers hesitantly moved down the gangplank. Thea told Kirk good-bye and promised to write.

The customs were extra cautious with baggage clearance. With grave faces, Mother and her daughters boarded the train for the long journey to Calcutta. They sensed the quiet before the storm. This could very well be a repetition of another station uprising like that of Bowani Junction. The natives on the train were suspiciously inclined, while the Britishers were at their mercy.

The train clattered past the miles of desolate terrain, and Thea couldn't believe that she had returned to this chaotic country. She was reminded once more of August 15, 1946, the day of Indian Independence. In Calcutta, the traditional storm center of politics, the refugees attacked and plundered, and Thea and her family experienced a siege and food shortage. It was a legacy of hate and destruction. The five hundred princes were in a dilemma in their provinces. The British rule neared defeat with a stiff upper lip.

She vividly recalled June 21, when Louis Mountbatten had handed his office of viceroy over to the new Indian government. Governor Rajagopalchouria had arrived at Dum-Dum airport in Calcutta, and was greeted by the first all-Indian cabinet. A front-page photo appeared in the morning issue of the Statesman newspaper. Conspicuous in the group picture was Thea's father. He adorned the new governor with a garland of marigolds around his neck, a greeting in the Indian tradition.

The aftermath of war had taken a toll on the new government, which had ended the British Raj. At this time there had been a general exodus of Britishers who scattered to all parts of the Commonwealth, to begin anew. They had been subjected to such slogans as "Quit India." The fact was that the era of empires had fizzled out. Then India had three hundred and forty million citizens. The British had molded the country to their own greed, and left the Indian cursed with ignorance, idleness, and idolatry. One Indian child out of twelve could read and write one of the two hundred and thirty-five languages in the country. If they mastered one, it was sufficient for them to get by on.

After having lived abroad, Thea had mixed feelings returning to these shores. She had a romantic nostalgia for the country of her childhood, for India she wished to remember. Her mother spoke about the glories of ancient India, and the good old days. Now this city that she once had called home, seemed unfamiliar. The withdrawal of the English was irrevocable. Yet England wasn't her home either. She felt that what once seemed whole was now washed away. How could she have forgotten the circumstances before their departure for the U.S.? There were the riots and bloodshed on the streets and the stench of dead bodies disrupting the main thoroughfares, on her way to and from school. There were the vultures and crows feasting on their prey, until only skeletons remained, which were not removed for days on end. Her father's Rolls Royce had been the only vehicle on Park Street, as he commuted from one end of the city to the other, the car flanked on either side with both Hindu and Moslem flags. Not showing partiality, his only concern was to bring home the food. His wife and daughters were the captives of circumstances, whilst they awaited for him. The servants had fled out of town, for fear of their lives. Since those days the country had deteriorated even more.

Thea now put her arms around her mother and Lydia, as the three of them stood by the door of the compartment, and the train slowly came into Howrah station. "It feels strange being back here, doesn't it?" she said. Apprehensively, they alighted onto the platform, as coolies dashed madly toward them to carry their baggage. They were mobbed by beggars, and the never ending influx of refugees. Famine was ingrained in their pitiful faces, as many lay prostrate on the ground, which made it difficult to walk without having to step on them.

"Where is Father? He will never find us in this dreadful crowd."

The three women were jostled by the masses, until they finally got to the parking lot. Thea caught sight of the familiar face of dear Ramnareese their chauffeur, who immediately came to their aid. Mother was most perturbed by now.

"Where is the Sahib?" she asked.

"He is in Pakistan on business, Maimsheib. He told me to meet you at this train today. I have been here all morning; the train is late."

She turned toward her daughters. "Can you imagine, at a time of unrest, and in all this confusion, he isn't here to meet us. Isn't that just like your father?"

Ramnareese drove them through unfamiliar streets so as to avoid the masses, and Thea felt as though she were a tourist, visiting here for the first time.

Finally even Park Street looked obscure, as the car neared their mansion, which looked the worse for a coat of paint. The girls jumped out of the car as it came to a halt under the porch. Popeye was there to greet them. He wasn't as young as they remembered, but he was still as friendly. The cook and bearer were at the top of the stairs to welcome them. A scrumptious dinner awaited the family, which the bearer served around their vast ornate mahogany dining table.

"Who would imagine," remarked Thea, "after hamburgers, hot dogs, fried chicken, and rabbit, and rations, we would be here to eat cook's wonderful dishes, as though we had never left. He is still the best in all the world, I'm sure."

They ate in silence, each deep in her own thoughts! Thea looked at the clock on the wall. Father had been the only one to handle its temperamental mechanism. She noted it had stopped at the time of their departure, over two years ago. Obviously it hadn't been in use since then. Hadn't he dined here at all?

The servants were only permitted to speak when spoken to. Thea knew they were anxious to hear about her trip abroad, but they daren't ask questions until she volunteered. Mother was served her coffee as usual on the veranda by the bearer, and Thea entered the pantry where he did the washing up.

"Thea baba," he said smiling, "Let me bring cook, and you must tell us all about the strange places you have visited!" Thea, the famed narrator, started to elaborate in detail about ships, storms, and skyscrapers. She spoke to them in Hindustani, and they savored her experiences. Their eyes widened, and their mouths fell open, as their heads shook from side to side. No bona fide story was complete without the head shake. It seemed to enhance the authenticity for them. After she had captivated their interest enough, she demanded of them, "All right now tell me, where is the Sahib?" Their faces went sullen with fear.

"He is out of town Missie."

"Now that's enough lies. You and the driver have collaborated between you what to say to us if questioned?"

"You know Miss baba, the Sahib is always away on business, he only comes here each month to pay us, and then he's gone."

Thea tripped happily down the backstairs, on to the back compound, and in the direction of the stables to visit the horses. There was a dim light to show the way to the stalls. Some of them were asleep, and some neighed at her intrusion. There wasn't any new blood amongst them she thought, as she stroked Red Rose on her velvet nose. "Maybe you can tell me where Daddy is?"

Now at seventeen, Thea pondered as to her future here. Her friends were scattered all over the world, except for Katherine. Would she at least remember where they had left off, or maybe she, too, had other interests. Friends, somehow had been outgrown and left behind. Some would be resentful of Thea's experiences, looking upon her as a stranger. The girls in school had never left this city. Thea had to go forward, and returning here was going backward.

After a good night's rest in her comfortable room once again, Thea awoke to a bright new day, forgetting momentarily where she was. She got dressed and headed down Park Street in the direction of Katherine's house. She passed the deteriorated post office, which looked the worse for wear. The Indians came in and out of the building spitting mounds of beetlenut against the walls and all over the pavement. She was stunned at the filth that surrounded her. She tripped herself on the uneven side-walk. The beggars squirmed toward her begging alms. This had been the first time Thea had walked on the street unattended by her Ayah, or her nanny. She brushed past the mob hurriedly but with composure. It would be disastrous for them to get the better of her.

She passed the Chinese shoe store, where she'd had her custom shoes made in the past, and then the furniture store, which had its front windows smashed. The chemists still looked familiar but there was an Indian staff instead of English. She had now reached the traffic lights and was unsure of crossing the street. Yes, indeed, this didn't have many traces of the past. Finally she reached Katherine's house. She got into the wretched, shaky elevator that she'd always been afraid of, and pushed the button. Even that failed to work, so she walked up the three flights of stairs. She rang the front door bell, and the bearer answered. Katherine was playing the piano in the living room. She turned around to see who it was.

"Thea! When did you return? How wonderful to see you after such ages!" Thea kissed her on the cheek.

"I got back last evening, and I don't mind telling you I feel lost. Everything is all so weird."

"Well my dear, you have been gone awhile, and there have been some changes. I'm sure it was a lot more exciting where you were."

"No it isn't that so much. Everything looks so dilapidated. Besides which I haven't seen my father yet, and nobody knows of his whereabouts."

Katherine looked at her friend in a dubious manner, as though she was holding back some information.

"Do you know something, maybe, that I don't?" Thea asked.

"Well I wouldn't want to be the first to tell you, but you will no doubt hear it from another. Rumor has it your father has gone bankrupt so he's conspicuous by his absence."

"What do you mean bankrupt? What gibberish are you talking?"

"Now Thea, I knew I shouldn't have said anything to you, but you asked me. You had better not repeat it to your family, if your mother doesn't already know it. It's common knowledge on the turf, and amongst those you know in this city."

"He's never given any indication over low finances while we've been abroad, or else I'm sure we would have returned a lot sooner. Don't worry I've already forgotten it. I just find it hard to believe."

Thea and Katherine were as different as chalk from cheese. Yet over the years they had been the closest friends. Katherine was an excellent student, whilst Thea was mischievously inclined and never worried about her grades.

"Did you finish school in England?" asked Katherine.

"I suppose I did something of sorts. As for finishing, does one ever really do that?"

She laughed. "Same old Thea. You'll never change. But you are a barrel of laughs, that's for sure."

"Well now that you have completed according to the standards of Loreto, what's next?"

"I'm now in college, and then I'm off to London, to join in the Royal Academy of Dramatic Art, known as RADA. You know I've always yearned to be an actress."

"Darling don't we all? You just want to make it a profession."

"Well, you've been overseas, and so has my sister, Sara. She's just returned after four years in Oxford, my brother Ara is at UCLA in California. So now it's my turn. I'll never return here."

"Well good luck to you, I'm sure you'll make it. I wish I hadn't returned. But then again, I don't think I'll be here long either."

Thea slept over at Katherine's that night, and the girls giggled at Thea's interpretation of the kids, both in New York, and Walton-on-Thames. Katherine couldn't believe her friend's experiences abroad.

Like most teenagers in those days, the girls were impressed by Hollywood movie stars. They imitated their dress style, and hairdos and lived in an imaginary escapism. They were Liz Taylor, Jane Powell, and Debbie Reynolds, all rolled into one. This was probably because of their sheltered upbringing. Neither Thea nor Katherine, had as yet had a serious date, or even aspired to one. So they'd lose themselves in the movies, and in Modern Screen and Photoplay magazines.

Thea's boredom drove her in the direction of her old school. She entered the massive wrought iron gates onto the red gravel path, past the aviary that had stood there since kindergarten, around the fish pond, across to the main building. The school had been rebuilt and added to, during World War Two. She continued through the main corridor, up the grand stairway, toward the senior classrooms. School was out, so she sat herself down at her old desk, and reminisced as she listened to concert practice across the playground at the assembly hall. Her eyes wandered to the playground below, and to the basketball fields, where she had spent her happiest moments as a child. The huge tamarind tree overshadowed the grounds. Here she'd thrown rocks at the boughs heavily laden with tangy fruit, filling her pockets to snack on during class. This, too, is where she had gathered crowds, and gotten in trouble in doing so. Ah! It all seemed like a world apart now. She walked carefully down the stairs, and past the big clock on the left where she had often been punished for many long hours. She could almost here the echo of the voice of the nun in charge, berating her, until her time was up, and she could leave.

She hesitated before proceeding to the assembly hall. She stood by the side door, and hoped she'd go unnoticed, as if that were possible. The sister that conducted the choir, flicked back her veil impatiently. She felt distracted. She heard a whisper from her group.

"Isn't that Thea Martin watching us?"

The same old fears came over Thea as when she had been reprimanded in the past. The nun now walked in her direction, a faint smile of disbelief on her face.

"It is you, Thea! We never expected to see you again."

"Good morning, Sister Michael. Yes it's me. I've recently returned from overseas."

Within seconds the girls jumped down from the platform and rallied around Thea. Patricia, who was doing her final year, exuberantly hugged her old friend.

"Oh Thea you look wonderful, welcome home."

Thea wept with happiness to see her again.

"Hey girl, you've grown so tall! Bet you play a mean game now."

"Er, not like when you were here. We were a team."

Patricia had never left the city, so she took Thea aside and questioned her about her travels. They walked out of the hall onto the grounds and chatted for quite some time before reaching the main gate. The native children with their pot bellies and grimy hands still clammered for small change by the church doorway. Time still progressed the same old way, as Thea remarked.

Weeks had passed, and Thea had to reach a decision as to her future. She wasn't the type to sit and wait around for something to happen. She had to make it happen. There was so little choice in those days for a young lady. If you didn't train as a stenographer, or a nurse, what else was there? She deplored study, but she found out that without it, she was stuck. Lydia had secured a job in the new showroom of the General Electric Company. Mother had her social life, and Father occasionally passed through to wind the clock and pay the bills.

He wasn't as financially flush as in the old days, but they weren't exactly with limited funds. Thea still continued her track outings with him in the mornings, and he encouraged her with her schemes and ideas.

"Don't worry, Mickey Mouse, you will find your vocational place one of these days. And when you do, you'll be the best in it. Don't listen to your mother and sister. They don't know it all. Look at me, I came into this world with nothing, no parents, no home, nothing! You are not a sheep, that is why your mother will never understand us. You have a solid foundation, you are not stupid, and you can do anything you set your heart on. Remember this forever."

Thea loved her dad for his encouragement. Unfortunately he was never around long enough for her to listen. She needed plenty right now, because all she did hear was the same old, "You will never come to anything, you don't care enough about what you do, and you have a wanderlust." If only her family at home would allow for her development, she could proceed to adulthood.

Mother gasped at the dining table. "Beautician of all trades! What makes you think you will qualify, or tolerate women?"

"I won't know until I try; do I?"

"Pray, where are you going to get this training?"

"I've been shopping around the neighborhood. There is an English cosmetologist who will train me privately at a price. She has a shop here in Park Street with an excellent reputation."

"Well, we'll make an appointment to see her, and I'll make the necessary arrangements for you. If it's a price I have to pay, young lady, you had better stick with it, that's all I'm telling you. I don't have money to throw down the drain."

During the next eighteen months, Thea trained, explored, and exhausted her creativity in all the well-known salons of the neighborhood, until she was forced to work for herself, and this she did with great gusto. She began with friends. Her mother's thought her too young and inexperienced, so she charged little. Then a Canadian lady with a business heard about Thea's capabilities and asked her to work with her, but not for her. She accepted.

Thea now nineteen, was still restless. It was summertime, and the first of many when they didn't journey to the hills. It was a long hot summer, and a group of film producers from England were in search of local talent for Rumor Godden's play, *The River*. It was to be shot as a movie in and around the city. Thea asked her mother if she could audition for a part in the cast.

"Honestly child! You think up such harebrained ideas. I wish you had concentrated as much on your studies as you do on the movie industry."

Her next attempt was an interview arranged by her father, as an airline stewardess, which she could have secured, but it meant flying.

"Once and for all Thea, I will never permit you to fly, or live on your own, until you get married. And as you don't even date yet, get all this gibberish out of your head."

Father shrugged his shoulders. "I did try, Mickey Mouse, you know how your mother is about your welfare, so just forget it."

Adding to Thea's plight was her father's withdrawal from the racetrack. He was disqualified from the Turf Club, for the alleged mismanagement of his affairs. This left him little choice but to race a handful of his horses at the Gymkhanna racetrack at Tollygunge, on the outskirts of town, which wasn't strictly affiliated with the Royal Turf Club in Calcutta. Thea's concept at the time was vague, but she was somewhat aware of the corruption and deceipt of racing. It had been her father's whole existence, and his sentimentality and superstition had led him to self-destruction. He had certainly given a lot more to the sport, than he had received from it over the years. Until now he had been one of Calcutta's most successful owners. The pity was that a gambler never knew when to quit. He had lived and worked hard for his folly for over thirty years. Thea was most saddened for her dad. He seemed to have lost his lust for life, and he hardly ever smiled anymore.

Thea yearned for faraway places. It seemed the girls her age that remained on in the city, were pressed down like flowers into marriages. She loved her family dearly, but the time had come for her to discard her innocent, vulnerable adolescence. In her mind, she had conjured this exuberant dream of her future: Her Prince Charming on his white horse would enter her dreary life and carry here away to some distant land. As her dad would have said, "It was kismet."

Kismet, the transmigration of souls, as well as strict karma; you get what you are. Her nirvana, the promise of heaven, is the reward of release from the wheel of existence.

Part 2

Thea and Howard

Chapter Ten

Through ages four to ten, both Thea and Lydia had participated in the Christmas fancy dress celebration, which was held at Calcutta's prestigious Grand Hotel. Mother had spent months in the preparation of her daughters' costumes, with the idea of them winning first prizes each time they paraded the grand ballroom.

Thea would strut proud as a peacock in her dress of real plumage. The feathers gracefully adorned her minute frame, and she'd obtain her goal in the final march. Lydia clutched her little sister's hand as she, herself, won her prize dressed in the attire of a Calcutta policeman. At five, Thea won again as the familiar logo of Johnny Walker on the Scotch bottle, and Lydia depicted the nursery rhyme of Mother Goose, as she clutched a real live goose in her arms. Each year Thea would draw the attention of the judges in the final march, as she'd make them aware of her claim. When her mother eventually ran out of ideas, and the children had outgrown their performances, it came to a close.

Now Thea at nineteen, and Lydia at twenty-five, attended Firpo's palm court concerts, each Sunday morning on the veranda. After church service, it became a weekly ritual to be seen at the concert with their friends, to catch up on the local gossip.

On one such occasion, Thea and Lydia made their usual grand entrance, as the orchestra always gave them special recognition upon their arrival. The sisters were identically dressed, and all eyes were riveted in their direction. Thea's curious eyes were hidden behind her sunglasses, as she observed a stranger amongst their group of friends. Who was he? She had to know before she left the company. He was tall, slim and ever so handsome. He had blue-gray eyes, which when they looked at her, showed his mutual attraction to her.

Unfortunately, he wasn't seated close enough to share in their mutual enthusiasm. As time went on, he appeared rather amused from a distance at her conversation. She was now temporarily distracted as her name was called from the bandstand for the lucky ticket number drawn for the prize of a picnic basket, chock full of goodies! She hastily jumped up with glee.

"I won! I won!" she exclaimed, as she ran toward her prize. She enthusiastically received the large hamper, and upon her return to the table, she stopped and whispered in the stranger's ear.

"I'd like very much to share this with you."

He whimsically smiled in return, not prepared for her impetuosity.

The concert came to a close at one o'clock. The crowd dispersed for lunch in the dining room. Each Sunday Mother awaited her girls for the elaborate curry lunch prepared by cook. Lydia and Thea sat in their respective places at the dining table, with Mother at the head of the table. There were always a dozen or more of their friends to share in this weekly ritual. The bearer served each course until everybody had his fill.

Thea gasped! There he was sitting opposite her, having lunch, still smiling.

"Who invited you here?" she asked.

"Your sister did."

"She doesn't even know you. You followed the crowd here."

"I beg your pardon, I am not that presumptuous, young lady."

Oh dear, why hadn't she kept her mouth shut. They had gotten off to a bad start. After luncheon was over, Thea and Katherine proceeded into the drawing room, as Thea watched the handsome youth follow her mother to the veranda for their demitasse. Their friends, contented with full bellies, relaxed to Thea's choice of music on the gramophone.

After a while Thea's curiosity overcame her virtues, and she slowly moved toward the veranda.

"Thea darling, I don't believe you've met Howard Wrenn. He is fairly new in Calcutta. The poor chap has had a unfortunate series of circumstances happen to him since his arrival here."

"Is that a fact? Such as what?"

Mother continued to relate the tale, as though he weren't able to himself.

"First he came down with the chicken pox, then with typhoid fever."

"Oh that's dreadful! Didn't you have your immunization shots before coming to this filthy country?"

"Of course I did, but I still got sick."

"How long are you here for?" asked Thea.

"Four years if I make it that long."

"What company do you work for?" she continued.

"It's a world renowned air-conditioning and heating company. We install machinery on ships and for commercial businesses."

"Where does your head office operate from?"

"Thea dear, that's enough questions," said Mother.

"That's all right. It's in London. This is my first overseas tour."

"Didn't you read about India before your departure? This is a dreadful country, with its loathsome diseases, some of which get the better of you."

"One never really knows enough until one gets here does one?"

"True! Unfortunately, you are experiencing things at their worst now. You will never know the country as it was."

Mother said, "The European population enjoys the prosperous lifestyle here, but we are saddened at its decline. So many of our friends have emigrated elsewhere."

Mother was definitely entranced by this newcomer. She had never taken such deep interest in any of the other gentlemen that had visited for the first time.

"Well, Howard, you must feel free to visit again. Our home has always been a home away from home. During the war this house was brimful of uniforms, and both my daughters entertained the troops. I myself did a lot of voluntary work, and Thea helped in the canteen. You must ask her to show you the 'hut' where it all took place. Now it stands empty and closed to the public, but it's a landmark on the *maidan*. I'm sure you have many such places in England."

Howard lacked sophistication and aggressiveness, but he was willing to learn and partake of this foreign country. As the company took leave of them for the afternoon, Howard seemed reluctant to go. He shyly moved in Thea's direction, on the pretense of selecting a gramophone record to hear.

"Here's one I'd like to hear. Would you please play it?"

"Music! Music! Music! That's an oldie, but Theresa Brewer has made it popular again."

Howard bravely took Thea by the hand and they started to dance on the marble floor.

"I can see you enjoy dancing," he said. "I'm not good myself, but I do like it." The music changed to Nat King Cole singing a sentimental ballad.

"What is the name of this one?" Howard asked.

" 'Too Young.' It's his latest," she replied.

"How old are you, Thea?"

"Eighteen."

"I'm twenty-three. I guess we are too young."

"You are rather. Especially to be abroad at such an age, on a responsible job, and already sick a couple of times."

He laughed! "Yes some of us get all the breaks, and others have to learn the hard way."

"Would you like to join us this evening at the cinema show? It's the one evening my father spends with us. You'll meet him if you do."

"I'd enjoy that very much. This is the first time I've felt so comfortable in a home since leaving mine in London. Your mother is a most gracious lady, and I enjoyed talking to her. Of course I also like dancing with you. You're easy to be with."

"Have you dated any since being here?"

"I've met some young ladies, and I was invited to my boss's home for dinner. But I can't say it's left an impression. Just in the line of duty you know."

Ramnareese awaited the family to appear at the front entrance, and he opened the car door for them. They drove toward Chowringhee Road, and came to a halt at the MGM theater, which was showing Esther Williams in *Bathing Beauty*. As they alighted from the car, the eternal beggars swarmed around them with their grimy hands out for alms. Cows strayed stupidly in their path. Calcutta had become an outdoor garbage heap, and the refuse from the street had an unbearable stench. Mother and Lydia clutched each other's hands, as they walked in the general direction of the foyer. Thea clung to Howard's arm avoiding the mobs, which they impatiently brushed past. They headed toward their reserved seats which were for their use each Sunday of the year, in the first row of the dress circle. Father was waiting for them. Thea rushed into his arms for a hug. She introduced Howard to him. During the interval, the two men had a drink at the bar, as was the custom, and the ladies chatted in their seats.

After the show, they went to dine at Firpo's Italian restaurant. Father accompanied his ladies toward their special table in the corner. The bearers in their fine gold and white uniforms and turbans catered to their orders, and the impressive management was at their service. Howard was overwhelmed at this VIP treatment, which even his boss had never experienced. Father excused himself as he strolled toward Mr. Firpo's table, and joined him in conversation. Howard watched Mother's reaction closely. It was obvious the man of the family wasn't questioned, and didn't require any excuses made on his behalf.

"Shall we dance Howard?" requested Thea.

Howard excused himself politely from the table. He wasn't sure of his next move, except to follow Thea to the vast, uncrowded dance floor. He smiled as he drew her to him.

"You all seem rather popular at this famous restaurant, with everybody's undivided attention," he said.

"Yes I suppose it must appear that way to you, but these folks from the bandleader and his orchestra, to the owner, have known my family since I was knee high to a grasshopper. So it's only natural."

During the weeks that followed, Howard and Thea were constant companions. After their respective jobs each evening, they would meet at Thea's home, where Mother was always present.

Frequently they would drive around the Strand, and stop by the river. "Do you come here often?" he asked.

"I used to in the past with my family before we left for America. Daddy and I visited the stables at Hastings, where he kept his thoroughbreds around the corner from here. It was all so different then."

"I'm sure I will find it difficult to reestablish contact at home when I return. Everything is so ordinary where I live. People move, get married, and you don't fit in anywhere."

"Well you don't have to worry about that right now."

"What is it like to grow up in a country like this?"

"I haven't lived here constantly. We've traveled extensively. In fact the last time we were gone so long, I never expected to see these shores again. But I knew we had to return."

They continued to drive toward the Victoria memorial, and once again Howard parked his car beside the huge monument.

"Let's take a walk on the *maidan*," he requested.

They walked hand in hand along the tree-lined avenue of monkeys, which Howard named Monkey Avenue. The monkeys were totally harmless, almost domestic, as they sought recognition. He was terribly amused by their pranks. Thea told him about her childhood here, when she was escorted by Phoolmia, and for a few pennies they would be entertained by the monkey keeper. The monkeys, dressed in vividly colored silken rags, were trained to dance, get married, and die, all in the same performance. It was the highlight of her day, and then a bag of peanuts was shared between her and the animals. Howard laughed and said he could visualize it.

"There is the Rondelshay Hut Mother was talking about. Boy! Was it an active hot spot in its day."

It was a moonlit evening. As they came to a halt by a huge tree, Howard drew Thea in a fond embrace as he kissed her for the first time. It was a sweet, innocent vibration, to which Thea responded. She was drawn instantly to his strong clean masculinity. It gave her the feeling of being a fragile nymph. She had only ever been in the company of young boys and had never been truly kissed like that. Howard was definitely her knight in shining armor.

"Thea, I never had the courage before to hold you in my arms. I've gone home so frustrated after our dates. You probably thought me a jerk. You are so worldly for your years, I felt very inadequate. But I couldn't resist you this evening, you look so beautiful. I think I'm falling in love with you. Do you feel anything for me?" he asked.

"Yes, Howard, I look forward to seeing you each evening. I enjoy your company, and most of all I am not acting when I'm with you. I always seem to be someone else with most folks."

Oh dear, Mother liked Howard well enough, but now that Thea wished to reveal a steady courtship, she might disapprove. Maybe for all concerned, she should keep it her secret. She had never kept one as yet; it was going to be most difficult. How could she not talk about Howard to Katherine? Her girlfriend knew her too well, and they were constantly in each other's company. Howard suggested he would write his parents first, and then their parents would automatically assume the inevitable.

Thea hadn't ever had a serious discussion of this sort with her mother. So she didn't rightly know how to cope with a subject as sensitive as her affection for a man. Mother was a romantic, in every sense of the word, but when it came to her girls, she was plain conventional. Lydia never spoke of such matters either. Thea, just had to confide in Katherine. She had to have her opinion. Most evenings Thea and Katherine would visit the Armenian club on the park, and play badminton. They had social activities in which girl met boy, but again the girls had grown up in the community, and were still considered children.

"Katherine, what would you say to Howard and I getting engaged?"

"I'd say you're crazy! He's the first man your mother has given you permission to date. Your assumption of this cannot be taken seriously. It's just delusional, Thea."

"Well, we intend to, and get married soon after."

"It won't last, Thea. You're too impulsive. You know little about him, and he knows less about you. I've known you all of your life, and I don't think you're ready for a commitment as yet."

"Don't you feel he's a good catch?"

"Thea, you're talking marriage. Not a catch!"

"Oh what difference does it make? Nobody seems to care about happiness. Everything has to be a cut-and-dried affair. What experience is expected of one when it comes to the affairs of the heart? Howard is handsome, good natured, attentive, holds a good position, and he is going places. What more would I require?"

"Goodness me, child," said Mother, "Why must you get serious, in so short a time? Get to know each other, introduce him to your friends, go out to more parties, don't continue on a one to one relationship. There is plenty of time to settle down. Marriage is a responsibility, something foreign to you."

"Oh Mum, left to you, I'll be an old maid."

Well so much for opinions, both girlfriend and Mother didn't seem to understand her.

The political unrest had worsened, and it wasn't even safe to walk on the *maidan* anymore.

One evening Howard brought over a handsome gent from the past. Colin was in the insurance business, and had stopped in Calcutta from Hong Kong. He was introduced to Lydia, and for the first time ever, the sisters began to double date. Within weeks Lydia announced her engagement to Colin. Both Mother and Thea were flabbergasted! She informed them that she had decided to fly to Britain with him, and they would marry there. Once again Mother had been deprived of a wedding regalia. Lydia had made no secret of her disenchantment with Calcutta. All of her friends had emigrated to South Africa, Australia, and England, and now it was her turn. Thea didn't want to think about their lives minus Lydia. She was the first born, and her departure would cause an upheaval in the household. However time would tell. . . . The two of them left for England as planned.

Thea introduced Howard to the Gymkhanna races. He wasn't a gambling man, and he thought it a bit rich for his blood. He treated the whole affair like a carnival, as they enjoyed the afternoon tea on the green by the clubhouse. He watched the intensity of the gamblers by the tote and commented they were a strange breed. Howard was extremely unsophisticated, and his myriad questions exasperated Thea at times. He'd speak of his London suburban life-style. His recreation time was spent scrambling on his motorbike with youths his age. He drank socially at the local pub, enjoyed a game of darts, and he voted for the conservative party. He was an only child, and he wished he had sibling. He was overwhelmed by Thea's affectionate attention, and most unsure of her impetuousness. She in turn succumbed to his possessiveness at social functions. Nightclubs, concerts, dining at the finest restaurants, and horse racing were part of her accepted life-style. She was always the center of attraction, and her wardrobe glistened to mother's perfection. At the popular Golden Slipper nightclub they would dine, wine and dance till dawn, until the band ended with "I'll See You in My Dreams." Thea could never have enough of Howard's company. And he would leave her at the garden gate frustrated. Her sophisticated innocence was captivating. He wasn't familiar with the sophistication of company directors, and the executive class. Englishmen on their first contract overseas were not accustomed to such a lavish lifestyle.

Their salaries wouldn't have covered a night's tab at any of the restaurants they now frequented. Their simple bread and butter ladies were glorified charwomen, the highlight of their entertainment was a church bingo game, or a gin and tonic at their local pub. Now they had gotten accustomed to club membership of the golf set, and learned the niceties of mah-jongg and bridge. Sundays were spent on the polo grounds. Polo was an Indian invention, now a British sport, and also an American pastime. They had servants at their beck and call, and they paraded around at garden parties with their frilly umbrellas, to keep the nasty sun from burning their milky white complexions. No wonder the Indians had wised up, and threw their slogans at them to "Quit India."

As time went by Howard's physical condition had weakened, and his tolerance toward the heat of Calcutta decreased significantly. At Thea's suggestion he took a two-week leave of absence, and went for a holiday to Gopalpor-on-sea. His departure left Thea despondent. She thought to herself, his abstinence from sexual activity had probably not helped any. After all how much could a young man have tolerated on a daily basis, without copulation. Mother was most anxious over his poor health, and advised Thea to free herself from contemplating marriage. But Thea had her plans made, unknown to her mother.

Upon Howard's return from his holiday, he looked the picture of health. With his bronze suntan, and blue eyes, he stood before Thea, tall

80

and slim, dressed in his complementary whites, with an intricately tied cravat round his neck. He glowed with pride, as he'd glance with private admiration and amusement toward Thea dressed in her frills of tuile and organza. They truly made a handsome couple as they set out for a night on the town.

"Now don't be late," was Mother's admonition.

Thea had sipped on her umteenth glass of champagne, and she amorously kissed Howard on the dance floor.

"Darling, let's go for a drive by the river, and then to your place. I've never seen where you live," she whispered.

"Thea, do you know what you're implying? You've had a little too much bubbly."

"Yes, Howard, I know what I'm implying. I wish to go to your place. About time don't you think?"

Howard didn't know how to react to this outburst.

"I believe you're trembling, dear Howard. Don't you want to take me in your arms and make mad passionate love? I'm still a virgin you know, and if we are supposedly so enraptured with each other, there should be no cause for hesitation. Should there?"

It was her imprudence that determined their future. He couldn't possibly deprive himself any longer of this delectable sensation offered him. He trembled with uncertainty and awkwardness, as his trousers fell to the floor of his bedroom. His forehead had beads of perspiration, and he prolonged foreplay. She eagerly kissed him, and they were engulfed around each other, as he penetrated himself inside of her for the first time. She agonizingly winced! She wasn't overwhelmed with passion as she imagined. Their passion had lost momentum, and he couldn't release himself, as she clung to him clumsily.

"I'm sorry love, if I hurt you. But it won't be that way again."

"Look at my beautiful taffeta petticoat. It's all bloody. I must wash it this instant, before I go home."

She was upset at having lost her virginity, and he showed concern for his negligence.

"This making love is a messy affair, isn't it?" she said.

He laughed loudly.

"What's so funny? That you had a cherry, probably the only one you ever had—it's nothing to laugh at."

"No my precious, it's your innocent expression that I adore."

Because of their social conditioning, Howard felt he had robbed

Thea of her guarded chastity, though she had voluntarily entrusted it to him.

"Howard, you know now we have to get married as soon as possible don't you?"

"Darling, because you are no longer a virgin, doesn't mean you're tarnished for life."

"Maybe where you come from, that's so, but in this country, a lady of virtue and breeding is a virgin when she marries. So if you don't ask my parents for my hand, I can never see you again."

"Are you serious?"

"Never been more so in my life, so you had better do the honorable courtesy when you next come over to my house."

For the past year Howard and Thea had been inseparable. He had vowed his never-ending love for her, and now because she had given herself to him, he had stopped visiting overnight.

Thea had never known such despair. A week had passed, and he hadn't called. Mother questioned his whereabouts. Thea didn't know how to react to the hurt she suffered.

"He must be sick," said Mother.

Day followed day, as Thea assumed one thing and another. But she didn't pick up the phone to find out. He had always called her, and on principle, nice girls didn't call their men friends.

Katherine and Thea went to the Elite cinema theater to see Doris Day in "Lullaby of Broadway." Thea was so disturbed, she could not watch the movie to the finish. The taxi came to an abrupt halt outside of her house, after she had seen Katherine home. She woefully dragged her feet up the stairs to her front door. She stopped outside the door, with the key in her hand, as she heard voices from within. It was past midnight. Who could be visiting at this late hour? They were the voices of Mother and Howard. Thea's heart skipped and she felt nauseated as she turned the key in the door.

"I can't possibly leave here without Thea. I had no idea how much a part of my life she had become. I realize I cannot offer her the life she is accustomed to, but I will certainly love and take care of her to the best of my ability."

Mother was mute as Thea rushed into Howard's arms.

"Howard! Howard! I've missed you dreadfully, are you all right?"

"Darling, will you marry me?"

"I thought you'd never ask! Of course I will."

"I'm here pouring out my heart to your mother. I'm being sent home in a month before my contract is completed. I'm costing the company too much in doctor's bills. So now we can get married and leave here together."

"A month is all we have? Oh Mum, that isn't much time for wedding arrangements. There's so much to do."

"I must phone Daddy. Where could he be? I hope he's in town," Mother said, as she gave them both her blessings. "I must see the church in the morning. And call Angelo Firpo, you'll have your reception at Firpo's. Howard, you must get the rings, and a new suit to be married in. I'll start right away."

So Mother got her wedding, even though it wasn't the one she had planned on. She was excited about the affair as any proud mother would have been.

Chapter Eleven

It was 3:00 P.M. on a beautiful, sunny, mild December afternoon in Calcutta, as Thea awaited the arrival of her unpredictable father. He dashed up the stairs as he always did, mopping his brow.

"Mickey Mouse you look like a movie star!"

The adoration on his face brought tears to Thea's eyes. Mother fussed attentively over her daughter's dress, as she glared at her spouse.

"You're late as usual. Let's go," she snapped.

Father and daughter got seated at the back of the car, as Ramnareese smilingly drove toward the Catholic church.

"Are you nervous, Mickey?"

"I feel a bit strange, but that's to be expected. I'm happy, Daddy, not nervous." She smiled.

"I can't believe this whole affair, but if your mother approves, and you love him, he seems nice enough. It would have been nice if you both could have lived here awhile before departing from this country so soon."

Thea looked exquisite as she slowly walked up the aisle on her father's arm. Her full-length white gown of guipere lace and taffeta, was a replica of the one worn by Elizabeth Taylor in the movie, "Father of the Bride." It was then that the film star had married Nicky Hilton. There was profound silence amongst the guests, as Thea glanced at each and every guest seated in the church awaiting the bridal couple. There were wellwishers known to her over the years, and some that weren't familiar such as Howard's two bosses and their wives. She now reached the altar steps, where Howard stood alongside of his best man, Marshall. Here Father stepped to the left of the bride and joined Mother. The solemn ceremony began with the Belgian priest, as they took their vows loud and clear. Howard's strong hand was a trifle nervous as he slipped the small wedding band, next to Thea's diamond clustered engagement ring, which he had given her three weeks prior to this. He smiled as he gently lifted the veil off her face, and kissed her saying *"arp cupsourith hi,* you're beautiful." She smiled as they walked down the aisle to the organist playing the final Mendelssohn march on their way out. They were indeed a radiant couple as the groom assisted his young bride into the car. They were driven first to the photographer's studio, which was situated on the corner of Park and Chowringhee Streets.

The glorious reception at Firpo's restaurant awaited them, as they gracefully walked up the stairs. Casanova, the talented maestro and good friend of the family, had his orchestra play the wedding march as the couple entered the beautiful ballroom, with its splendid imported Italian murals, and tinted mirrors, which were delineated with Spanish dancers. From the high elaborate ceiling hung spectacular chandeliers, the largest of which focused on the fifty-pound fruitcake, a gift from Angelo Firpo.

Mother and Father danced the first waltz, as Howard and Thea danced alongside of them. They changed partners, as was the customary gesture. Father proudly smiled as he waltzed with his daughter, around the highly polished wood floor. The orchestra then drifted to the tune ''My Foolish Heart.'' Father handed his little girl to her husband, as that was their courting song.

Howard and Thea were totally involved, as they gazed into each other's eyes with adoration. They had been having such a wonderful time at their wedding, they didn't want to leave the happy reception. Thea hurriedly changed into her going-away attire, with Mother's assistance in the powder room.

The bride and groom clasped their hands with excitement, as they ran down the stairs and friends showered them with confetti and rice. Thea tossed her bouquet of pale purple orchids to Katherine. Father awaited the couple at the foot of the stairs, as he gave Ramnareese final instructions, to drive around the Strand nice and easy, before delivering them to their honeymoon suite at the Great Eastern Hotel on Esplanade Road.

Father kissed his daughter, as he held her tightly. He shook hands with his son-in-law and bid him a safe trip back home to England.

''Look after my Mickey, and be happy,'' he said.

''Oh Howard, wasn't that a marvelous wedding? Did you ever think in your wildest dreams, we'd live to see this day?''

''I must admit your parents did us proud. I wish my folks could have been here. They have never experienced anything like that in their lives. For that matter neither have I. I must say you conducted yourself with terrific diplomacy, darling.''

Ramnareese finally came to a halt outside the Great Eastern Hotel.

"*Chota Baba*, do you wish me to take you home after the weekend? Your mother wishes to know when I should fetch you."

"You tell my mother we will call her."

Howard took his jacket off and unfastened his tie, with a sigh of relief, or one of anticipation. He drew Thea toward him. They kissed passionately, and they were both excited about the intensity of each other's expectations.

The couple couldn't honestly pride themselves over their erotic experiences on this their wedding night. It was the novelty of discovery that made it enchantingly exquisite. Thea loved Howard with every breath of her body, as she entwined herself around him, making him a part of her. Howard's masculinity couldn't refrain from thrusting himself inside her, making them whole.

For Thea a first love was very special, and could never be recaptured, or forgotten. For Howard, he had made his life a commitment to her never to be broken.

It was New Year's Eve, and Marshall, their best man, had arranged a farewell party for them at his home, which wasn't far from their honeymoon suite. The next morning they brunched with Mother at the homestead. There hadn't been time for sleep, as they got dressed in their party clothes for another night on the town. The bride and groom's final week in Calcutta was spent at Thea's home. Mother was most attentive to her daughter's requirements, and cook prepared her favorite dishes. Thea had no concept upon her departure, how her mother's heart ached as the trunks and cases were packed also for the last time. The servants lined the driveway, as they bid the "missie" good-bye. Some even had tears in their eyes. Poor old Popeye treated it as just another day, as she hugged him with tears. At Howrah station some of Thea's closest friends stood on the platform awaiting the train to depart. Mother showed no signs of anxiety, as the final whistle blew, and Father wasn't anywhere insight. His Mickey Mouse eagerly sought for his face in the teeming crowds, but she secretly knew he wouldn't be there. He had never been brave when it came to farewells. Thea had promised herself she wouldn't get emotional, but with Howard's arms around her she cried bitterly. This time she was aware of leaving this station forever, never to return.

The shimmering Howrah bridge was now in the distance, as the train widened in a circle. The city's twinkling lights in the dusk of evening faded away. Thea was now alone in the compartment for two, with her husband. From now on it wasn't me but us. Not till then had she paid heed to his feelings, and the responsibility he had, returning to his home with a new bride.

She awoke in the early morn, as Howard slept peacefully. She gazed out of the window of the fast moving train, at a day that was widening the distance between herself and her homeland. She thought of her previous train journeys, through terrain much like this, to Mussoorie and Darjeeling, and the hours she had spent as a little girl looking out of the window. Now she was married, and her childhood was behind her, retreating just as the rural plains of India disappeared, possibly forever on either side of the onrushing train. Calcutta was a city that could inspire all sorts of feelings, from repulsion to fascination, but that couldn't leave anyone indifferent. This had been her destiny, before she came into the world. As the train came to a halt at Bombay's station, Thea didn't let go of Howard's arm for minute. She felt so totally helpless.

Although Thea's father hadn't said good-bye she hadn't been slighted. He had made sure that his racing friends in Bombay would show his daughter and her husband a good time, whilst they were in transit at the Ritz Hotel for a week before they departed on a ship for England.

The newlyweds were exhausted as they lay in each other's arms in their hotel suite the next morning. There was a knock on the door. Howard answered it.

"Come on you lovebirds, we are waiting on you."

Thea jumped out of bed as she heard the voice at the door.

"I don't believe my eyes." The three prosperous jockeys of the season with their respective wives had surprised the newlyweds, as they stood there by the door. They, too, were living at the Ritz.

The week that followed was one champagne party after another. During the days they toured the city, and at night they scarcely slept. After a hectic whirlwind of events, the couple had a final send-off in their cabin on the ship.

Chapter Twelve

The P & O Strathaird was the sister ship to the Strathmore, which Thea had previously traveled on. However this was a cruise ocean liner, which pleased Thea, as it was Howard's first ocean bound experience, and he was ecstatic over the idea.

Slowly the large ship moved away from alongside the jetty in the dusk of evening. From where they stood the impressive arch of the Gateway of India was silhouetted against a crimson sky. As they were distanced from Bombay, they smoothly sailed into the Indian Ocean.

Thea apprehensively smiled at her husband.

"I can't believe I'm never to return to these shores again. It's almost frightening," she said.

She was just beginning to register the drastic change of life-style she had undertaken. Pensively, she held Howard's hand in hers, and hesitatingly smiled at his handsome face.

"What's the matter dear?" he asked.

"Oh, I suppose all new brides feel this way."

"What way is that?"

"A little awed."

'You awed!" he laughed. "Never! You have too much adventure in you."

The tears slowly ran down her cheeks.

"Howard I've never left my mum before, and when I don't have her to return to, what will you do?"

"Come come now, my darling. You are my wife now. You must stop this little girl illusion. Sure it's all strange to you now, but it will get better. We are on the brink of a new life together."

"You make it sound so easy. I've never told you before, but I loathe England. How can I make it my home when I've never really liked it?"

"I think you're just a little homesick. You'll get over it. Let's enjoy this fabulous two weeks on this ship. It may be a long time before we can again. You shouldn't compare your short experience of London after the war to returning now as a married woman.''

"Well! I'll tell you my idea of typically English. It's a quality that challenges, and is challenged, by all that is foreign to them. It's a code of behavior that is provincial. They are stuck up, arrogant, stuffed shirts. And I am not!''

"Oh dear me. You don't look at me in that manner, do you?''

"No! Because you have conformed. But every so often you get a bit typically English.''

Within the first week on board ship, Thea and Howard made friends with an Australian couple on their way to England, and also an English family returning from Australia for the second time, having not liked it. Margaret, also nineteen, conveniently overlooked Thea's marriage status, and she sought her companionship whenever Howard wasn't by his wife's side.

"I just can't imagine anyone my age getting married,'' she said to Thea.

"If you met the right man, somebody like my Howard, I bet you would.''

"I bet you won't feel the same way you do now in ten years.''

"Oh yes I will. Howard is my life. I will love him even more.''

Their last port of call was Marseilles, France. Howard and Thea deserted the passenger tour of the city, as they got off the bus on the Cambiare for a shopping spree, which they indulged in until it was time for the ship to leave the port.

They had now left the sunny Mediterranean behind them, and they entered a choppy Atlantic, and finally sailed into the bleak English Channel. As they sighted the shores of England, Thea looked forward to Lydia meeting them. If not for her what would she do? She couldn't have tolerated her new surroundings without some member of her family present.

Thea anxiously scanned the crowd on the pier in the distance, as the ship neared the port of Southampton.

"There she is, there's my sister! Howard wave, wave to her so she can see us,'' Thea yelled. "Lydia, Lydia, here we are.'' Who was the dapper gentleman that stood beside her with a quizzical expression on his face? He had on a bowler hat, and in his hand carried a folded umbrella. He slightly resembled Howard, and was engrossed in conversation with Lydia.

"What do you know, Dad has come to meet us, too. By jove! What an attempt for him."

"Why shouldn't he? My sister did."

"You don't know Dad."

Thea was one of the first passengers to rush off the ship. She embraced Lydia with a bear hug. "Where is Colin?" she asked.

"Shush Thea! I don't know. I left him shortly after our arrival here. How is Mum?" she asked.

"Mum and Dad are fine. Daddy never said good-bye, but he arranged for his friends in Bombay to give us a great time." Thea hadn't even glanced in Howard's direction until he said, "Darling, I'd like you to meet Dad."

He circumspectly shook Thea's hand.

"Welcome, young lady. Your sister and I have kept each other company, since we got here a couple of hours ago."

"Howard darling, please get our luggage together, I must chat with Lydia. There is so much to tell her."

They then proceeded toward the boat train for London. Howard and his father followed the sisters, as they were deeply engrossed in conversation.

"Tell me why you didn't marry," Thea said.

"I just didn't. He changed completely after we got settled here. So I got a job as a secretary. I live in Hartfordshire, which is quite a ways from here. Mum wrote and told me to meet you on the day of your arrival, so here I am."

They got settled in the train, to which Lydia was well adapted by now. Howard's father observed his new daughter-in-law closely, and his eyes rested upon her ring finger.

"How much did that rock throw you for, Son?"

Howard smiled awkwardly, holding on to his wife's diminutive hand.

"Not as much as it should have, Dad."

Lydia compassionately smiled at her little sister. Thea smiled back and wondered why her sister hadn't gotten married yet.

As they drove through the narrow streets of London toward the north side, Thea was convinced she would never develop an enormous appetite for this great city. Howard had never discussed or made plans to make it their permanent home. In fact they had spoken little of their future.

Chapter Thirteen

It was a tidy unimaginative neighborhood, with rows of little red brick attached houses, on an apple tree-lined street. The people that dwelled here were as unassuming as their weather, which was the topic of conversation upon meeting. Food rationing, which was still in existence, troubled all concerned.

The car halted outside of Howard's home, by the garden gate. His perplexed, pallid mother anxiously awaited her prodigy. Howard embraced her for a lengthy period, and then he turned to introduce his wife and sister-in-law. Thea's mother-in-law, Mrs. Wrenn, affectionately embraced both sisters, as they proceeded through the main entrance into the living room, which was used only on special occasions. Here a roaring fire was ablaze, which reflected on the highly polished furniture and floor.

Thea stood in the center of the room with outstretched arms and said, "This is like a doll's house."

Howard smiled. "Yes dear, the houses here are small, and we don't have servants to keep them clean. Mother does all her own work." They were taken on a house tour. The dining room, which was most used, was heated by an economical coke fire. The table was set with fine fresh linen, English china was used for high tea and holidays. A glass door led into the wintry garden and frozen fish pond. The bedrooms upstairs were completely devoid of heat. Howard's mother placed stone hot water bottles in each of the beds each evening. The tour completed, they all sat down to high tea. Thea was most thankful that Lydia had been invited to stay over for the weekend. Festivities had been planned, as the neighbors anxiously awaited the newlyweds from abroad.

The couple repeated the wedding celebration in a simpler manner. Thea wore her beautiful bridal attire, as she walked down the stairs, to meet Howard's three uncles, who had traveled from far and wide for the celebration. Mrs. Wrenn took great pride in serving the top layer of the wedding cake which the couple had brought back very carefully. She had saved weeks of food rations to splurge for the party.

The excitement of their arrival now concluded, Thea had to appropriately settle down in her austere surroundings. Howard diligently returned to his head office, the reality of which disturbed him, after his overseas position. Thea familiarized herself with the neighborhood and London transport. She secured a position in a beauty salon in Golders Green in North London. Both her home and work life had become catastrophic, before she had given either a chance. She hadn't any idea how difficult she had made it for herself. But then she had never been one for compromising.

Her father-in-law diligently returned home each evening at 6:00 P.M. dressed in his conservative office suit and bowler hat, with the *Daily Express* newspaper folded in one hand, and his umbrella in the other. Howard followed within minutes from the train station, after having ploughed through the crowds on the tube from the city. They'd be seated in front of the coke fire in the dining room, awaiting their supper. Thea was of little or no help, for fear of criticism. She felt totally confined. Each evening after supper, Lydia would call to enquire how her sister fared. She knew only too well how that was.

Sundays were exceptional. It was their one morning in the week to sleep late, and none of them went to church. Mrs. Wrenn outdid herself with their traditional roast beef, and Yorkshire pudding for lunch. Monday's came round only too soon, and they were back to the grind.

Howard never complained, and he was most tolerant with Thea. Thea should have treated it all as an experience; instead she felt pressured. The short winter evenings were dismal, and she and Howard seemed to spend little time with each other. Between them they didn't earn enough to leave his parents' home. Thea's mother wrote faithfully each week, and informed her that her father had returned to the homestead permanently.

Spring arrived and the crocuses and daffodils were the first to appear in the back garden. The English are recognized for their passion for gardening, and summertime was a burst of color everywhere. At the first hint of blue skies and sunshine, Howard and Thea went to the London Zoo and Regent's Park, where amongst the flora and fauna the couple boated on the lakes, and took a picnic to Kew Gardens. They had walked for miles, never tiring of each other. Truly their happiest days were now. Often Lydia accompanied them to the theater, and Katherine now performed with the greats of the London stage, and gave her old friend complimentary tickets. The stage was truly her one and only love.

The summer months lasted only too briefly. Thea's initiation seemed rather slow, as she struggled with domestic duties. Howard patiently helped her with cooking and ironing, after she had burnt many a good shirt of his. Her first attempt at cooking lamb chops caught on fire. Howard rescued them and completed their dinner, while his mother shook her head with disapproval.

When they retired to bed, they were too exhausted to make love. And when they did make love, they had to be very quiet. To say this was for the birds was an understatement. Even they had their privacy in the trees and bushes.

Thea's patience had grown threadbare. Each evening after work, she'd purchase the local paper, secretly in search of apartments for rent. It was like searching for a needle in a haystack, but that didn't hinder her. She had never shared a bathroom with her own sister, let alone a household of strangers. After weeks of frustration, she found a listing for a comfortable, clean bed-sitter. Naturally one shared the bathroom and kitchen. But before she even rang the doorbell to the establishment, she vowed she'd take it with the little money she had saved from her salary. The Viennese-Jewish landlady was reluctant to accept her money in advance without her husband's approval. Thea assured the woman her choice would be all right with him. She mentioned her husband's reputable company, and her job in a local beauty shop. Joyful at her achievement, she jumped on the bus to her in-laws' home. How was she to break the news to Howard and his parents? She rushed into the house, as they were finishing supper as usual.

"Thea, where have you been? You have been late all week for dinner."

She sat down in silence, and not a word was uttered in anybody's direction. After dinner, she wished the dishes would disappear, as her poor attempts at washing up were not appreciated.

That night as Thea lay beside her husband, she felt doubtful over his reaction to what she had done. But done it was, and she had to tell him.

"Howard are you ready to move into a flat as yet? We can't live here forever."

"Thea we've been over all that, we don't make the money to go on our own as yet."

"Well! I found us a place today, and I have put two weeks' rent down. We can move in next week."

He jumped up, and sat bolt upright in bed.

"Are you crazy? Where did you get the money to put down two weeks' rent? And how much is it?"

"I saved it, and you will like my choice, and we are going to move," she insisted.

"Tell me pray, how do we come up with the same amount each week, from then on?"

"We will have to budget, won't we?"

"Where is this place you have found?"

"It's in Hampstead, you can take the train, as you do from here, and I the bus."

Thea tried every which way to humor her spouse, but he wasn't falling for it. He withdrew from her, with disregard for her insensitive feelings. This was probably because she had made the first move, against his wishes.

"I know you feel pretty much secure here. But left to you, we will never leave your parents' home. We can't have our privacy here, not even make love, without you shushing me. Besides it's not fair to your folks. We must go on our own way now."

He put his arm around her, and said, "I guess you're right. Left to myself, I wouldn't make the first move. It's so difficult to readjust to this country on limited funds. I miss the life abroad so much, and must try and get back overseas."

"I don't think you're in a position to as yet. The company won't grant you that privilege until you're stronger."

Winter was around the corner. Thea hadn't developed a blissful marriage. Their fairy-tale beginning now seemed nonexistent. Her restlessness caused their relationship to develop into one of confusion. Howard had never spoken of future plans, and she felt a lack of permanence, as her compelling obsession was to leave the shores of England. He secretly thought if he didn't secure an overseas position for them soon, their marriage would end.

They moved as planned to their first bed-sitter in Hampstead. Each evening Thea invariably got home from work before he did, and she prepared supper with their meager rations. She couldn't look at another spam fritter or sausage and mash in the face. Sharing a bath and kitchen was repulsive. With eager eyes she searched the street from her bay

94

window each evening, for her husband's return from work. He was never late, and she knew from the expression on his face, whether he had had a good day or a bad one. He had very little in common with his colleagues at work. Thea would rush down the stairs to open the door and welcome him.

The months passed, and he waited hopefully for an overseas position. It seemed endless. Finally the day arrived.

"I got it, I got it!" he bellowed from the garden gate below.

"Tell me! Tell me! Where? And what did you get?"

"We have a choice of two countries, neither of which are familiar to me. No doubt you will make the final selection. One is Khartoum, the capital of the Sudan, in northeast Africa. The other is Aden, which is in the Arabian Sea. We have already passed through there."

It didn't take Thea too long to make her decision.

"How long is the contract for?" she asked.

"Two years."

"Tell the company you request Aden. It's by the ocean, and I think the weather's better than in the Sudan."

"I think we should think it over awhile. There's time."

"You tell them immediately that you want to leave as soon as possible."

"Thea, who in their right mind wants to go to Aden?"

"We do! Right away Howard, or else you'll be too late."

Howard had to be approved by his company doctor, and by the medical staff at the Hospital for Tropical Diseases, after which it took six weeks to get the necessary immunization shots, and their passports in order. The redtape attached to an overseas assignment was a serious affair.

Thea was so excited over their latest development, she promptly telephoned Lydia in Hartfordshire. Her sister was pleased, as she was aware of Thea's discontent in Britain. Thea didn't care where they headed, just so long as it was a warm climate and Howard would make a better livelihood.

Chapter Fourteen

On a gray foggy afternoon, Thea and Howard flew by BOAC to their first stop, Cairo, Egypt. Lydia, her devoted sister, was at the airport to wish the couple a safe journey, as she waved them good-bye.

Thea lay her head back with a sigh of relief in the comfort of her first-class seat, as she glanced over to her husband.

"Do you feel as good as I do?" she asked.

"I won't know until I get there, but I do feel good, yes."

"Umm! This French Champagne hits the spot. It's been so long, I almost forgot the niceties of life. Cheers darling, here's to our new life."

At Cairo airport, the couple were greeted by Howard's company associates, and driven to the Metropolitan Hotel, on Soloman Pasha Street. This was to be their residence for the weeks to follow, whilst Howard took intensive training.

They stepped through the front doorway to the luxurious hotel, and into the elevator to their suite of rooms, the balcony of which overlooked Soloman Pasha Street. Thea looked up at the blue sky. She had never been so starved for sunshine before, and she appreciated its warmth. She swore she would never take it for granted again.

"Howard, isn't this wonderful? I feel as though we are on holiday. Whoever thought we'd be in the land of pharaohs and pyramids, surrounded by the river Nile."

In the early morning, they were awakened by the call to prayer from the mosque in the distance. It was music to Thea's ears. The cock crowed outside the window. This was certainly nowhere as harsh as an alarm clock. The reluctant mules and camels startled them as they walked beside them on the streets. The familiar aromas of the bazaar were nostalgic.

The amenities offered Howard for a life abroad were most welcome; a new car, a furnished home, three-month paid vacation at the end of his contract. In Britain it would never have happened.

Howard started work at the office at eight and returned for a long lunch period. Whilst he was at work, Thea browsed around the local shops. She discovered that the Egyptian shopkeepers and merchants fluently spoke French, Arabic, and English.

The senior staff of Howard's office graciously accompanied her and her husband around their beautiful city of which they were most proud. Their first visit to the Pyramid of Giza was fascinating. When Thea and Howard attempted their first camel ride, she felt the arrogant beast wasn't to be trusted, and it was common knowledge they were the carriers of venereal disease. They scaled the heights of the musty interior of the pyramid, with the help of the guide and an oil lamp but they couldn't decipher the hidden tombs within. Thea posed for a picture by the aged sphinx. On their return, they stopped by Mena House, notoriously known for ex-King Farouk's opulent orgies. They visited the ancient museum of the Egyptian dynasties, which dated back to 4500 B.C. and saw the preservation of mummies, which took a couple of visits to absorb. The Egyptians were proud of their zoo, which was the nicest Thea had experienced. Last but not least was a visit to the magnificent Muhammad Ali Mosque, which stood upon a hill, surrounded by lush gardens and tall poplar trees reaching toward the sky. From here to as far as the horizon lay the city of Cairo, old and new.

The interior of the mosque was fragile mosaic of translucent alabaster, unlike any that Thea had ever seen. Women and tourists were allowed to walk through when there wasn't a service.

Although the archaeologists had excavated the city of its relics, it was still breathtakingly cinematic.

The conclusion of their month's stay here was completed by dinner at the boss's home. The meal was typically English, and the conversation centered around business and Howard's future position at the Aden office.

Thea and Howard departed from Cairo on Aden Airways, and in a matter of hours, they would be in yet a totally different environment.

Chapter Fifteen

Aden was a fishing village in 1839, when the British moved in to curb pirates. It became important as a coaling station, when the Suez Canal opened a shortcut to India. The oil refinery made Aden the main fueling station for ships between Europe and Asia. Tankers were now outgrowing the canal, and airplanes drew passenger traffic away from ships. The commercial need for Aden was dropping. In the early fifties there was still much of a boom trade, as the oil refinery was under completion by the British-American Companies, known as Bechtel/Wimpey. As with most of Britain's possessions, she was slowly closing her grip on this small but extremely important peninsula.

Thea and Howard arrived in the late afternoon at Khormaxcer airport, near where the Royal Air Force Base was situated. They were driven to the Metro Hotel, which was situated in the Crater, located in the heart of an Arab bazaar. It was a far cry from the glorious Metropolitan they had just left behind in Cairo. Pioneering had its disadvantages.

Crater was approximately seven miles from Steamer Point, where Thea had previously stopped on various ships. It served as the main shopping center as well as the center of government businesses. The couple lived amidst rock, rubble, clay shacks, and match box apartment buildings, which were constructed overnight and were much in demand. It was surrounded by miles of white sandy beaches and ocean.

Their first weeks of adjustment were difficult. Even the healthiest digestive system experienced "Montezuma's revenge!" But it was compensated for by the warmth of the climate and the ocean. Each evening they dined on the hotel veranda, along with other guests, several of whom were British and Americans, and a few nationalities unknown to them. Amused, they would watch the activities on the street below. The half-clad natives, squatting by their dwellings, cooked their meals over a charcoal fire, while others intently played to a rhythm on a variety of tin cans, kerosene drums, hand made flutes, and tom-toms, until they drove themselves to a frenzy. As the night went on their singsong got more boisterous, but nobody would complain as they wouldn't have got any results from doing so. The aroma of their shish kebob made of goat's meat appealed to Thea, more than the hotel food on her plate. An unfamiliar mixed breed of goat and sheep, called "shoats," roamed in and out of the native shacks.

Each morning Howard and Thea started with an early breakfast together, after which Howard would kiss his wife good-bye and continue on his work schedule with another Englishman, who had been brought from the Nairobi office, to introduce Howard to his new and various tasks on the island. Once the initial work had been achieved, Howard was on his own, to train the Arab labor. After the two years of organizing was completed, the company would be handed over to Howard's replacement. Howard was most conscientious over his new position. It was a challenge, and he hoped Thea would understand the responsibility they had both undertaken. In the two years they had been married, Thea had worked at her profession in London, and she wanted to be occupied. However, from her observation of the women on the island, there seemed to be little use for her trade here. Howard would have appreciatively welcomed her help in his office. But she hadn't considered herself an office person, and she wasn't about to change now. Because of her obstinacy, she complained of boredom. She wrote her mother weekly and mentioned to her that she was totally wrapped up in Howard's life, and she herself had no identity. She tried to show interest in his achievements, but she wasn't in the least interested in his work.

Mother never sympathized with her daughter on this. In fact, she wrote that it was time Thea grew up and assisted her husband in their life together—that it was difficult enough for him under the circumstances without her lack of cooperation.

"Howard! I'm sick of living in this hotel. We've been here six months now. When will we have a home of our own?"

"Darling, just bear with me a little longer. There are no suitable flats available right now."

The permanent residents in the hotel spent much of their leisure time at the beach club. There were a few young mothers, and some airline pilots and stewardesses in transit. Thea took long walks on the beach and visited the bazaars. She discovered a fair size Indian population in the colony, so she'd converse with them, and she enquired about new residential flats in the area. Her monotonous life ended when she was introduced to Carla and her husband, Miles Fox. Miles had met Howard through business, and he in turn brought his delightful wife over to meet Thea.

Carla was from the north of England. She was tall, blonde, with brown eyes, and Thea instantly made a friend of her. The Foxes lived in a flat in Malla, an area between Crater and Steamer Point. They had already lived in Aden a couple of years. Miles was president of one of the banks, so they had become established residents. They introduced Thea and Howard to the British community, and got them membership to the Gold Mohure bathing club. Gold Mohure was a fenced-off beach for swimmers, and was comprised of a bar, and a dining area under a huge tree. There were dressing rooms, showers, and cabanas scattered around the beach. It was an absolute haven for women and children, with no occupation. So Carla, with her five-year-old daughter, would fetch Thea daily, and they would spend either a morning and have lunch at the club, or else an afternoon, and dine at the club with their husbands.

One afternoon, as the women chatted on the beach, a dark handsome youth with curly black hair, clad in a brief bikini, nonchalantly came up behind Carla and kissed her on the neck.

"Hello love, I wondered where you had got to! Dino, this is my friend Thea; she hasn't been here long."

He clasped Thea's hands with both of his.

"How do you do, young lady," he said.

Thea didn't wish to seem inquisitive, she looked away from his glance. He drew up a chair and put his arms around Carla in a suggestive manner. Thea thought to herself that they were obviously having an affair. After a few minutes he went in for a swim, and the ladies were on their own again.

"That's my sweetie," said Carla. "Isn't he handsome? He's terrific in bed. Italians are wonderful lovers. He's single, and he works on an oil rig out in Little Aden across the other side of here. I try and see him every chance I get."

"That must be kind of awkward," Thea remarked.

"Oh Miles is aware of the fact, but there's nothing much he can do about it. Says I'll outgrow him one of these days. But it's been two years now. I'm crazy about the little bastard."

"How long have you been married, Carla?"

"Seven years. But I've always had a lover. It's good for the morale, keeps one young, and makes life a little more interesting. Miles has such

100

a low profile, I couldn't tolerate him as a daily diet. How do you feel about another man in your life?''

"I've not been married long enough to answer that. Besides, what's to be gained by promiscuity? Surely, it's an illusion that ends in frustration on both sides.''

"Not if you treat it for what it is, just an affair. Then nobody gets hurt.''

"How is that possible? Doesn't love come into it? He has nothing to lose, you have a lot.''

"You wait until Howard has to leave town on business. You'll answer your own question.''

"I couldn't ever cheat on my husband. There isn't anybody that could take his place. I've never so much as looked at another man.''

"Well! Then you don't know do you? You have nothing to compare with.''

That evening Howard worked late, as he often did, and Thea dined alone at her little table on the veranda. She thought over her conversation with Carla and shuddered at the thought of it. When Howard returned later that evening, he informed her he would be leaving town on business for a week. Her immediate reaction to that was Carla's comment, and she had to tell him of it. He laughed!

"Howard, you can't possibly leave me in this hotel alone. You know I'm afraid of the weird types that creep around these hallways at night. I've never been left alone in my life.''

"Darling, I know that, but this outburst of yours is ridiculous! You were aware of the fact that I would have to travel from time to time before we left the U.K. So don't make it more difficult for me.''

Thea spent even more time with Carla after Howard's departure. She dreaded it when night approached and all the sounds that went with it. She didn't sleep a wink. She never questioned herself about what she was so afraid of.

Shortly after Howard returned from his business trip, Thea celebrated her twenty-first birthday. Howard was aware of his wife's sentimentality about birthdays, be it hers or anybody's. So he gave her a party on the rooftop of the hotel, to which he invited a few of their friends, and a conglomeration of permanent guests that resided at the hotel.

Thea dressed in her resplendent white gown, and felt ecstatic, as she joined their guests. Howard tried to recapture the feeling of their past. He was aware of her desire for constant attention, and the lack of public functions of which there had been few since leaving India. They danced the night away and retired happily intoxicated.

Thea asked herself why she could never be satisfied and what was she constantly in search of. She was bored with Howard's eternal devotion toward her, and she almost wished she could find fault with him. But she couldn't! He was confident, and he had even acquired the necessary initiative in practical matters, which he didn't have when she met him. She had broken her neck to catch him, yet she was unfulfilled. Maybe they were not really suited, but as Carla had remarked, she hadn't any comparison, so how would she know?

One evening as the couple dined on the veranda, Thea was distracted by a handsome blond, blue-eyed gentleman, seated behind Howard. Had he always been there, she asked herself. Or had it been negligence on her part that she hadn't observed him before today? Their eyes turned toward each other. He smiled at her, and she smiled in return. Howard wasn't aware of this open flirtation behind his back. She wondered who he was and how long he had sat at that table. Presently, he was joined by another equally handsome man. This flirtation continued until dinner was completed, after which he got up from his table and proceeded toward Thea and Howard.

"Excuse please, I don't speak English good, but I wish very much to thank you for inviting me and my friend to your birthday party. We haven't been in Aden long, and we don't know much people." He then felt a little awkward, so he turned to his colleague to assist him with his English.

"This is Hans Sperber, and I am Helmut Weber. We are both from Hamburg, Germany, and we work together at the shipyard in Malla."

The men shook hands upon introduction, and kissed Thea's hand in a formal gesture. Howard had invited them and acknowledged their presence at the party, but they hadn't conversed much, and Thea didn't remember them at all.

A few days later, Thea was breakfasting alone at her table, when she was suddenly distracted. Her heart raced as Hans stood in front of her in white shorts and an open shirt.

"Good morning Frau Wrenn, I forgot something on the job, so I came back to get it. Are you alone this morning?"

"Yes, my husband is at work. I'm always alone, the plight of most of us that don't work."

"I see you walk sometimes on the beach at the back of the hotel, I watch you from afar."

Thea felt her cheeks flush.

"Yes I do most days; it's so peaceful there. I have never seen anybody frequent that beach except me."

"Except us," he said.

He bid her good day and left.

As Thea paddled by the water's edge, her mind was on Hans. It was his suggestive manner that troubled her. She had appeared terribly awkward in his company. He had come on too strong, and she hadn't made her stand. She scoffed at herself, as she kicked the sand beneath her feet. *Who does he think he is anyway?* she thought. She sat herself down by a huge rock and gazed out at the ocean. Her privacy was suddenly intruded upon. She was overcome by his shadow alongside her. His desperate eyes scorched her. She awkwardly brushed away the sand and stood up.

"Why did you follow me? You know I am married, and my husband would not appreciate the attention you are giving me."

He smiled, "And you don't appreciate it either?"

"That's not fair," she said, "I'm not supposed to."

He gazed into her eyes and gently caressed her chin, his quivering fingers stroked her cheek.

"You are a gypsy woman, your eyes sparkle like coal. They say to me, I want you, but I can't have you."

With this he closed his eyes and kissed her on the mouth. Thea passionately reciprocated to his warmth. She had never been kissed like that before. Slowly she backed away from his strong arms.

"Hans, you must never do that again, you must never, never come near me."

She turned around and hastily walked away, leaving him in the distance wondering what he had done that was so terribly wrong, except he was fully aware, as she also was, that no good could ever come of such advances toward each other.

A week went by, and both Hans and Helmut were conspicuous by their absence. Carla called around as usual for Thea, and they drove out to the Gold Mohure club. Thea appeared rather restless, which didn't go unnoticed by her girlfriend. However, Thea didn't disclose her immediate feelings to Carla, probably because she, herself, didn't understand them.

The women swam across to the permanent raft anchored in the

103

swimming area. Thea lay back with her eyes shut, as she languidly bobbed to and fro, listening to Carla's voice in the distance. Until she felt drops of water drip slowly on her face. Startled she opened her eyes. It wasn't Carla, but Hans standing over her. Her immediate reaction was, to remain composed. Carla was most interested in this masculine image that had appeared in their midst.

"Hello, what's your name? And where did you come from?"

He watched Thea with a smile on his face,

"I'm Hans Sperber, a friend of Thea's."

"Sure I remember you from her birthday party. You and your friend sat alone in a corner, not saying much of anything."

"Excuse please, I wish to speak with Frau Wrenn alone."

"Sure, I understand. You're probably the reason for her sudden silence."

"How are you, liebling? Did you miss me?" he asked when Carla left.

"Was I supposed to?"

"No, I suppose that was most presumptuous of me, but I had you on my mind. We were on business in the Yemen, and what with the language handicap, both Helmut and I returned very frustrated. I needed to speak with you, and that is why I'm here now." Thea's heart pounded at the sight of his handsome physique, as he stood before her in his tight blue swimming trunks.

"Thea, would you please teach me to speak English properly? I pay you for lessons, please."

"I should think Arabic would be the language you'd want to learn, so as to be able to converse with your boss and your workers."

"No! It is English that handicaps me. I can get by with Arabic pretty good."

"I'm sorry Hans, I am not free to give you the attention you desire. This is a small community that we live in, and my husband would never agree to it. As it is Carla is watching us from a distance, and I am sure she isn't thinking well of us."

"Why are you so afraid? We are just friends. I am friendly with your husband also, no?"

"I don't think you understand me, Hans. My husband wouldn't agree and I think you know this."

Thea jumped into the water, and he followed her back to the table. Smiling, he ordered a round of Beck's beer, as he briefly excused himself.

"Well love, it didn't take you long did it? How could you keep such a gorgeous apparition a secret? You didn't say a word all this time, but you didn't fool me for a minute."

"Oh Carla, don't jump to conclusions. He is just lonely, and doesn't know anybody here."

"Aren't they all, love? That's the first signal of something new."

When Hans returned, he sat near Thea, not for a minute taking his eyes off her. He made small talk about the Yemen to Carla, as Thea enthusiastically listened. She desperately wished to be left alone in his company. They had been seated with their backs to the club entrance, when from behind, Thea felt a pair of cool hands across her eyes. She was totally familiar with the touch of those hands. Howard felt his wife get tense. It was the first time in their married life that Thea was resentful of her husband's intrusion. Howard drew up a chair, and conversed amicably with Hans. Both men intensively watched Thea's reaction. There was none.

The scenic drive from Gold Mohur to Steamer Point, with the white-capped waves beating across the irregular coastline, was much to be desired. The harbor with the passenger liners and cargo boats was forever busy with traffic. Not a word had been uttered by husband and wife. There had never been cause for disapproval, Howard had trusted his wife, and she in turn had never had cause to question his behavior. She had only lost composure momentarily!

They had reached their hotel and were seated in their respective chairs. It was later than usual and they continued their silence over dinner. The soup plates were removed, as the bearer brought the main course. Howard wiped his mouth with the serviette in deep thought. He cautiously observed Thea's face and continued to eat.

"Thea, I prefer if you didn't encourage fraternization with the Hun."

Thea didn't know how to react to such an accusation, and she felt immediate guilt come over her. Howard continued, as she listened.

"If you are so bored with your time, you could help me at the office. To take full charge of a new company isn't all joy you know. It's a bloody responsibility. You can't expect me to work and play nursemaid to you as well. The trouble with you is you sadly need to grow up. You live in a dream state. Hans is single, with no obligations in his life. I have a responsible position on this island, and you as my wife are expected to cooperate."

Thea silently left the dinner table and withdrew to their rooms. She felt so hopelessly alone. To reprimand her severely must have been more difficult for him to do, than it was for her to accept. He had never spoken to her harshly. What was happening to them? Was it all really her fault? The door opened as she felt his presence in the room. He put his arm around her.

"Darling, I'm not angry, I love you. We are living among strangers in unfamiliar surroundings. They don't care about our welfare. I'm just giving you word of caution."

Thea resisted his embrace, as she felt defiance and hostility rise within her.

"How dare you treat me like a child? Just because I'm your wife and wear this ring on my finger, doesn't give you the right to put a ring in my nose."

"Oh, dear you haven't heard a thing I've said, have you?" Howard replied. "Don't you understand, if we can't communicate with each other, then all is lost before we even begin our new life together."

"Howard, you're jealous and too possessive of me. I'm a person not a pawn."

He was at a total loss for words and rejectedly got undressed and went to bed.

In the morning Howard had already gone to work, when Thea awoke with the sun shining across her face. She got dressed and went to breakfast. Hans was alone at his table smoking a cigarette and having his coffee. He reproachfully glanced in her direction and said good morning. She drew a chair to his table and ordered a light breakfast.

"Do you still wish to learn English?"

"I feel your husband is threatened by me. He is a man same as I am. I cannot blame him. I would feel the same if you were my wife, and somebody else paid you attention. He treats you like a child, not a wife. This is the first mistake he makes with you."

"I told him last night that I didn't require my childhood to prevail in our married life. I hoped that ended when we married, but it seems to have gotten worse."

"I have been a gentleman, no?" Hans asked.

"That is his trouble, he's worried you won't be for long. That's not saying much for me."

Hans uttered words in German, as if in protest.

"He is a good man, your husband. But he will eventually lose you if he doesn't change his ways."

"According to him, I am the one who has to change. I have been bound to his world, and I feel I can't breathe. He objects to my friendship with whomever I come in contact. I am not the submissive little wife he thinks I am."

From that day forward, Thea and Hans met each morning for elementary English lessons. During this time Hans told her about his work, and the problems with the Arabs' procrastination at the shipyard. Time was of no consequence to the Arabs, and at this rate his one year tour could become two.

"Would you like to visit my place of work? I take you now and bring you back directly."

They got in his jeep and drove toward Malla. She got a tour of his boats, his help, and the conditions he worked in. She showed interest, but her anxiety intensified, and she hurried Hans to leave. If Howard should pass in the neighborhood, not only was she in the company of the Hun, but also in an Arab boat yard.

"Don't worry, he not see you. Here we go now," Hans assured her.

As they drove in his open jeep, the breeze from the ocean carelessly blew his hair, and his mischievous blue eyes sparkled in the sunshine. Thea's brown eyes wandered to his thighs in sexy brief khaki shorts. She had made no secret of absorbing his sensuous masculinity. Gosh! Was he gorgeous! She didn't in the least feel embarrassed about her thoughts.

She found it most difficult to ignore his endearments, as she, herself, had always been demonstrative. He left her off at the hotel entrance, then spun around and drove away on the dusty road.

Thea stopped in her tracks before climbing the stairway. She decided to walk toward Howard's office, which was a short distance from the hotel.

"Hello. What do I owe this surprise to?"

"Oh I was just curious about where you worked, that's all," she said.

He had done exceedingly well in this barren Crater. His staff had a great deal of respect for him. Howard was as assiduous about his business as he had been with his private life. Perhaps this was the cause of Thea's dilemma. She lacked his dedication, and hadn't worked at their marriage, which was hardly his fault.

The following week, Howard revealed he would be leaving again, this time for French Somaliland. Here was another trial Thea would have to face. Howard was aware of her dislike of being left alone, but business was his priority, and he couldn't be intimidated, not even by her.

He flew out by Ethiopian Airlines for Djibouti.

That night Thea's restlessness had prevented sound sleep. The streets around the hotel rumbled with traffic all night long; she felt as though she were in a railway station. The next morning Hans joined her for breakfast and invited her to attend the cinema that evening.

"I think that would be against my better judgment. My husband is out of town, and I'm expected to be the dutiful wife."

"Aw come on. There is no harm in going to a picture show with me."

"Okay! I accept your invitation."

It was a crystal clear evening, and they dined on the rooftop of the Crescent Hotel. The illuminated sky full of stars, enhanced the brightly lit ocean liners berthed in the harbor. After dinner they went to the open air A.S.T.R.A. Cinema where Lana Turner was starring in *The Merry Widow*. Thea felt a sudden release from her anxiety, as the lights dimmed and the crescendo of Franz Lehar's "Merry Widow Waltz" enveloped the intimate RAF theater. As the story progressed, and Lana Turner's dramatic acting became more torrid, Hans reached for Thea's hand in the darkness, and she searched his face.

He caressed and gently kissed each of her fingers, as their eyes met, and her heart raced. He smiled as he kept time with the waltz, and whispered in her ear.

"Do you like to valtz?"

"I love the waltz," she answered.

The movie came to an end, and the harsh theater lights flooded upon them. Feeling guilty she jumped out of her seat, as she beckoned him to hurry.

"Let's get out of here before I'm discovered by someone I know."

It seemed to take forever as the crowd ambled out toward the front entrance. Thea was stopped a couple of times by mutual friends.

"Thea, where is Howard?"

She smiled reluctantly as she rushed out toward the parking lot. "Let's hurry up and go," she said to Hans.

"You worry unnecessarily. Take it easy."

"You would too, if you were in my shoes," she replied.

Steamer Point behind them, they drove on the sparsely lit road relying on the jeep headlights to guide them toward the Crater. All of a sudden Hans took a sharp turn to the left onto the dirt track which led to the big rock on the beach. He knew full well she sought consolation here. The tide was out, as he helped Thea out of the jeep. They strolled slowly on the sand, gazing at the stars above. The quiet rippling waves caressed their bare feet. Thea felt as though she were walking on air. Not a word had been said between them. Hans picked her off her feet in his strong arms and twirled her around and around. He set her down gently as his lips devoured hers with exuberant passion, and she reciprocated with indulgence. He was tender, yet aggressive, as he kissed her eyes, and nose, and moved down to her throat and back again to her lips. In so doing, he expressed words of endearment in German. Thea had never thought German a romantic language, until now. When he did release her of his grip, she unwillingly let go of him. The moon shone on his handsome silhouette and she strongly desired to make love to him. She threw her head back in ecstasy.

"Hans, Hans, you can't stop now, I want you, I must have you."

His eager pulsating penis thrust against her groin awaiting release.

"Not here let's return to the hotel," she said.

He composed himself as they got back in the jeep. Holding her hand all the way back, he assured her he would never cause her grief.

They arrived at the dimly lit hotel and cautiously walked up the stairs, toward his room. With his key he opened the door. The electric fan hummed over the oppressive indoor air, the street light filtered through the venetian blinds as Thea awkwardly stood by his bed. He rested his hands on her shoulders, and kissed her back, as he unzipped her dress that fell to the floor.

"You smell so good, what is the perfume you use?"

"It's French. It's called Indiscreet."

The hum of the fan comforted them as they lay naked beside each other. Thea had never experienced another man, and he didn't know what was expected of her. Hans gently eased her on top of him as they enveloped each other with warm sensualism.

The faint aroma of his cologne mixed with his masculinity was like a vintage wine. He caressed her back as though she were a fine velvet. She winced with delight as they became one. Her eyes had never teared before when making love. She had never been told that her bosom was beautiful, as he sucked on her nipples. Her body was a mass of goose bumps.

"Are you shy, my liebling?"

"No. I've never felt such an extraordinary sensation before, perhaps it's because you are different."

He wanted so much to please her. She could tell from the expression on his face, as she gasped for breath!

"Oh! Oh! Oh! Don't stop, Hans!"

"You come my beautiful one, come as much as you wish, I don't stop until you finish."

She repeatedly climaxed, and then he spent himself powerfully. He didn't withdraw from her, as he said that was the most desirable time in making love. One should never leave one's mate when she requires you the most. Yes he was different. With her husband she had always taken precautions, and they were constantly in fear of her getting pregnant.

As the dawn's early light crept through the room, a soft knock disturbed Thea and Hans. It was Helmut speaking in German on the other side of the door.

"I must get ready for work, liebling; you stay here if you wish."

Thea watched him get dressed. Then he playfully returned to her side.

"You are a strong lady, you know that."

"What do you mean by that?"

"You have made me tired. You are like that jellyfish I removed from your leg the other day. You cling tight."

"Are you complaining?"

"Never! I see you this evening on my return from work, okay?"

Thea stood by his door to make sure the coast was clear before she scuttled down the passageway toward her room to take a shower. After sleeping alongside of Hans, she was full of exhilaration, so she went for a brisk walk, which led her to an unimpressive Catholic church. She stepped within the small clay building and sat herself down. She hadn't attended church services in years. Howard wasn't in the least religious, but this didn't impede her beliefs. She watched the candles flicker in the dimly lit church, as she questioned herself. Was she really a sinner? Who would be the judge of that?

According to her early conditioning in the convent, she had broken one of the gravest commandments, and now she truly believed she wasn't any good. She requested a priest who was in deep prayer to hear her confession. As she knelt in the confession booth asking for forgiveness outwardly from a total stranger, she didn't honestly repent inwardly. What was the point of all this hypocrisy if she didn't feel guilty about her actions? She felt terribly confused as she walked out of the house of sanctum.

Exhausted from her mindful actions, she fell asleep, and would not have awakened if not for Hans knocking on the door. He had been anxious when she hadn't come out for dinner.

"Come with me, you need some fresh air. We go for a drive."

She obediently followed him, as he persuasively took her by the hand and led her out of the hotel. They got out of the jeep at the Crescent Hotel. "I'm not dressed to go in there, Hans."

"Nobody will see us, we sit at a corner table and have a nice drink."

He ordered a Pimms No. 1 for her and a Becks beer for himself. They were in deep conversation when they were intruded upon by one of Howard's associates. The man looked at Hans directly expecting a formal introduction. Thea gestured that they were on their way out.

"Damn it! Wouldn't you know it? He is the last person I should have met up with."

It was 9:00 P.M. when they got to Gold Mohure for a swim. Carla and Dino were the only members sitting at a distant table.

"Well hello stranger. I can see you have been busy," said Carla.

"Hello Carla, hello Dino. We didn't realize we were coming here, and I'm minus my bathing suit."

"I'm sure Hans won't mind you skinny dipping. There's nobody here but us."

Thea laughed! "I guess there's a first time for everything." Thea and Hans walked out of sight and swam in the nude to the anchored raft. She giggled at her audaciousness.

"There are a lot of nude beaches all over the world, I don't think I'd care for that. But this is surely delightful," remarked Thea.

Hans bent across and kissed her, and they played like children until they fell off the raft. Like dolphins they swam in circles in the tepid water. She rode him piggyback until they were entwined like a knot, as though they were some deep sea creature that had surfaced. She had never fornicated in the ocean before. She burned with delight in more ways than one. She floated on her back and looked at the stars.

"This is the closest I'll get to heaven."

"Wow Hans, Hans, stop! I'll drown!"

They were alone on the beach. Thea's limbs ached with delight.

"Nobody should sleep now, it's the nicest time in the whole day.

111

Do you know of anywhere in the world, where one can feel so blissful for free?'' she said.

Hans turned around toward her. ''You are a terrible romantic, and have been suppressed too long young lady. Come here to me,'' he said.

They slept on the beach until the beautiful sunrise welcomed their new day. The seagulls paraded around them, and the ocean caressingly embraced their nudity.

''You know Hans I could easily be a beach bum with you. You could fish and I would cook, and we could sail around the coast on a raft. That's living. Tarzan and Jane were no fools, they had the right idea.''

They hadn't considered that time had raced against them. All week Thea had awaited Hans's return from work each evening, and the rousing of her heart as he'd whistle their song, ''I'm Walking Behind You.'' And she'd rush into his arms. She didn't think for a minute of Howard's return, and how she would cope with the situation.

Chapter Sixteen

Thea had planned her evening as she happily took her shower. Hans had asked her if she liked to waltz? Well! Tonight would be as good as any to find out at the Regal cafe. She turned off the shower, and entered the room to dress into something appropriate.

The front door flew open, and lo and behold, it was Howard. He looked the picture of health, with a bronze tan, and a radiant smile as he rushed toward her.

"Hello my love did you miss me?"

Thea still in the nude, stood in the center of the room in a state of shock!

"Look what I brought you. Italian candy, wine, cheese, and a fresh salami. I got here just in time, didn't I?"

"Yes dear just in time."

"I've missed you dreadfully, darling, come here before you get dressed."

With an apathetic expression on her face, she distastefully rejected his embrace.

"Howard, please, I'm not a machine. I'm not in the mood for making love."

He abruptly sat on the edge of his bed and observed her.

"Maybe I got home too soon for you."

Her back was turned to him.

"You answered your own question," she muttered.

"What's the matter with you? I've never seen you this way," he said.

"I amused myself, and discovered being alone has its compensations," she said.

"Would you like to go out to dinner?"

"That's not what I had in mind."

She realized her little escapade would have had to terminate sometime, but this was so sudden. She hadn't prepared herself, but then how did one do that?

They joined Carla and Miles at the beach for supper. Carla whispered in her friends ear, "The party's over, eh? Don't feel bad, I know the feeling."

Thea sat motionless amongst them, as her mind wandered back to the previous evening. It had been only a few hours ago that she was so enraptured with Hans. Now she was back in harness. Howard spoke endlessly about his trip. It bored Thea to tears. She swam toward the raft. She needed to be alone, away from the chatter. Carla followed her directly.

"When did he return?"

"Who cares? He did it on the wrong day. I had planned such a nice evening, and he ruined it."

"Don't look around you now. Hans and Helmut have just arrived."

The headlights of the jeep shone on the women on the raft, and Thea's heart raced.

"Take it easy Thea, the first time is always the worst," Carla warned her friend. "What are you going to do now?"

"You tell me, you seem to know all the answers."

"I bet he swims out to us."

"Then he's a bigger idiot than I would take him for. He must have known Howard was back, when he called for me for our date this evening. Found I wasn't there, and has brought Helmut with him for moral support."

Suddenly the girls were disturbed as the raft pitched. It was Hans. "You thought you wouldn't see me this evening, because he has returned. Well you are wrong."

"Please go away, don't make trouble for me."

"Liebling, I'm going to speak to him."

"No, you will do no such thing. Are you crazy?"

She jumped off the raft and swam back to her company. She was sure Howard had seen them together, as he was at a loss for words when she sat down. Her stomach churned and she was positively nauseated. The sight of food before her worsened her condition. Howard ate in silence and did his meal justice. This farce continued until conversation became an ordeal. Howard finally excused them and said goodnight. They walked toward their car with great tension. It was parked near the

114

jeep in the lot. As they reached the intersection at Steamer Point, Howard came to an abrupt halt and shut the engine off.

"I have warned you once, and I won't again. If I see you talk to that Hun one more time, I will break his neck. I ask little of you, but now I demand respect. Do not insult my intelligence, or underestimate my actions for one minute. We are husband and wife; he is an intruder."

Thea didn't retaliate. He had saved her from making excuses and telling lies. They returned back to their abode in silence. Howard undressed and retired immediately. She did likewise in the bed opposite to his.

She watched him sleeping peacefully, as she lay awake. Of course he had been correct in his accusation, and she couldn't blame him a bit. She had been impulsive toward another, and hadn't planned to upset her spouse. Howard had always been considerately attentive at all times toward her.

The next morning she breakfasted alone, and she felt the worse for her behavior. She had broken the trust her husband had in her. They would never be the same again. She thought back to his arrival and his happiness to see her, which instantly turned to frustration. Only she could mend this situation. To be involved with two men at the same time could only end tragically. Her privacy was suddenly disturbed by Carla at the table. She was most sympathetic to her friend.

"Well does he know?"

"He suspects. Howard is very proud, but very sensitive."

"Oh I wouldn't worry about it anymore. Let's go to the Sweepers for a change. A different place." The Sweepers, a tennis club, was situated in Crater. They left there for tea at Gold Mohure, as neither of the women wished to return to their homes. Carla parked her car beside Hans's jeep. This gave him the excuse to visit with the ladies. Thea took a stroll around the club with him.

"I suppose you can't see me as long as he's in town."

"Hans I feel worse than you do. I have no experience with a dual relationship. I am married, you are not. You know we are not doing right."

"I know what you are saying, but you don't love him do you?"

"He is my husband. He loves me and needs me. I care for him in a different way. Besides I believe it is possible to love two men at the same time."

"Ahh come on, Thea. Where is your heart, or for that matter, your mind?"

Thea got uptight and began to blabber at him.

"I bet if I were married to you, I'd be a full-time house-frau. There wouldn't be any of this wine and dine. You'd probably keep me barefooted and pregnant. I know you European men."

"You are such a child, Thea. You want to have your cake and eat it, too."

"My husband is the provider. He has to endure and tolerate my many moods. You don't even know me. Making love is one thing, but a steady relationship is another."

Carla approached hurriedly. "Howard is here love, come on let's go." Carla put her arms around Thea. "The best thing left for you to do is to move into an apartment. You must get out of that hotel."

"That's easier said than done. I've been on Howard's case since our arrival."

That night the four of them dined at Carla and Miles's home. Carla inquired as to when they would be moving into their own flat.

"Pretty soon I hope. There is a new development being completed in Moghul Valley, to which I have been given first choice when completed. We have outstayed hotel living. I can see how it's affected Thea," was Howard's reply.

Howard appeared affable toward his wife when they returned home from the Foxes. She felt terribly restrained. They retired in their respective beds with a goodnight kiss. Should she have made the first move now that his feelings had been hurt? Would he have accepted, or rejected her advances? She didn't have the desire to make love to him, yet her guilt bothered her. She had enjoyed Howard until now, the comparison test had got in the way. She was unsure of herself after indulging with another.

"Howard are you asleep?"

There was no answer. The clock ticked away the minutes, as she watched the luminous hands pass over the hours. In the distance she heard a haunting whistle, to the tune of *"La Vie en Rose."* Hans wasn't asleep either. She clutched the pillow over her ears, as she couldn't fight her untamed desire for him in the still of the night. He repeatedly continued with defiance, until she got out of bed and opened the door gently. In bare feet and baby doll nightdress, she hastened toward his room. His door was ajar, and she ran into his arms. They clung fiercely to each other.

116

"Why? Why do you tease me so? You know how difficult it is for me."

"Because you belong with me, and I won't let you escape."

"Do you realize we have no shame! My husband is asleep down the corridor, and I am making love to you."

"Does he satisfy you more than me?"

"That's not fair. But now that you mention it, maybe I require more and that's why I'm here."

He snickered as he got his way with her. She rode her lover with frenzied desire. Urging him deeper and deeper, there seemed no end to her capacity for his ultimate penetration. With ardency she burst forth convulsively.

"Hans! That's it, that's it, don't move I'm coming! I'm coming."

"Sweetheart I feel you, now we come together!"

"Ohhh Hans, more, more. I can't stand anymore. Now stop." She sobbed uncontrollably with her head on his chest. "Damn it! I've never had this happen before. You know you have beguiled me."

"That's not true. I have made a woman out of you. You're alive, you function! That's how you are supposed to be." She rolled over on her back.

"Spoken like a true arrogant German."

"I speak the truth."

"I have to go now. If he's awake, he can only kill me."

Howard hadn't moved from his position, from the time she had left the room. *God!* she thought. If she persisted to play with fire she would get burnt.

Howard awoke and got dressed. Thea with eyes closed pretended to be asleep. In actual fact her body yearned for Hans, but both her men had been called to duty. So she had to stifle her desire.

That afternoon Howard returned earlier than usual, to inform Thea he had secured their new flat in the valley. Would she care to go along with him to see it? The building was now completed, and they had the nicest choice of three floors. She should have shown some enthusiasm, as they drove through rock and rubble to the dead end street. The match box buildings had been constructed during the time of the Moslem religious holiday of Ramadan, hence the delay for their moving in. Now they were renting at a high premium.

Howard was most excited, as he anxiously described decorations and furniture, which would all be provided at the company's expense.

They would be the first family in the area with a telephone, and air-conditioning. He put his arms around his wife as they stood on the balcony.

"Hotel living is not for us. You have had enough! We need a home of our own, and we are long overdue."

They had never had a home of their own, and now that it had transpired, Thea was remorseful. She silently thought how marvelous it would be to live with Hans in it. Instead of eliminating him from their lives, she was already contemplating his participation. Howard tried desperately to hold on to their marriage. When he made advances toward her, he trembled with uncertainty as to her reaction. He hoped she would get over her self-indulgence, but she was in deeper than she'd care to admit.

The next day, Howard took an early morning flight to Djibouti. Thea had planned to meet Carla for lunch. There was a knock at the door. She smiled at Hans as they embraced each other.

"It didn't take you long, did it?" she asked.

"I saw him at the airport this morning. I watch every move he makes and I know where you are. I have taken the day off so we can go on a picnic."

The hotel had prepared a delicious hamper with an assortment of foreign treats. It was a lot more desirable than their normal menu. Naturally Hans had ordered to his specified taste, including chilled German wine. They drove as far as Malla, where a motor boat waited to take them round the coastline. Hans operated the vehicle past the harbor and into the ocean. Thea hadn't viewed the coast from this angle, it was truly a gorgeous day. They had passed the Gold Mohure where the usual crowd sat on the beach sunning themselves. They hadn't been noticed as they continued for some miles to the other side of the peninsula. Here he stopped the boat by a hidden lush cove. They got out and spread a blanket on the sand.

"This is such a change from the usual things we do. Have you been out this far before?"

"One time Helmut and I went fishing in the boat, and I told him I would bring you here on a picnic."

She lay comfortably in his arms, and told him of her move.

"Yes I know where you are moving to. We have secured a flat around the corner, and I can see through to your place from our living room window."

"Why you're incorrigible! Why did you do that?"

"Because I will not let you out of my sight."

She sat up abruptly.

"I don't believe you would stoop so low." Secretly she relished the thought of his devious attention. He chuckled as he teased her, and they started to play tag, running in the dunes, and splashing in the ocean until she was out of breath, but not too tired enough to make love. It gave them both second wind to satisfy their compulsion for each other.

"Now I have another surprise for you," he remarked.

"You mean the day is long enough for another one?"

"Tonight we go dancing! Nothing will stand in our way this time."

Thea and Hans complemented each other in their formal dress, as they met on the hotel veranda. At thirty he was ravishingly handsome in his tuxedo, with an abundance of assurance in his haughty European manner. He kissed her hand and excused his jeep as a means of conveying them in their finery.

"We reside in the desert my love, not in the city of Hamburg. I forgive you." She chuckled.

They arrived at the open air restaurant and were seated by the orchestra that played the romantic music of the fifties. The piano player played "*La Vie en Rose*."

Hans and Thea danced cheek to cheek as she closed her eyes in profound ecstasy. She loved this man tremendously and she wished they could be together permanently. She had accepted the fact that she could never feel the same again toward her husband. In affairs of the heart, who was to say what was right or wrong, except for the two people involved? If this was forbidden love, and Hans had allured her for his own satisfaction, then he had tricked not only himself but also her to such an extent, she would never trust another man as long as she lived. He kissed her on the brow. . . .

"Are you here, liebling?"

She opened her eyes and looked into his.

"Can you feel our hearts beat together?"

"Always I feel that."

That week had been the most glorious and happiest time of Thea's existence. To quote Hans: "You and I we have the same temperament, each knows what the other is feeling. We learn from each other and where there is love, there is trust. I will remember you when I am an old man, because we found happiness under the most strained circumstances. I started you on your journey of discovery.''

Once more the time had passed too soon, and she was filled with resentment. Each time Howard returned from one of his business trips, it got more difficult for her to be apart from Hans.

Each evening after Howard had completed his day's work at the office, he would proceed to decorate their future flat. At first Thea would accompany him, but then she couldn't spend her final days with Hans at the hotel. Howard persistently painted each of the rooms with enthusiasm, and never got through before midnight on his project.

One night as Thea played cards with Hans and Helmut on the veranda, Hans suggested they visit Howard at the apartment.

"Poor fellow he is working alone each evening. Let's take him a cold beer.''

Thea didn't think this appropriate. Hans would get impetuous at times toward her husband. It went against her better judgment to encourage his gesture, as she was aware of Howard's attitude toward Hans. Helmut thought him crazy and didn't want any part of it. Thea was apprehensive as they entered the flat together. The front door was ajar as they both faced Howard who was on a stepladder. He was diligently painting with the aid of a solitary electric bulb. Thea took one look at his enraged face and realized her mistake.

"What the bloody hell do you think your doing here in my flat?''

"Please Howard, don't be angry. I wish to be friends with you. I brought you a beer.''

Howard descended slowly down the ladder. He turned toward Hans, and delivered a sharp blow to his jaw.

"I'll kill you, you bastard.''

"Howard! Stop it, stop it!'' shouted Thea.

"You had better stop it, if you know what's good for you,'' said Howard.

He continued to hit Hans who hadn't defended himself till now. Both men were enraged, as Thea stood helplessly in the way.

"You had better get out of here while you can still walk,'' Howard yelled.

Hans turned to leave and Thea followed him out. The beer bottles lay smashed on the floor.

"If you go with him now, don't bother to return, do you hear me Thea?''

She walked down the stairs with Hans, and they got in the jeep. When they reached the hotel, Hans spoke rapidly to Helmut in German.

"I told you both this would happen, but you would not listen to me. You are a German in a British Colony. The Englishman can have you sent away from here."

Hans opened himself a beer as he tried to compose his anger.

"It's no good Hans. Neither of us can possibly expect happiness from a sordid affair. It will only get worse for us all. We must stop seeing each other now," Thea said.

"Are you afraid of him?" he asked.

"No! I'm not afraid, but I know we are wrong. I can't live with this sneaking around corners and secret meeting places. I can't function this way." She left the table and went to her rooms.

Thea was in bed when Howard returned that night. Enraged he put the light switch on.

"Thea I've told you for the last time, I won't have you persist in your promiscuousness. You had better choose between us. I have taken all I can from the two of you. We were fine until that bastard crossed our path."

"Howard, we were far from fine, and you know it. He just agitated a hopeless situation."

"What the hell do you want from me?" he yelled.

"It's not either of our faults, it just happened!"

"Thea, you're impossible. Life to you is one big party. I took you from your home, and carried on where your mother left off. I have catered to you and your whims. But this I will not put up with. I thought at one time you loved me. But I can see now I am hanging on to a myth."

"I'm sorry, Howard. I do care about you, but I love him. I just can't explain it."

"Well I have given you an ultimatum. Take it or leave it."

Chapter Seventeen

The couple were in the throes of moving into their flat, when Howard was urgently called upon to assist at the office in Khartoum, Sudan.

Thea was most distressed, as this time she was obliged to accompany her husband for a period of six months. Howard wasn't about to leave her in Aden for such a lengthy time. She didn't have the time to convey this sudden development to Hans, as she hastily left the island with her husband.

Khartoum in 1956 had got freedom from Egyptian control, and at the same time from the British. It was the first of the black African countries to do so. The principal streets of the city were laid in the shape of the Union Jack, as a permanent mark of the British boot, upon what would become the capital once again. Glassy hotels and sand block buildings were thrown up in a way that was reminiscent of Aden.

After a long dusty drive from the airport, they reached the prominent Grand Hotel in the dusk of evening. A conglomerate of Britishers sat on the green lawn sipping on their whiskey sodas, and gin and tonics. Here Howard and Thea were introduced to the company superiors. Naturally the business discussion was carried to the dinner table. Thea was the only woman present, and she condescendingly joined in the conversation when it was directed toward her.

Arrangements had been made for Howard and Thea to reside in a private bungalow owned by an Englishman. Once again Thea was to live in another's home. It felt strange for her to share an abode that was in good taste but not of her choice. In those days there was little or no air-conditioning. Homes and public buildings were cooled by the desert air-cooler. This was comprised of window units run on electricity, through an attached filtered water hose. As in most deserts, the days were hot, and the nights cool enough for blankets. Through choice they slept on the rooftop. However she had never gotten that close to nature and the sounds of the desert. Each night she was awakened by an extremely offensive urinal odor that enveloped the atmosphere. A clattering camel cart passed the compound below and stopped to collect the portable toilet receptacle from the outhouse.

This was referred to as the Midnight Express. The bungalow was surrounded by an abundance of sweet smelling jasmine trees, the perfume of which was highly concentrated. The mixture of the waste matter and the flowers made Thea nauseated. She couldn't lull herself to sleep. Apparently nobody else was effectively disturbed by this strange nightly occurrence.

Thea would lie awake on her cot gazing at the stars as her thoughts floated toward the beaches of Aden and her nights with Hans, until she finally fell into a drugged sleep.

She awakened before dawn, as the first flight of birds passed over her, and the hens cackled in the backyard. She amused herself of a morning collecting the fresh eggs from the coop, and later she'd take care of the garden. She had never done either of these chores before, and she enjoyed them, even though the household belonged to another.

Howard had already left for the office, after an early breakfast cooked by the houseboy. Although there was a lack of communication between Thea and the servant because of the language barrier, he was most congenial at all times. His smile was one of approval.

The Sudanese were a haughty race, dressed mostly in white. They wore white turbans, not checkered like the Arabs.

Time lay heavy on Thea's hands, so she'd take long walks by the river Nile. One early sunrise as she approached the river bank, she observed a middle-aged man sitting in khaki shorts with a sun hat on his head. He was painting a canvas and he had a huge box of paints and brushes by his side. He looked askance at Thea's intrusion, but smiled politely.

"I'm not disturbing you am I?" she said.

"No not at all. Nothing could disturb this beautiful scenery. Mind you, I can't capture it all in one sitting, and it does change from day to day. But I'll do what I can for today."

"I used to paint many years ago. But I haven't attempted a canvas like that. I have all the time in the world to do so, but not enough patience to sit for hours as you're doing." Thea said.

"Oh yes it's taken many years for me to cultivate my passion. But now I have earned it."

"I detect an accent. Where are you from?"

"From Belgium. I was born and raised in France. I came to the

Sudan just after World War Two and made this my home. I am a retired archaeologist."

"How very interesting. To call this your home."

"Where are you from, young lady?"

"I was born in India, but unfortunately I have no place I could be proud enough of to call home as you do."

"Yes, I have spent my time between Egypt and this country. The Nile holds much fascination for those that know her. You know of course that there is a Blue Nile and a White Nile. Over beside the White, the soil was laid down by the flooding of the Blue. The White flows more than sixteen hundred miles from Khartoum from Lake Victoria in Uganda. The Blue Nile falls 4,600 feet through many cataracts and volcanic highlands to our city. The White slides through swams and declines 2,500 feet. The blue carries seven times as much water, also a great deal more of silt, which is why it's called Blue."

"Well! Is that a fact? Now I can say I know the difference."

"I take it you haven't been in Khartoum long."

"Only a few weeks. I'm here with my husband who is on business. We hope to return to Aden in a few months. Well I had better let you get on with your painting. Perhaps we will meet another day."

"I'll be here each morning until I have completed my sunrise."

Thea continued to walk along the river's edge, thinking of what the gentleman, (who's name she hadn't even asked) had said about the river. In the silence she unceasingly thought of Hans, and wished so much that he could have shared this timeless serenity with her.

Thea and Howard toured the ancient city of Omdurman, situated on the Nile opposite Khartoum. Omdurman was built by the Mahdi* in 1885, after his seizure and destruction of Khartoum. Here on September 2, 1898, the dervishes were defeated by the British and Egyptian troops under Sir Herbert Kitchner. Thea had learned this in her history lessons, but she'd never thought she would have the experience of being in its midst. They were shown the historical events of General Charles Gordon, who was also a part of this era in history. He was besieged by the Mahdi at Khartoum on March 12, 1884, and was killed in the storming of the city, January 26, 1885. Both these Englishmen had left their mark in the poignant traces of their past here, of which now only stood crumbled walls.

*Mahdi: According to Mohammedan belief, a spiritual and temporal ruler.

The Britishers that Thea had encountered at the club over the months of her stay in Khartoum seemed content with their acquired life-style. Several spoke of making it their home. Thea felt very much in transit, and wished to return to Aden.

Chapter Eighteen

After a wearisome flight from Khartoum, Thea and Howard were reinstated at the Metro Hotel in Crater, and they instantly retired in the late evening.

Now that Thea had returned and breakfasted alone at her table the next morning, she had mixed emotions about their future here—perhaps for fear of what she may find, or had already lost, or never had to begin with. If only she could occupy her time in a purposeful manner. She had always worked, and now she felt most inadequate. Whilst she cogitated, Hans appeared around the corner, and their eyes fixed upon each other. He had already got settled in his new flat, but he periodically passed the Metro in search of her.

"When did you return?" were his first words.

"Last night," she replied.

"Couldn't you have at least said good-bye before you went?"

"We left hurriedly. Besides, there wasn't anything more to say."

He drew up a chair alongside of her and ordered a coffee. His blue eyes penetrated through her, making her uneasy, and he was aware of how she felt immediately. He sipped on his coffee.

"Do you know how wretched I felt after you left, not to know where you had gone? Nobody could give me any information as to your whereabouts. That wasn't fair, do you think?"

She shrugged her shoulders, to hold back her anguish, and then she wept.

"Oh Hans, I'm so painfully unhappy. I thought of you every day these months we've been apart. I feel sorry for Howard, but I can't continue in this pathetic manner."

He grabbed her by the hand as they rushed out of the hotel and got in his jeep.

"Where are we going?"

"I must talk with you. We go for a drive, away from here. Why didn't you write me, just one letter to tell me something?"

"I didn't see any point to it. I was telling myself we were finished. That while we were apart maybe you would have a girlfriend and that would be the end."

"You talk like a silly child. You think you can dismiss somebody's feelings when you wish. No Thea, you don't have that right."

They drove in the direction of Little Aden across the bay toward the oil refinery. He came to an abrupt halt on the beach. He helped her out of the jeep, and slowly their lips met as they passionately kissed each other. He held her tightly, so much so that she had to gasp for breath.

"I've missed you more than words can say, my mind hasn't been on my work. Poor Helmut didn't realize how bad it was for me. Liebling I must have you by my side, to come home to. We can't go on like this."

"Hans, you know that's impossible. I cannot leave Howard, I married him for better or worse. You are Catholic, the same as I am. You know there is no divorce in our religion. And we could never be happy at his expense."

"Look in my eyes and tell me that you don't love me. Tell me!"

She sobbed uncontrollably.

"I do, I do. I always will care about you. I can't stand not having you in bed, loving me the way only you can do. But you must help me, Hans, to stay away from you. Please help me."

They both sought consolation from each other, as they sat on the lonely beach watching the sunset, and the close of another day.

"We have been apart all these months, and now we're together again, only to be parted once more. Life is so unfair," he said.

They headed back toward the Crater. Thea watched his solemn face. She felt doomed; their timing had been wrong. If this be a lesson to be learned, then it was cruel indeed. She had only experienced Howard and Hans, and never compared the two. Before Howard she hadn't had any experience. With Hans she had bloomed from a cactus to a flower, but now she was aware she couldn't come out smelling like a rose.

Thea and Howard moved into their new flat in the Valley. From the balcony one faced a steep rocky hill. It was said that those who climbed that hill successfully would never again return to Aden.

During the first three years of marriage, Thea desperately tried to be a homemaker. She sought new friends, most of whom were new to the neighborhood. Howard had fulfilled her many requests for custom furniture, and all that it took for a new home. They both anticipated a new beginning in this first flat of their own. They drove miles to the

Sheik Othman gardens to purchase flowers, foliage, clay pots, and window boxes. Thea painted them in gay assorted colors, and she placed them on the balcony. Howard assembled a wooden trellis along the outside wall on which he encouraged the growth of sweet smelling Jasmine. Thea stayed busy in order to change her frustrated life-style. Howard wasn't as yet sure of his wife's capriciousness, but he hoped that pursuing her interests during these weeks would give her more stability. But alas! When all was in order and completed, he felt threatened by her irrationality.

The street below was under construction by the British Installation Calendar Cable Company. They were in the process of digging miles of ground in and around the Crater area, for the installation of new telephone equipment. Howard's company was on the priority list for the first telephone in the area, as there were none to be obtained for months to come. Each day Thea would observe the Englishmen working in the heat and dust with shorts and sun hats, and bare bodies exposed to the sun. She felt compassion for them, and occasionally would take a jug of lemonade and sandwiches to ease their discomfort in the course of their long hours. Naturally the men were most appreciative of this kindness, and as the weeks passed, both Thea and Howard encouraged their countrymen. So when the Wrenns had their housewarming party, they were all invited, and they all accepted.

The living room overflowed with guests, booze, and food. Howard as always was the perfect host, and Thea at most times the hostess with the mostest. . . . She was most genuine when she entertained, and in her glory hoping the party would never end, until of course, she had succumbed to enough Scotch for consolation. Fully inebriated she victimized a youth, whom she knew was infatuated by her. She lured Jimmy into suggestively dancing with her in a dark corner of another room. He was a handsome clean-cut lad, and a good conversationalist. Of which there was little at this time.

Their kissing and necking was disturbed by Jimmy whispering in her ear.

"We are not alone my love, we are being watched by your lover on the rooftop of the house across the street."

"Hummm w-h-a-t did you say?" she said, slurring her words.

"You heard me, let's go in the other room."

She glanced across the street and her eyes came in direct contact with Hans. He stood his ground with a Becks beer in his hand, as he motioned toward her and his lips signaled *cheers*. She turned her face away in anguish, and she couldn't resist his face or her pretense a minute more. It was now or never! She ran out of the apartment two steps at a time, until she stood by his jeep across the street. In minutes he was beside her and they drove away, without a word between them.

It was just around the corner that the jeep came to a halt. Hand in hand they rushed up the stairs, in the direction of his bedroom. She gasped for breath, ripped off her dress, and jumped onto the bed, as he stood beside her fully dressed.

"Why you drink so much? You are drunk," he said.

"You're damn right I am, so would you be if you lived in a cage."

He slowly took his clothes off and slipped in beside her, and in her.

"Oh God! How I've missed you," she said, as they entwined around each other in ecstasy.

"Liebling don't cry, not like this, this is not the way, please let me help you."

"Just make love to me, hold me tight, lie to me, make me feel like you used to."

Their lovemaking endured relentlessly. Now sober she stood by the window with a slight headache.

"Well I'll be damned, I can almost count the guests in my living room. You weren't kidding when you said you could look into my apartment."

"It's late I don't want you in trouble," he said. "I see you home now."

"No! I need to get some fresh air to clear my head, before I can face that lot, that goes for Howard, too."

She walked briskly toward her apartment building, still feeling the warmth of Hans's body and the smell of his cologne upon her warm flesh. He was so utterly masculine. What a beast!

Howard wasn't particularly thrilled by her sudden reappearance, as the lingering guests started to leave. Thea poured herself a triple Metaxa and played Edith Piaf's record "*La Vie en Rose*," feeling as pained as the singer with each word.

There were still a few guests sitting around reluctant to leave. Thea felt relieved she didn't have to confront her husband at an awkward time. Jimmy was still hanging in so Thea took advantage of his presence, and they continued their unfinished dance with decorum.

"Don't you think you should conclude your night while you're still

129

ahead? Howard is seething, and I for one wouldn't want your fate when you are alone with him today. I should think you've had your fill for one night. Call it a day Thea.''

"There is never enough of a good thing, or don't you know that? I know you want me, so don't take pity on Howard.''

"I'll take a raincheck, if you ask me nicely.''

"Sweetheart, I'll never succumb to a man for his pleasure, damn you.''

With his self-conscious laugh he bid her goodnight. Thea didn't remember much as she fell asleep on the couch. She was awakened by Carla at noon.

"Gosh! what a mess. Where is your bearer? And how is Howard after your absence last evening?''

"I guess he will start arguing all over again, or he may even give me another ultimatum. I don't know, and I don't care. To hell with everything.''

"Why didn't you treat this liaison for what it was? Just an affair. Then you could have had the best of two worlds.''

"I guess because I don't have your experience, my love. I happen to care about him more than I ever did Howard.''

"Rubbish! You listen to me. Hans has nothing to lose. You have everything! Why he'd be the first to run in the opposite direction, if you both truly confronted him. He's been rather smug with this arrangement for as long as it lasts.''

"Is that what you truly think? Can you imagine my mother's face if I mentioned the end of my marriage. Now I think I have another problem. I may be pregnant.''

"Thea you're not serious! You wouldn't know what to do with a baby.''

"Oh, I couldn't be, silly Hans said that to see my reaction.''

"What the hell did he say that for? It's a serious accusation. The man's a nitwit.''

Thea laughed! "I need a drink. Hair of the dog. A nice spicy Bloody Mary should make it all well.''

That evening upon Howard's return from work he confronted her.

"Well what do you choose to do? I am not here to be the laughing stock of the island.''

She looked at him vacantly.

"Don't get coy on me Thea, it doesn't suit you. You have tested me as far as you possibly can, I find you rather tasteless."

"Howard please refrain from playing your broken record, I don't wish to listen."

"Hah! The bastard hasn't the nerve to confront me, I'll talk to him if you wish. I hate for you to look absurd in his eyes, but if that's what you have come to, then so be it."

"How can you subject yourself to such demoralization if you already know the outcome?"

"You are the victim my dear. I just want to get our facts right, and to show you where you do stand in his life."

"You won't have to stoop so low on my account. It's finished!"

Thea now endured the most difficult task ever, by avoiding Hans completely. She swore to herself this was the finish! Hans persistently drove by her apartment morning and evening, tooting his car horn for recognition. She pretended she hadn't heard him.

As the weeks passed, Howard and Thea persevered to recapture their past. They attended dances and friendly meetings at the Alliance Française Club, they mingled with mutual friends who had feared their marriage was over. Howard dedicated more of his time to his wife's whims.

One evening Thea nonchalantly asked Howard if he thought they should start a family. He choked on his soup at the dinner table.

"What did you say?"

"Well Howard we have never made a true commitment between us, I think a baby would draw us closer. I feel terribly restless and selfish living here. So let's stop using the birth control, and get on with it."

"Somehow I don't visualize you in the parent role," he remarked.

"I know we have never spoken of having children, but maybe it's time we did."

After that very night of consummation, Thea imagined having morning sickness. She lived in anticipation for her next period, and when it didn't occur, she was sure it was Howard's seed she conceived and not Hans's.

As the months passed, she suffered from fits of depression. Each time she passed a mirror, she shuddered at the sight of her voluminous body. What was supposedly a time of joy was misery for her. Howard showed concern for her personality change, and requested her mother to visit them, hoping maybe she could communicate with her daughter where he couldn't. Carla was Thea's only sympathetic friend.

131

Once again Howard was away on his business trip in Djibouti, and Thea was alone in their apartment. One night there was a gentle knock on the front door. Thea wasn't sure if it was the high winds that kept knocking, so she hesitantly answered it. When she saw who it was, her hand immediately covered her stomach in embarrassment.

"What do you want?" she demanded.

"I had to see you, to know how you are."

She asked him in. She placed a Becks beer in front of him as he sat on the sofa. They stared at each other in silence. She felt uncomfortable in his presence. She knew full well that she still cared no matter how many changes she endured. He watched her with a saddened expression.

"I had so much I wanted to say, and now words fail me. When is the baby due?"

"In June sometime."

"Will you inform me when your time comes near?"

"I don't think it is any of your concern."

"You are wrong. I must know when you go to the hospital."

"I think it's best you leave now, Hans. This is Howard's home, and he wouldn't appreciate your visit. I'm sure he'd be most perturbed. I have nothing more to say to you."

She heard the jeep drive away as she poured herself a scotch on the rocks. Even the booze tasted nasty! All this good living had sapped her vitality. She stood by the window of her darkened bedroom and watched his lighted flat. Why did he come around? She had been so strong willed until now. She hurried down her stairs, along the dirt road and hastily entered his building. Breathlessly she ascended the stairs and pushed open his front door. Hans and Helmut were engrossed in a game of chess, and they looked up at her intrusion with astonishment. Hans immediately came forward with his hand and requested her to sit down. In German he asked Helmut to excuse them.

"I'm not sorry I came here; you upset me."

He held her face in his tender hands and drew her to his chest. She withdrew from his embrace and started to weep.

"Hans I'm frightened. I have never been so scared in my life. It's nobody's fault. I don't feel in the least maternal. It was you that suggested I might be pregnant, so I asked Howard if we could start a family. Why did you say that?"

"Because I thought it would solve your dilemma."

"From you, or him?" she asked harshly.

132

He turned away from her.

"Damn it! It's not enough you fuck my life, now you tell me how to live it."

"Thea! Listen. Listen to me. Don't upset yourself, not now. Think of your baby. Not Howard, not me, but your baby!"

"Go to hell! I hate you for this. Howard is right. You're a selfish demanding brute. All you men are bastards!"

Hans had never seen her acting so delinquently before.

Thea felt weary as she lay on his bed. He sat alongside of her holding her hand.

"Do you wish to be taken home, or will you stay the night here?"

She shamefully opened her arms out to him, as he lay his head on her chest. Now in her seventh month, she desired copulation with the man she truly yearned for.

Thea and Howard stood by the jetty at Steamer Point awaiting her mother to disembark from the ship. It had been over three years since mother and daughter hugged each other with delight. Yes! Thea was long overdue for the sight of the woman who had been her lifelong anchor. Although the lady didn't understand her daughter's motives, they had an inseparable unity that Thea couldn't banish.

The first weeks of their visit flew by rapidly. They spoke of old friends in Calcutta, most of whom had immigrated to Canada, Australia, and even Great Britain. Thea wished her father could have accompanied her mother, but he never left the shores of India. Thea's friends in Aden were enchanted by her mother, and she in turn with them. Mother was familiar with Steamer Point as most day trippers were, but to actually take up residence in Crater was beyond her mother's belief. Mother soon realized with anxiety that her daughter's behavior had worsened since they had last seen each other. Probably because of her present condition.

Thea had always caused her mother alarm because of her unpredictable nature. She now hoped becoming a parent would establish the necessary commitment required of her. Howard may have been her mother's ideal paragon of perfection and the answer to curb her daughter's restlessness, but this had no significance on their relationship. As it appeared, both Mother and Howard seemed despondent over Thea. Mother would in due course solve her daughter's dilemma.

Howard was out of town on business when Carla came around to take Thea and her mother to the beach. Thea was now self-conscious over her condition, so she didn't swim. However the ladies had tea on the beach. Thea was distracted by Hans in the distance who got her attention. She excused herself and strolled toward him behind the dressing rooms.

"I can't stay long as my mother will be suspicious."

"Our work has been completed here. Helmut and I fly back to Germany in a couple of weeks. I must speak with you alone before my departure."

'I'm sorry that's out of the question, as my mother is constantly with me, and I cannot get away."

"I'll arrange it with Carla to keep your mama occupied while we see each other. If you agree to this."

The next morning while Thea and her mother were dining with Carla and Miles at their home, Carla whispered to Thea that Hans expected to meet her at the big rock on the beach at 8:00 P.M. She would keep her mother occupied during Thea's absence. It was already seven forty-five. So Thea excused herself and told her mother not to be anxious, she would be back presently. Carla and Thea drove hurriedly toward Crater.

Hans was already at their meeting place and watched Thea approach in the distance as Carla drove away. He put his arm around her and lit a cigarette to calm himself. She watched his distressed expression.

"Leibling, I know we have run out of comforting words, but you must know I love and care about you and your baby, no matter what you say."

They got seated on the beach as they had so often done in the past, and he caressed her stomach.

"She kick a lot no?"

"Don't call it a she, it's a he."

"I say you have a she. You will see I am correct." He proceeded to say, "The day of Queen Elizabeth's visit to the colony—in ten days I think it is—I will meet you on the Crescent Hotel rooftop. You wait for me until we meet, okay?"

Thea's body throbbed with anxiety, and her provoking infant seemed tuned in to its mother's remorse. Hans tenderly kissed away her tears with empathy, as he helped her back on her feet.

"You had better drive me home now. I'm sure my mother will demand an explanation for my disappearance."

"You will meet me on the Crescent rooftop?"

"Yes Hans I will, if I'm not already admitted to the hospital."

Hans had delivered Thea to her apartment entrance. Mother and Carla were seated in the living room when Thea entered.

"Where were you, baby? Carla said you had to take care of some important matter. What was it?"

"Mummy, my dear Mummy! I hoped to spare you the details, but I have never kept secrets from you, and you know me well. You are aware of the circumstances between Howard and me. Though you would never interfere. My husband sent for you for a grave reason. It wasn't because I'm about to give birth to your grandchild! For the past fifteen months I have gotten myself involved with a German fellow, and my marriage was threatened. Now the German is returning to his homeland, and he wished to say good-bye, so I was with him this evening."

"Goodness me my child. How could you ridicule a good man like Howard with such shame. A daughter of mine making such an admission. You literally spun a web for Howard. Anybody can get married! It's to stay married that's the test. You want what you can't get, and when you get it, you don't want it. You were always a problem, and with age you seem to worsen. The German, whoever he may be, obviously has no scruples. He belonged to Hitler's Germany, he was probably a Nazi. You could never have been a part of his life. What were you thinking about, child?"

"Mummy the man is only thirty. We never discussed such matters."

"Maybe you didn't. He knew exactly what he was up to! You were a sheltered little girl from a respectable background. Germany was aggressive with the Hitler youth movement, and he was part of that culture, such things unknown to you, or us, for that matter. I don't know this man, and I don't wish to. Howard is a gentleman in comparison. If I were Howard I would have let you go with this wretched man. Your poor father, what would he say to your foolishness?"

Thea screamed at the top of her voice! "Stop it! Stop it! Save me the sermon on the mount. Yes Mother dear, I would have gone with him, if he had agreed to take me. I will never be the same toward Howard, baby or no baby. I only got married to get away from your watchful eye, and our financial circumstances in India. Now I know I should never have married."

Mother was horrified! This had been a side of her daughter she wasn't in the least familiar with.

"The baby! Is it his?"

"Fear not, Mum, it's Howard's. I didn't disgrace him, I only betrayed myself, if that's any consolation to you."

Mother now faced Carla. "I suppose you were aware of this sordid affair?"

"Yes dear, but don't blame Thea. She had her first unforgettable experience, which she should have handled differently. As you say she was brought up very sheltered. I feel Thea has strayed from the fold, and will probably encounter more of the same in the future. Perhaps next time she will handle it with discretion."

The colony was decked out in all its splendor. The Union Jack was conspicuous on all the buildings, and hung from every street lamp. The crowds in Steamer Point anxiously awaited Her Majesty Queen Elizabeth the Second to alight from her ship, the *Gothic*. She looked radiantly beautiful in buttercup yellow with white accessories. By her side her handsome husband, Prince Phillip, was dressed in full naval uniform.

Howard had returned to the colony just in time to chauffeur his family through the endless crowds to participate in this regal visit. Thea felt as though she were back at the Victoria Memorial on the Mall in London. The British with their customary pomp and ceremony carried out several marches. The Arabs and the English were dressed in their spruced whites and khaki for the royal occasion. The Queen conferred a few important sheiks with the rank of knighthood with the usual ceremonial protocol. The fanfare of trumpets accompanied marching soldiers to a well-rehearsed brass band, as camels and horses joined in the parade. Howard took photographs of the spectacular color on the parade grounds. The evening ended with a fantastic array of fireworks in the harbor, as the ships sirens wailed.

Thea searched for hours for the sight of Hans on the rooftop. She stood where he had told her to, but no Hans. Her eyes followed every jeep on the colony. She felt nauseated. She heard Howard's voice in the distance.

"Come dear, we have to leave now. The Hun has departed. I saw him leave at the airport yesterday. It was his turn to take the plane out this time. And he won't be returning, thank the Lord."

Chapter Nineteen

The clock in the distance chimed 3:00 A.M. Thea peeped into their respective bedrooms, both Howard and her mother were sound asleep. She had consumed enough Mataxa the night long, to provide her the courage of satisfying her curiosity. In her inebriated condition she circuitously approached his dark flat. Laboriously climbing the stairs, she reached for the light switch, which had been disconnected. In sheer exhaustion she crept into Hans's empty bed, from which the sheets hadn't as yet been removed. She hugged his pillow with self-reproach and wept bitterly. Her cumbersome body vibrated with remorse, and she wished she were dead. Daylight drifted through the window, as she looked around at the stark realism of her loneliness, within these walls that once held love and laughter. She slowly walked away from the strange abode.

Now as she sat on the couch in her living room, she felt a weird sensation. Her dress was wet through, and the water trickled down her legs. Not in the least anxious, she moved toward her mother's bedroom. Mother was awake saying her morning prayers, when she was disturbed.

"Baby! Your water has broken. It's time to go."

"Is that what it is? I guess I'm ready to unload this burden."

Howard jumped out of his bed, and came to his wife's side.

"I have your bag packed, we had better leave now," he said.

Thea was ushered into the delivery room and propped up on a hard table. Her feet were placed in cold metal stirrups, and her legs abruptly pulled apart. Her contractions were consistent and sharp. She stared at the white ceiling of the sanitized room, and her mind wandered to Moll Flanders. Hah! A far cry she was from a gentlewoman. With each contraction she now let out a scream. The little competent Scottish lady doctor wasn't in the least sympathetic.

"Push lass, keep pushing, push again," she persistently persuaded in a monotonous tone.

The nurse alongside of Thea held her down with a periodic sniff of ether across her nose.

137

"Damn it I can't push anymore."

Thea's mouth was dry, and her face sweaty. Her body quivered as resentfully she yelled once more.

"You're getting there, lass. Give another big push. Come on now, you can do better than that."

One final attempt and Thea heard the shrill of new lungs enter her dismal world.

"Get me a gallon of hot tea," Thea said.

"A beautiful bonny bairn. Do you wish to see her now?"

Thea had fallen asleep, and the next thing she heard was her mother's voice.

"Is she all right? Is everything all right?"

Howard's conversation with her mother outside was clear to Thea now.

"I will never permit Thea to endure such pain again. It was positively dreadful to hear her anguish."

Thea's private room was upstairs of the clinic in Crater. As she lay in her bed, she gazed across at the blue ocean and the peacefulness of a new day. The sun shone on the whitecapped waves that rippled on the sandy beach. Clearly now she observed "the rock" reminiscent of her past with Hans. That seemed real to her, and this imaginary. She was in a deep altered state of consciousness, smiling to herself she expected at any moment for him to wave to her from down there. Little did they realize at the time that this room even existed. Her thoughts returned to the present.

"I wonder where in Germany he is at this moment," she said to herself. It was because of him she now sat here, with a new commitment. Not for a moment did she consider that it had been her choice, and her path, she endured.

Howard stepped into the room and stood beside his wife. Holding her hand he said, "We have a little princess. She is the longest, and most perfect baby I ever did see. She has a head of black curls, and smells so sweet."

"When do I get to see her?" Thea asked.

"Well you've been resting so the nurse didn't bother you. I'm sure she'll bring her in directly."

Howard looked the proud father, indeed his expression told all. Thea felt saddened at his benign endurance, as he kissed Thea on the forehead.

Grandmother stood on the other side of her daughter proudly smiling. Thea wished she could have felt some of their exuberance.

Thea was awakened by the nurse, and presented with a wee bundle in her arms. She cautiously uncovered the infant's head, and marvelled at this miracle before her. A peculiar bewilderment came over her. To think such a perfect baby could be created during such a traumatic pregnancy. Thea cradled her in her arms as she scrutinized her from head to toe.

"My you have the longest fingers, I wonder what you will do with these artistic hands? Your skin hasn't a blemish. I thought all newborn babies looked like cabbages. You look three months old already. I'll call you Laura, you're a face in a misty light. I can't promise you a rose garden. You see I feel unworthy of someone as beautiful as you."

Thea never ceased to marvel at the wonderment of breast feeding. It truly felt awesome, as Laura's tapered fingers held her mother's breast with such urgency. Thea was fearful that something so great, yet so small was totally in her possession. She had always been so irresponsible about herself, and now she had a new life to take care of.

Nights as baby Laura slept so contentedly beside her mother, Thea would silently weep as her mind wandered to Hans and what he had said.

"Once you have a baby, your life will dramatically change, and you will live only for your child."

Thea hadn't considered herself a selfish woman. But she had the tendency to drift from one thing to another. She had never asked herself why. She did this or that, in an impetuous manner, never thinking over the situation until it was too late. Even then she'd get into yet another awkward situation.

Grandmother was most attentive over her grandchild. She probably recalled her own daughter at infancy. The only difference was she totally lived for both her daughters and never neglected her duties as a parent. Thea had been spoilt by both her parents into adulthood and she didn't have her mother's characteristics and fine quality.

Within the first six weeks of Laura's life Thea hired and fired three nannies. Then came Shiela from Somaliland. Shiela was tall, black, and skinny, and she functioned wonderfully with only one eye. She was a meticulous person, and a hard worker, and Laura's constant companion.

Laura grew rapidly in the climate of Aden. She loved the beach and the ocean at a very young age. After she had been christened at the

Catholic church in Steamer Point, her grandmother left for Calcutta. Thea felt a terrible letdown once again after her departure.

Laura now ten months old, wasn't prepared to leave Aden with her parents, and to bid farewell to her devoted Sheila. Howard's job had been completed, as he handed it over to a Greek from the Athens office. Thea had mixed feelings as she clung to her long lost fantasy. A mirage in the desert, and the only home she had had.

Carla and Miles drove the family to the airport. Thea drove past the Regal gardens for the last time on the road that led to Little Aden and several landmarks of her past escapades. Although she never did climb the mountain opposite her house, she felt she would probably never see the shores of Aden again.

The powerful jet signaled their takeoff as Thea placed herself near the window seat. The plane circled on the runway, and Thea couldn't hold back here tears, as she bid the colony farewell. A lot had transpired here for her future awareness, but was she sensible enough to recognize her romantic illusions? Sadly enough she hadn't become a woman, and she clung to her naivete.

The plane was now in the clouds, and Aden was just a dot in the vast ocean behind.

Chapter Twenty

Before their arrival in Great Britain, Thea, Howard, and Laura vacationed for ten days in Vienna and Amsterdam. From here they boarded a KLM flight to London.

Lydia was at the airport in London, as always, to meet her sister and family. She was thrilled to hold her niece for the first time, and delighted to cuddle and coo at the baby who looked at her with interest. However Lydia's allusions didn't go unnoticed by her sister, when she remarked, "Thea, I never associated you in the role of parenthood. I can't believe you're a mother."

They drove through the bustle of London's traffic, and Thea felt even more removed from this city then when she had last left it. London to most was a glorious experience; some even accepted its lousy weather, but to Thea it only reminded her of the austerity she'd faced when she arrived from the U.S. in her teens.

They checked into a hotel off Baker Street, most comfortable but cold. A roaring fireside in the foyer was deceiving. After they got unpacked, she missed Sheila's presence and assistance, as she had been fully responsible for Laura. Although the child was a treasure, her mother felt confined and confused. Howard, as always, was most supportive of his wife and helped tremendously.

In the morning after a hearty English breakfast at the hotel, they drove into the country to Howard's family. Mrs. Wrenn was delighted with her only grandchild, and she took on full responsibility to Thea's delight. Howard planned a scenic tour of the English coastline to Devon and Cornwall in the weeks to follow, after their new car was delivered.

To Thea's delight it was one of Britain's warmest summers, as they began their holiday through England's quaint villages and towns. They started out in Banbury.

"Oh!" said Thea "This is associated with the nursery rhyme Mummy used to sing to me when I was little. I remember it well: 'Banbury

Cross to see a fine lady upon a white horse, with Rings on Her Fingers and bells on her toes, she shall have music wherever she goes.' "

This was truly appropriate of Thea. She had to have music wherever she went, and whatever she did. Music to her, be it jazz, classical or rock and roll, was far more than a source of entertainment. It was a vital food that nourished her daily.

Their next visit was a drive through Cheddar Gorge, famous for the cheese. Here they stopped for the night at a roadside inn, after which they visited the Roman city of Bath, and finally they spent a week at Stratford-on-Avon, Shakespeare's birthplace. Howard and Thea briefly shared happiness with their baby in the peace and tranquility of the Avon Hotel. Here they fed the gracious swans on the river bank, and laughed together.

They continued through Somerset and arrived the coastline of Cornwall. Not far from here they visited Howard's uncle and aunt in Paignton Devon for another week. It was a glorious home surrounded by white sandy beaches, and an ocean view. The weather highlighted their stay. On the return drive they detoured through mystical Stonehenge. This is a circular arrangement of prehistoric monoliths set up in the neolithic period on Salisbury Plain.

After a month on the road, the family returned to the hotel in London. Howard checked into his office for a briefing on his next tour. This gave Thea the opportunity to indulge in a refresher course in hairdressing in London's West End. Grandmother Wrenn looked after Laura.

Thus their three-month vacation period flew by rapidly.

Lydia spent most weekends with her sister attending the theater, and shopping. Thea enjoyed London's West End, the assortment of its people and color never bored her. The excitement of Regent and Oxford streets was ever changing. The two movie extravaganzas *Around the World in Eighty Days* and *South Pacific* were a must which they enjoyed.

Marshall, their best man from the wedding, was home on leave from Calcutta. He surprised Howard and Thea by treating them to a night on the town at Edmundo Ross's night club with its Latin orchestra.

Howard and Thea responded to each other like old times. Lydia wished them good-bye once more, as they flew out to the Middle East.

Chapter Twenty-one

Baghdad . . . not only the capital, but the heart of Iraq, with no equal on earth either in the Orient or in the Occidental countries of Europe and America. It has an abundance of water and a healthful climate. People emigrated to it from all countries near and far. It was stretched out on two banks of two large rivers, the Tigris and the Euphrates. Merchandise was brought from India, Sind, China, and Tibet. It was the land of the Turks, Khazars, and Abyssinians. It was extremely hot in the summer, and moderate in the winter, though parts of Iraq could get colder.

Howard and his family were met at the airport by an English rep, sent out from the company in Scotland. As they drove through the city, the contrast of old and new fascinated Thea. She felt instantly she was going to like her five-year stay here. They had reached their destination in the center of the city on the main thoroughfare called Rashid Street. Their temporary home once again was the Metropolitan Hotel, renowned for its French cuisine. It was certainly a far cry from the Metro in the Crater. As comfortable as it appeared, the readjustment for Laura was difficult. Rashid Street was a congested hub, where American cars were predominantly chaotic as in Cairo, and the pedestrians were as whimsical.

Howard immediately got down to business, while his wife and daughter got adjusted to their new environment. The hotel stood on the banks of the Tigris, and the guests lunched and dined on the green lawns from where they could observe the endless river traffic, as the Arabs steered their dhows with a slow motion. In the evenings after the sunset, the sky would be invaded with a flock of river buzzards. Huge bats flew overhead, which at first gave cause for alarm. But soon they became just another peculiarity associated with the surroundings.

Across the river the constant flares of the Dora oil refinery expelled its gasses. The picturesque sunsets were reminiscent of Aden.

After a month Howard secured a house in the Alwyiah residential district, not far from the British club, which they became members of instantly. Thea hired a maid, and an Indian speaking cook, though they could both speak English.

Jessica and Cecil Turner, their immediate neighbors, were from England. They had lived in Baghdad many years. Their son, Keith, was a year older than Laura, so she had an instant playmate. Housewives spent the majority of their leisure time at the club, and their husbands worked strenuous, but shorter hours than in Britain. In the evenings friends would get together at the club bar, and the men enjoyed a game of billiards. The club provided the necessary pleasures and rendezvous for both old and new members. Saturday nights alternated with dinner dances or bingo. Thea had introduced the new sound of Bill Haley's rock and roll, and Elvis Presley to home parties. She had met a new friend, Joni Davis, an impish Shirley Maclaine type, who was the life of any party. Joni was an airline stewardess for Qantas airlines, that flew from Sydney to San Francisco. She now stopped in Baghdad. Thea and Joni got well acquainted when they performed the Charleston together at the club ballroom.

In the evenings the diners sat on the lawn around the open air swimming pool, where they were accompanied by a carpet of croaking frogs that mischievously jumped around their feet. Although the pool was constantly alive with folks, Thea missed the lure of the ocean and walking the miles of sandy beaches. Time passed congenially as they made new friends, a group of people that Thea nicknamed "our gang." The gang was comprised of a dozen Britishers that met each Sunday morning at the bar. This was followed by the club curry lunch. It was customary to play tennis or swim after that, making it a whole day affair. During the week the same clique socialized at each other's homes, at the club, and many times ended their evenings at one of Baghdad's night clubs. Thea's life-style had become most acceptable to her now, more than any place she had lived during her married life.

Howard's responsibility was to take over the existing agency that had represented his company, and to establish a new office. Thea had already shipped out her hairdressing sundries from London, and she thought it appropriate to be occupied for the years ahead and earn her own pocket money, working at home. She affirmed her confidence once more with her husband, and he in turn was assiduous about his marriage. His family came first. From all appearances they seemed to be a united family.

A year had passed, and Thea's phone rang for business as usual.

One morning around eleven, an unfamiliar male voice surprised her on the phone.

"Who is this?" she inquired.

"You mean you don't recognize my voice after all this time?"

She chuckled. "It's Guy, how are you? What's happening?"

"Oh I'm in your neighborhood, and I thought I'd visit awhile."

"I'm sorry I'm working," she replied.

"How about tomorrow around this time?"

"You mean you'll be in my neighborhood again tomorrow?"

"Yes, in fact I'd like to take you to lunch."

"I can't do that, Guy, my husband comes home to lunch with us. Laura and I look forward to that break in the day."

Guy and his wife Ethel were from England, and been married for sixteen years with no children. They appeared to be independent of each other, at parties they were together yet apart. Guy was forty-six, not handsome, but he had sex appeal. He was of medium build with brown wavy hair, brown eyes and a good personality. Ethel was in her mid thirties, pleasant in appearance, quite tall. They were both avid tennis players and socially orientated.

Ethel worked as a private secretary in a downtown law firm. Guy was a geologist, and worked for British Petroleum. They had both previously lived in Lybia. Thea hadn't displayed any encouragement toward him to warrant a personal call, so she dismissed the thought instantly. The next morning at eleven Thea answered her front door bell.

"Guy! You took a chance in visiting before calling, don't you think?"

"You're not mad are you?"

"No, but you know I work at home, and I have a client in the next room, so please wait in the living room."

"I woke up this morning, and said to myself it's now or never."

Thea smiled. "I don't think I follow you."

He playfully swung her around and kissed her on the cheek.

"What's wrong with a little diversion in one's life, huh? We've known each other some months now, and my eyes haven't deceived me. You need a man to be aggressive, so I am. You pretend to be indifferent, but I know you better."

"I'm sorry, you don't know me at all. I have no intention of endangering my family ever again."

"I knew it. I knew it from the moment I met you. You've had a past affair."

"I think you owe me an apology, so you had better leave. I don't have the time to talk with you."

"All right, maybe I do, I'm sorry, still friends?"

"Yes, Guy, still friends. You'll excuse me now, good-bye."

A few days passed and the phone rang again at the same time. Thea was almost sure it was Guy, so she wouldn't answer it. It persistently rang, until she was forced to prove herself correct.

"Guy I wish you'd refrain from calling. I'm busy."

"Thea please don't hang up. I must speak to you."

"Guy, I accepted your apology, so please refrain from your foolishness." She hung up on him.

No sooner had she done that, Howard came through the door. He kissed his wife as he always did, and they sat down to lunch. Laura was at the club with her friend Keith next door, and Howard drove Thea there after their lunch was completed.

"Hello Jessica. How is my daughter behaving?"

"Just fine. We just finished lunch, and she and Keith are playing in the sand pit."

"I guess I'll wait awhile before I go in for a dip. It's such a lovely day."

"Thea, was that Guy Markham that I've noticed a few times visiting you?"

"Yes, he has called round. Today it was to invite us to a party."

"A word of caution, beware of him. He likes the married women, especially a new face in the community."

"Well! You'd hardly call me new. But thanks for the warning."

Thea immediately felt guilt come over her. Why had she lied to Jessica? She didn't have to seek her neighbor's approval for her actions. Like most women, Jessica was inappropriately inquisitive. Being neighborly these past months was one thing, but now Thea had to beware of her.

"Speak of the devil," she remarked. "Here he is."

"Hello ladies! May I join you on this beautiful day?"

He placed his chair next to Thea.

"How come you manage to get away from work during the afternoon, while our husbands can't?" said Jessica.

146

"Probably because I start my day earlier, and I'm not bound to office hours."

Laura came toward Guy with her little rubber duck in her hand and placed her wet bottom on his lap. He jumped!

"Not on my good suit, baby."

Thea laughed. "It's obvious you're not used to children. Come here darling, Uncle Guy is upset. We must be leaving presently."

"You can't leave before afternoon tea," he said looking at his wristwatch. "At least let me order some tea and cakes."

The bearer came round with an assortment of sandwiches and cakes, as Jessica poured the tea.

"Now isn't this pleasant? Howard should try it sometime, wouldn't that be nice?"

"Howard should try what sometime?" came a voice from behind them.

"Hello darling," said Thea. "Isn't this a lovely surprise."

"Daddy, daddy," said Laura, running into his arms.

"Hello my love. I came to have some of that chocolate cake with my daughter. Then I must rush. Have to leave for Basra this evening. I'll probably have dinner on the plane." Guy glanced in Thea's direction.

"Do you travel much, old chap?" he asked.

"I've managed to avoid it so far, and I've been lucky till now."

Howard carried his daughter on his shoulders, as they bid their company good-bye. Thea had a feeling she would hear from Guy before the evening was out.

"One more, Mummy, just one more story please."

"Sweetheart, I've read enough for tonight. Now to sleep." The phone was ringing downstairs, and Thea ignored it as she kissed Laura goodnight. The phone stopped, and Thea got undressed to retire for the night. Her mind wandered to Guy. She wasn't in the least enamored of him. She heard the phone ringing in the distance, and she was getting angry at it. Finally she picked it up.

"All right what do you want? Make it brief."

"What took you so long?"

"I should think it would be obvious. I don't want to talk to you."

"That means you do. I'll be over in a jiffy."

Thea planned her next move as she sat in the darkness of her living

147

room. But she hadn't enough time for deviousness of any sort, as a gentle knock on the door got her attention.

"You're too much. Don't you ever give up?"

"How can I give up, when I haven't even begun?"

"Guy, must you park your car so obviously behind my husband's in the garage? My neighbor is most curious, and nothing would delight her more than to gossip about me."

"Ahh, you're not afraid of the women in the club, are you now?"

He promptly followed her into the living room, as she turned on the light, only for him to turn it off again. He aggressively hungered for her lips, which didn't astonish her. She didn't put up any resistance to his fondling her body. On the contrary, she contributed to his lustful desire. He picked her off the floor in his arms, and carried her upstairs to the bedroom, as he hurriedly disrobed himself.

They immediately began to erotically satisfy their lust for each other. "Wow!" she gasped, "whatever gave me the impression the English were passive?"

He became intense, which roused her curiosity over such accessible stimulation.

"You know, Guy, I've been warned that you are a reprobate. However I never take heed of gossip."

"The woman next door, no doubt. I've seen her at the club, but she has a face that leaves no impression. It's amazing how women that are not sought after, will be the first to warn women that are."

"Speaking of gossip. Do our friends discuss Howard and me?"

"I've heard it said in conversation that he would rather not fraternize with us as much, but he does so on your account."

"Do you think that, too?"

"Yes, it's possible. You are both so mismatched. Your husband is very much in love with you, however you're in love with love, and it need not necessarily be his."

Thea sat up in bed and continued to question him. He smiled as he brushed his lips over her bosom.

"I feel at sometime in your life young lady, you may have had a romantic relationship that probably jeopardized your marriage. For some apparent reason you have never forgiven yourself for this. You've taken a guilt trip."

"Is that what you think?"

"Thea, not all women are prepared for a commitment, and I myself think you take shelter with Howard. Yet I sincerely think you have tried to be a dutiful wife and mother, but a lot of women are not cut out for marriage. You did what was expected of you because of conditioning. But you had choices. I'd say you took the easy way out." She slapped his face, and straddled her legs across his abdomen.

"All right wise guy, let's really see what you're made of. I think you have bitten off more than you can chew this time."

How had Guy termed it? "What's wrong with a little diversion in one's life?"

"Okay," she said to herself. "This time I will play him at his own game. I won't get too involved, and I admit he'll make a pleasant play-mate. It's time I had the attention of another." Her heart quickened, and she looked forward for that 11:00 A.M. jingle.

"It's past midnight! Don't you care or wonder where your better half is at this moment?"

"Not really, I know where she is. With her lover."

"How long has this been going on?"

He turned round to face Thea, as the huge eastern moon shone on her nudity. His quivering fingertips moved over her sensitive mouth, and on her cheeks, across her nose.

"You ask a myriad of questions at the most awkward of times, young lady. What do you think Howard could be doing at this time in Basra?"

"Oh I'm sure he's fast asleep. By himself!" said Thea.

"You're probably right at that," replied Guy.

"Well, my dear, I think we had better call it a day," she said to him. "I won't be fit to receive my clients in a few hours. Sleep is calling."

"Yes! Besides, that moon is brightly shining on my car and we don't want the woman next door to be inquisitive do we?"

For the duration of Howard's absence, Thea spent much of her time with Guy Markham. He had a desperate need for acceptance from her. With his wife he felt like an old shoe. The context changes with the fascination of a new conquest. Sometimes they would lie in bed and he would discuss various aspects of his business, which by this time probably bored his wife. He explained about oil, its resources and production levels, its multinational corporations. His job was to examine samples as they were brought to the surface, and thereby to keep in touch with the stratigraphic progress downward. He had the prime responsibility for discovering the oil. The drilling was carried out by crews and petroleum engineers. He as a geologist was involved as a participant and consultant. His work spanned between Bahrain, Kuwait, Jeddah, and Baghdad, which was his base.

In 1956–57 the anti-British attitude in the Middle East after the Suez crisis resulted in the sabotage of the pipelines of the Iraq Petroleum Company, where he was presently. He predicted a lot of problems in the future of this country, and he had to achieve results while he could, as time was already against him.

Thea stroked his forehead with compassion. "Is that why you consume more Scotch than you should?"

"I like to drink, and I can hold it. I don't get inebriated like our friend Steven. Poor chap, one of these days he'll be fired."

"Yes, he is a pitiful old chap. It's a shame to watch an intelligent handsome fellow like him serve no purpose in society. Howard's job entails a lot of responsibility, but he is a true company man. It's interesting to watch the first timers on a new contract, breaking ground in these foreign countries. Some are true to their cause, and others can't take it."

"Thea, you are delight to be with, and if it was caused by my lust to get close to you, I am not sorry."

He got dressed silently and covered her with the bedsheet as he kissed her on the brow.

"I'll call you tonight, maybe we can dine and wine on the Tigris at the Embassy night club. Maybe even dance around to that fantastic orchestra. I know you'll enjoy that." She smiled as his footsteps disappeared down the stairs, and the front door shut. His car drove away through the main gate. It was dawn.

Neighbors! Jessica would soon be on her front lawn reading the newspaper with a cup of tea.

"Good morning," she'd sing in her inane fashion.

Mornings were so peaceful. The summer mist hung above the lawns, the sparrows were in flight as they chirped their morning song. The cock crowed in the distance, welcoming another gorgeous day. Laura would join Thea on the veranda in her pajamas, her sleepy eyes not awakened fully. The bearer brought breakfast on a tray with the morning paper. "Good morning Meimsheib," he'd say.

Chapter Twenty-two

Thea was cautious that morning when she answered the phone. Howard's voice from the other end informed her that he would be delayed another week. He left her a phone number where he could be reached in case of an emergency. No sooner had she put the phone down when Guy called. He had tried calling at his usual time, and she told him of Howard's delay.

"Good I'll have you to myself awhile longer, see you tonight at seven."

Thea had read Laura her bedtime stories, and Shufi, the nanny, was at hand to take care of her for the night.

Dressed in a beautiful blue tulle cocktail dress, Thea wore her silver shoes, and was getting her purse organized, when Guy arrived. She kissed Laura good night. She always fussed when her mummy took leave of her, more so as it wasn't with her daddy.

They tripped out the front door, as Jessica and her family observed her in her finery with raised eyebrows. Guy smiled as he assisted Thea into his car.

"You look positively ravishing. It isn't difficult for them to disapprove of you. That lady is so terribly homely."

"Shush Guy, that isn't nice."

The couple looked rather spiffy as they entered the club. The "gang" was in full attendance, which surprised Thea. She muttered in an undertone, "Is this your idea of a quiet evening on the Tigris?"

He replied, "There's method in my madness. If we show ourselves here now, we can spend the rest of the evening alone."

Guy directed Thea onto the dance floor as the band played "Teach Me Tonight." He pressed himself close to her and they scarcely moved around the floor. She submissively succumbed to his pranks, until his better half passed them on the floor with her partner.

"I love your dress Thea. It's beautiful."

"Guy let's get out of here, I don't feel at all comfortable."

151

"We will in due course, just a little bit longer, my dear."

After they returned to the table, the band started to play Elvis' "Don't Be Cruel," and bashful Steven was keeping time to it, but he never danced at any time. So Thea got him by the hand.

"Come on lazybones, let's cut a rug. If you can't dance with me, you never will with anybody."

"No! No! Thea I've never danced in public. I don't know how. Please don't."

But she had got the better of him, and he awkwardly tried to keep in step. She believed in his fashion he enjoyed every minute of it. Thea's light manner made him feel at ease, while he was still sober.

It was already past midnight, the air was sultry, and the music played on as Guy removed his jacket for comfort.

"Okay you can gently retreat after this dance, we won't be returning to the table, and I'm sure we won't be missed," he said to her.

She walked toward the ladies room, but met him in the parking lot. Guy was already in the driver's seat, as he blinked the head lights upon her for attention. They both sighed in relief to make a quick getaway.

"Where are we going, Guy?"

"To Baghdad's lover's lane."

"Oh! And where might that be?"

"You haven't been there as yet. I think you will enjoy it. You're not afraid are you?"

"Should I be? I love adventure, and I trust you."

They had driven for some miles toward the desert, when they finally approached a huge ancient clay arch. It seemed as though it was the remains of a ruined city in the past. It stood on the Tigris illuminated by a beautiful moon.

"This is Ctesiphon, isn't it romantic?"

"Well! It is different. It is indeed an obscure place. Nobody here but us. Suppose we were suddenly attacked by Bedouins. Do you come here often?"

"Where is your adventurish spirit?" He drew her to him and kissed her passionately. "No I don't come here often. I wished to share it with you, besides," he said, "I carry a pistol at all times. Now does that answer all your questions." She smiled.

They took off their shoes and walked on the cool sand. "Wait here for just a moment." He reached for a blanket and an ice bucket from the trunk of the car. "Okay you pick the spot where we'd be most comfortable.'' She slowly undid his tie, and the top button of his shirt, as he impatiently discarded it. She caressed his hairy chest with her long tapered manicured fingernails, moving toward the buttons on his waistband releasing his trousers. With the flick of his wrist he unzipped her dress.

"You truly bring out the animal in me,'' he said as he tasted her lustfully. He opened the magnum of champagne and poured it in two glasses.

"Umm, the nectar of the gods. I feel positively nefarious.''

"You are my love,'' he said.

They made love with exuberant ecstasy, the sand beneath her nakedness sensually stimulating her limbs alongside of his. She felt the pulsation of his penis erupt, as the mystic sounds of the desert in the early dawn brought them to a powerful climax. They hedonistically submitted to passion in an Arabian Desert.

Chapter Twenty-three

Laura was a pensive child, and at times appeared terribly languid. On this particular day she had developed a high temperature, accompanied by a rash. It was obviously the measles. Jessica had warned Thea that many of the children in the neighborhood had come down with it. The doctor was called for, and both mother and daughter were confined to the house.

Thea warned Guy not to visit as they were both in quarantine. His reply was wild horses wouldn't keep him away from her. He insisted on taking care of them. Before long as Laura improved, Thea came down with a worse attack than her daughter. Howard returned home to find his family sick, and felt guilty about having left them. He asked his wife why she hadn't called him? She said there hadn't been any need to. During the daytime while Thea lay in bed, Howard would call her frequently from his office, and Guy visited at his usual time. Thea was in fear the two men would collide before this was all over with.

The weeks passed and the Moslem high holiday of Ramadan drew near. As usual the Arabs virtually came to a standstill at work. The Wrenns had already experienced this in Aden.

The "gang" had planned a five-day cricket vacation to Northern Iraq, to a place called Kirkuk, another oil refinery town. Howard had no inclination for the sport, and even less to leave home. Thea pleaded with him to go, but he refused. However he told her not to let that stand in her way, she could go with her friends, not for a minute thinking she would.

"Yes I will, even if it is a caper to another town. After all most folks will have left here, and it is a holiday."

"You know nothing about cricket, but I suppose that isn't your reason for going is it?"

"Howard you can be such a stick in the mud sometimes."

"You go along and enjoy yourself. Laura and I will make our own fun."

"You do that."

The gang had planned the trip weeks in advance, and the arrangements had now been completed. About five cars set out at the crack of dawn. Thea traveled with Guy and Steven. Guy's wife, Ethel, accompanied her boyfriend, Malcome. Archy and Diane, happily married for over thirty years, took along Richard and Norman, and Angela, the only single female, rode with Caroline and Ian. Alex and Sydney went in their car. So in all there were fourteen of them that met at the club parking lot, in their respective cars, before filling up with petrol at the station.

Most roads were comparatively new in Iraq. Their first stop was at a *chi-khanna* (teahouse) which gave the appearance of a miniature oasis. Everybody got out here for a stretch and a cold Coca Cola chilled in a cool mountain stream. The men discussed the route on their road maps and the course ahead. They continued through the desert, with nothing to mar their vision, except for camels in the distance, and the periodic abandoned limo. Sheiks and Arab men of means abused their Cadillacs, and when the gas ran out, they were discarded by the roadside.

Guy drove all of the way, with Thea alongside him. Steven was seated in the back and provided them with refreshments from time to time. After several hours of heat and exhaustion, they sighed in relief at the lights of Kirkuk ahead of them. The British cricket team welcomed them as they were given a tour of the club and their residence. After everybody was allotted their respective rooms, they retired for the night. Thea and Angela, being the only females with no spouse, shared a room.

Thea awakened at the crack of dawn, to the sound of hooting pigeons that were nestled in the eaves of the building. She glanced across at Angela who was still asleep. Thea jumped out of bed and took a shower and got dressed. This was the best time of day to go for a walk. The scattered oil flares couldn't go unnoticed, as they overpowered the senses. Her walk completed in and out of the maze of pathways, she went into the dining hall. It resembled that of an army post, with long orderly tables covered with crisp white linen and starched serviettes.

"Good morning chaps. I'm starved."

Both Guy and Steven assisted Thea into her chair at their table. The hearty menu was relished by all of them, and the crowd anxiously looked forward to the day's events. The game commenced on a partly shaded green field. The onlookers sat under a huge tree with an awning and folding chairs.

Cricket is a serious sport and not one of distraction. Guests spoke in whispers, only when they had to. Other than the sound of the bat and ball, and comments from the umpire, silence ruled. Of course when there was a score, everybody clapped. The men looked extremely spruce in their starched whites. Steven was an excellent player and outdid himself on the field. In the heat of the noonday sun, the players took a short break, splashed their red faces with ice water, and had a cool drink. Tea with light refreshments was served in the tent at 3:00 P.M. The game ended at sunset. The men were in their glory, as cricket had been a pleasurable escape from their daily routine. After an early dinner, everybody moved in the general direction of the piano in the lounge. Thea sat herself alongside of Arthur on the piano bench. He had been an RAF officer in World War Two.

"Arthur, I hear you play the oldies. Do you recall 'Lambeth Walk?' "

"By jove! A girl after my own heart." He played the tune and drew the crowd around him. Thea got them all to sing "The White Cliffs of Dover," Vera Lynn's "We'll Meet Again" and "Underneath the Arches." No sing along would have been complete without "I've got a loverly Bunch of coconuts."

The men were totally rambunctious as the beer tap flowed, and their energy along with it. Thea, quite exhausted by now, took a walk with Guy in the compound. They strolled hand in hand looking at the mass of stars above them.

"I can't remember when I sang with such vigor; it was wonderful."

"Where did you learn all those old songs?" Guy asked.

"In Calcutta. I did volunteer work with my mother at the canteen. I was always asked to sing with the boys at the piano."

Guy and Thea strolled toward her room, where they momentarily stopped outside the door, as they heard voices within. Angela had company.

"Now what do we do?" exclaimed Thea.

Guy slowly tried the door handle. It was open, so he walked in, as Thea cautiously followed him. Angela was in bed with Norman, and not in the least perturbed by their visitors. They started to giggle, as she gleefully beckoned them in to join in a glass of champagne. There were several empties rolling around the floor, and part of one in an ice bucket. Guy poured two glasses and invited himself to sleep the remainder of the night with Thea in the bed alongside of Angela and her beau.

Guy keeled over and passed out. Thea removed his shoes and jacket.

She got undressed and crept in beside him for the remaining hours. She didn't get much sleep because of Angela and Norman making love.

"Guy wake up, wake up, you must get back to your room." He squinted at Thea with blurred eyes, then looked across to the other bed, where their friends lay fast asleep.

"Umm, that's not fair, I didn't get any."

He got on top of Thea with much enthusiasm and her lack of sleep didn't discourage her from the enticement.

At the breakfast table the men looked a sorry hungover sight. Thea thought to herself the day ahead should prove interesting. Before the game commenced and the visitors sat in the big tent. Guy and Steven clinked their glasses together.

"Cheers! Hair of the dog that bit, old chap."

Thea watched Steven competing on the field as he sang "Mad dogs and Englishmen go out in the noonday sun." He was truly high spirited.

The final night they attended a special dinner dance. The men dressed in their Red Sea attire which was comprised of either black or white trousers, a black cummerbund, and a white open neck shirt, tie was optional. The women wore cocktail dresses. The men honored each other with innumerable toasts, and applauded the winning team. The return game would be held in Baghdad. The dance ended on the strains of "Goodnight Sweetheart." Thea got solemn all of a sudden. "Is something the matter?" questioned Guy.

"I was thinking about my husband. This used to be our song, in days gone by when we were young and in love."

The next morning they got in their respective cars for their journey home. Steven's affection toward Thea hadn't gone unnoticed. He had always paid attention, now for the first time she sensed that he desired recognition for his past efforts. She pretended she hadn't noticed and overlooked his gestures.

Thea arrived in Baghdad at sunset. She said good-bye to both Guy and Steven, as she got out of the car. The porch lights were still on, as she entered the house. She tiptoed up the stairs and looked into her daughter's bedroom. Laura was still asleep. She then entered the master bedroom, where Howard appeared to be asleep. He awakened at her presence in the room.

"Did you have a good trip?"

"Yes, it was different. But you didn't miss much."

"I'm sure you didn't either."

Chapter Twenty-four

Laura was going on her fourth birthday, and her parents planned to move from the well-established Alwyiah neighborhood to the new development called Masbah. She was to begin kindergarten at a private school supervised by two young lady teachers, one of which was American, and the other English. From all accounts it was favorably recommended. Until now Laura's introversion disturbed Thea. However Howard assured his wife that after their daughter met little girls and boys her age she would find herself. Being an only child explained shyness.

Thea enthusiastically began to decorate and plan their beautiful new three-bedroom bungalow. The impressive front garden gave the appearance of a Persian carpet, inlaid with colourful shrubs of crimson, gold, and shades of green. It was as decorative as a precious rug. The beauty was contributed by the Persian gardener whose dedicated hours resulted in his desired achievements, both in the front and back garden.

The Wrenns celebrated with a housewarming on Thea's twenty-seventh birthday. With the assistance of cook, Thea prepared a feast fit for the gods! The evening commenced with Howard's famous scavenger hunt. Each couple was handed a copy of the following:

A piece of string, and button black.
A matchbox full of sand.
A paper clip, and drawing pin,
A signature from the Auberge band.
A wishbone of a chicken, and the hair from a horse's tail.
A postage stamp from a letter
And a ruddy great six-inch nail,
The cork from a bottle, for this you must try.
The last is easy, 'tis only a dead fly.
Now off you go, and make it a race.
Let's see who's first back at our new place.

Their immediate neighbors with whom Thea and Howard were not as yet acquainted, were amused by the shenanigans as they watched with curiosity. The party ended as daylight became visible.

On one side of them lived a prominent Armenian family from Tehran, Iran, and on the other was a delightful Iraqi homesteader. Both became Thea's good friends in the years to come. They adored Laura, who spent more of her time in their homes, than she did in her own.

The following day Heneretta, the vivacious middle-aged Armenian lady, invited Thea to accompany her to a classical recital which was held at the United States Information Service Cultural Center downtown. Prominent musicians from the world over periodically performed here. To Thea's delight it brought back old times in Calcutta, when she frequented such concerts with her mother.

Heneretta also introduced Thea to the ancient city of Baghdad. They shopped at the gold and silver bazaars, and walked miles in the souk, where Heneretta bargained with Arab merchants over fresh produce as Thea watched the performance to see which of them would reach a mutual price bargain. The chauffeur stayed close at hand and would carry back the purchases to the car. It was all very reminiscent of Thea's childhood in India.

On festive occasions, and name days, Thea attended the Armenian church with the Samoghian family. Marco Samoghian, the head of the family, was a prosperous architect and had designed many of the new developments in and around the city. The couple had two talented adopted daughters. The younger Anoush became Laura's constant companion. The family held extravagant banquets in their vast mansion, and cooked ethnic foods familiar to Thea, who gave her assistance to many a party. She had never before experienced the preparation of a hundred or more chickens on the spit. Thea and Howard introduced the new music of Bill Haley's "Rock around the Clock," as they all learned how to rock and roll to this strange sound. She had now discovered this vibrant cultural community, which she had very much become a part of. Thea was of British background, and married to an Englishman. She felt comfortable with the Armenian people, for she was part Armenian, as well.

Heneretta's perceptiveness hadn't gone unnoticed. As their friendship grew, she was aware of Howard's tending to exclude himself from their social activities. Which she felt was due to his estrangement from Thea, rather than directed to the Samoghian family personally. So as the months went by Laura and Thea spent much of their time with this family. They filled a void in Thea's life.

159

Once more Thea awaited for her telephone installation, as her home was comparatively newer than her neighbors and the lines hadn't as yet been connected.

Guy continued his morning visits if and when Thea was home. Because of her latest newly found friends, he accused her of having deserted her old friends. She disagreed, explaining that she couldn't center her recreation around the British club, as it bored her.

Chapter Twenty-five

Early one morning after Laura had gone to school, Thea stood by the front entrance of their home, when she noticed a station wagon parked across the street. A handsome gentleman walked toward her.

"Good morning, I am looking for Howard Wrenn's residence, I wonder if you could direct me," he said.

"I'm Thea Wrenn. My husband left for work minutes ago, in fact he's probably in his office by now."

"I'd like to introduce myself. I'm Kurt Voight. I have recently joined Mr. Wrenn's company. I have a message for him, we must have crossed paths on the road. It was a pleasure meeting you. I had better reach him." Kurt couldn't have gotten farther than a couple of blocks, when Howard pulled into the driveway from the opposite direction.

"I have to leave for Basra on the next plane out, dear."

"Kurt Voight was just here. That's probably the message he had for you."

"He's recently arrived here from Geneva, Switzerland, and he seems to be a real nice chap. I'll stop by the office and park my car there, and he will drive me to the airport. I'll ask him to chauffeur you around and take care of you in my absence."

"Umm! I'd like that, he seems most conscientious."

Howard left the house at 10:00 A.M. and Guy drove by at eleven.

"You just missed my husband. Pray! How would you have explained your presence here?"

"Easy, you don't have a phone as yet, so I came to invite the two of you to dinner."

"You're never at a loss for words are you?"

He smiled as he drew her toward him and kissed her.

"Guy it's too early in the morning for romance."

"You never complained before. I've noticed a change in you. Anyway I'll be over this evening, I know how you deplore being alone. You did mention Howard was out of town didn't you?"

"What gives you the right to say I'll be alone?"

"Ah hah, you have someone else do you?"

That evening after Thea had bathed her daughter, Laura pleaded to spend the night with one of her neighbors. The child knew full well if she timed it right with her mother, she would get her way. The two Iraqi girls, Netzi and Keri, were sisters of a warm and tender nature. Netzi, the older, was engaged to be married, and adored children. Keri was still in high school. Invariably around suppertime, Netzi would hop over the wall and pick up Laura for the night.

"Darling you can't bother the sisters every night. You must sleep in your own home sometime."

She pouted as Thea sprinkled her with baby powder, and dressed her for the night. She noticed the smile on Laura's face, and turned round to see what had got the child's attention. Netzi clapped her hands together in a gesture to carry her away. That had settled the discussion promptly.

Thea hurriedly took a shower and got dressed. Guy would be there at any moment. As she applied her makeup, she couldn't resist the thought of handsome Kurt, and silently wished it was him calling on her instead of Guy.

Kurt was fair with brown hair and eyes, tall and slim with broad shoulders. He resembled TV star Bruce Boxleitner. Her thoughts were interrupted by Guy whistling through the front door.

"Ummm, you look good enough to eat," he said.

"Shall we go? Please leave the light on in the foyer, I deplore returning to a dark house. Well! Where is it to be tonight," she asked.

"Let's dine at the Auberge, it's a beautiful evening, and we haven't been there lately."

When they reached the parking lot, the orchestra was in full blast playing the popular "Cherry Pink and Apple Blossom White." Thea gestured to the rhythm, as she strutted toward the main entrance. The waiter ushered the couple toward Angela and Norman's table. Thea noticed Ethel and Malcolm dining in a quiet corner of the ballroom. They waved and Thea smiled.

"What is this a family affair?" she remarked.

"Come on Thea, we live in a confined community, it's to be expected." Guy was drinking excessively, and began to rest his hand upon Thea's thigh under the tablecloth. She repeatedly withdrew it, and excused herself to go to the powder room. Here she was joined by Ethel.

"You know Thea, you and Guy make such a nice couple, and he's terribly fond of you."

"Is that what you call it? Well the feeling isn't mutual I'm sure. He's not my husband, Ethel."

Seated at the table during this ridiculous evening, who should walk in their midst but Kurt. "Oh no," said Thea as she lowered her eyes and wished she could vanish from the scene. Kurt was shown to a table directly across from them, and couldn't be avoided. He waved to her and she smiled in return.

"Who is that gorgeous man?" enquired Angela.

"His name is Kurt Voight. He is a new addition to Howard's office."

"Oh Thea, do ask him to join us."

Guy got hold of Thea's arm and directed her toward the dance floor. He was the worse for liquor, as he held on to her for support. His forehead was sweaty, and she suggested they sit down.

"I'll be fine, just hold me close. We can't leave right now, it won't look right."

Kurt pensively ate his dinner, as he watched them on the dance floor. The music came to a halt, as the band took a break. Thea sipped on her scotch, as she longingly gazed in Kurt's direction. He intuitively approached her table, and she introduced him around. He hadn't summarized the situation and where Thea fit into this group. She wouldn't tell! The band started to play.

"May I have the pleasure of this dance, Mrs. Wrenn?" he asked. She smiled acceptingly and accompanied him to the floor. A beguine was played, and they danced in a professional manner.

"You are a terrific dancer, Mrs. Wrenn."

"So are you Kurt. Please call me Thea."

Thea felt as though they were dancing on a cloud. Other couples stepped aside in admiration, as the couple nimbly stepped through a medley of Latin tunes completed by Tico-Tico, the popular samba. After such eloquent footwork, she was returned to her table by her gracious partner. He bade her good night with a kiss on her hand.

"The show-off, who does he think he is, Fred Astaire?"

"I think we had better call it a night Guy. I want to go home."

Guy came to an abrupt halt outside of Thea's house. She wished him good night, and requested he drive away immediately, as she felt they were being watched.

"What makes you say such a foolish thing?"

163

"Because I know we are. It's late."

Thea shut the front door behind her. She observed Guy light up a cigarette and drive away. While she got ready for bed, she knew she was through with him.

The next morning Thea went about her business as usual. The ladies came for her professional services, and their discussion centered on the telephone being connected. All of a sudden as though it were magic, the phone rang. "Oh do you hear it? It's my phone," said Thea. "Hello who is this?"

"Good morning, it's me Kurt."

Although she was deprived of his expression on the other end of the line, she could sense he was smiling.

"How did you know I had my phone connected and the number? I don't have it myself as yet."

"I rushed the order, and was given the number, naturally."

"Oh, thank you Kurt, I'd like to reward you if I may. Would you have dinner with my daughter and me tonight?"

"I would enjoy that very much. Is seven o'clock all right?"

"Just fine. See you at seven."

He was dressed immaculately in a light grey suit, and his white shirt displayed a handsome pair of gold cuff links. He had the whitest teeth when he smiled. He handed Laura a gold foil box of Swiss chocolates. Thea directed him to the living room and offered him a drink. Laura sat beside her mother and gave Kurt her approval. Soon after the cook announced dinner and the three of them got seated. Kurt was charmed by Laura, and he politely answered her many questions. After dinner, Thea excused herself as she got her daughter ready for bed. Kurt browsed over the library, and when Thea returned, he mentioned he enjoyed mystery stories.

"Please help yourself. Howard is a science fiction buff."

"Would you care to sit outside on this beautiful starry evening?"

His conversation was decorous, and Thea was most interested in his conventional background, compared with the easy going ways of the Middle East.

"Well! I didn't realize time could go so fast. Thank you for your hospitality. By the way this is your new telephone number. Please feel free to call me anytime. Mr. Wrenn asked me to take care of his family. It is indeed my pleasure."

"Thank you Kurt, I will."

"Perhaps you would care to have dinner with me tomorrow? We could go to the Embassy on the river, and maybe continue dancing where we left off."

"Could you make it Saturday evening? I'm busy tomorrow."

Had she said busy? She was bored to tears at the party on the club lawn. To her dismay, Steven stalked up from behind and put his arms around her waist, affectionately kissing her neck.

"Watch me carefully, I'm about to capture you away from Markham."

"Don't talk a lot of gibberish. I was never his to begin with."

"You've both been playing footsie a long time now, while I've witnessed this pathetic charade. Poor Steven! Poor Steven! He's the bastard. I'm the one that cares about you."

Other than being terribly self-conscious, Steven was over six feet tall, and a totally wasted alcoholic. His most favorable asset was that he resembled the movie actor Mel Ferrer.

Thea brushed past him disdainfully, toward the ladies room. She picked up the phone in the lobby and called Kurt who answered on the second ring.

"It's Thea. Am I disturbing you?"

"No! no, not at all. Is something the matter?"

"Would you do me a favor please? I'm at the club, and would appreciate if you could meet me at the entrance, as soon as possible. Thanks."

Kurt's headlights blinked in her direction as he drove toward her. He got out and opened the car door.

"Thank you Kurt, I had to get out of there. I am sick of these boring affairs."

"Do you wish to be driven home, or go for a drive?"

He swung the car around as they drove clear across the city, over the bridge to the other side of the Tigris.

"Sometimes when I can't sleep I come here for a cup of Turkish coffee. Have you ever been here?"

"No! I haven't. I stay pretty much in my neighborhood, except when my neighbor takes me to the souk bazaar."

He ordered a couple of coffees in perfect Arabic, to Thea's astonishment.

"Where did you learn to speak the language so well?"

"One almost has to, to communicate with the locals."

"I've picked up a little, especially in reference to the cost of things, otherwise the merchants get away with it."

"Am I wrong in thinking you appear to be restless? Don't you like the Middle East?"

"Oh yes, I like it very much. It's just that I temporarily get myself into awkward situations, and then have to find a way out. Like tonight for instance. We could have been dancing, if I had accepted your invitation last evening."

"Well I'm flattered that you asked me to come to your rescue."

They drove home in silence in the wee small hours of the morning.

Chapter Twenty-six

In the morning Thea awoke to, "Mummy, Mummy, come and meet my new friend. She has just come here from Germany, and she lives beside us."

"Umm darling a little later, okay? Let Mummy sleep a little longer."

Laura took her mother by the hand to meet her new friend Elke, and her mother Annabelle, who was cheerfully plump and pretty, in her mid-thirties. Elke was six, skinny and cheerful, but she didn't speak a word of English. They had moved to a little house on the right of the Wrenn's. Annabelle was in the throes of unpacking a household, so she excused herself and shook Thea's hand.

"As you can see we have just arrived from Europe, and the house is a mess. But we can take a coffee break. My husband and his colleagues work for a German automobile company. Laura and my Elke play well together, maybe your daughter will teach my daughter how to speak English. Laura had breakfast with us this morning."

"Laura has made a lot of friends since she started kindergarten and both our neighbors have her over constantly. I can't keep track of whose house she's in. Now she has one more to visit. Well I won't keep you any longer, thanks for the coffee. Please feel free to call on me if you need anything."

Kurt was over at seven promptly. He was dressed in formal black tie and white jacket, with a perfect crease in his trousers. Thea wore a white organdy cocktail dress. He lifted an eyebrow at her radiance when she opened the door to him.

Kurt wasn't familiar with Baghdad's night life, and he didn't belong to any clubs. This was his first tour abroad.

They dined by candlelight by the dance floor at the Auberge. Time went by most pleasantly, as they were totally relaxed—until Guy and Steven appeared at the front entrance. Kurt immediately felt Thea's tension, as he asked her to dance. He was a man of perfection, especially when they danced together. The floor was all theirs, as few attempted the dramatic tango, which changed to the frenzied rhythm of the mambo. They smiled at each other, they were a team.

"Kurt would your mind if we left now, I feel claustrophobic."

"Have you ever driven outside of the city limits?"

"No I don't have the time to. Where do you have in mind?"

They took the road to Ctesiphon. He asked her if she came here with here husband.

"No, come to think of it I don't think he's been here either."

There was silence as they reached the arch. He turned the engine off, and did what he thought was now expected of him, in the quiet desert. He kissed her very gently, and she responded just as gently. He then drew her into his arms and they got rather emotional. His clean-shaven face was enticing to her lips. She kissed him over and over; he reciprocated to her demonstrativeness. She was sure they would make love instantly in the driver's seat. But he composed himself and backed away.

"I think I had better drive you home. I would not like myself in the morning, and I do not wish to regret a weak moment."

"I asked for that. You are a gentleman, and you have respect for my husband."

They drove home in silence, so he put the radio on so as not to cause anymore embarrassment. When he got to her driveway, he politely opened the door and thanked her for a wonderful evening.

Laura sat on her daddy's lap the next morning, as he'd returned early before breakfast. The two were engrossed in conversation, when there was a knock on the front door. It was Annabelle and her husband, accompanied by two other men.

"Good morning Frau Wrenn. I bring you a coffee cake I just baked. This is my husband, Max, and Herr Gunther, and Herr Ernst. I hope we do not intrude on you, but would you mind very much if I show my husband and friends your home. It is so much larger than ours. We were speaking about the difference in size. You don't mind, no?"

"Sure, come on in, folks. This is my husband, Howard, he just returned from Basra."

The men shook hands, and Max asked, "You travel a lot, Sir?"

"I do my fair share; sometimes more than I'd like to." They browsed from room to room speaking in German, then Annabelle chatted briefly with Howard before they left the premises.

"Thank you very much Frau Wrenn."

"What was all that about?" asked Howard.

"Beats me! I suppose they were curious as to how other people live around here."

"Well I had better take a shower and change. See what's going on in the office. By the way, did Kurt take care of you?"

"Yes thanks. He was attentive."

One evening Howard was working late. Thea had put Laura to bed, and was playing her classical records as she often did when her husband wasn't home. Howard wasn't much for the classics in any form.

Thea took to alcohol only when she became melancholy, which had been four years ago. She realized once again she was drinking too much Scotch. She desperately desired to be free of this encumbrance. It was her problem, to which she hadn't any solution. She had been convinced both by her mother and Howard that she could never survive on her own. Besides which she now had Laura to consider.

She heard a voice call her name in the distance. She moved toward the garage door and came in contact with Max from next door.

"Good evening Frau Wrenn. Would you and your husband care to come to our party? It isn't anything fancy. We welcome a new colleague of ours just arrived from Stuttgart."

"My husband isn't home. He's working late. However I'd like to come if I may," she said. She splashed her face with cool water, got dressed, and soberly walked next door. Annabelle greeted her at the garden gate. She had platters of food in her hands, and she beckoned to her husband for assistance. She introduced Thea to their company, all of whom were speaking in German, and now directed their conversation toward her in English. When Germans fraternized in a group, they became very boisterous, talking rapidly, as each interrupted the other for attention. Or so it appeared to Thea at this moment. She noticed a jovial character playing an accordion on the veranda, to which couples were singing and dancing.

Like a phantom from the past appeared the guest of honor. Their captivating glances fixed upon each other. Thea broke the silence.

"Welcome to Baghdad."

"Thank you" he said.

"Where in Germany do you come from?"

"I flew out from Frankfurt, but my home is Stuttgart. And where may I ask do you come from?"

"Well I guess from London, but originally I was born in India."

"Have you lived in Iraq a long time?"

"Almost three years, though it feels much longer."

"My name is Jurgen Berger. I am a salesman, and I represent my company for the Middle East," he replied.

"That sounds most impressive. I wish you success in your achievement."

They moved away from each other, as his colleagues demanded his attention. However he glanced in Thea's direction from time to time, and she relished his interest. The accordionist played happily as the couples sang and danced to a polka. It brought a smile to her face, that from her utterly depressed mood, she was now in the midst of such gaiety. The music and lyrics weren't in the least familiar to her, until the tune changed to *"La Vie en Rose,"* and Thea's heart skipped a beat.

"May I have the pleasure of this dance?" he said.

She ardently clasped him to her, as he held her close to him. Her face was over his right shoulder, she figured he was about five ten in height. He had wavy brown hair and light brown eyes, a good physique and a sound command of the English language.

"Jurgen, forgive me if I was discourteous upon meeting you. You reminded me of someone I once knew."

"Was he someone close to your heart, or an enemy?"

She smiled. "He was my lover, and he came from Hamburg."

"What happened to him?"

"What happens when one is married and the other isn't?"

"I apologize for my curiosity, it isn't any of my business. I didn't know you were married."

"I didn't say I was, but I am. My husband is at work, and Max asked us both over. He wouldn't have come if he had been home, and then I wouldn't have met you."

"Well! I'm glad we did meet, and I hope we will again. Have you been married long?"

"Six years, but it seems I have all of my life."

"I detect a lot of sadness in your voice. Yet you appear to be a happy person. Am I wrong?"

"I'd rather not discuss me. Tell me about yourself."

"Oh, there isn't much to relate. This is my first overseas tour, I have never left Germany before. Like most of us here, I was tempted by good wages to work in these Arab countries. We work and save our cash to return to our homeland and buy a nice house, get married, have kids. It is exciting to travel, learn different customs and get experience from it. I am thirty-seven, never been married, have a lady friend back home, but there are no commitments. I have come here for three years, and then intend to return to Germany.'' He smiled. ''That's about it.''

''I wish I could pride myself with such a sound self-analysis.''

''If you desire something with your whole heart and mind, you work toward it, until you get there. After all, life is but a challenge isn't it?''

As much as Thea didn't wish to leave Jurgen's company, she had to in all good faith. She thanked Annabelle and Max for the evening, and walked toward the gate. Jurgen wasn't far behind. ''Please! Let me escort you home,'' he said.

''Oh, I live next door. There's no need to, thanks.''

''It's my pleasure, I want to—okay?''

They held hands as they strolled toward Thea's home. He then gallantly kissed her hand. ''I hope we see each other soon Frau Wrenn. I enjoyed your company immensely. Sleep well.''

Such chivalry! She trembled all over as she entered her house.

Howard was sitting in his chair in the living room, engrossed in a book.

''Where have you been? It's past two o'clock in the morning. Since when have you taken to leaving Laura alone in the house? Suppose she had awakened and not found you here?''

''Howard, I was just next door. She would not have woken up. It's a pity you didn't come along. You were invited.''

''I wouldn't on principle. You know my feeling about Germans.''

''You feel that way about all our neighbors. Be it Heneretta and her family, the girls next door, and now the Germans. Well tough! I'm home a lot more than you are, and I need friends.''

As Thea lay in her bed alone, her thoughts reverted back to the pleasant hours she had spent next door: her conversation with Jurgen, the friendliness of Annabelle and Max. They were so enthusiastically different when compared with old British reserve. What was it that attracted her to Germans? They were a tough, hardworking breed, she could never fit into their life-style. Yet wherever she went, she seemed to clasp them to her bosom. Since Hans in Aden, she had completely estranged herself from Howard. Thea finally gave in to sleep.

One morning Thea received an anxious phone call from Steven. It appeared his tour had been terminated because of his excessive drinking, and he was to leave on the next plane bound for England. This was inevitable, so she wasn't surprised. He begged her to be at the airport on a certain day and time, and not to mention the incident to any of their friends. He said she was the only person that truly mattered to him. She promised she would be there. After she hung up, she phoned Kurt and asked if he'd drive her to the airport on that day. Kurt remained in the parking lot, while Thea went in search of Steven. She found him looking terribly dejected as she came toward him. He hugged her with all his might, tears in his eyes.

"Oh Thea, I thought you wouldn't come. I had to see you one more time before I left."

"Steven, you know I wouldn't have disappointed you. I'm here am I not?"

"Thea will you write me?"

"Sure I will, we'll keep in touch."

"Thea I know you pity me and consider me a bum. I could never aspire to someone like you. But I've loved you from the first time we met."

Thea's heart went out the poor pathetic wretch. She kissed him hurriedly and departed from the scene. As she walked away she yelled, "While you're in London don't forget to visit Scott's bar in Picadilly Circus, and ask for the famous Baghdad visitors book that we have been informed about here. I'll look for your name and address when I get home on leave, okay?" He waved to her as he got in the plane. She watched the overseas Comet taxi down the runway from the glass window in the lounge. She couldn't help but feel sorry for him. What a blow it must have been to his ego to leave in disgrace. She walked toward Kurt in the parking lot. He started up the engine.

"Who was that?" asked Kurt.

"A friend who didn't have a friend except me."

As Kurt drove toward the city, he mentioned Howard would be leaving town once more. "Mr. Wrenn asked me this morning to take care of you, and to take you dancing, as you were most enthralled with the night life here, and he couldn't always accommodate you. I said I would, only if you wished it."

"You make it sound more of a task than a pleasure. I'll be just fine, Kurt. You don't have to be helpful on my account thank you."

Howard took umpteen trips during the next few weeks. Life continued in much the same manner. Until one morning . . . Annabella, Max, and Jurgen visited the Wrenns.

"As you are aware that Jurgen lives presently in a hotel, and he takes his evening meal with us, we wondered if it isn't an imposition for you if you would condescend to rent him your third bedroom. He will pay handsomely for this, and it would be most convenient for us. There was utter silence in the living room, as all faces turned toward Thea for acceptance or rejection. Howard spoke first.

"You know we only have one bathroom, what do you think, Thea?" She knew only to well how he felt, so she wanted him to answer his own question.

"It's up to you, Howard. I know you like your privacy."

"When would you wish to move in?" asked Howard.

"Right away. I can give you the rent now if you wish."

"Well all right, the room is yours."

Jurgen took out his billfold, and handed Thea a couple of months generous rent. After they left, Howard glanced at his speechless wife, as she slowly unclenched her fist full of Iraq dinnars.

"My word that's more than generous!" she exclaimed.

"You are aware of my feelings in this matter. I hope we won't have a re-occurrence of the past."

"If you didn't approve, Howard. You could have said no!"

"And have your friends dislike me even more?"

Chapter Twenty-seven

Thea and Howard's lives had now changed for the better. Their daily trivial arguments had subsided and Jurgen and Howard became good friends. Thea and Howard participated socially with Jurgen's colleagues next door, and from all appearances the couple seemed to have a new lease on life.

After only a few weeks of association, Jurgen and Howard planned a weekend to a mountain resort called Sarsang in North Iraq. This included Thea and Laura. They traveled with Jurgen and Gunther, who was an excellent driver, as he was the owner of an exceptional automobile.

The four of them set off at dawn. Thea had prepared a delicious picnic basket for their long trip ahead. Their first stop was a *chaikhanna* situated around a minute waterfall which trickled from a distant mountain, beneath which they stored tiny bottles of Coca Cola served chilled from a rapid stream. As the journey continued, the only thing in sight was the occasional caravan of camels plodding through the windswept dunes. Jurgen's observation in his rearview mirror of Thea hadn't gone unnoticed by her. In the early evening they approached lush greenery with sparsely scattered houses, indicating the last lap of their journey. Around dinner time they had reached the Sarsang Hotel, a giant white structure sprawled along the mountainside.

It was late at night when they checked into their respective rooms. The night air was exhilarating and comfortable for sleeping. They retired on individual cots on the rooftop, covered with blankets, beneath the twinkling starlit sky.

Thea awoke at the break of dawn, while Howard and Laura slept on. Jurgen and Gunther, whose cots were in the far corner, glanced toward her with a smile, as Jurgen stretched his limbs with a sigh of contentment. He then took a stroll around the terrace, and Thea lost sight of him. Shortly after Thea followed his course around the building, where he stood admiring the mountain range that surrounded them. She crept up from behind and surprised him.

"Good morning Jurgen. Isn't this beautiful?"

"Yes the tranquility of this wilderness is mystifying. I could spend longer than a short weekend here. I wonder what folks do here for a pastime? This hotel is a good size to attract visitors, so there must be a tourist trade."

She watched him closely, and she knew he felt uneasy over her expression.

"You know Thea you look very lovely in the morning, like a little girl."

"I do?" she said moving closer to him. She brushed her lips past his ear, to which he immediately responded.

"Thea! Thea! You have no idea how much I desire you daily. At night I imagine you in my arms, and you are with Howard in your room. To be so close under your roof and yet so far is tormenting me. I have to shut myself in my room to free my mind of evil thoughts. Howard is my friend. I could never betray him."

"Shush! Shush!" She put her fingers over his lips. "Don't you think I feel the same way?"

He kissed her again and again, until she tore herself away from his embrace.

"I had better get back. See you at breakfast."

Thea had never fully liberated herself of the nightmare of Aden. It seemed not since then until now did she have the same longing for Jurgen as she did for Hans. It was as though she were acting in a sequel to her movie, same plot, but a different actor.

Both Howard and Jurgen took turns to piggyback Laura, as the four of them started to climb the mountain at the side of the hotel. The higher they climbed the more beautiful the picturesque scenery was. Jurgen took innumerable photographs with his German camera. Howard and Laura had walked on ahead, and had been completely out of sight for sometime. Thea lingered as she clung on to Jurgen's arm for support. His hand held hers, as she shamelessly encouraged their intimacy. Once more her imagination confused the issue. This was not Hans, and what she was doing endangered the both of them. He held her close to his chest, as she had stepped on a rock and lost her balance. Their eyes met, and they amorously kissed each other. He backed her into the dense bushes demanding instant pleasure.

"Jurgen! Jurgen! Not here. Please we can't make love now. This

175

isn't the place or the time. Howard may already be wondering about our disappearance. We must catch up to them."

Now that she was conscious of Jurgen's feelings for her, she had to be cautious. She thought to herself, *I won't get emotionally involved like before. Enjoy it for what it is. Concentrate on him, and forget the others.*

One night after they had said their respective good nights at home, Thea was restless. She tossed and turned in bed, until she reluctantly walked out on the front patio, and sat on a chaise lounge. She wasn't alone. Jurgen was smoking a cigarette as he walked to and fro.

"You can't sleep either?" she said.

"I have a lot on my mind," he said coming toward her. "I leave for Mosul in a few hours and will be gone a week. I wish you were coming with me, Thea."

He sat alongside of her, and they spoke in whispers. The moon above was as bright as daylight upon them. He took her hand in his, and smiled.

"You know I never wished this to happen; you both have been so kind. Perhaps it would be better if I move when I return. I feel this to be my home, but it isn't. It is Howard's and yours. I must go now; good morning."

Thea returned to her bed, and Howard was peacefully asleep in his. She couldn't help but hear Jurgen's moving about in his room, as he packed his bags to depart. The door shut, and his footsteps faded toward the front door. He started his car and drove away.

Thea couldn't sleep as she was attacked by mosquitoes. She wandered toward the kitchen with bare feet for the insect repellent. In doing so she stepped on a scorpion. She immediately screamed as though she had been electrocuted. Both Howard and Laura came promptly to her side. Howard switched on the light to find her in excruciating agony. The venomous sting had floored her. She pointed toward the scorpion, which crept along the floor. Howard consequently grabbed Laura in his arms, before she stepped on the insect. In his dilemma he got a hold of his razor and tried to extinguish the sting, that didn't bring relief, so he sucked the blood from her heel. Nothing helped. He was forced to drive her to the hospital for attention.

For the next forty-eight hours Thea lay propped up in bed on her pillows. Howard had to leave town on business, and the neighbors showed great concern for her. Kurt visited evenings to keep her company.

One night her foot throbbed more than usual, which deprived her from a good night's rest. She heard the front door open.

"Howard is that you?" She got no response. She called again.

Jurgen stood by the door to her bedroom with his bag and briefcase in hand. "Are you alone? What is the matter?"

"I got stung by a scorpion the morning you left," she said helplessly.

"Where is Howard?"

"Out of town as always," she replied.

He threw down his case, and came toward her.

"Does it hurt terribly?"

"It's better, just aggravating. It has to take its course, I guess."

He lifted her off her bed and carried her to his room. He placed her gently in the center of his carefully made bed. She watched him take off his tie and shirt, and put his trousers carefully on the chair back. He then bent down and kissed her.

"Don't say a word, just let me hold you as I lie beside you." His warm lips moved slowly over her eyes, and the rest of her face, his strong limbs encircled her. All discomfort seem to instantly vanish, as she responded to his lovemaking.

"Oh Jurgen you're wonderful. I want more, more," she kept saying. "I knew you would be fantastic. This is how a woman should function, with her whole being. I've been so dishonest in making love."

Jurgen and Thea spent the following evenings exuberantly involved. They knew they were on borrowed time. It was too fantastic to last. Their final night together ended in a nightmare! They were sound asleep in their nudity when suddenly the overhead light shone upon them. Startled they jumped up in a daze. Howard was standing in front of them with a disgusted expression on his face. He didn't seemed shocked, it was almost as though he expected this infidelity.

"Get out of here you bastard, and take her with you."

"Take it easy my friend, it isn't Thea's fault. I am just as much to blame. It was bound to happen. I can't say I'm sorry."

"You're no friend, and she's no wife. You belong together. Get out of my house this very instant."

Thea stood in the center of the room without flinching. Then she stalked out to put her robe on. She sat in the living room half clad as Jurgen hurriedly packed his bags and left the premises. He got in his car and drove around to Annabelle's house. Now no doubt they would hear the sordid details. Howard came into the living room and said, "You still here?"

"Oh shut up! I'm glad you found out, and it's in the open. Maybe now I will do something about my life."

"You haven't the nerve or the sense," was his reply.

"When we return to London I want a divorce," she continued.

"You want a divorce! I should get one from you. These bastards wouldn't take you on, on a bet. You're just easy bait for them, and I'm stuck with you."

"Not anymore your not, we were finished a long time ago. Howard, you can have your divorce. I want nothing except to be free. I've never had that privilege. It's time I did."

It was May of 1958, and there was a lot of political unrest in Iraq. A number of Iraq army officers of brigadier level secretly agreed on a rough course of action. Whosoever among the first found himself in or near Baghdad with the requisite ammunition and equipment, would strive against the government. On July 13, Brigadier General Abdul Karim Kassem and his subordinate officer, Abdul Salaam Aref, got orders to proceed with units to Jordan, via Baghdad. On July 14, Colonel Aref led his columns into the city. The results shocked the Western world. The Crown Prince Abdul Ilah opened fire and in the gun battle the boy King Feisal, about to be married, and most of the Iraqui Royal family were killed. The young King was an object of pity rather than hatred.

A Republic was proclaimed in Baghdad on July 14, 1958, as the result of a military coup d'état. The poor of the city acted crazed, and their released anger and vengeance were in virtual control of the streets. The radio blasted day and night with reports of chaos throughout the city. The British and American civilians were told to stay home.

Thea hastily visited Nitzi and Keri, whose brother was in the Iraqi Air Force. They had lost touch with his immediate whereabouts. She then visited Heneretta and her family, who were equally distressed. Annabelle managed to speak to Thea on the request of Jurgen, wanting to see her. Thea said it was best left the way it was.

The British and American people in the city were evacuated in droves daily. Armored tanks and guns rumbled past the residential areas, and downtown was a prohibited area.

Thea hurriedly packed the family's personal belongings, and gave their cat, Sheba, to Heneretta for safe keeping. It was indeed a calamitous conclusion for all concerned.

This prompt evacuation transferred them to the turbulence of Beirut, Lebanon. Here the Wrenns took refuge at the Excelsior Hotel, one of several beautiful hotels situated on the beach, and demolished during the street fighting. The battle raged on for days, and Thea was in fear they would not get out alive. Their personal problems were put aside, as Howard's only priority was the concern for their safety. They were finally given a military escort from the hotel to the airport. Once more Thea faced the fanaticism of this country, which was reminiscent of India.

Howard, Thea, and Laura safely boarded the jet in the late night for London.

Chapter Twenty-eight

Thea and Laura trudged through greater London in search of anything that half way resembled suitable accommodation. They subsequently secured an attic apartment in the Holder's Hill area. It looked as though a crawl space had been renovated into a tiny bedroom and kitchen, for renting purposes.

The one general bathroom on the landing was shared by the household. It was a clean, makeshift and reasonable rental for the London area. Laura's comment was, "Mummy this is like a doll's house."

"Yes dear, that's exactly what I said to your grandma when I first arrived here with your daddy."

Howard was awaiting his next overseas assignment, and he shared this tiny abode with his wife and child. They had all been abruptly removed from their carefree secure life in the Middle East, to this uncertain situation.

Thea at this time was planning a visit to her father and mother in Calcutta. She longed to be with her parents, and for them to enjoy their granddaughter who wasn't aware of their existence.

It was one of those particularly dreary Sunday mornings that is associated with Britain. Howard was called to the telephone in the main lobby, as Thea awaited the result of the call. He finally returned with a dismal expression.

"Who was that? What is the matter?"

"I'm afraid it's bad news."

"What? Is it Mummy? Has something happened to her?"

"It's your dad. He's gone, Thea. He had a heart attack walking home. He was alone, and it was too late to save him."

"Oh my God!" Thea screamed hysterically, as Howard tried to console her. She beat upon his chest, and sobbed from room to room, as though she were trapped in a shoe box. "It's all your damn fault. I should have been there already. What the hell am I doing in this damn place? Oh God! Do I have the most wretched luck? I was so near, yet so far from seeing him. Now I never will again.''

Poor little Laura started to cry alongside of her mother.

"Don't cry Mummy, please don't cry, I'm here with you."

Thea rushed out of the room to dial her sister's number. Lydia, at a loss for words, kept sobbing.

"He's gone Thea! He has been poorly for sometime now, but they didn't want to interfere with your visit. They were both looking forward to it. He never complained, it all happened so quickly."

Thea had never prepared herself for the great loss of a loved one that came to everybody at sometime. She brooded for weeks, and couldn't function to say the least. Mother had previously informed her in letters, that her father had lost his zest for life when he had stopped racing his horses. He was fearful of old age, and now at fifty-eight, he had made his transition.

Howard agreed to continue his wife's monthly allowance for her support in London, and begged her not to give up completely before she reached a definite decision. She was saddened at his departure for Greece. He had been so tolerant of her impetuosity, but then again, she had brought him so little happiness.

Mother arrived in Tilbury not long after Howard's departure. Her long sought dream to retire to her beloved England, had at last transpired. It had been six long years since Thea had seen her, and even longer for Lydia. The two of them had been inseparable, and more like devoted sisters, than Thea and Lydia could ever hope to be. It never truly bothered Thea that she was their obtrusive child. Thea had always imagined them to be a close family, but in fact, Thea was a comparative loner.

The time had arrived to divulge the conflict in her marriage. Lydia had always come to her little sister's rescue, so as Thea was nervous of her mother's reaction, she asked Lydia to reveal the worst to their mother. However it took care of itself.

"How long will it be before you join Howard?" Mother asked.

"I'm not," was her younger daughter's reply.

"What do you mean by that? Laura should be your main concern. You're not free to think about yourself as usual. You have a commitment to your daughter. What is this great happiness you crave? You call having affairs with men happiness. My child you have a lot to learn."

"Mummy I can't continue my marriage the way I am. I believe I

181

should live on my own awhile. I am terribly confused. Marriage is demanding, and I am not prepared to sacrifice my life, as you did for us.''

"You can't possibly survive here alone! You have never accepted this country for any length of time. You're accustomed to the life in the Middle East. This is too humdrum an existence for you. I would think twice if I were you.''

Thea loved and respected her mother and sister dearly, but there had always been a lack of communication with them. She was getting a little old for them to constantly reprimand her.

Thea and Laura continued their suburban life-style together, and relied on Howard's financial support. Neither of them were in the least bit stable with the situation. Laura longed for her father constantly, and Thea wished to work and be independant of her estranged spouse. Mother devoted her evenings to her grandchild, but she had little patience for children now. Howard pursued with affectionate letters hoping Thea would come to her senses. But alas! She wouldn't. It never entered her mind to register Laura in a day school, and find a job for herself. The child's persistent longing for her father could not be countenanced by Thea much longer.

On one of Thea's many trips into the West End, she stopped at Scott's bar in Picadilly Circus. Upon entering the cellar, she requested the famous Baghdad visitor's book. She flipped the pages over, and nobody seemed familiar to her. So she signed her name and phone number, and returned it to the bartender with a thank you.

Weeks had passed and Thea and Laura were having their supper in their attic kitchen, when Thea was called to the telephone by the landlady.

"Hello Thea, guess who? I found your name in the visitor's book.''

"Steven! What are you doing here?''

"I just returned from Africa. Why didn't you reply to my letters?''

"Probably because I didn't receive any.''

"That figures. I wrote them care of your husband's office. I bet after he got through reading them, he tore them up. Where is he? Are you still together?''

"Howard is in Greece. We are separated.''

"By the way I saw your old flame, Guy, in Africa. He and Ethel got divorced.''

"Well! That was inevitable, wasn't it?''

"When can I come out and see you?''

"Oh Steven, I don't know. It's an hour by train you know.''

"Distance is of no consequence, when it comes to you. I've waited long enough already."

"Are you on vacation, or between jobs?"

"Give me your address, I'll be there tomorrow evening, and I'll bring you up to date."

After she hung up, she thought to herself, *Steven was trouble, and she didn't require anymore at this moment.* She wasn't in the least flattered by his attention, yet she was pleased to hear from him. It was someone from the past, and she needed comforting in the worst way. But then again, he drank too much, and she couldn't handle that. To sympathize with him in a crowd was one thing, but to be on a one to one basis, would be another.

Steven was over the next evening, and took her and Laura to supper. It was raining heavily when they returned. And the train to London had stopped running after midnight. Thea made some coffee, and put Laura to sleep in her cot by the kitchen window. They sat in the other room talking of old times, and their dislike for the life-style they now led. Steven was comparatively shy and unpretentious. He had been an only child, and his parents divorced when he was a lad. He had been educated in one of England's finest universities, and had always managed to secure good positions, but lost them because of his addiction to alcohol. Laura did not approve of her mother keeping company with another, and told her so. "I want my daddy. I don't like this man."

During Thea's brief association with Steven in the past, she had neglected to discover the cultured side of his personality. He was informative on several subjects, and he spoke correctly in his English manner. He chose his newspapers with discretion, the *Daily Telegraph*, and *The London Times*. He enjoyed a battle of wits with both Mother and Lydia regarding the *Times* crossword. He was truly an intellect, which was a pleasant contrast to the Steven who had always caused embarrassment among friends.

As they strolled hand in hand in beautiful St. James's park on a sunny Sunday afternoon, he began to disclose his traumatic past to Thea. His days at university, the disillusionment of his parent's divorce and how lonely he had always felt. He was awkward with the opposite sex, and one encounter in particular with an Oriental woman in Kuala Lumpur during his impressionable years discouraged any effort to pursue again. He started drinking to get his kicks. If he had followed his good intentions, he would have acquired an executive position on his first contract abroad. "Is it because you are fearful of achievement?" Thea asked.

"No! I just don't have what it takes."

"I think it is fear, and you shouldn't refuse professional help."

"I enjoy drinking, and if society cannot accept me the way I am, then to hell with them," he insisted.

A couple of weeks had passed and Thea hadn't heard from Steven. Although she was slightly disappointed, she was also relieved. They were both at a disadvantage, and couldn't be honest with the situation so as to have a friendship.

One late evening there was a knock on the front door, which the landlady answered. She disapprovingly let him in, as she watched him climb the stairs toward Thea.

"Steven! What are you doing here at this late hour?"

"Thea forgive me, but I must talk to you right now."

"I wished you had called, my landlady has already warned me over your visits, and said if you planned on spending the night here, she would give me notice to leave."

"Oh to hell with the old bag, tell her you will next chance you get. I have been giving us thought this period of silence on my part. Why don't you let me be correspondent in your divorce? Howard hates the thought of me, so if he should know we are keeping company, he'll let you have the divorce."

"Oh no, Steven, I could never do that to him. I've already hurt him beyond words, I'll do it my way eventually."

"Thea, divorce is never nice. I've loved you from one continent, to another, just give me a chance. You probably think I'm a bad risk, and I can't blame you. But please consider it."

"Steven, please don't embarrass me, I have Laura to consider, and she doesn't like you one little bit. I just can't."

He drew her to him, and wouldn't let go of his grasp on her. She weakened, having pity for him, and yet she was curiously aroused. Never in her wildest dreams did she imagine that she would permit this man to make mad passionate love to her. He was completely sober and most aggressive. Her appetite for experience was once again voracious as she savored each valuable moment of a new love affair.

Six months later Howard was well-established in his business and residence, and hoped by now his wife would have tired of living in

Britain. His regular letters of endearment made her even more rebellious. Thea's mother was terribly opposed to a divorce in the family. She had always admired Howard, and she felt her daughter was his responsibility.

Thea and Laura had by this time moved in with Steven at his Kensington Apartment in London. There was constant friction between her daughter and her lover. Neither of them could tolerate the other. So Thea requested Howard fly out and fetch their daughter as she needed to attend school and get proper care, which she obviously didn't give the child. Howard replied hastily saying he was aware of Steven in her life and was horrified at the thought. He could have accepted another, but Steven was bad news. Not only was he shocked over her choice, but also terribly saddened. He would never expose his daughter to the likes of him, and would certainly come and get her. He felt the divorce should wait, as he was sure she would come to her senses, when she had had enough of Steven.

Thea met Howard at her mother's home in Hampstead, where she handed Laura over to his care.

"I'm sorry you have reached this conclusion. Of course your allowance will now be terminated, but if you should change you mind please get in touch with me. I wish you the best of luck. You'll need it! The plane leaves at seven this evening. We will wait for you at the airport. You may still change you mind."

Thea wept. "Bye bye darling, you look after Daddy and be good to each other." She turned around at the front door and caught a bus going downtown. As she sat on the top deck of the bus, she felt mortified at the expressions of her mother and Howard upon her departure. Mother had never looked so miserable, as Howard awkwardly picked Laura up in his arms. Thea could never erase those expressions from her mind. Never! Nine years went down the drain, all because she didn't know what she wanted out of life.

As irony would have it, Steven had to be at London airport at 6:00 P.M. to meet his mother who was expected from Singapore. The lady had a job in the Peace Corps, and was visiting her son in London. When Thea reached the apartment, she found a note scribbled by Steven. "Meet us at the BOAC terminal at the airport. Mother and I will wait." Thea got a taxi to Heathrow. She had butterflies in her stomach all the way there. She wasn't prepared to meet his mother on this sad day.

For all the traveling that Thea had done over the years, she was ill at ease in airports. The incessant crowds and traffic paralyzed her, she could never understand how friends were delighted to meet there. Upon arrival she stepped on the escalator to the second level. She hurriedly passed the restaurant, and then retraced her steps. Howard and Laura were eating at a snack counter. Thea hid from sight, so as not to be seen by them. They both looked sad, as Laura anxiously held a glass of milk in her hand, and her father wiped her chin with a serviette. Howard then looked at his wristwatch, and was about to look in Thea's direction. Had he seen her? No! She tearfully watched them, and wanted to reach out to her baby. What could she do? She shook with despondency. A fraction of a minute could determine their three lives, and it was her decision. "God! I must be crazy. Do I know what I am doing?" They now left the counter and headed in her direction. Thea stepped backwards, so they'd miss her. Her eyes followed them until they were out of sight. She kept walking in search of the BOAC arrivals. She was out of breath, and her mind wandered. She wasn't in any condition to meet Steven's mother. She stepped into a bar and requested a double scotch on the rocks. The noise in the confined room made her nauseated, her eyes focused on the clock above the cash register. It was 7:00 P.M.

The noise of the powerful jets in the distance couldn't go unnoticed. "My baby is now airborne to the sunny Mediterranean, I'm happy for her. She's a lot better off than I am here." She consoled herself assuring Howard to be the substantial parent, which she never was.

Thea's thoughts were disturbed by Steven and his mother joining her at the bar.

"Where have you been?" he asked her.

She shook her head despondently.

"I saw Howard and Laura here. I'm sorry I can't talk."

"We understand," he said. "I told Mother all about us."

His mother looked at Thea very disapprovingly with no comment to say the least. She was tall and slim with grey hair and blue eyes. Her son favored her in looks. She was in London for a week, during which time she lived with her sister, but monopolized her son's attention most of the time. Thea didn't feel hospitable toward her, as she had her own problems. During the week's visit of Steven's mother, Thea went into hibernation. She would sit in the dark and gaze at the cot Laura had slept on. Her tiny teddy bear lay on the pillow. Thea picked it up and said, "Laura you forgot teddy, you'll miss him."

The weeks that followed became a rude awakening for Thea. The absence of her daughter had left her in a deplorable condition. She had realized how she had dispersed of her little girl to suit her addiction for Steven. Her conscience bothered her from morn to night. Steven had never married or had the responsibility of parenthood, so his patience with Thea was limited.

She was working in a beauty salon in High Street, Kensington for some weeks now. During the time she was at work, she was forced to forget her personal problems and cater to the elegant clientele of Mayfair. At the end of her day she was too exhausted to prepare dinner, or to cater to her lover's demands. He suffered with excessive hangovers and was in bed early. Thea until now had never exercised her temper. She abhorred degeneracy, and he was a supreme example of it. She was used to Howard, who never evaded his work, not even if he was ill. Alcoholics were truly afflicted in their cloistered, demonic world.

It was summer of 1959 when Thea and Steven set out on their first vacation to the glorious Lake District in the North of England. Steven had secured yet another sales position, this one for a world-renowned printing company that provided him with a car.

They started their drive in a British Austin from London on Britain's new motorway the M1. After they had passed through the industrial areas of Birmingham and Coventry, they entered the picturesque green moors with their breathtaking mountains, which mirrored themselves in the surrounding lakes. The clouds were like spun cottonballs against a blue sky, and the rhododendrons tumbled down the mountainside. This tranquil spot was home for many of Britain's famous poets of the past. Steven had rented a thatched roof cottage for two weeks surrounded by acres of daffodils. They drove to Lake Cumberland and walked for miles around. They watched the sheepdogs rustle the herds, and for the first time since they had been together, Thea enjoyed the serenity of this beautiful country.

She fought fits of depression in silence. She missed Laura's little face, and myriad questions, and her affection which she showed Thea in abundance. At times Thea would awaken from one of her nightmares in a cold sweat, and Steven would hold her consolingly as if she were a little girl. Her divorce had begun, but the procedure was slow because of the parties residing in different countries. Howard wasn't in any hurry to be free of his wife.

Steven and Thea lived together for nearly two years. They both deplored the monotony of crowded London. He missed Africa, and she was restless. On occasion he'd ask her where her choice would be if she had one, for her ideal life-style? Without hesitation she'd reply the Fiji islands.

"Why Fiji?" he asked.

"Because it hasn't as yet been exploited like most. The weather is ideal, and much of the population are Indians. India is my past, and if I could recapture my visionary Utopia, I know it would be Fiji."

"Then I will start to search for a position in its capital, Suava. Let's read up about the country, in the public library."

"No! Steven I have no intention of ever marrying you. Fiji is my dream, and I will go there someday on my own. Besides you would be a bad risk as a mate!"

One day Steven returned home from work with a smile of achievement on his face. He had met his two cousins, Trevor and Hugh. They, unlike Steven, were enterprising. They both owned their own travel agency. Thea and Steven had been invited by his cousins to dine at the Angus House restaurant in Knightsbridge.

"My! My! Things seem to be looking up for a change," she exclaimed.

The three gentlemen hadn't seen each other since their attendance at university together. They were both as handsome as their personalities, which, of course, contributed to their business. Neither Thea nor Steven could have afforded the likes of the Angus House, so Trevor and Hugh did them the honors.

Thea felt enraptured as she stepped into the luxurious restaurant. The brothers were seated at a round table for six, with their ladies, Jill and Heather, as Thea and Steven joined them. Steven glowed with pride as he introduced Thea to his cousins. The drinks had been ordered, and the maitre d' handed them vast menus. Trevor was obviously the elder and more authoritative of the two, as he requested the wine list, and ordered the best steak the house had to offer. Thea smiled as she haughtily remarked to Trevor, "Your savoir vivre is most refreshing, and it comes at a good time. I've missed my life of luxury."

"Oh Thea! I'm delighted you both are here with us."

Later while they all sipped on their drinks in a Chelsea flat, Trevor whispered in Thea's ear.

"Are you serious? Or is this just a joke," she asked, amused.

"I'm very serious young lady, and I want your reply, before I proceed to ask my cousin Steven."

Steven was already in his cups.

"Hey Trev, stop flirting with my woman, I've been watching you all evening."

"On the contrary old chap, I just wanted her okay before I went any further. I asked her if you two would care to have a two-week holiday with us in Yugoslavia? All expenses on us. We leave Monday morning, all you need is your bag packed, and your passports. We fly to Zagreb with our party, yes or no that's all."

Steven said, "I'm ready, but she's too conscientious about her job."

"The invitation is to you both, I accept a yes."

"The job will still be there when I return," said Thea.

"That's right," said Steven. "We don't get invited on a free trip to Yugoslavia everyday. Sure the answer is yes, cousin."

They flew out by chartered plane to Zagreb, and from there got on a bus to the Opatija Riviera. They journeyed around the rural mountains toward the beautiful Adriatic coastline, which gently caressed the miles of white sandy beaches, as they approached their destination. The narrow coastal road lined with old houses and gardens, blossomed with masses of roses. The bus halted halfway through the town center. Trevor and Hugh, with new ladies fair, Amanda and Hazel and Thea and Steven all got off the bus.

The Slavijia Hotel is a classical old structure built a century ago, with ornate ceilings and chandeliered lobby, plush velvet couches and chairs. On a thick red carpet, they walked toward the guest register. All their passports were politely confiscated until their departure. They were ushered to an old-fashioned lift, that took them gently to the third floor. Thea and Steven were shown to their handsome suite, and private terrace, overlooking the ocean and palm-lined avenue below.

Opatija came alive at night, as tourists and the town residents were in perpetual motion. Thea discovered that the resort had an Eastern environment, and most of the people were of Moslem faith, as they attended the mosques on Friday evening. The food was of Islamic cuisine, and their national khebab was *chiap-chi-chi*, a spicy hamburger cooked on charcoal.

"Steven let's stop here at the Blue Cellar and order some of that huge lobster, I've never seen them that size. That wonderful band on the terrace is playing such romantic music. Come let's dance."

"Here you go again. I haven't had enough to drink to dance yet, let's just sit awhile."

The Slovenes were a jolly people. They drank and made merry on the least pretext. The six of them sat on a beach past 2 A.M. drinking the local brew made of potent plum wine, called "slivovitz." It numbed the senses instantly, and in a short while they were inebriated enough to skinny-dip. Thea and Steven discovered a sheltered cove far from where they had started their evening. There wasn't a soul in sight, except for some fisherman in the distance. The effects of the wine and holiday spirit aroused their early morning desire to make love, after which they took an invigorating swim together.

There appeared to be an extreme amount of confusion among the fishermen, which distracted Thea, so she got dressed in her wet briefs, and walked down the beach in their direction. They had ensnared a huge whale. Earlier on before the dawn, Thea and Steven had been watching the mammal frolic not too far from where they had sat on the beach. Now all the commotion was nearing finality, as the enormous creature was trapped by human hands. The battle raged on as the fishermen attacked the defenseless whale with long spears. The sun shone over the shiny black body, as inquisitive onlookers stopped to watch the poor creature succumb to its death. Thea saddened at this persecution of it being dragged on the beach, as it continued to strive for its life. Finally it lay prostrate on the sand as the onrush of people rallied round to inspect this alien from the deep. The harpooner sat himself on the mass of blubber. The poor mammal's eyes were fixated upward in defeat, and now it was free from its suffering. The fishermen and local inhabitants immediately began to dissect it. Thea couldn't endure this cruelty, and she walked away. Steven watched with the others and gave her the full reports later when she indulged in her lobster dinner. As he watched her relish each mouthful of the succulent food he said. "That lobster you're enjoying was immersed in hot water before it was put on your plate. There is little difference between the killing of that whale or your lobster."

"Oh, Steven, you're positively disgusting. I just lost my appetite." she said.

They had reached the end of a delightful two weeks, and spent all of their time on the beach. They sunbathed on the rocks, as the Adriatic circled its warm waters around their bodies, and at high tide they rode the crest of the whitecapped waves. Their last evening they were entertained by a group of Slavic performers that danced and sang on the hotel terrace. They were all in a jovial mood and drank enough slivovitz to assist their flight back to harsh realities.

Chapter Twenty-nine

In Steven's many wanderings, he had by chance stumbled on an all-night private club-bar that was accessible to him after pub hours. The Blue Dolphin was hidden in a basement apartment building in Knightsbridge. This became his home away from home. This was the first mistake he made. The second was to insult Thea's intelligence. he would presumably dress for work, instead of which his footsteps automatically directed him to the club. One Monday on Thea's day off, unknown to him, she followed him, because she had to prove her suspicions were correct. He had been there all morning.

As she entered the bar, he was sitting on a stool with his arms around a whorish woman, who no doubt inflated his ego so he paid for her drinks. The astonished guilt upon his face at the sight of Thea was ludicruous. Thea picked up his beer stein and threw it in his face. She focused her eyes on the woman, and said, "He's all yours. Good luck, you'll need it." She stalked out of the joint, and went back to the apartment to pack her bags. She had had enough of him!

To her mother's utter disappointment, her daughter had returned back to her doorstep. To live with Mother and Lydia, was the lesser of two evils at this time, but by no means convenient for Thea. She now worked doubly hard for seven days a week between two beauty salons, so as to keep out of the house.

Although Thea was now divorced from Howard, he had invited her on a holiday to the island of Cyprus, and she accepted. She longed to see her daughter after such a long time, but it hadn't crossed her mind how Laura, now eight, would react to her estranged mother.

Steven had tried desperately to lure Thea back, by saying he had gotten a job in Suava, Fiji. She flatly refused, informing him she was leaving the country to get away from him. Cyprus was the answer to disappear from Steven's sight, it was far enough so he couldn't reach her ever again. He was a closed chapter.

Cyprus, which is situated in the eastern Mediterranean, stands as a crossroads between East and West. It was declared an independent Republic in 1960, after a hard struggle for liberation from some eighty-two years of British rule.

At the time of Thea's visit, the National Organization of Cypriot Fighters had not as yet achieved its political objective. She arrived at the heavily guarded Nicosia airport. As she alighted from the plane in the night to the warm tropical breeze of the island, she had mixed emotions about her trip. After she had passed through customs, she saw Howard waiting for her. He smiled as he embraced her fondly. She found him to be a great deal more mature, as his expression could not conceal his secret from her. She knew him too well. He had obviously encountered a serious love affair with another woman probably older and a lot more mature than Thea was.

As they drove along the quiet streets in silence. Howard explained that the city was under curfew. She remarked that he had always seemed to be situated in troubled countries, and was it worth it? He stopped his car outside an exceptionally pretty home.

"Here we are, I think you will enjoy your stay here after roughing it in London. Laura is asleep, but you can peep in and see her."

Thea walked in through the front door, and Howard took her luggage into the bedroom. She observed the familiar pictures and trinkets of their past together, none of which she had requested of him. She now glanced at an unfamiliar portrait, which resembled Thea in looks.

"Who is this?" she asked him. He nervously chuckled. "I left that out on purpose for your comment. I have nothing to hide, she's my girlfriend."

"Is that a fact? Where is she now?"

"She's living in the mountains while you visit."

"How convenient and condescending of her."

"You didn't expect me to live a life of celibacy, did you? We are divorced, and I needed her to take care of Laura, she is a good woman."

"I'm sure I'm pleased for you both."

"As things stand with us, I have given her two alternatives. If you return back to London, she has the option to return to us. But if you and I remarry, she and I part forever. So the ball is in your court, Thea. Actually your mother and I planned this trip together. She hoped you would reconsider your mistake, and we could begin again. We have a child's life at stake. Laura is the one to suffer."

"I'd think you are both doing a lot better than I am. But then I am the culprit. Please Howard, don't hold me so tight. I came here to see our daughter, that was all."

The little night-light was on her bedside as Thea admired her sleeping child.

"Gosh she's a big girl, and she's so pretty, too. I'm fortunate that she has you, Howard. I know you'll give her the best that life has, even a stepmother. I wish you both happiness."

"Thea, you are her mother, nobody can replace a real mother. We have tried to live our lives under strained circumstances. The first months of readjustment were so painful. Laura stayed with the lady next door, through fear of being alone. She thought Helaine, our neighbor, resembled you. It was heartbreaking."

"Well she has gotten used to this woman of yours, who will probably be a better mother than I could hope to be. I have no patience with children, you know that."

"Damn it woman! Why the hell did you come here? She will awaken to see you, and once more you are about to leave her again. She has feelings, and she is a very sensitive child. When I think of how your mother spoilt you. Don't you even care?"

"That's probably why I am the way I am, Howard."

The smell of eggs and bacon carried through the air, awakening Thea, who for a moment didn't know where she was. She heard voices coming from the kitchen. She put on her robe and walked toward them. Laura was comfortably chatting with her father, until she saw her mother in their presence. She stopped talking.

"Good morning Laura, do you have a kiss for your mummy?" She obediently came toward her mother and placed a little kiss on her cheek. Thea felt the restraint.

"Isn't this a beautiful place you live in? The weather is perfect, and that blue sky is like a picture postcard."

Howard was rather cheerful, as he replied. "It could be yours as well you know. You'll excuse the rush, I have to get Laura to school. Laura will you get your clothes in order please. The ones I've washed and ironed for you to take for the week."

"I have them ready, Daddy. They are at the front door in my case." She looked at Thea with her large hazel eyes.

"Have you come to stay, or just for a holiday? Daddy said if you stayed I wouldn't have to be a boarder anymore. I hate being a boarder."

"I've come for a holiday. I won't be staying, Laura." The child left the table pouting, as she headed for her father's car.

"You didn't have to greet her that way. It could have waited."

"She asked me a point-blank question, I see no point in beating about the bush."

Howard cleaned up the breakfast table, and said they had to leave.

Thea sipped on her tea, admiring the view from the kitchen window. The unique little houses built along the mountainside all around, were truly Mediterranean. She wondered about the life-style here, as she walked back into the living room and browsed around. Everything was in immaculate order and good taste. She had missed a pretty home, and Howard had always provided her with one. She shudderingly thought back to the various abodes she had endured in London, and was rationalizing because of pride. She was even more obstinate than when she came here, as she studied the woman in the portrait.

"You're no fool! You have it made with a good man, when I leave. My loss is your gain. Then again if I was smart, which apparently I'm not, I'd stay and hold on to what rightly belongs to me." Thea could not let bygones be bygones, because of her dreadful programming. She was on a guilt trip, and wild horses would not change her mind. More's the pity!

Thea now stood on the front patio, and watched the houses alongside. She was distracted by a voice on the left of her.

"Good morning you must be Laura's mother, Mrs. Wrenn. Would you care to have coffee with me?" Helaine was an attractive brunette, married with two sons, one of whom was Laura's age, and good friend.

She prepared fresh Turkish coffee and Greek shortbread, which she placed before Thea in the kitchen.

"I've heard a lot of good things about you Helaine, and I thank you for being a friend to my family. I suppose you disapprove of me as a mother, being as you are such a devoted one. Everybody is different."

"I am pleased you are visiting our country, and I wish you would stay. Have you finished your coffee? I can read your cup if you like that."

"Sure why not? I love that sort of stuff." Helaine's large brown eyes enlarged at the thick mass of coffee grounds in the saucer. She had waited about half an hour before she continued.

"I see a mass of confusion. You are in a storm; you take shelter under a big tree. This tree's branches reach out to you in protection.

194

However the tree gets struck by lightning. You are not hurt by the tree, but you suffer in silence. You are forever seeking despair in your life. You never give yourself a chance to catch your breath. You are constantly running. I see an ill-fated marriage, and you will suffer a great deal. You mother worries about you, and is constantly protecting you. She cries out to you, but you don't listen."

"You mean to tell me this mess in front of me predicts all this? I'm sorry Helaine. I don't intend to marry so your reading isn't true."

She smiled! "I'd like for you to keep in touch and let me know, okay? Mrs. Wrenn it is none of my business, but I am older and wiser than you, I have been married many years. Please think this matter over seriously, for your own sake. Do not be threatened by another. Your husband loves you very much. He has confided in me many times. I beg of you one woman to another, do not leave them again. Also I have done this reading in confidence. I trust it will not go any further than us."

"Helaine I am touched by your concern, but Howard and Laura are far better off with this other woman. I am not able to fulfill a commitment. Marriage isn't for me. I need freedom."

"You feel hurt, and it's only your ego that stands in the way. When Howard and Laura first moved here, they were terribly lonely. It broke my heart to watch them help each other along. Laura was with me everyday, she would hug me and say, 'You remind me of my mummy.' Howard told me you were a dreamer, and always in search of the impossible. He said you lacked stability and would never grow up. I think he's wrong."

"Helaine, you know it all, so there is little to discuss anymore. I hope we will be friends while I'm here, and sometime maybe we can visit the Turkish sector during the day. I'm told it's not safe, but if I go with you, I'll be taken for a local inhabitant. I promise to keep my mouth shut, once we get there."

Howard had a varied mixture of friends, mostly Americans. Christmas had arrived on the island, and Laura was home for the holidays. Mother and daughter attended midnight mass at the sixteenth century Holy Cross Catholic Church. It was situated in the interior of the ancient part of Nicosia. The congregation had an aura that Thea presumed resembled Biblical times.

"Peace on Earth and goodwill toward all men." In the distance the sounds of guns had quieted for the holiday period.

Each day Howard drove his family to various picturesque spots in and around the island. The car hugged the fantastic curves and slopes of the precipitous Kyrenia Mountains, which were capped with delightful wooded areas, and medieval castles, alternating with valleys red with oleander. All around the hills for some forty miles ahead they were surrounded by the glistening amaranthine sea.

Thea's tricky mind periodically drifted to unpleasant thoughts of Steven in London. This life-style would be so easily accepted and gotten accustomed to, compared to the drudgery of Britain.

One evening Howard and Thea sat on the balcony with a highball that got them both in a nostalgic mood. He played some of the old songs they had danced to in Calcutta. "My Foolish Heart" played and they began to dance. This is where it had all begun, and the memory lingered on. The last record was "Be My Love." Howard broke the romantic spell, by saying. "This is the tune associated with my present lady."

Thea backed away.

"You truly are very tactful dear," Thea whispered in his ear, "Goodnight sweetheart, tomorrow is another day, and I wish you love."

Thea's last days on the island were most painful to her. She was tormented by her failure as a parent and a wife. She was stubborn and insecure. Where there was no trust, how could there be love?

Howard drove a devastated ex-wife through the beautiful countryside for the last time. Thea never said good-bye to Laura as she retired that final night.

They now drove twenty-five miles in silence. Howard looked straight ahead as they drove past miles of olive groves. They arrived in Larnica by the delightful seafront, palm-lined avenue that resembled a miniature Cote d'Azur. The Italian liner Santa Maria was berthed by the dockside. Howard accompanied Thea for the last time as he attended to her needs and made sure she was comfortably situated on the ship.

"Good-bye, little one. I hope you find what your looking for. I wish you would stay, but I know you better than that."

He kissed her as tears fell down his sensitive face. He turned down toward the gangplank, and waved one more time as he got into his car for the long, lonely drive home. He felt very responsible for the little girl he'd once married, and had truly cared for. . . . Or so her mother told her at a later date!

Part 3

Thea and Jason

Chapter Thirty

Thea had lived in bondage for the most part of her life. She had never thought of the day when she would actually be by herself. She never dreamed of living alone and taking responsibility for her own welfare. In those days there was no such thing as Women's Lib. In fact it was frowned upon. Her philosophy had been one of marriage and living happily ever after. Because of her inhibitive conditioning, she hadn't as yet realized the serious step she had taken. At the back of her addled mind she was returning home to her mummy! So long as her mother was there to perpetuate her daughter's inability, it was of little consequence to Thea.

Thea stood by the rails of the ship and watched it being cut adrift from land. In all her wanderings and travels, she had always been chaperoned. Well so much for that! At this moment she was unaware that she was closely observed, and had been from the time she got on board. A gentle voice from behind approached her.

"Would you mind very much if I kept you company in your trend of thought."

She was stunned at this approach, and taken back at the handsome face.

"My name is Adam Spencer, we dined earlier on at the same table."

"Yes, I remember you sat across from me. I'm Thea Wrenn, I'm pleased to meet you, and you may join me."

"I watched you get on at Larnica. I also noticed that the gentleman who escorted you, seemed disturbed. He nearly lost his grip on the way down the gangplank."

"That was my ex-husband. I had spent some time with him in Cyprus, and I hated to leave the beautiful island."

"Are you traveling to the end of the line?"

"Yes. That's Venice, then I get on the train to Paris, and on to London, which is my home."

"What do you do when you're home?"

199

"I'm a beautician by trade, and I'll probably live with my mother, and find a job. Sounds dull, huh? What about you, Adam?"

"I go as far as Venice, too. Then I plan to drive through Europe, until I reach England, and pass through London. I have taken a year's sabbatical to travel the world. I'm an anthropologist, and I teach in New York City."

"How different that sounds, and exciting I bet!"

"Before I attended college, I had this infinite curiosity about human frailty, and social behavior. So I am taking this world tour to broaden my study of exotic people."

"I take it you're not married?"

"No! I haven't as yet found the time for that. I'd like an honest to God relationship with somebody that understands my work, and isn't threatened by it, or consumed by me. I enjoy freedom, not ownership. I believe everyone should have his space."

"You're right. I think that's been my problem. I've never researched my priorities. I'm terribly impulsive, and that gets me in trouble."

As they strolled arm and arm around the deck, she secretly observed his sensitive chiseled face. His eyes were even darker than hers, almost coal black. He had a sculptured soft beard and mustache. Until now Thea had never been attracted to men with whiskers, however they enhanced his professorial image. He was five feet ten with a good physique. She was fascinated by his rhythmic voice as he spoke.

"Growth is a natural factor, and hurt is a part of development, and until you decide to allow yourself this philosophy, you'll be in a constant turmoil."

He stopped momentarily and kissed her on her nose. "Do you know," he continued, "the normal eye contact between strangers lasts less than seconds, unless two people concerned are attracted to each other, then it lasts a second or two longer. This expresses sentiment. For instance your smile says more than your words, your lips parted as they are right this minute, say you're approachable. It was your laughter and humor that put me at ease with you right away."

She kissed him on the cheek.

"So in other words I'm an open book to you. Am I suggestively implying we explore each other in bed?"

He chuckled. "Your impetuosity is delightful, and I'd be a fool not to accept. It's kind of chilly out here. Shall we turn in for the night?"

Her heartbeat raced as they walked toward the lower deck to the cabin.

"Adam! My cabin is in the opposite direction. So I'll bid you a very good night, and see you at breakfast."

"Are you leaving me now?"

"Yes it's been a long day for me; I'm not too receptive. We'll begin anew in the morning, okay?"

Her restless mind prevented a good night's sleep. She didn't encourage Adam, because she was weary, and thought it appropriate that she save him for the next day when she would perhaps be more affable.

In the morning she was late for breakfast, and noticed immediately that Adam had changed places with another of the passengers at the breakfast table, so as to sit near her.

"Good morning" he said first. She smiled.

"Did you not sleep well?" he asked.

"It took me awhile. I had a lot on my mind."

"Perhaps if we had spent awhile longer together, I could have had a tranquil effect on you."

"On the contrary, you would probably still be analyzing me."

"I'm sorry, I promise I won't do any of that again."

Now in the glorious Mediterranean, Thea and Adam, spent their time playing shuffleboard, and quoits. She hadn't been as confident as in her school courts. Now after she had thrown her second quoit overboard, she nervously laughed, "I give up!"

Their first and only port of call was Piraeus, Greece. They disembarked with excitement as they accompanied the rest of the passengers on a train ride to visit the Acropolis. They spent all of the day among the ruins as Adam took innumerable pictures in and around the Parthenon. He had promised her the pictures when he visited London. They lunched at an open air cafe, and continued to tour as long as time allowed. They rested awhile by the open-air arena, where the motion picture, *Never on Sunday* was being filmed. The song was most prevalent at this time. They joyfully returned to the ship at dusk.

During the course of the day, Thea's amorous infatuation had developed toward Adam. As they dined quietly, now at a table for two, she knew they would be spending the night together. After all, there wasn't enough time to stand on unnecessary ceremony. She had been drawn to his magnetism from day one, and they hadn't been apart since their meeting. As she listened to the melody of "Love Is a Many Splendored

Thing," her romantic illusion intensely moved him toward her cabin door. Out of breath they bounced onto the lower bunk in a fixed embrace. They disrobed each other so as not to waste precious time.

His tremulous lips moved across her face toward her sensuous limbs. She harnessed his head with her legs, as his soft beard titillated her pubic hairs in the act of cunnilingus. He savored the delectable urgency, as he spent himself with excitement. His perpetual motion modified until she reached an orgasm. In Thea's past one-nighters, men would get over-anxious to force their eagerness during copulation, and invariably inhibited her desire. Perhaps his study of the human race contributed distinctiveness. She had never thought of herself as promiscuous. She had this violent desire to experience variety, for which they retaliated. In her mind she had formed the idea that sex was imperative in a relationship. In marriage one became submissive, until there seemed little or no excitement. In her affairs she encountered and mastered the art of making love expressively. No two affairs were alike, so there was constant variety.

They climbed to the top bunk and gazed out of the porthole at the new break of day. Mesmerized by the silence and the dawn's light on the horizon, their short-lived fantasy was that of two ships that passed in the night. As Thea lay in Adam's arms, her recollection came to mind of Howard's and her inadequacy, of their honeymoon on the ship, and how it should have been. Her fear of getting pregnant interfered with the spontaneity of copulation.

Thea and Adam walked hand and hand around the deck, as he talked and she listened. "In the six days that we have been together, I have been studying your aspects of human experience. The way I see it your curiosity toward sexual behavior in your past and present, could very well create a problem in your future. I feel I am right to tell you, you are overoptimisitic in your choice of mates, and your ability to control them. You are not recognizing the expectations you wish them to fulfill. You have this need to fit them into a mold of your making. If they don't, you lose interest very quickly. You inhibit their sexual response toward you, and this causes a character change in you. Also you retreat when least expected."

"I didn't feel you were inhibited when you made love to me. If anything you were very much in control. In fact we both contributed equally as much in the act."

"Thea my dear, dear romanticist, sex is one thing, love another, you have got the two terribly confused. You let sex dominate your life. Until you learn to accept a better self-image, you will persistently draw to you that which you deplore most—an apprehensive relationship. The men in your life haven't cared enough to discuss this matter with you."

"So when can I expect this transformation to take place?"

He smiled. "When you stop running from yourself and blaming others."

Their last night together, they had stayed awake all night, as the ship neared its destination. Here in the romantic city of Venice, Adam and Thea stood on the station platform in a fixed embrace. Thea recaptured a mental image of a movie she had seen in her teens, of Jennifer Jones and Robert Walker in *The Big Clock*. Now she herself was saying farewell to Adam under a big clock, and the train indicated departure. It started to move along the platform, and she jumped on it. He waved saying "I'll see you in London, take care."

She wept silently as she turned away from the compartment window. Once again she was alone, and instantly she missed Adam's reassuring hand in hers. Loneliness could be such a sad affair. The train rushed into the night, and she was surrounded by unfamiliar faces. Most of them were Greek students drinking Ouzo and eating homebaked bread and feta cheese. They merrily sang the lyrics of "Never on Sunday." Thea wearily sought comfort in their hilarity. In the morning she had arrived in Paris, where she changed trains. The final lap of the journey was the crossing of the English Channel on the ferry on which most folks got frightfully seasick. Thea braved it with a cup of hot English tea in her hands, to warm the chill within her. She finally arrived at Victoria station past midnight. Her dear faithful mother hadn't failed her daughter. Thea saw her from afar, and she rushed toward her arms weeping despondently at the sight of the only one who ever really cared about her.

Chapter Thirty-one

Thea had lived in London a month, and secured a job at a Baker Street beauty salon. She was already bored with her nine to five routine, and the rigid house rules. She had been accustomed to a lot of freedom, and to suddenly acclimate to the discipline was more than she could tolerate.

One evening as she sat in her mother's living room, she browsed at her little black book of addresses and phone numbers. Her next move couldn't get much worse than spending evenings in the front room attached to the "boob tube" or could it? If she had had a crystal ball and gazed into her future, and seen the prediction it had in store for her, she probably would have smashed it to bits.

Before she had left Nicosia, Cyprus, an American friend of Howard's had given her the name and phone number of a naval associate of his in the Philippines. She was told to look him up, but not to get involved. She pondered at this for a while, before she followed through. *Why not?* she thought, *I have nothing to lose.* So she dialed the navy office in Governor Square, and asked to speak to a Jason Travis. The voice on the other end said he was off duty, but if she wished to leave a message, it would be related to him. A week passed, before Jason returned the call.

"Hello this is Jason Travis speaking. May I speak with Thea Wrenn?"

"This is she."

"Hi hon, I have this message to call you. We don't know each other do we?"

"Not yet we don't. I was given your name by a buddy of yours from the past, Bert Nielson."

"Sure! I remember Nielson, we served together in the Philippines. Are you navy?"

"No, I'm civilian and British. I met Bert in Nicosia. He is presently stationed there with his family."

"What do you know? Well hon, it's like this. I work three watches, hear? The day, eve, and midwatch. I have just completed my days off, so I won't have time until next week to meet you. Maybe we can have dinner together. Does that sound fine by you?"

"I guess. You get back to me, you have my number, and we'll take it from there," she said.

Three weeks later, Thea sat at a spaghetti joint opposite the navy building, a few doors from the beauty shop she worked in, waiting for Travis. She had no idea as to his appearance so she sat at a table by the entrance, where she could be noticed as he came in. A cheerful, blue-eyed, smiling face blew in like a whirlwind. He had on a rumpled raincoat like that of the TV character, Columbo, minus a few buttons. Under the coat he was dressed meticulously in a suit and tie.

"You must be Thea. I'm sorry I'm late. I had to wait for my buddy to relieve me. Gee you're cute."

He had a southern accent, and he resembled the actor Brian Keith in looks and stature.

"Gee what took you so long? Where have you been all my life?"

She thought this a bit presumptuous of him, but then again he probably showed his self-expression in this manner. Within a few minutes he disclosed that he was a confirmed poker player, enjoyed hard liquor, fast women, and country music. She thought him capricious, and she wondered how she could get out of an awkward situation directly after dinner. He pursued the conversation as though she were a tourist, and he would show her his London. After being in Adam's company, this was surely an awful let down.

It had stopped raining, and as they stepped onto a wet pavement. Jason took her hand affectionately, and slipped it in his pocket as they strolled down Baker Street.

"Honey, I don't have a car as yet, so we'll get a cab here to my place which is along Little Venice Canal, off the Edgware Road."

"I'm sorry I must get home before the bus stops running for the night, so you get your cab. My mother expects me home about now."

"You mean you're not coming home with me?"

"I don't know what gave you the idea that I might. I'm not a fast woman." Thea jumped on a passing number two bus and waved good night.

He was definitely not her type, and he wasn't getting a second chance to prove otherwise. When she got home, her mother was still awake, as the hall light was left on until her daughter's return. She had to be sure her baby was home before she retired for the night.

"Well, what was the American like? You didn't go to bed with him did you?"

"No Mum, I don't make a habit of that on a first date."

Persistence was the key, so far as Jason was concerned. He wasn't about to give up before he had even begun. Each time he phoned, Thea's mother would make excuses for her, until she had run out of them. Finally, Thea had to take the initiative and let him know she wasn't interested in seeing him anymore. Before he could speak, she put the phone down.

Weeks went by. One evening Thea returned home from work to find Jason sitting in the living room engrossed in conversation with her mother.

"Hi snugglebug!" he said. "How is my beautiful brown-eyed darlin' today?"

The nerve of him, thought Thea!

"What are you doing here?" she asked.

"I came to meet your family, and ask them to dinner. Maybe you'd care to join us?"

"No way, I just got back from the jungle, and won't return till the morning."

"Well honey, you wouldn't turn down some good American chow, would you now? I'm taking them to our Douglas House in Lancaster Gate."

"I think you have us figured all wrong. The war was over a long time ago, we are not in need of American food or any other handouts you may have in mind." Thea looked at her mother and sister. "You're not truly serious on taking him up on his offer are you?"

"Now Thea, there is no need for such hostility, please get dressed and come with us. It will make a pleasant change for us all."

"Yes, snugglebug, we'll take the subway right to Lancaster Gate, and be there in half an hour."

"Stop calling me that ridiculous name, I'm nothing to you." She thought to herself, *were they in for a surprise! Jason wasn't a man of decorum, but they would no doubt find out their error, and it would serve them right.*

Jason escorted them to Douglas House with great pride, as he presented his naval identification at the entrance. Mother and sister followed him in. Thea wasn't in the least impressed. The bartender acknowledged him upon sight, as did his buddies, and a few stray females who attracted his attention. He passed them all with great bravado, as Thea looked on at the foolishness. They got seated at a table, and were handed menus. Jason's idea of good food was a T-bone steak, so he ordered everyone the same, whether it was their preference or not. Mother at no time had been a meat eater, but she was too polite to refuse. Lydia smiled pathetically with no comment. Thea didn't do the meal justice. The music in the distance was the best part of the evening.

"Snugglebug, ain't you glad you came? Don't you like this place? You finish your steak like a good girl, and I'll take you for a shuffle round the dance floor." Thea thought this man insufferable. He didn't stop talking for a minute, and he was full of himself. He had danced with both Mother and Lydia, and he finally got to Thea, who thought him a pitiful dancer. He was by no means in the same league as Kurt, Hans, or Jurgen, but at least he hadn't stepped on her feet.

On their next date together, she had discovered he had little or no tolerance when he drank, so she left him at the bar and got herself home to Mother, only to discover that Adam had visited to give her the pictures taken of them in Greece. Mother had entertained him in Thea's absence, and remarked what a gentleman he was. Thea was terribly disappointed at having missed him.

Thea decided around this time to visit her old friend Carla from Aden, who was living up north. Carla had left Miles in Kampala, Uganda, along with her two daughters, which Thea had never expected her to do. She was living in North England with her family, and said she had a business with her boyfriend there. It was wonderful seeing her again, and they had a good visit together.

Thea was reluctant to see Jason, but he surprised her by meeting her at her place of work one evening. He was wild and mischievous, and wouldn't be discouraged by her. So she agreed to have dinner with him at his basement flat, which resembled a dungeon. It was dark and surrounded by little windows with bars across them. The pedestrians walked on the pavement above, periodically sneaking a glance in their direction. A vast fireplace monopolized the length of one wall, above which hung old English spears. The floors were covered with ancient carpet that was the worse for wear, the kitchen was cold, and the cabinets were well-stocked with American canned goods purchased from the navy commissary.

Thea timidly sat herself down on the corner of a huge clumsy couch.

Jason fixed her a Southern Comfort on the rocks. She took a sip and said it was a wicked sweet drink.

"Snugglebug! Tonight I'm going to capture you."

"I feel as thought you already have in this dungeon."

"Hon, I don't think you understand me. You're not going home tonight."

"I'll be the judge of that, if you don't mind. I realize the bus stops running by midnight, but I shall be on my way before that."

"Snugglebug, don't you like me even a little bit? I like you."

She turned her eyes up to the ceiling.

"Jason let's get one thing straight you are a drinking man, and a gambler, two things I abhor, so what's to like?"

"Okay but ain't I pretty?"

She laughed.

"Since when is a man pretty? You mean handsome."

"Whatever, don't I appeal to you just a little."

"No! Quite honestly you don't."

He dialed her home and said, "Mama Martin, I ain't bringing snugglebug home tonight. Don't you worry about your daughter, we are listening to Hank Williams, eating steak, and doing some serious talking. She will be home when the bus starts running in the morning."

Oh my God! thought Thea, *this guy is crazy. How do I handle this character*?

"Honey, I have to educate you. Mothers are fine, if you handle them right. See she didn't say a word, she was young once and understands where I'm coming from."

Thea had had all she could take of "Your Cheatin' Heart" and rejected the record of Fats Domino's "Blueberry Hill." Jason's choice of music was a little on the morose side. His record collection was comprised mainly of the blues. He got more repetitive in his conversation, and had tears in his eyes speaking of home and family. He had two sisters Faith and Hope, and two brothers, Curtis five, and Luke twenty-five.

"You see snugglebug, I am terrible lonely, and wish I knew another life apart from the navy. It's tough living in strange countries with no family life. You wouldn't understand."

Little did he know, but then again he didn't really care. That was how he felt and thought. He interrupted her each time she started to say something. Finally he passed out on the couch. She had consumed enough Southern Comfort to do likewise on the opposite couch. She hadn't slept soundly, as she was aware she wasn't in her bed. When she awoke, the light in the living room was still on, but Jason wasn't there. What time was it? Her wristwatch had stopped, and she felt most uncomfortable in this man's apartment. She got up and went in search of the bathroom, next to which Jason slept soundly in his bedroom. At a time like this she wished she had a car, so she could have driven home. She had to bide her time until daybreak, and the London transport available to her. Or so she thought. She had a bad taste in her mouth from the liquor, so she rinsed her mouth with Listerine. Not fully awake as she stood in front of the wash basin, Jason suddenly approached behind her in his under-wear.

"Snugglebug come to bed; you need some sleep."

"No Jason, I'll be just fine, I'll be going home shortly." He defiantly picked her up and laid her on his bed.

"Now just relax awhile here with me."

His urgency for sex had no boundaries and he forced himself upon her. He lacked finesse, and she wasn't in the least aroused by him. He hadn't any desire for her, it could have been anyone. Lust was his master. He was a sexual grizzly bear, wanting to devour his prey. She turned her face from side to side. His body was a burden upon her. She squirmed and winced in disgust. But he had to spend himself over and over, until she finally fled from his grasp on her.

"I don't enjoy being mauled. You make me sick."

"Snugglebug, please love me, please try, nobody has ever cared about me. I want you in the worst way."

How pitiful, she thought. After the warmth and sensuousness of Adam, she had let herself be subjected to this clumsy befuddlement. Neither of them had taken the necessary precautions, and she warned him she didn't want children. He laughed to scorn her.

"Honey, even you can't make a baby the first time around."

"That's all it takes mate." she replied. "The way you came would make four babies."

She was totally disgusted with herself. She dressed hurriedly as he gave way to sleep. She ran out of his front door, and briskly walked along Little Venus Canal, through the early morning fog, to the Edgware road bus stop. Never again! She said reproachfully. Sometimes she de-plored her lack of morality.

A couple of weeks had passed and she and the family had retired for the night. Thea was awakened by a rustle in the bushes outside of her bay window which was situated on the ground floor, overlooking the garden. She lay awake quietly in the dark of her room. There was a full moon out that night, and she could distinctly see a silhouette, which stumbled into her mother's hydrangea bushes. She sat bolt upright now, and could see him clearly as the streetlight shone upon his silly face pressed against the window.

"Jason! What the hell are you doing here? Disturbing the peace?"

"Snugglebug, get up, get up, and let me in."

Anything for peace and quiet, she did just that.

"Hon, I know it's late, but I just got off work, and I had to talk to you."

"Jason, this isn't any time to talk. We all have to go to work in the morning, and if I don't have my rest, I'm not fit to face the public. So you had better leave right now before my mother gets here."

"Snugglebug, why did you leave me the way you did?"

"I should think you'd be able to answer your question. I don't enjoy being mauled against my wishes."

Mother and Lydia both promptly entered the room, with disapproval. Jason immediately apologized for his intrusion, leaving them confused. Lydia spoke first, as she was exasperated by his intrusion. Thea watched him closely as he was under attack. His forlorn expression mellowed Mother and she quieted down and decided to hear him out.

"I only came here to ask snugglebug to marry me, that was all."

The three women simultaneously answered, "You're truly crazy."

"She's the only one to make an honest man out of me. Ever since I met her I've wanted to settle down and have a home."

"You've picked the wrong woman." Lydia said. "She was just divorced from a very conscientious husband, I'd hardly say you fit the bill. So run along and don't bother us anymore."

Mother left the room to make a pot of tea. It seemed the logical custom in an awkward situation.

"Snugglebug, all I ask is a chance. I know you will be good for me."

"Jason you don't seem to hear too well. I don't love you, and above all I want to be free for a while. I am not marriage material."

At that moment Mother came in the room with a tray of tea, and four cups. Thea horrified at the sight, left the room and followed Lydia to her room. She wished at this moment, that she had never called or set eyes on him.

"Mummy is sympathetic at the wrong time. I fail to understand her. As for you, you sure pick 'em," said Lydia.

"You both encouraged his invitation to dinner, so he's taken advantage of it. As for me I don't ever wish to see him again."

In the morning Lydia fixed breakfast for herself and her sister. Mother came in the room where they were seated.

"I feel sorry for the poor chap. He misses home terribly, so I chatted with him until he fell asleep. He's still here. When he awakens, Thea, show him out and don't say anything to provoke him. We just won't answer his phone calls. I honestly don't think he's for you."

On a rare occasion the sisters had a serious discussion, and Lydia confronted Thea.

"Are you pregnant?"

"Gosh no! Why do you ask me such a silly thing?"

"You have the look of an expectant mother that's why."

"Come to think of it I didn't have a period this month, and I never miss."

"I don't believe how negligent you are," said Lydia. "But if you are, it doesn't give you cause to marry. We can have it taken care of. You can't possibly go as far as America with a man like him. Mind you he's all right I dare say. He's just terribly immature and lacks polish."

"I'd rather not jump to conclusions. But if I am, I intend to go through with it. I would never abort because of my negligence. It's ironical that I terminated my marriage to Howard, and gave Laura to him, to get myself into a worse predicament. I who never wanted children. Would you call it retribution, or self-punishment?"

"Now maybe you will understand why Mummy and I worry about you. You never stop to think of the consequences. Neither you nor Jason show me your qualifications for a good marriage, much less a child. He has a totally different life-style from us, and we know nothing about his background or family. Haven't you learned anything with all your affairs—at least how to take care of yourself properly?"

Thea fretted for days on end, each morning at work she felt nauseated, but she wouldn't admit to herself that she was pregnant. For the second time in her life she was bearing an unwanted child, and to make matters worse, she wasn't married, and the man concerned didn't even appeal to her.

Weeks had gone by, and she couldn't keep it a secret any longer.

Jason was the last to know. He appeared on her doorstep without any warning, and she screamed at the sight of him.

"It's all your damn fault. Get out of my sight."

"What's the matter little doll?" he asked.

"Don't you little doll me. I'm pregnant, you bastard."

"Well honey, you should be more experienced in these matters than I am. You are the one to be divorced; it's not fair to blame me. I'm willing to make an honest woman out of you. That's my baby, too."

"Some prize you are! Well let me tell you right now, I'm a bad risk, all of my life I've been manipulated into situations. I don't want children, and I don't love you, and never will. I hate a drinking man, and will not tolerate one, so there."

"I'll still marry you, so we had better discuss our wedding day. I have to get permission to marry a foreign national. You do right by me, and I'll do the same. That's all I can say for the time being."

Mother was aghast at her daughter being called a foreign national.

"The nerve of the man!" she remarked. "What do we know about him? Probably laid around the globe, and now settles his oats on you. Thea you never did have much sense."

In Thea's fourth month of pregnancy, she married Jason Travis at the registrar's office in Hendon, Middlesex. They rented a cottage not far from her mother's home, where their wedding reception continued around the clock. For the first night they partied, and the second Jason and his buddies played poker.

The sun shone through the concealed drapes of the living room. The lights had been left on since the wedding. Thea awoke to the sound of poker chips, swearing, and ill-tempered voices in the background. There were cigarettes burning out of the full ashtrays, some spilled over on the furniture. Stale drinks sat on the tables, and the remains of food lay on the carpet and on the couch. She was sick to her stomach. Jason turned around to his bride with closed eyes.

"Snugglebug, why don't you clean up this mess, and make us a cup of strong coffee, huh?"

Thea was of a compliant nature, and didn't get easily angered. But this morning all hell broke loose!

"You make your own bloody coffee, and all of you get the hell out of here. The party's over. Don't you all have a home to go to?" Jason spun around his chair and slapped Thea across the mouth. She didn't flinch and stood her ground.

"Woman when I say make coffee, you jump and do as I say." He aimed another blow at her head. One of his mates reached over to hold him back, because Thea didn't defend herself, or retaliate to his cruelty. Her mouth was her superior weapon, and she provoked him in his anger.

"What did I expect from an idiot that's all brawn, and no brain."

She ran out of the room and locked her self in the bathroom. He furiously followed her and broke open the door. He continued beating her all over her body, with a final blow to her eye. If not for one of his buddies getting him off her, she would have probably fared for the worst. In his drunken stupor, he pushed her out of the bathroom and stood under the shower to cool down his wretched temper. She was glad to see him get dressed and leave the house. She opened all the windows to let out the stale stench of bodies and booze. She was too embarrassed to phone her mother and sister. They were not accustomed to such brutality, and would have reported him to the authorities, and of course humiliated her with "I told you so." She cared little about his being, however she carried their child. All it had been was a merger of two different people locked together in destruction. Her vulnerability seemed to provoke his violence against her. He had never known how to love anybody, because of his poor self-image.

Thea's trepidation worsened with her advancing pregnancy, as she was aware of Jason's schizophrenia. It was a forgone conclusion, that if the two of them remained on together, one would most definitely reach a violent end, and it sure as hell wasn't going to be her.

By her ninth month of pregnancy, she had quit her job, and she spent most of her time at her mother's home. She didn't have a husband to go home to. If he wasn't at work, he was out gallivanting, and often he didn't return home at night.

One evening as Thea lay her cumbersome body on the couch in her mother's living room, there was a ring at the front door. Her mother answered it.

"Howard! What a wonderful surprise! And Laura what a big girl you are."

Oh no, thought Thea, *I'm in no condition to see them*. It was too late. They entered the front room. It was embarrassment for all concerned. However Howard was a gentleman as always.

"Well this is a surprise, we didn't expect to see you here. Laura, say hello to your mother."

Laura hid behind her father, with her finger in her mouth as she observed her estranged mother. She wouldn't speak.

"Well Howard, here on leave again?" Thea asked.

"Yes only for a short time. My wife and I and Laura were visiting my wife's family in Italy. I thought I'd bring her along to visit with her grandmother."

"Yes that's nice. Mummy is happy you did, I'm sure."

"So when is your baby expected?" he asked.

"Anytime now."

"It's ironic I always wanted Laura to have a sibling. My wife can't have children."

"What's the matter Laura? Cat got your tongue, or don't you remember me anymore?"

"I think she's surprised to find you here, and she's also a bit of an introvert."

Mother got her grandchild by the hand and took her to her room. Howard was at a loss for words, so he just smiled at Thea.

"Well, Howard, where is your next tour to be?"

"Africa for the next three years. What about you? Are you happy?"

"No, Howard, I'm far from happy. I'm beginning to think I'm a masochist."

"Anything but, my dear. Whom did you marry? I presume you are."

"Yes to an American in the navy, Bert Nielson's friend."

"Lord no! What did you do that for?"

"To look at my condition should explain that."

Howard looked very saddened for Thea, as her mother returned back in their company with her granddaughter.

"Well I suppose we had better be on our way, sorry the visit was short, but my wife is awaiting us."

He glanced in Thea's direction.

"Take care little one, I hope all goes well for you and the baby," he said.

That was the last time Thea met with Howard and Laura. It was January of 1961.

Thea would lie in the quiet of her mother's living room, while both Mother and Lydia were at their respective jobs: Mother at real estate and Lydia at a law firm. Thea would reminisce over their days in India, about beloved father who had showered her with adoration, her mother always at her side, and their secure family life. Howard at least had perceived her background, the sophisticated cultures she had been accustomed to. It all seemed like a dream now, and her present condition was truly a nightmare.

She hadn't as yet visualized her future in America. Her past visit there as a little girl, would hardly be helpful to imagining life with Jason and whatever he might have to offer.

Resting her hand on her abdomen now, was reminiscent of eight years ago, when she had expected Laura. She felt sure this was a boy, and that he'd be spared of his father's psychopathic personality.

The night she had been rushed to the naval hospital in Ruislip, Middlesex, Jason was inebriated. Both Mother and Lydia accompanied Thea to the delivery room. The discomfort of childbearing was of secondary importance, in comparison to the presence of her husband. Thea begged both doctor and nurse to keep him out of her sight. Giving birth this time was even more difficult than when she had Laura. Thea's intolerance hindered her delivery, and the doctor immediately relieved her stress with a spinal shot.

After hours of struggle and misery, Marc appeared into his world from the warmth of his mother's womb. He was a beautiful bonnie baby, and Thea felt at that moment he was worthy of every minute of her discomfort. Nothing mattered to Thea except to live for her newborn son. He would restore in her the hope and strength to continue a loveless marriage.

Jason temporarily became humanly domesticated. He adored Marc, and was most attentive toward him, but not to Thea. On one occasion when she was breastfeeding her new infant son, Jason sat alongside of them, with tear-filled eyes. Thea almost felt compassionate toward him. Then he matter of factly informed her about his little native woman and their baby he had left behind in the Philippines.

"You know, snugglebug, I had a beautiful son by her, and looking at the two of you now reminded me of them. He was my first boy, must be around seven or eight now. I often wonder about their welfare. She didn't speak English, but she sure made beautiful babies—just as you do."

This wasn't Jason's first faux pas. Thea discovered he had spawned more than one bastard.

A month passed, and Thea certainly had no desire for intercourse.

She pleaded with Jason to leave her alone. Between his erratic work schedule, and her taking care of Marc, she could all but keep her sanity. Like a spoilt child he stayed inebriated, and between hangovers she yielded to his debauchery, to keep him off the streets. When it came time for her postnatal checkup, the doctor, who was familiar with Jason's cruelty toward his patient during the nine-month period of her pregnancy, was floored at her negligence. Dr. Mackinley shook his head.

"Thea, I think you are a glutton for punishment," he said.

"It's a pity he can't be castrated," she replied.

Mother was devastated at her daughter being pregnant again so quickly.

"You're not capable of parenthood, and Jason is a misfit." she said.

Marc was now nine months old, he had been christened at the Catholic church in Golders Green, and he was his grandmother's pride and joy. Her heart ached to see him leave the shores of Britain. Jason hadn't been too informative about their U.S. destination, and Thea showed little interest. She wept bitterly as she departed from her mother and sister, but she felt in due course she would return to her family.

Chapter Thirty-two

It was September of 1962, when their Pan American flight touched down at New York City's John F. Kennedy airport. After Thea had been cleared upon entry by Immigration, they continued their flight to Washington, D.C.

Jason had spoken from time to time of the beautiful Shenandoah Valley, and his growing up in Virginia. Thea had envisioned a gracious life-style in the South, something in relation to *Gone with the Wind*. After all what did she know?

They had taken a train out of Washington that appeared to be moving rapidly for some time, until it crept round the creeks to the course of the Roanoke River, and finally came to a complete halt on one of its bends.

Jason would chuckle every so often at the expression on his wife's face.

"Snugglebug, you're not anxious are you?"

"Would it make a difference if I was? I just thought we could probably walk a lot faster than this train."

Roanoke was situated in a bowl formed by the Blue Ridge and Allegheny Mountains. Thea hadn't encountered this part of America before, or even heard of its existence. There were unsightly poor homes on the hillside, beside junk heaps near historical landmarks. Virginia was a rugged state with vast coalfields, and blue grass pastures, and fertile farmlands. Mining communities huddled in the valleys, and coal dust smeared the surrounding area. From where she now sat on this slow train it looked a dismal sight. They had reached Bluefield and transferred to a bus. Jason and Marc sat by a window seat, while Thea and her unborn sat directly alongside. Thea's eyes widened with each mile at the sight of poverty and the dwellings. The sunken porches, with torn up refrigerators, old stoves, and washing machines, were all burnt out and of no use to their owners. The junk heap of assorted automobiles and trucks had been left to rust. Jason said "There's a lot of money there, don't kid yourself." Disheveled children with no shoes on their feet, with faces so weary they looked like old people, ambled in front of the bus. Thea's stomach protested now as the vehicle lurched to and fro. The bus jounced through the unfamiliar terrain, until they finally reached their destination of Grundy, Virginia, the late evening.

Grundy, seat and principal settlement of Buchanan County, looked like a respectable little town. As they got off the bus, Jason's impression of his hometown was that of a tourist, and he expected Thea's assistance.

"Have we arrived?" she asked.

"Yes, I think so. We have to get a cab home now."

"Lord give me strength," she remarked.

It was a crisp fall evening as the sunset hid behind the colorful hills. Thea briefly flashed to her youth in Darjeeling, but one could hardly compare coal trucks, tipples, and a muddy river to the serenity of the Himalayas. Both were primitive, yet far removed from each other, as were Thea and Jason.

While driving around the hills in the taxi Jason remarked. "You know, snugglebug, this part of the country was prominent territory during the Civil War. The Yankees were driven back by way of Grundy, and Pikeville into this here Big Sandy Valley, and the Big Sandy River ahead of us."

Finally the cab came to a halt at the bottom of a steep hill, when the driver refused to go any farther. Jason argued the point with him, saying his cab could make it. As they argued, Thea got out and started to climb the hill slowly, until she reached a strongly built brick house. Fatigued at her attempt, she sat herself down on a swing on the porch, and watched Jason carry Marc toward her. Slowly the screen door opened, and a middle-aged woman appeared with a bewildered smile, and glasses on her nose that were spattered with white paint. She seemed all of four feet seven inches tall.

"Marm!" Jason embraced the little woman. "This is Marc, the oldest son of the oldest son in your family, and this here is snugglebug, my little woman."

She timidly expressed joy at the unexpected arrival of her son, as she put her arms around him, and her new daughter-in-law.

"I didn't expect you home so soon. I'd hoped to be through with the house painting before you got here."

"Aw Marm, don't fret over little matters. We had a long trip home, and I could sure do with a drink. Where does Dad keep the whiskey?"

"Why honey, we don't keep that stuff around us. There's either pop or milk if you're that thirsty."

Mother relieved her son of her grandson, and as she examined him carefully. "My are you a pretty boy, with all that black hair, and big brown eyes, just like your marmie."

While mother and son chatted inside the kitchen, Thea strolled around the front yard and observed a little wooden house across the driveway. This was the home of Maw and Paw, who became her constant companions in the weeks that followed. Maw was part Cherokee Indian; she was slightly taller than Mother Travis and had salt and pepper hair tied in a knot behind her head. She had a sallow complexion, with strong features, and a soft spoken voice. Paw resembled the film actor Walter Huston.

The old folks came out of their dwelling to welcome their new member of the family. Maw embraced Thea as though she were one of her own. Thea liked her instantly, there was something awesome about the lady. Thea felt as though Maw and Paw were old souls from another place in time. Maw was definitely a very old soul. Mountain folk held tenaciously to their individualism and customs. Within the hour the room was full of chatter, as neighbors and relatives wandered into the big house. It was nightfall as faces turned toward the front door. There was immediate silence as everybody watched the man of the house enter. He was dressed in dark green coal smitten overalls, and a hard hat to which was attached a light. From the hard boots on his feet to his head he was covered with coaldust. The amazement on Thea's face, brought a tired weary smile to his face. He approached step by step toward her, as she sat spellbound in her chair. He set his lunch box on the table nearby, and gave her his large black hand as a welcome. His soulful expression, was one of warmth and his blue eyes fixed upon her. He moved in the direction of his son, who clasped him to his chest.

"Dad, it's been a long time. Snugglebug's hardheaded, but I won her just the same. This is Marc, your new grandson."

Grandfather sat himself down in the largest chair in the living room, and his wife promptly hastened to draw her husband's bath. That signaled the end of his work day. The silence broke, and he disappeared from their presence.

As Thea sat among her newly acquired family, she couldn't help but feel as though she was acting out a Tennessee Williams play. Life here was as unsophisticated as she had ever experienced. The primitive

Appalachian country had its cold reality, and the pattern of these hill folks had gone unchanged for a century. An outsider such as herself required an enormous amount of human insight to understand or even come close to understanding these people. The mountaineer not only had his peculiar mode of speech, their folk superstition and suspicion of the outside world required special understanding. Paw monopolized Thea's attention, as he hungered for information about "life across the ocean." She smiled in the same manner as she had years ago, with her servants in Calcutta, after she had returned from her overseas trip as a teen. Once again she was narrating her experiences.

"It's like this Paw. There are several aspects to many parts of the Continents, which I'm sure we will eventually cover, that would be of interest to you."

"You see I ain't been no place in all of my life. This is the only world I know. Mind you we have some beautiful country right here, but I'm curious about where you come from."

Jason and his Dad made themselves scarce, and thought they hadn't been missed in the roomful of people. Mother and Thea were shrewdly aware of both men's addictions. The old man had his hiding place in the basement, and from the sound of their boisterousness, Jason had at last found the whiskey.

The days drew nearer for Thea's confinement, and she nested with the old folks. Paw and Thea played endless games of gin rummy, and checkers, which Paw won most times. Maw would stand over her wood stove and fix their supper of corn bread and pinto beans, which Thea had developed a taste for. Paw was Maw's second husband, and made no bones about his low esteem for Thea's father-in-law.

"I don't care for a drinking man. Nothing but trouble they are."

The old folks spoke little of their personal feelings, they were both in the evening of their lives, and were grateful for their little house on the hill, and their pension check. He was retired a long time back from the railroad company. He was a gentleman in every respect, and when Jason behaved degenerately Paw would stand tall and hold his ground.

"You let the girl sleep now. It's long past your bedtime, so move along in where you belong. She'll return in the morning directly, after Maw has made her some breakfast."

Jason would kick the dust with his shoe in disgust at not having got his way. Thea would be pretending to sleep in the old folks' guest room, relieved that she had been spared Jason's drunkenness.

Thea attempted to write her mother weekly, as she had always done when they were apart from each other. She wondered what her mother and Lydia would have said about her manner of existence. Somehow letters couldn't describe her loneliness. They would never had exposed themselves to the unknown, so they wouldn't understand any of it.

Mother-in-law was the wife of a miner, the only life she knew. She was an educated woman, but lived in complete bondage to her husband as did the rest of them.

Thea saw such bondage as a detrimental sense of self, but her concept meant little. She knew it was better in her ninth month to keep silent, as there was little she could do to change her situation. Inwardly she rebelled every minute and wouldn't allow herself to be destroyed again by any more mistakes. She conveniently omitted that she made her own heaven and hell. Nobody had pushed her into this situation. She had gotten herself into it, and only she could get herself out.

On a dismal wintery December day, Jason ploughed his wife through the heavy snowbound highways in his Ford convertible toward the hospital. Here Thea gave birth to their daughter, Fiona, who weighed in at five pounds, one ounce. She was adorable with a head full of black curls and slanty light brown eyes. Thea knew nothing of her delivery as she'd had a general anesthetic. Both mother and baby were home for Christmas. Marc welcomed his baby sister and was most attentive to her.

Thea had lost all composure, if not one, then the other child required her attention. Mother-in-law assisted Thea most of the time, yet Thea seldom could sleep of a night. Both women prowled around the house attending to the babies. Mother Travis had a fantastic disposition toward family. She seemed to fill everybody's needs and requirements. Thea had now been introduced to the rocking chair, she wasn't sure if it was the answer to the babies falling asleep, she certainly didn't.

The Travis family had a special reverence toward Christmas. The lack of funds didn't discourage them in their festivities. Presents were wrapped and put under the tree, everybody received acknowledgement, and there was plenty of food on the table, cooked by various members of the family. The enthusiasm of this breed was extraordinary. For all the miles Thea had covered, and the various societies she had experienced, Virginia and Kentucky dumbfounded her. She had discovered the women had stamina, yet they submitted to the weakness of their men, a lot of whom drank to excess, and lived without respect for society and the law, as did Jason, and his brother Luke, whom Thea had yet to meet.

221

Appalachia was rich in natural resources. If you were not aggressive enough to demand your share, you only had yourself to blame. A person's day to day life depended on his abilities and requirements. The endless hardships took the romance out of this desperate area. The wealthy folks lived well, while the poor sat on their swings on the porches, and talked of rocking chair money, deaths, wakes, births, and marriages. The men tanked up with moonshine and local brews, and then spouted their limit knowledge of politics.

They'd lived in Virginia for nearly a year. Jason got out of the navy, discovered his limited qualifications, realized he wasn't of any value in these parts, reenlisted in the navy, and got his orders for Guantanamo Bay, Cuba.

Thea gave a sigh of relief, as she packed his bags for his departure. He had to secure housing for his family before they could join him. Thea wasn't in any hurry, as she received her monthly allotment check, on which she managed far better than she ever did with her husband.

Chapter Thirty-three

Five months and several ham telephone calls from Jason in Getmo later, Thea followed out with her two babies. She began her long journey by bus from Grundy, Virginia, to Norfolk. Here they checked into the Tides Motel for the night, and requested an early wake up call at the reception desk. Later that morning, they got the MATS flight to Guantanamo Bay U.S. Base.

Guantanamo Bay Naval station, situated in the inlet of the Caribbean, was all of twelve miles long. For Thea it was paradise, and a perfect environment for a family. Their home was situated near Kittery beach. It was comfortably furnished, one of four units. A smiling Jason met his family with great enthusiasm, as he relieved Thea's arms of Marc.

"Snugglebug, you're going to love living here, it's like being on one long vacation."

Jason spent his leisure time fishing off the coast with his buddies. Thea would barbecue enough red snapper for all their new friends on the block, at the provided pits on the beach next to the cabanas. Saturday nights they attended the dinner dances at the NCO Club, and Jason proudly introduced his wife. The naval wives welcomed Thea. There was one in particular, Valerie Preston, whose husband was a chief. They lived in the corner unit and became Thea's closest friends. Although living conditions were restricted, the navy was considered family, and at times became too close for comfort.

It didn't seem possible that the Travises were already celebrating their third wedding anniversary, if one could have called it that. Thea had invited their closest friends over for dinner at their home. It all seemed too good to be true. Toward the end of the evening, the familiar dread from the past had started to surface. Valerie was the last to leave the party. In doing so she whispered in Thea's ear, "If you have a problem with him, bring the children with you to me for the night," Valerie had four kids of her own, and she was very family oriented.

When Jason was the worse for liquor, he went against his wife. She still hadn't learned to get out of his way. She had always been his direct target, and she invariably got a black eye or a busted head. The babies got frightened and most times hid under the beds, until the coast was clear. Thea couldn't tolerate his degeneracy any longer. He could be as charming as a prince, in front of company. But when he got his days off on a stretch, it was his time to unwind with poker and booze. His cohorts like himself, had no concept for family or privacy. They always used his home for a base.

Alcoholism was a sickness that needed to be treated professionally, and his escapism had become a tragedy. Thea had little choice but to take drastic measures. She was on the "pill," and as the shipments were scarce, her fear of having another baby became catastrophic. This led to estranged behavior on her part, and provoked his anger toward her. He was a lousy lover, and she couldn't tolerate him.

One night when Jason was on the midwatch, Thea strolled over in the direction of the admiral's quarters without an appointment. She beckoned the guards at the gate to let her in, as it was a matter of life and death. She was shown to his office to wait for him. She had sat for practically an hour before the admiral appeared. She had had enough time to contemplate the seriousness of her presence here.

"Yes, Ma'am! What could be your urgency at this time of night? If it's a domestic problem, you should confide in your husband's CO."

"I'm afraid it's gone beyond that, and it concerns your authorization, Sir. I am requesting my husband's immediate removal from this base. He is a chronic alcoholic, and the medical treatment he has received here has not helped. He must be removed for the sake of his family."

"Are you sure you wish to jeopardize your husband's career?"

The admiral requested Jason's work chart, from an orderly standing to attention by the doorway. He read it carefully.

"I see no signs of defectiveness, if anything he has an exceptional record. He works up on John Paul Jones hill and is never late."

"Sir, I am not here to question his work. We have been here a year now, and he has been picked up by the shore patrol umpteen times, for disorderly conduct in the home."

"I'll have to speak with his CO before I sanction the necessary validation. You'll be hearing from me one way or another Ma'am."

Thea walked away a bit hesitant, yet sure the admiral would act upon her behalf. The following week Jason came home from work as

224

usual, preparing himself for another binge. His CO planned to act accordingly during this period of his time off. Thea had been warned to stay away from their home with the children. So she took the babies over to Valerie's home next door. Jason went on the warpath when he realized they were gone. There was also a hurricane in force, and Valerie bolted and shut all the windows. Valerie's four children were petrified at the sounds outside the building, so the six children sat on the living room floor. Her husband was at work, so the women were alone in all the confusion. Thea heard Jason's voice outside the front door, demanding she come home. Valerie yelled back at him to go home and that she wasn't going anyplace till the storm was over. It had been a sleepless night for everyone, but the morning appeared quiet.

A knock on the door by the shore patrol required Thea's signature, to remove Jason from their residence. So she did just that. He was to stay at the brig and be kept under surveillance, until their departure date was established. Although Thea's last days on the island were tedious, Valerie had helped her to regain her self-respect, and lectured her about the outcome when she and Jason met again. She lectured them not to be intimidated by his cruelty.

On the day of their departure, Valerie accompanied her friend and the two children to the airplane. Jason was already seated in the aircraft with two military aides on either side of him. He reached out to hug his babies, but he slighted his wife. His only words to her were "Snugglebug, you'll pay for this." She ignored him as she got seated as far away from him as possible in a limited space. He truly revolted her by this time.

They arrived Fort George Meade in Laurel, Maryland. Jason had been warned by the military authorities, that if he gave his wife and children the least hassle, he would suffer grave consequences.

Now demoted in his job, he became unusually passive toward Thea, and she trusted him even less. This justified him to stay away from home altogether. She was alone with her kids in a strange environment with no money, food or friends except for some kind neighbors that took compassion on her. In those days Thea was ignorant about shelters or Legal Aid, there was never anything mentioned on this topic. She wasn't a frightened person, but she wasn't clear in her thinking either. As a last resource, she would have to contact her mother. So far she had prevented herself from doing this.

One cold wintry night in subzero temperature, Jason exploded with a final episode of violence. He had been sitting in the living room in a

225

drunken stupor, when he suddenly rushed into the children's bedroom, where they were fast asleep and carried them out one under each arm out of the apartment building into the snow, to his unheated car in the parking lot. He placed them in the backseat and locked all the doors. Fortunately for Thea and her babies, the car wouldn't start.

"I warned you woman, I'd get even with you, today is the day I do. I'm taking the children back to Marm. They have been yours too long already, now they belong with me."

Thea didn't panic. She called the police immediately, and they were there in minutes. Observing Jason at the steering wheel, and the babies in tears, they got the children back to their mother, and took Jason into custody. Thea was warned to take the necessary precautions before Jason would be set free by dawn the next day.

Thea called her mother in London, and requested flight tickets for her and the children. She advised her mother to send them to her neighbor's address. In the meantime American passports had to be obtained for the children. Thea's British passport was validated. She wasn't anxious over Jason's returning in a hurry. In fact she was positive that after he had been let out, he would go to the nearest bar and stay there with any available woman who'd listen to him. Thea and the children were driven by the neighbors to Baltimore's Friendship airport within twenty-four hours.

Needless to say it wouldn't be true to Thea's course to have left in peace. She was pregnant one more time!

Chapter Thirty-four

Mother and Lydia awaited the Pan American flight arrival at London's Heathrow airport. They were saddened at Thea's plight, but at the same time joyous that she had brought the children home.

Lydia was enthralled with Fiona, and she reacted with even more enthusiasm than when Thea brought Laura to London when she was a baby. In fact she deemed Fiona to be the most beautiful baby she had ever seen. Thea's mother felt as strongly about Marc. He was the son she had yearned for and never had. When they got home, Thea removed her overcoat revealing her condition. Mother gasped!

"How come you look so pregnant dear?"

"Probably because I am again."

They were both horrified at Thea's complacency.

"Goodness me, girl, haven't you learned anything with your traumatic life with this man. Who pray is going to take care of all these children?"

"Don't worry, Mother, I'm so pleased to be away from him, everything will be okay, so long as I am not hounded by the likes of him."

Their first weeks in England, the children were installed in a nursery school for the mornings. Grandmother had made arrangements at a private school across the street to take care of them, as Thea toiled with great discomfort. A domestic helper came in the morning. Thea visited the U.S. Naval Hospital where she had had Marc, for prenatal treatment. She was now in her eighth month, and the doctor that had delivered Marc attended to Thea once again. His opening words to her were, "I don't believe it! Same man is it?"

"Yes doctor, what's more, there's one in between, a little girl I had in Richlands, Virginia. This time I've left him, and returned to my family."

In May of 1965, exactly eleven years later to the day, Thea gave birth to Philip, Laura's half-brother, about whom she knew nothing. Laura was in Africa at this time with her father and step-mother.

So now Thea had had four children, two of each sex, all beautiful and healthy, except for her ineligibility as a mother. She couldn't very well expect the support of her mother and sister forever. Lydia had been married a short while, and was past having children, she never wanted them. However at this point she offered to give Fiona a home and lots of love, and a private school education. Mother offered the same for Marc.

They tried to reason with Thea that a reconciliation with Jason would be preposterous. He had called several times over the past eight months, and insouciantly requested Mother to send back his family. His impertinence vexed Mother who told him he didn't have to listen to his demands in the middle of the night. He hadn't supported his family, or even asked about his latest addition.

"If you wish to see your children, why don't you send for them?" she asked. "You have caused my daughter enough grief, and she would be better off without the likes of you."

Now nearly a year had passed, and Thea reluctantly decided she had to return to the States. She couldn't cope with the situation any longer. It cost her mother the flight tickets back for Thea and the three babies. The day they departed from the house against Mother's better judgment, she and Lydia both wept. They hated seeing them return to Jason's depravity.

Mother and Lydia had never had the least confidence in Thea. She was about to surprise them, and herself, and show that she was a born survivor.

Chapter Thirty-five

The plane touched down at Chicago's O'Hare airport in the late afternoon.

During their year's separation, a few changes had taken place. Evidently Jason hadn't comprehended the failure of his past endeavor of coping with civilian life. He had gotten out of the navy once again after Thea had left him in Maryland. He was now supposedly in construction. That was a laugh, a tall story. A pencil pusher, with softer hands than the average woman, was now in construction? She discovered he had aged considerably for his thirty-three years. He looked a lot older than Thea; in actual fact he was two years younger. Habitual drunkenness and lying around with an older woman, had far-reaching repercussions.

The instant their eyes met at the airport, her mind registered his submissiveness to another. His guilty expression gave him away. Now that she had returned, she was about to play him at his own game, but she would be the victor, not the victim. His salacity was about to become a legend! Snugglebug maybe, but a fool she wasn't.

They drove out of Chicago. It was now dusk as they arrived at a dreary part of the country near Kankakee, Illinois. This sudden transition from her mother's comfortable home to a second-hand trailer remotely parked in a cornfield, led Thea to suspect treachery. Her indecisiveness hadn't as yet reached any conclusion, as she stalked around the interior that looked disheveled from recent use. It was a cold November day, yet the trailer was devoid of heat. Thea and the babies sat in the living room awaiting fuel, which brother Luke had supposedly gone out to get.

In walked trouble! "Cool Hand Luke," her handsome brother-in-law. Thea was amused at his amorous expression which he didn't even conceal upon their meeting. She saw a replica of a youthful Tony Curtis. Luke had black hair, blue eyes framed with eyeglasses. He was physically more appealing than his brother, and six years younger than Thea, which made him thirty. He, too, was a little the worse for wear, and seemed a lot more mature for his years. He definitely charmed the opposite sex. He affectionately embraced his new sister-in-law.

"Your a lot prettier than your pictures," he said.

"You're the mysterious maligned brother."

"Yes I'm the black sheep of the family."

That's great, Thea thought to herself.

Jason's parents had now moved to this part of the country, and her father-in-law had purchased a Texaco gasoline station. Both his sons worked for him, and between the three of them, they drank up the profits. Jason also helped build a motel across the way from the trailer, owned by an older woman. Although her mother-in-law was close at hand, she seemed very disoriented having moved from her home in Virginia. This made Thea even more suspicious.

Luke was divorced and living with his parents. Jason was living with somebody who was a mystery as yet to unfold. Thea and her three children were living in the trailer.

It was Halloween, and the brothers had planned to take Thea to the VFW dance in Kankakee. Jason had neglected his responsibility toward his family. So far Thea and her kids were at the mercy of Luke and his parents. It was a bit late for her to regret returning to such deplorable conditions. Besides which, she hadn't returned to Jason, her motive had only been to return to America. Her situation had led her to this time and place, and in due course the pieces of the puzzle would fit.

From the time Jason entered the trailer on that doomed evening. Thea noted his offensive behavior. They had both been estranged people at the best of times, now even more so. He wasn't smart enough to lead a double life, but he was dumb enough to think Thea would tolerate it. To even go out with him was a sham. She gave a sigh of relief when Luke cut in on Jason on the dance floor and finished the dance with Thea. Luke then walked onto the bandstand and announced over the microphone, "This song is for my beautiful sister-in-law." He ardently began to sing "Misty" to Thea. This provoked Jason instantly. He cut the song short as he pounced on his brother. Within seconds they were in a fist fight on the floor, causing Thea much embarrassment. Couples stepped aside while the brothers let loose their rage toward each other. Jason got the worse of it, and Luke took a jug of ice water from the dinner table and poured it over his brother's face.

"Damn it Jason, won't you ever learn? You could never whip me, even when you fought dirty." Luke grabbed Thea by her hand, and ushered her out to his car.

"Luke, you're crazy. I know him, he'll kill you."

"He's a chicken shit. He's a wife beater. I'm sick of watching this charade between the two of you. You know he's shacking up with a woman older than Mom. She is supporting him, and that's her trailer you're living in. I'm going to take you all out of there."

"I think you had better attend to your own homework before you take on anymore. From all accounts your wife hasn't had her fair share of support. If not for her mother coming to her rescue, she and your kids would be on the street."

"Don't you worry about her, she's a lot sharper than you give her credit for. You'll be on the street before long. How far do you think you'll go with three little ones?" They hastened toward his mother's to get the kids out of bed. Mother sided against Thea and Luke, and she held on to the kids. Before long Jason had arrived on the threshold, and he reached for a carving knife in the kitchen drawer. Luke and Thea fled out of the side entrance and jumped into his car. He drove like a madman, as time was against him. They came to an abrupt halt outside the bus terminal. He jostled Thea toward the bus, and told her to lie low.

"What are you saying? I can't leave my children because of you two nitwits. I wouldn't have taken them to England, and brought them back, just to run away. You drive me back, I'm not scared of him."

"This isn't my car, I'm leaving it here. Jason means business, he's told me more than once he'll do you in, that you've been nothing but trouble for him."

"That's a laugh, the bastard! He wouldn't know a good thing if he saw one. He'll come to a violent end, so help me."

"Well I'm sure he will. But let him do it at his own risk. You have to stay out of sight for now. It's his story against yours. The story won't hold in court. Remember you're a British subject. Mom won't give up those kids. You haven't a leg to stand on. You should not have come back to this mess. Now you have to pay for it, but you don't have to get killed in the bargain. Listen to me." In Thea's dilemma, she hadn't time to change, or even pack for a getaway. She was dressed in party clothes, and she carried a small evening bag that held her passport and green card in it. She had left behind all her personal effects, jewelry, and wallet. She felt like a fugitive on the run, listening to Luke all the way. Sitting at the back of the bus, she worried about her children, yet the thought of Jason's raging face frightened her too much to return.

Luke didn't appear too troubled traveling light with a heavy burden. This last bus for the evening was traveling to Chicago, with few passengers. They sighed in relief as they drove out of the terminal.

"Have you ever been to Chicago?" she asked.

"No but I have a friend there, and I'm sure he will keep us until we get ourselves situated."

"How do you figure to explain me?"

"He and his wife never met Carie, so you can impersonate her."

"Do you expect me to answer to the name of Carie? You're crazy."

"They don't know that to be her name. I was stationed with Eddy in the Air Force in San Antonio, Texas years ago, neither of us were married at the time."

"How did we meet? You've never been to London."

"Don't worry about trivialities; we are not staying long with them. I'll go along with whatever you say."

"Well I'm not a good liar, and this won't work. I can't just disappear from the scene, because of Jason being crazy."

"Thea, please stop worrying about the children, and what you're going to do. I don't make a habit of running away with my sister-in-law every day. We couldn't stay there the way it was. You're lucky that I was around to get you out of it. You have to trust me."

After they arrived at the Greyhound bus station on Randolph Street in downtown Chicago, they got a cab to Cicero, Illinois.

They drove a long distance and ran up a handsome cab fare. It was a strange time of night to land on a friend's doorstep—a friend he hadn't seen in years. Thea hoped he was still at the address they pulled up to. He was. After the introductions were over with Ed's wife, Cora, pointedly observed Thea's dress and light-colored shoes worn in the depth of winter.

"Yes, I'm not dressed suitably for all that snow out there. Kind of left in a hurry," Thea said.

"You don't have to explain a thing to me, hon. We are friends, and ask no questions of you two. Just rest some, and you'll think clearer in the morning, that's what I think."

Within two days Luke secured a job in the corrugated box factory. This enabled them to move into a sleazy apartment building situated alongside the tracks of the el train. Thea discovered many hillbillies here

232

who were at ease in their own neighborhood, which was in uptown Chicago.

Luke was fully aware of her utter remorse about her separation from her children, and he refrained from making advances toward her. She believed him implicitly when he indicated she was an alien, and Jason could have had her deported back to England as an unfit mother. She didn't have the money to fight him, and her mother was too far away. So she took refuge with Luke, who had taken care of her honestly. However she contacted her mother-in-law to enquire about their welfare. The lady begged her to return, and said that Jason wouldn't threaten her. The babies were fine, but they needed their mother.

"I'm sorry Mother Travis, I will never return to Jason again. As soon as I'm situated I'll find a way to get the children to me."

Thea had gotten her bearings around the neighborhood, though she wasn't brave enough as yet to secure a job around their apartment building. The poverty and deplorable living conditions astounded her. You could take the man out of the country, but not the country out of the man. On Broadway and Wilson, the Southerner tossed his garbage into the alleys, as he did in the creeks back home.

Luke started making his moves on Thea. His supreme debauchery attracted her, and his passion for cunnilingus fueled her with constant exhilaration. She had never experienced sensuality such as this, or as often as he wanted it of her. He drank every bit as much as Jason, or even Steven did, but his compulsion for making love was boundless, and drove her wild. She lived only for the lovemaking of Luke.

They had been to see Paul Newman in *The Hustler*, and Luke imagined himself as Fast Eddie with a pool cue. On Friday nights he exploited and duped the guys at the local tavern. He only frequented the bars to gamble and win their Friday night paychecks. They lived precariously, and changed apartments, as frequently as he changed jobs. He went from foreman at several box factories, to printing lithographically. He worked the longest at a sheet metal shop. He always made a good living and took care of Thea. But she had to work to be occupied. She started her rounds of beauty shops, always the best in the city. She had discovered that Chicago was a good place to make a living. There were choices, and money.

"Honeybear," he'd call her, "You have to lie a little, or else you get cheated on. In the hills we wrap ourselves in a cocoon, in some sleepy 'hollar.' Here in Chicago, we have to learn to fly right."

"Why do you have to lie?"

"Because folks here think us dumb hillbillies. I ain't about to spit in the wind, for it to end in my face."

Saturday nights they'd dance at ballrooms to the big band music. She was introduced to country and western. Luke would play guitar and sing in bars. He attracted young and old, and Thea felt threatened. She had never shown jealousy until now. She felt his love for her would fade.

One evening after they had eaten supper, she noticed Luke was apprehensive. He said he had talked with his mother, and although he had promised not to tell Thea, he couldn't restrain himself any longer. Mother had informed him that Jason had been serving time in prison for nearly a year, and she couldn't take care of three little ones. So Marc was in her care, but Fiona and Philip were with foster parents.

"How dare she take the matter into her hands without consulting me. I am their natural mother. I have family in England that would take in their own. Strangers—who gave her the right?"

"Honey, your in no position to take three children. It's best left this way. If you take this matter to the law, you have to prove you can give them a good home. We move too fast, we are not suited for responsibilities. Besides, you need big money to fight your case. Be honest with yourself."

Thea phoned her mother immediately. She went into instant shock! She took the matter to English solicitors, and they in turn corresponded to lawyers in the U.S. After the case had been hashed over. The decision was that Thea as a mother had chosen to run away, leaving her children with their American grandparents. How could Thea's mother, a noncitizen take the matter into her hands? Perhaps if her daughter had remained on in Britain, then things would have been different. But as they stood now, her daughter was living with her brother-in-law, which wasn't exactly ethical. Either way Thea felt beaten, and she didn't put up any fight. Instead she kept Luke company in his heavy drinking. She went from job to job, and she couldn't tolerate herself or her brother-in-law any longer. She had told him she could provide for herself and didn't require a wet nurse, that if he wouldn't leave she would. She had packed her belongings and was on her way out, when Luke came home with a couple of steaks to barbecue in their backyard.

"At least have dinner with me before you leave," he said.

"Well all right I'll have dinner, but then, Luke, I have found a place to stay, and please don't follow me. I need to be alone from now on."

They had gotten started with the salad, which Thea had prepared, and the steaks were just about ready to be taken off the coals, when before their eyes stood as large, and as ugly, an enraged Jason. Thea and Luke were paralyzed as one looked at the other in shock! Jason had come through the back gate and walked toward Thea with his cynical smile.

"Lookie, lookie here, how the two lovebirds have their supper."

Luke got up from his chair.

"Jason we don't want any trouble now."

"There's not going to be any trouble brother. I came to collect what rightly belongs to me."

"Jason, she ain't coming with you."

"We'll see about that, won't we, snugglebug?" He came toward her and grabbed her by the ear. "Now that you've caused enough grief all around, your coming back to me and your son Marc. I've lost the other two, because Marm couldn't take care of our children."

"You don't scare me, you bastard. You better get the hell out, the same way you came in."

He bashed her head against the range in the kitchen. All she remembered before she passed out, was Luke getting him by the hands. "She's out, let her be. I have to get an ambulance."

Thea opened her eyes slowly to see a troubled Luke standing beside her bed in a hospital.

"Where is he?" she asked.

"Another jail for the night," he replied.

"How did he find us, Luke?"

"Mother told him."

"How could she do a stupid thing like that? Does she really think he's playing with a full deck?"

"Ah, you know Marm, she weakens when it comes to Jason. He spun her a yarn about getting you back to take care of Marc."

"I hope Marc will be spared ever being in his father's company. He'd be ashamed of him I'm sure."

Thea's memory lapsed as she lay in the hospital. Her eyes closed almost as if she didn't care anymore. Life seemed so pointless. Over the years her fears stemmed from the lack of this long sought after love she yearned for. Her thirst for sex produced anxiety and a very poor self-image. She didn't want to be possessed. Luke had never loved her, he needed a mother the same as Jason did. They had derived a false emotional strength from each other. She had to learn that real love seeks to liberate the potential and possibility in one's partner, not to take possession of them. Possessive love is the mother of jealousy, and jealousy is a form of fear. It's the emotional reaction of someone threatened, so this made their love imperfect. Luke wasn't aware of his actions, and maybe he never would be. If he had been in the least secure, he wouldn't have had the same problem as Thea. She at least had made the decision to terminate their sick relationship. She had to end up in a hospital to see the light.

Thea returned with Luke, to stay with him until she regained her strength and could return to work once more. Only then could she find another apartment and live on her own, as was the general plan before Jason had appeared.

Two weeks before Thanksgiving Day of 1967, Luke and Thea were asleep, when the phone rang at 3:00 A.M. Thea groped for it and she incoherently listened to the party on the other end. She awoke Luke.

"I can't understand what this man is saying," she mumbled.

She put the light on, as Luke fumbled for his glasses, assembled pencil and paper, and began to scribble.

"Yes, yes, right away," was all she made of the conversation.

"What is it?" she asked.

"It's Jason. He's been in an auto accident. We have to leave immediately for the La Grange Hospital."

"How did they know where to reach you?"

"I don't know, honeybear. I'm not even fully awake. Hurry, let's go."

Upon arrival at the hospital, they were both ushered toward the intensive care unit. Thea was admitted in first. She had always feared hospitals, and could never accept them as a place of cure, only death. Before her lay an unconscious Jason, surrounded by complicated apparatuses to keep him alive. His body had swollen to three times its normal size. His eyes were closed. He had tubes in his nostrils that continued to the base of his throat.

"My God!" was Thea's only reaction.

Luke stood alongside of her with tears in his eyes, as he held his brother's hand. She felt sympathetic toward Luke, but showed no emotion toward Jason. It had been a first time for her to experience a sight like this; she walked out of the room and left the brothers together. *What a waste*, she thought, *Jason had been his own worst victim*. The story was that Jason had been driving along on the Stevenson expressway, which was under construction at the time. He was driving against traffic, and got on to an off ramp, in the course of which three teenagers were killed instantly, and another was hospitalized the same time he was. His mother and Marc flew out directly within the hour.

"Well, honeybear, I guess my brother won't be on the warpath with us ever again." Luke wept bitterly. "I can never forgive myself for not making amends to him. I loved my brother, even though I know he never had a good word for me."

"Jason didn't love himself. You can hardly blame yourself for this situation, Luke."

Jason died the day before Thanksgiving. Thea didn't attend the funeral. She couldn't subject herself to any more grief. Luke accompanied his family with the body to Virginia to rest in peace. Thea went her own way at last.

The mythical unity once shared between them had at last crumbled.

Part 4

Thea Continued

Chapter Thirty-six

Thea's positive attitude gave her a new lease on life. She didn't have a friend in Chicago, but she was tenacious enough to hold on to her convictions.

At first she had frequent nightmares, in which she was continually escaping from both of the brothers. She'd awaken at night in a cold sweat, and turn on all the lights in her apartment. She doublelocked her front door in fear of the suspicious characters living in the building. She heard voices in the hallways all through the night. Each evening she'd hurriedly walk home from work, fearful that Luke would be following her. He had already called her several times at the beauty shop, but he didn't know where she was living. She knew he would never give up, so she had to disappear from her job. More the pity, because it was the best she had gotten.

To spend the Christmas holidays alone was another hurdle for her to get over. She lived off Michigan Avenue, and after supper she often took walks and gazed at the beautiful store windows, as shoppers scuttled by with their shiny shopping bags full of goodies. The spirit of the holiday season embraced Marshall Field's and Carson's as Thea stood among the crowds with memories of her past.

Oddly enough she didn't feel deprived of her children around her. She temporarily escaped back to her youth, and she was in her living room in their beautiful mansion, and she and Lydia were decorating the tree with all the presents around it. They were dressed in their new crimped dresses, had attended Mass, and had returned home for their festive lunch. The girls would then hand out gifts to the servants, which each of them accepted with smiling gratitude.

The vast veranda overflowed with colorful baskets of an assortment of exotic fruits, nuts, and sweetmeats bestowed on the family by Father's factory help. The girls went in search of treasure which was tucked away in the baskets. Gold coins better known as sovereigns were covered in colored tissue paper waiting to be found by them. Each time one was found, they'd laugh with glee as to which of them collected the most. Then they were handed over to Mummy, who had the coins assembled into bracelets by the family jeweler. Thea felt as though she had died and gone to heaven. Now she watched the Nutcracker Suite in the Marshal Field window. With tears in her eyes, she slowly wended her way back to her lonely abode on Chestnut Street. That evening her mother called from London.

"Thea baby, come on home for Christmas. Don't stay there in a strange city alone."

"I can't, Mum. This time of the year I'm busy in the shop, and I have to send Marc his package. He's the only one I'm in touch with. I don't know where the others are. But maybe I'll come for Easter. It's nice hearing your voice, you seem so close by."

Thea couldn't visit her son in Kentucky, because she was sure Luke would be there with his family. Their mixed feelings toward her would certainly not be festive.

Thea's assumption of excommunication from the Catholic church hadn't deterred her from attending services at the Holy Name Cathedral. After all she had been brought up in its faith, and she required a full share of spiritual comfort right now.

New Year's Eve, she sat alone with a bottle of champagne, watching the countdown on TV on both State Street in Chicago and Times Square in New York. She thought back to her first impression of the Big Apple, and of the excitement she shared with her family and Captain Fortisque in the forties. It seemed like a dream. Maybe that was what life was, a dream state, and these were lessons to be learned on the way.

Soon after, the construction of the John Hancock building had begun across the street from where Thea lived. The block of buildings was to be demolished so she had been given notice to move. So if she was to move from her residence on Chestnut Street then she would have to find another job. She wouldn't be able to walk to her place of work at the Ambassador Hotel on State Parkway. Her next move was to an efficiency apartment on Sheridan Road, on the opposite side of which the one time famous Edgewater Beach Hotel was also in the throes of being dismantled. That, too, was as much past history as Thea was.

Thea had gotten used to her many moves and job placements. Each became an improvement. However her life was to take on a totally different aspect.

Until now Thea's knowledge of homosexual life was limited. She wasn't in the least familiar with their life-style. Her new friend, Jeremy Grant, was lively, talented, and he related to her like a school pal. They were both hired the same day at a salon in Wilmette, Illinois, and became good friends instantly. Jeremy and his lover, Don, included Thea in their weekend activities, going to the theater, gay bars, and gay parties. She was intrigued over their mannerisms, frustrations, anxieties, and addiction to each other. Thea was now referred to as a fruit fly, or even worse, a fag hag. They enjoyed her company, as they found her very uninhibited, but she didn't participate in their habitual drug or irresistible attraction for the same sex.

Although her sister-in-law, Hope, was a lesbian, Thea had never queried the matter. To each her own. She didn't know enough—or anything for that matter—it was beyond her comprehension. Thea had had her fill of alcoholism over the years, and her adventuresome nature was certainly not one of a degenerate.

Beauty salons in the Chicago area hired shampoo girls, some of whom traveled from the South side of the city to make a livelihood on the North Shore. One such was Alice. She was a friend to all in the shop. Alice was black, proud, and lively, always smiling. One day she seriously confided in Thea.

"Thea child, do you keep friends with black folks? I'd like very much to ask you to my home for Easter. That is if you're not doing anything else. You shouldn't be alone on a holiday."

Thea hadn't prepared herself for this, yet she was fond of Alice and accepted her invitation.

On Easter Sunday morning Alice and her husband, Vernon, called for Thea in their shiny black Buick. Alice was festively dressed for the occasion, and was smiling more than usual, as she introduced her husband to Thea.

Thus far the South side of Chicago had been a mystery to Thea. Presumedly where the Jewish folks once lived, it was now taken over by the black community.

Alice opened the front door to her prosperous home. She chuckled as Thea followed her in.

"See. Miss Thea, you assumed I was a poor shampoo girl, didn't you? I live good don't I?"

"Alice you shouldn't put yourself down, I thought no such thing." Alice laughed nervously as she showed Thea the rest of her home. The dining room was prepared for Easter lunch. The table was beautifully set with fine china and silverware. There was a centerpiece of tulips and daffodils cut from her garden. At the far end of the room sat a man behind a newspaper. Thea observed his black tapered fingers clutch the *Chicago Tribune*. He lowered the paper and gave her a friendly smile.

"I am Elliot. Have you heard only the best about me, as I have you?" He smiled some more.

"I guess you can say that," Thea answered.

He had a strong handshake. As he stepped back, Thea felt a little embarrassed for him, so she tried to put him at ease, as she directed the conversation toward him.

Alice outdid herself in cooking a baked ham, fixed chicken with all the trimmings, and homemade pies. Tea followed on a silver service.

They were truly a warm family. Elliot, was educated, charming, and Alice's only child. He resembled Harry Belafonte in looks.

Thea had never asked herself why she was prejudiced. She had been reared in India, with the snobbery of the British influence. As a child she was imbued with acute hostility toward the Indians. Not even the wealthiest Indian prince could have attracted her family or have been tolerated as suitable company. True, her father's racing and business associates were wealthy Indians and they socialized at parties and functions. But to fraternize with them on a personal basis, Mother would never have permitted. Thea's education was thus sadly neglected. She was about to discover more about the American black person's feelings in this sensitive matter. Elliott spoke of slavery and their heritage. His mother suffered with the age-old customs of their past. It was difficult for the poor dear to understand equality, and how hard they had striven for their place in society. He referred to hillbillies as cheap white trash. Thea didn't understand his dislike toward Southerners.

"Ah! They were superior because of their white skins," was his acute remark. "It makes all the difference for them to lord it over us. They can be cruel, uncouth, and ignorant, but they were superior because of the color of their skin. Why do you think the blacks have fought so hard to gain their rightful place? They have earned it. Even the Indians in your part of the world had enough of the British."

Thea wondered why he had exploded about racism on their first meeting. Maybe he required her to know how he felt.

"Yes I suppose you're right, but then it's gone on for centuries, hasn't it?"

"The centuries are finished young lady. We are dealing now with facts."

As he spoke she secretly thought to herself that as much as she would like to share her newfound friends with her family in England, she knew she couldn't because of their dogmatic way. She wasn't as bigoted as they were, as she had been exposed to a lot more than they would have thought conceivable. Elliott was sensitive on this subject, and he was aware of her differences.

On their first date together they attended a personal appearance of Sammy Davis in *Golden Boy*. On their next date Thea saw the movie *Guess Who's Coming to Dinner*. She was aware of his getting his message across. She finally got up the nerve to question him.

"Elliott, does our friendship bother you?"

"No, not at all. But it may you. I'm the first black man you have dated. Am I right?"

"Yes you are, but I don't hold it against you because you're black."

"I'm aware of the prejudice in India, and the beliefs you grew up with. It's not your fault. However you are trying to be more liberal, since living in this country. And I am your first experiment."

Thea felt shorn of her dignity, and she didn't know how to retaliate.

She had known Elliott for some weeks now, and it disturbed her ego that he had never made a pass at her. He was either afraid of rejection, or maybe he would contain his emotions until he felt a little more secure about hers.

One Saturday afternoon, she had just returned from work, and she came through her door to hear the phone ring.

"How are you?" he asked.

"Just fine."

"Do you have plans for the weekend?"

"Not so far I haven't."

"Would you care to drive with me to the Wisconsin Dells?"

"Sounds super, I've never been there."

"How long will it take you to get a bag together for the weekend?"

"Oh as long as it takes for you to drive from the South side."

He chuckled. "What if I told you I'm downstairs of your building."

"You rat, you're pretty sure of yourself aren't you?"

"I checked your whereabouts with Mother before I left home."

They stopped to have dinner on the way, and it was dark by the time they reached the Dells. Elliott drew into the parking lot of a motel, and checked in at the reception desk. Of course by now Thea was aware they were to spend the night here. She got a bit nervous as he put the key in the door of the room. He glanced over at her, as he apprehensively turned on the light switch. Taking off his jacket and loosening his tie, he sat on the chair by the window.

"We don't have to do anything you'll regret later. I thought we could spend some time together without being in my parents' home. I would never act against your wishes, Thea."

She came toward his tall stature, and put her arms around him.

"I believe you're terribly shy, and I do want to be alone with you. I think you've known that for quite sometime now."

She responded to his quivering tender kiss. It was as gentle as a whisper. He smiled awkwardly.

"One can't be platonic with you I found out."

"Why would you want to be platonic? It has been as long for you as it has for me. So there's no need for pretense is there?"

He trembled slightly as he lowered her head on the bed, circumspectly disrobing himself. *How sweet*, she thought.

Thea ran her fingers along his velvet limbs. He was so soft and beautiful, without a blemish. He had at last begun to relax, and this made her comfortable in his arms. He slowly undressed her kissing her all the while, giving him courage to go on. He penetrated her, as she winced.

"I'm not hurting you, am I?"

"If you call this hurting, then I enjoy pain, my love."

They succumbed together so naturally. He was a fantastic lover for a first attempt. He wasn't an animal that instinctively attacked. He moved with grace and ease. She responded to his unconditional gentleness. Until now she had felt like a crumpled dress that had been thrown in the closet. He had discovered and pressed her to perfection like new.

In the months that followed, they both derived warmth and consolation from each other. He worked in advertising, and held a worthy position. During the week he attended night classes, so they spent their weekends together. There was no end to the subjects they touched on. He was a pleasure socially; he didn't drink or smoke, and when they went out to dinner, he always ordered a fine wine with their meal. He was easy to communicate with. He would read Thea poetry that he had written. She had never encountered a gentleman such as him in America. In the year they had been together, there wasn't a fault to be found.

"One can't help but care for you. Your spontaneity is forever a surprise to me," he said.

One night she found him to be particularly pensive. She feared their days drawing to an end. So she made it easier for him.

"Elliott, we have shared some treasured moments together. I know it's beyond you to hurt anybody. So I'll make it easier for both of us." He had tears in his eyes as Thea spoke directly and truthfully.

"Thea you have such determination. I can't imagine how you goof when it comes to your choice of men. I have explained the situation to you more than once. Please promise me you won't sell yourself short anymore. You have so much going for you. Don't underestimate your potential. You can do so much in life that most people are afraid to even think about."

"I promise you, Elliott, I will try. I will do my damndest to make you proud of me."

"Never mind me. Do it for yourself. You owe it to yourself."

She never saw Elliott again. But he had passed through her life for a good reason. And she thought about him sweetly with kindness.

Chapter Thirty-seven

Thea's adventurous spirit had never deterred her boundless ability to routinize herself. Boredom invariably followed.

Oh what a tangled web she weaved!

Over the years she had kept in touch with her dear friend Valerie. While Thea had been hither and thither, Valerie had moved only once, and that was to a navy base in Maryland. Thea now planned to visit her girlfriend there, as she had become intolerant of her workaday existence.

Valerie met Thea at the airport. It had been years since they had seen each other, and both women were pleasantly surprised at the results. Thea had prepared herself for a quiz. Surprisingly Valerie did not bombard her at all. She did raise an eyebrow regarding Elliott but made no comment. If he had come to the rescue of her friend at a necessary time and helped her, that was all that mattered.

Valerie's husband was doing his last tour of ship duty before his retirement. Her children were still home, and she had a part-time job at the exchange. However she had taken off the next two weeks to be with Thea. Her home was not on the base, but she was there a lot of the time, and knew almost everyone in and around the community.

Their first evening they attended a double birthday celebration at the officers' club. The club was bursting with festivity as they entered. Thea felt comfortable among the navy family once more. It was a good feeling to be Valerie's guest, instead of Jason's wife. The band in the distance was playing the nostalgic music of Glenn Miller, which surprised Thea. It was so seldom heard anymore. Valerie was her popular self as usual, more so minus her husband's presence. She always attracted the male element and shared their attention with Thea. After they were seated, a handsome gent in officer's uniform caught Thea's attention. She obviously was attracted by him, because of his resemblance to Peter Strauss the movie actor. They smiled at each other, and he gestured to her to dance with him. She walked around the table toward the floor, where he joined her. They didn't say a word to each other. He held her close, and they kept time to the melody of "Moonglow." The music had stopped, and Thea went back to her chair. She glanced across to where he had been sitting, but he wasn't there. He didn't return, and she searched the crowded room, but there was no sign of him. She walked around the bar, and finally came back to Valerie.

"Did you see me dancing with a gorgeous apparition?"

She laughed. "Yes that was Robert Boyd, he's the dentist on the base, a real swell person. His wife is an alcoholic, and they are rarely seen together."

"That explains his vanishing. We didn't say a word to each other."

Valerie and Thea returned home late from the party. Although Thea had been disappointed over Robert Boyd, she was sure they would cross each other's paths in due course.

Valerie was a terrific lady when it came to motivation. She was a planner and always had something going on. They were never at a loss for activity. Her life centered around her five children, but she was still her own person. Although she worked at the navy exchange part-time, she was also taking a course in beauty culture, and she planned to work at home. Thea agreed that was the only way to go. She, too, was tired of working in salons and was never one for routine work.

One morning as Valerie was still asleep, Thea decided to take a walk around the countryside. Her house wasn't too far from the town center, yet it was far enough for a brisk walk.

It was a beautiful spring morning, and nature was at its best. The air was clean, free from ozone and the suffocating fumes associated with Chicago. Thea strode along in a vigorous manner. She was suddenly distracted by the beep of a car horn, and stopped. It was Robert Boyd.

"Can I give you a ride someplace?" he asked.

"Oh thank you, I'm supposedly out for a walk, but I don't know how far I've gone out of my way."

"Well you're nearing the base, and it's lunchtime, so let me buy you lunch."

"Thank you, Robert, I'd like that very much."

"That's not fair, you've had time to check up on me."

"I'm Thea Travis. We didn't have time to introduce ourselves on the dance floor."

"And now Valerie has told you I'm married, and I prowl around in search of good looking ladies to dance with."

"She didn't say any such thing. But I do know you are her dentist."

"You're not from these parts. How do you know each other?"

"I was a navy dependent at one time, and we were friends in Getmo."

"You say was?"

"Yes I'm a widow, and I live in Chicago."

"Staying here long?"

"I'm in my second week, I may stay a while."

"Would you have dinner with me tonight, or is that out of line?"

"How about an after dinner drink at the club. Val and I will be there together."

After a quick lunch, Robert drove her back to the house. Valerie was standing on the porch, wondering where her friend had got to. "Well here you are. Hi Robert, how's things?"

"Just fine, Val, hope to see you ladies later this evening, must be on my way."

Thea thanked him, and waved him on.

"It didn't take you long, girl, to find him again."

"Actually he found me. I was walking along a dirt road, and he picked me up and invited me to lunch at the club. Oh Val, he's such a nice fellow."

"Honey, he's very much married, so forget it."

That evening Thea and Val entered the bar, and he was already seated there on a stool, talking with a group of guys. When he saw them, he immediately came toward them and suggested they sit at a table. Val said the bar was fine, it was more friendly. Thea noticed Val and Robert were speaking in a subdued manner. It didn't bother Thea, as she directed her conversation to others sitting around. Shortly after, Robert headed toward the men's room, and Valerie whispered in Thea's ear.

"He asked me if I'd mind you spending the night with him?"

"What did you reply?"

"I told him to ask you."

Robert returned, and put his cool hand at the back of Thea's neck. "Let's go someplace quiet, where we can talk, okay?"

Thea looked at Valerie for approval. "Go on, you two. I'll be on my way home soon," Val said.

They got in his car, and he started up the ignition.

"Nervous?"

"Not really, perhaps a little apprehensive."

250

"Well be at ease, I don't make a habit of this. In fact, I'm the nervous one."

He had driven quite a way, and then said, "I have to be careful, wouldn't care to face anyone I know in the area. You know what I mean."

"Sure you have to guard your reputation."

He immediately stopped his car on the dark country road, and faced her.

"Thea, I like you, you're different. You're not at all the kind of female one meets everyday. You have class, your voice puts me at ease, and I'm terribly tense most of the time. I'll probably be very disappointing to you. But if you're willing to take a chance, so be it."

While he spoke Thea wanted to kiss him in the worst way. So she drew his head to hers and did just that! He was warmly responsive, and not in the least tense. They finally had reached a grand looking motel, which looked out of its league in these ordinary parts. She stayed in the car, until he got back with the room key.

"Nice place, eh? Pity it's only for the night," he remarked. He was so utterly handsome that she wished to treat this affair with kid gloves. She remembered what Adam had said in the past. So she attempted to bank her fires a bit, and not yield so easily. If he was as good in bed as his looks were, she wanted to etch every experience of this night into her mind and body. For once she wasn't going to be a roleplayer, creating it, instead of fitting into what he may have to offer. She wasn't going to challenge him. He was tender and tense, and she would wait her turn.

"You look very pensive dear, is something bothering you?" he asked.

"I was just thinking, that is all."

They both sat on the edge of the bed, each awaiting a first move.

He kissed her gently, looking into her eyes.

"What do they tell you?" she asked.

"That I'm pussyfooting around, instead of making mad passionate love to you."

He took off his shirt, and unzipped his trousers, and she watched him.

Men are terribly clumsy, when they haven't had any for a while, then they want it, and act silly she thought.

She took her dress off, and jumped him, as he laughed.

"There's nothing to it! It's doing what comes naturally."

He finally did make the second move, and they both were in seventh heaven. He moved with grace and urgency, and spent himself too soon. She hadn't even begun, but he felt good, and left her wanting more. They talked a while, and he seemed terribly relaxed in her arms. She became aggressive, and boldly went down on him. This renewed his endurance, and he performed at length, bringing them both to a violent orgasm. They had made love repeatedly until dawn, and yet she craved more. He didn't seem perturbed that he hadn't gone home, and she didn't pursue the subject. They finally took a shower together, and made love beneath the full force of the water. It was awesome.

After a hearty breakfast, across the way from the motel, he drove Thea back to Valerie's.

"Don't disappear from me in a hurry. I need to talk to you," he said.

Valerie agreed Robert was a well-liked person on the base. But that he would never leave his wife, and Thea wasn't the type to play second fiddle.

Their next date together was to the movies to see *Sweet Charity*. This was when he asked her to accompany him to Washington for a few days. She accepted immediately, as he brought her happiness, and she never thought about the consequences.

They took a leisurely drive to the business district of D.C. and checked into the Ambassador Hotel. The last time Thea had stayed there had been with her mother and Lydia when she wore bobby socks and oxfords. She had come full circle, and she felt as thought she were in the land of Oz. Robert was here on business, however he didn't neglect Thea. They explored the sights of the nation's capital, some of which she had forgotten. Besides one could hardly compare a visit as a child, to that of a woman. The city offered a varied assortment of wonderful restaurants, and they never tired of being in each other's company.

As they headed toward Maryland, Robert was quiet and in deep thought driving back. "A penny for them," she said. He smiled holding her hand.

"After these precious days with you. I must now brace myself for what awaits me when I get home. I wish it were you instead of her."

"As you probably noticed, I never touched on the subject."

"Yes I did. After all, there's nothing to be gained by dwelling on anything not associated with us."

After a month in Maryland, Thea realized if she continued to live around him, it could only lead to a calamity.

She assured Robert she would keep in touch, but to crowd him in so short a time wasn't fair to either of them. She had been fortunate to find him, and indeed could never forget his special treatment toward her. They never said good-bye. One afternoon she requested Valerie to drive her to the airport. Although she desperately wanted to see Robert, it seemed pointless to be agitated. To remember him as she had left him their last night together was far sweeter. As the plane took off, her eyes filled with tears at the thought of the love and laughter they had shared on borrowed time.

Chapter Thirty-eight

Once more Thea had arrived in the windy city, and secured an old-fashion apartment off Lawrence Avenue.

She was sitting in a booth of one of the Greek coffee shops, of which there were several in this neighborhood. She was circling job prospects in the *Chicago Tribune*. From a distance she was being eye-balled by a swarthy small-framed Greek, sitting behind the cash register. She was sure before long he would approach her. Sure enough he did.

"Excuse me, my name is Nick. I see you reading the job section. Are you new in town? Maybe I can help you."

"Yes, I am looking for a job. I'm new to the neighborhood, but I have worked in beauty shops downtown. However I would like to find something different."

"I have just the thing for you, which maybe you would be interested in. I am the owner of a barber shop in Rogers Park, and need a good manicurist. Top pay and excellent tips. It's a four-chair shop, I have one girl presently but require another, as most of my gentlemen take manicures."

"Yes I'm interested, but first of all I would like to see your shop."

"Are you married?"

"No, I am not married, and my name is Thea Travis. How do you do?"

She got in alongside of him in his Buick, and they headed for his shop. He had his eyes more on her than the road, and he spoke in broken English until they arrived at their destination.

Nick seemed to be a sincere character, and his dark eyes sparkled when he spoke. He proudly escorted Thea through his shop, introducing her to the barbers, all three of whom were Russian Jews. They had all come from their native lands including Nick who was from Athens. However he had lived in Montreal, Canada, prior to moving to Chicago. He had a wife and two children, from whom he was presently separated.

"You like my shop? You have the job."

While he spoke, Thea took stock of the other gal at work. She was resentfully watching Nick talking with another.

"Are you sure you require two manicurists here?"

"I offer you $200 a week plus you get extra in tips. You will do very well here, trust me."

The year was 1969 and Thea needed a job, plus the change she was in search of. It took Thea all of ninety days, to build up a substantial clientele. Her counterpart, Rosa, was most helpful with the barber shop procedure, and Thea was most confident with her new clients. Thea and Nick had a good business relationship, and he sought her companionship a few evenings a week. He'd dine her at the Greek Taverna in Greek town. They frequented the racetrack many times, though it was hard for her to be a participant in the crowd. She had been used to the members' enclosure and being a horse owner from an early age. It amused her to watch his eagerness at placing bets. He was a born gambler. He played poker as often as he could get his cronies together. He was addicted to any form of gambling, and it was probably the undoing of his family. He was a good friend to her, and that was all.

About six months had passed, when Nick confronted her with a request to move in with her. "Are you crazy?" she said, "I couldn't tolerate your thirst for cards every night."

"I help you pay the rent and the food, I take you out whenever you wish, you be the boss's girl."

"I'm nobody's girl, and I'm not cheap."

"You are a *basanos*. You know that?"

"What is a *basanos*?"

"There is no explanation in English. It means an endearingly aggravating and mischievous woman. This is my name for you."

Thea had worked in the barber shop for over a year now, and hadn't ever fraternized with her clientele. She was a woman of principle. A lot of manicurists were hungry to get ahead. Europeans came to the U.S. with the intention of saving their money, and eventually buying an apartment building for renting purposes, or having a business of their own. They could never aspire to self-fulfillment in their own countries. Divorcees were in search of business men, and younger girls hoped to meet Mr. Right. Thea wasn't categorized as any of these. Unfortunately at this time she didn't have a business sense at all. She had as yet to overcome her self-inflicted rule, to accept money lawfully from a client for services rendered. Nice women did not get anything for free. One Tuesday morning, she had completed a manicure at chairside and returned to her booth. Clients most times put a tip in her pocket, or in the basket on her lap, which contained her tools. She proceeded to go to the washroom, and in picking up her skirt, her tips fell out of her pocket. Among the dollar bills that fell to the floor, was a hundred dollar bill. She gasped at it! Thinking for a moment it was a joke, or play money of sorts, she examined it and saw it was for real. She instantly wanted to tell Nick, then she stopped in her tracks, and figured she would wait to find out for herself who it was.

One evening as she and Nick were having supper in her apartment, the phone rang.

"Hello, Thea, this is Irwin," the voice on the other end said. "I hope I'm not disturbing you. I wonder if your not busy this evening, may I see you for an hour or so."

"Whatever for?" was her reply.

"I'll explain when I see you. From where I stand now, it's a bit difficult."

"Yes, Irwin, by all means it's all right for you to visit." She gave him the directions to her flat and put the phone down.

"Nick, you had better make yourself scarce, I have company coming."

"*Basanos*, it's none of my business how you spend your time. But if that's a customer from the shop, I hope you know better than to encourage him socially. I don't like it."

"Yes, Nick, it isn't any of your business how I spend my time, and give me credit for my decorum."

Shortly after, Irwin entered her living room with a shy smile on his face.

"I see you have on a bowling shirt. Are you on your way for a game?"

"Supposedly I am. But I came to visit you instead."

He sat beside her on the couch and held her hand.

"I don't exactly know how to tell you this, without sounding foolish. You see in the past year I have gotten very close to you. You share your mother's letters with me, you speak of your travels, and I find you a joy to talk with. I would never interfere with your personal life, but would like very much to visit you once or twice a week on my so-called bowling nights. I never seem to relax as I should, and it would be so easy around you. Of course I'll pay you for your time. I don't expect to chat with you for free."

"Chat! That's all you want is to chat?"

"Of course, dear. You don't know how important this is to me."

Thea nodded her head skeptically as though he weren't playing with a full deck.

Irwin was an unassuming quiet middle-aged gentleman. He was very careful about his health and appearance. He owned a corrugated box factory (the kind Luke worked in) and planned to retire shortly. His yearly vacations were spent in Florida. It was the furthest from Thea's mind that a gracious prosperous man like him would want to have an affair with her. She felt a bit awkward over his request, and wouldn't have hurt him for the world.

"That reminds me. You didn't by any chance give me a hundred dollars on your last visit to the shop, did you?"

He smiled sheepishly.

"Yes I did, only because you work so earnestly, I thought you could afford to do something with the extra cash that you normally wouldn't do. Please accept it from my heart. Pretend as though it were from your father."

"You know it's funny you should say that. Not since Daddy has any man been generous with his money, without an ulterior motive. I've always felt unworthy of a gift of any kind."

"You shouldn't, my dear. You were brought up very differently to most I know, and you're selling yourself short."

"You're right, I am indeed."

When the time came for him to leave, Thea saw him to the door, and once more he folded money and discreetly tightened her fist over it.

"Please, Irwin, you don't have to do this."

"It gives me pleasure, and remember our visits don't go beyond these walls. I wouldn't hurt my dear wife or have her know I'm not bowling. I'll make an appearance from time to time with the boys on the team."

This time he had given her two hundred dollars, telling her to save it.

The next morning Nick called for Thea earlier than usual to take her to work. His curiosity had got the better of him.

"Good morning *basanos*. How was your evening?"

"Rather extraordinary, I'd say."

"Who was he, and what did he want?"

"I believe I detect jealousy in your voice, Nick."

"No point in my being jealous. You'd tell me to go to hell."

"You're right, I'm glad you answered your own question."

"*Basanos*, don't play smart with me. I know you pretty good, and this is no time to play around with the customers from the shop. The Jewish men are a clan, and you will become their topic of discussion."

"Oh Nick you are so insecure. What do you take me for? I wasn't born yesterday."

As time went on, Irwin's visits on Thursdays became beneficial for the two of them. He would sit beside Thea on the couch, and it was his turn to be the storyteller, while she listened with interest. He spoke in a whisper about everything from his adolescence to his present time. Now when he visited the barber shop, they exchanged few words as she manicured his arthritic hands. She continued to work in the chair next to him, as he watched her closely with a gleam in his eye. It was usually Nathan in the next chair; he was in the rag trade. Nick's suspicious eyes would follow Thea, as he silently wondered which of these men was sharing her company, the evenings she'd tell Nick to make himself scarce. Then again maybe it wasn't either of them. She was such an actress, one never knew where one stood with her.

It was a typical wintry morning in Chicago, as the snow accumulated rapidly outside the shop window. Thea's face was one of disapproval as she manicured Nathan.

"Thea! How would you like to be in Florida right now?"

"Anyplace, in preference to this."

Nathan turned around in his chair to get Nick's attention.

"Hey Nick! I'm capturing Thea for a week in Miami Beach. I'll take good care of her I promise. She needs a break from here." Nick's fiery eyes shifted with disapproval, between Thea and Nathan.

"She's a big girl, Sir. If that's what she wants, that's okay by me." Nathan winked smilingly at Thea. "I'd appreciate very much if you would play hostess to a group of my friends there. Will you?"

"Sure why not? I'm getting stale here. You're right I need a break."

That night when Thea returned home, she called Irwin. She was given a number by him in case of an emergency.

"Irwin, I'm leaving town for a week or so, I thought you should know not to come over for a couple of weeks. No! Nothing is the matter, I'll explain when I get back."

Nick tried desperately to talk Thea out of going with Nathan. Naturally it was a lost cause.

"Just because you never go anyplace, and never have enough money to take you there, doesn't mean I should suffer. I'm able to take care of myself. Nathan will show me a good time, and will pay all the expenses. I am so tired of counting my pennies constantly."

"Nothing is free, *basanos*, you are such a dreamer."

"If I didn't dream, I couldn't wake up in the morning."

Nathan and Thea flew out of O'Hare on a freezing night in February. They landed at the balmy Miami airport, where he was met by his friends. One couple was Jewish and middle-aged, close friends of both Nathan and his wife, who was vacationing in Las Vegas. And then there was Melvin, a paraplegic, who embraced Nathan with outstretched arms from his wheelchair. Melvin's Cadillac was designed for the handicapped driver. Nathan got seated in front with him, and Thea sat in the back seat with the Millers, Leah and Sy. After they had checked in at the Carriage House, they dined regally and Thea was most comfortable playing hostess with the mostest! Melvin then drove them all down the strip, and it was enchantingly different for Thea, as this had been her first visit to Miami. Their second night they dined and danced at the Fountainbleau. Nathan had never socially experienced Thea's company but he wasn't surprised at her abundant zeal for living. He was twenty-five years her senior, and she enjoyed his composure as he reminisced over his youth to her.

"Of course, my dear, I wasn't as fortunate as you were, to have experienced wealth and travel, but my parents gave us a lot of affection and a basic knowledge of values. Whereas you my sweet, were born with a silver spoon in your mouth, and readily settled for plastic. And you left home too early and too young. But you never fooled me. I'm sure working a barber shop isn't what your family wanted for you."

"Oh I could have done a lot worse, I enjoy doing what I do, and I'm not like several I know that deplore working for a living. I play, and don't have to answer to anyone but myself. That's not all bad."

During her week in Miami, they visited the Lion Country Safari, took a boat ride through the Everglades, and dined and danced at different night spots each evening. Of course it wouldn't have been complete without one visit to Stone Crab Joe's. It was wonderful!

Nathan had been a perfect host, and gentleman from start to finish. On their flight back, Thea momentarily excused herself while she freshened up a little in the powder room. She took only her makeup bag with her, leaving her purse on the seat behind Nathan.

When they returned it was snowing constantly. They managed to get a cab together. Nathan saw her home safely, and then continued his trip toward his Lake Shore Drive Apartments.

Thea retired past midnight, before which she had prepared her work clothes for the morning. In changing purses, she discovered a white envelope with her name written on it. This was a note enclosed.

"Thank you princess for a fantastic week of your company. My friends all loved you. Nathan." Attached to the note was one thousand dollars. Oh Lord! First it was Irwin, now Nathan. All this for being good!

No matter how carefree her attitude was at work, Nick seemed to get all the more disturbed over her.

One evening they dined in Greektown as often was the case. The floor show endlessly continued, as one belly dancer outbellied her counterpart. Thea and Nick had finished dinner, and the dance band finally gave them a chance to get on the floor together. Poor Nick pathetically shuffled around the floor, as Thea followed him. She couldn't help herself but compare him to Nathan's sophistication. Nick's heart was in the right place, but a barber he was, and a barber he would remain. He must have been born with scissors in his right hand, and a deck of cards in the other. He hungered for money constantly, and when he had some, he abused it.

From out of the blue he said, "*Basanos*, would you marry me?"

She stopped dancing and said. "Are you serious, or just plain crazy?"

"My wife has agreed to divorce me. She knows about you, and has consented to set me free."

"Dear Nicky, if you think for a minute that I would carry on where she leaves off, you're truly nuts. All you men need is a good mother, which I never was. So don't let's ruin a good business relationship. We work well together, and we can both be free together."

"What do you search for, *basanos*?"

"I don't know this minute. I take one day at a time."

"One day you will get old, and you will wish I was with you. We could take trips to Greece. My family likes you, we have a good business together. What more can anyone offer you?"

"Sure you'd play poker six days our of seven, we'd go to the track, you don't know how to relax, you grind your teeth in your sleep, and most important I don't love you."

"Then let's at least live together. The evenings you are occupied with your Jewish clients, you can give me the signal by leaving the bedroom light off. If you leave the light on, that means the coast is clear and I can come up. How's that sound?"

"You bastard, you'll be pimping for me next. Take me home right this minute, and if you're not careful I'll find another better job than I have with you. You don't own me."

When they had reached her apartment, Thea asked him upstairs for a while, as she wished to talk to him.

"Nick, I know you have always meant well toward me, but if we are to continue working together, you must refrain from meddling in my affairs. In my past the men I have associated with, I feel never allowed my sense of being. I allowed this because of my inadequacy. Ever since my teens, I was never asked my opinion, was always told what to do, and that I couldn't make it on my own. I have found out I am capable of living on my own, and I am not out of line in my affairs. So I don't need you to tell me what's good, and what isn't. We have only one life, and it's not right that we should be intimidated by another. If your wife wants a divorce now, living with me will not help your situation. Your differences began before we met, so it's hardly fair to me to say she's found out about us. You are not what could be termed as a dutiful husband or father. So maybe she'd be better off with alimony."

While Thea was speaking her mind, Nick nervously paced the floor chainsmoking as he did. He had stopped by the window facing the main street, where his car was parked.

"Shush, shush, I think I see my wife standing under the tree across the street, the street light is shining on her. She is looking up in this direction."

"It's 2:00 A.M. If it's she, she's as crazy as you are."

Thea stood alongside of Nick, watching a hesitant woman.

"Are you sure that is she?"

"After seventeen years I should be. She has threatened to come after you. She told me so, but I didn't think she would be so stupid."

"Enough is enough! I'm going down to settle this once and for all."

"No! No! Don't! She's crazy I tell you."

Thea ran down the stairs, and across the street, until she was face to face with the woman. The female lunged toward Thea with a huge

261

pair of scissors, fortunately for Thea she missed her target, swearing violently in Greek. Thea hadn't allowed for this drastic measure, and she swiftly got out of reach. Nick now beside the two of them, frantically grabbed the weapon, and pushed her aside. He took her by the arm and furiously shoved her in his car. The Greek language had never sounded so dramatic.

Phew! That was close, Thea thought as she saw them drive away. After an unrestful night, and no sleep at all, Thea languidly lay in her bubble bath with a strong Bloody Mary by her side. Her thoughts wandered back to Robert, and she wondered how much longer she'd be able to tolerate her frustration. She hadn't enjoyed making love since his tenderness. Just thinking about him turned her on. Her eyes were closed, but she felt she wasn't alone. Nick's appearance beside the bathtub didn't surprise her a bit.

"Oh! Not again, Nick. Don't you even rest on a Sunday?"

"After last night, who could rest? After I dropped that woman at her flat, I slept over at my cousins. I am so tired now."

"Make yourself a cup of coffee, and let me enjoy my bath." Within seconds he disrobed, and sat his scrawny body into her beautiful bubbles.

"Nick—Never on a Sunday," she yelled.

"With you anytime, *basanos*, you make me crazy, do you know that?"

His impatient penis throbbed to gratify his lust, as he groaned in ecstasy. He made love the same as he ate his food, hurriedly! It never took him any time to spend himself. What a waste of both, food and sex. Maybe he had been a rabbit in his last life. Thea stepped out of her wasted bath, and braced herself with a fresh turkish towel, and a splash of cologne. He sat stupified in the residue watching her move tantalizingly. She yielded to him once again, just for gratification.

That same evening Irwin surprised Thea by landing on her doorstep, with two dozen long-stemmed red roses. She was taken by surprise, and asked why he hadn't called first.

"I didn't get the chance to, my dear. I had to see you this evening. I'm being admitted into the hospital tomorrow for a checkup. I was concerned over your welfare, and I thought you needed this."

He set a roll of big bills on the coffee table and handed her the roses. She arranged the flowers in a vase, and asked him to be seated.

"I've been thinking seriously about you moving out of this neighborhood, and my purchasing a condo for you in the suburbs."

"Irwin dear, I don't drive, and a condo is a commitment. Living in the suburbs isn't for me. I like to be in town. But just the same that's very kind and thoughtful of you."

"How about getting you a small car then?"

"No Irwin, I don't enjoy driving and don't intend to drive.

"I'll tell you what. I would very much like to visit my family. They are now living in Australia. If you wish to pay my round-trip ticket there, I'd appreciate that a lot."

He promptly wrote her a personal check for the amount she quoted.

"But after your trip, you will still have to return to this flat."

"I'll cross that bridge when I come to it."

The following morning, a Monday, was her day off from the barber shop. Thea had begun to make plans to visit her mother and Lydia in Brisbane, Australia. She purchased her ticket, and informed her mother of her departure date. She asked Nick to live in her flat, and of course to pay the rent, until she returned. Nathan bought a brand new summer wardrobe for her. She purchased her American Express traveler's checks from the bank, and she was all set for her winter away from Chicago, going to the warmth of Brisbane.

Chapter Thirty-nine

It was winter of 1971 when she flew out of O'Hare by TWA to San Francisco and then Hawaii. Here she boarded the Qantas flight for Brisbane. In crossing the international dateline, it meant she left on a Wednesday, and lost out on Thursday in flight. So her arrival time was Friday morning. She hadn't slept a wink on the planes. She wouldn't have missed the transitional change from night into a breathtaking dawn. The sudden appearance of daylight, as it burst forth through the puffy clouds was awesome. At 6:00 A.M. the plane landed at Brisbane's tiny airport, which was situated some four miles from the city center. As the door of the aircraft opened, she immediately caught a glimpse of her mother and sister standing by the white fence, as they eagerly waved at her. After the hugging and kissing was over with, Thea passed through customs, and got seated in Lydia's Fiat to be driven to her home.

Lydia and her Hungarian husband, and Mother, lived in the neighborhood called Auchenflower. It was a pretty area and the houses and bungalows were built on high land that overlooked the residential area below. Brisbane was a holiday city that kept the rat race down to a comfortable crawl. After her lack of sleep, Thea welcomed a comfortable bed in which she slept the clock round with no disturbance. She was awakened by a strange sound of remarkable laughter of good humor, which repeated itself. Intrigued by it, she got out of bed around noon and went in search of it. Stepping out on the veranda that surrounded the house, on a nearby tree sat Australia's popular bird the "kookaburra" the sound of which was so human, she began to laugh back at it. She stretched her limbs to a new golden sunlit day, as Mother embraced her daughter after such ages.

"Oh Mum, it's so peaceful here, and so different to what I'm accustomed to."

Brisbane, Queensland, was founded as a convict settlement in 1824.

It stands on the banks of the winding Brisbane River. Prisoners from Britain were sent to this colony as punishment, calling it "down under."

Thea was rarely overcome by strange and new territory. Because of her eternal enthusiasm for new places and their people, she was insouciant toward circumstantial conditions. Her family of course was just the opposite and never stopped berating her for her "frivolity." All the pity that they couldn't recognize the adventure, without placing an obstacle in the way. Mother worried about matters before they even materialized, and she never did overcome this trait.

Lydia and her husband were the prosperous owners of the finest *patisserie*, the only one of its kind at the time, in the "valley," an area that boomed with immigrants. They both worked much harder here then they had in Britain. Mother had now retired. She devoted her time to the Red Cross. Thea was given a tour of these interests, and was introduced to the staff of both establishments.

Lydia drove her sister to Mount Cootha Forest Park, from which they got a panoramic view of the city. They breathed in the heavy aroma of the lofty eucalyptus trees, and the tropical shrubs dazzled with thousands of colored birds. The sisters meandered through the snake walk, which provided a changing view of the city and its suburbs. On the far horizon were mountains and the vast Pacific Ocean. This country was far removed from the rest of the world and had much to offer. Mother had planned in interstate tour for Thea whose knowledge was limited to the pages of an elementary geography book. All she had assumed of its history was that the first migrants traced their ancestry back to the British convicts. It had been a prison settlement, which opened up a big wave of immigration from Europe. The style of life here was cast in a British mould. The "Pommy" was used in a hostile manner and hurled at newcomers from the British Isles. Thea remembered from days gone by, at the Calcutta racetrack, of the animosity between the Aussies and the Pommy jockeys. Her father had always retained them both, and there was constant disagreement on the turf between the two nationalities. Reminiscent of Chicago, the Greeks here had carte blanche in the restaurant business. The Italians were in the construction business. Greeks and Italians, true to their peasant individualism, bought fruit growing properties, and they also owned cafes and grocery stores. Without the non-British migrant, the development of Australia would not have been possible. The same could be said about India. Both countries abhorred the interference of Britain now.

Mother and Thea traveled by bus to Melbourne, where they stayed with friends for a week. They saw the sights, after which they took a train to Sydney. Here they stayed with other friends from the past, a jockey who rode for her father and his wife, now retired in their homeland. Thea visited a public bar that unlike the pubs in England, was separated in three divisions: one for women, one for men, and one was mixed. She thought that unusual. The Sydney opera house was in the process of being built, in the middle of the beautiful harbor. Mother and Thea spent a day walking in the vast botanical gardens. After a week there, they continued to Adelaide in South Australia. Here they spent two weeks, the first with Thea's cousin Yvonne, and her family, and the second with some more racing folks from Calcutta, who had retired in their homeland. Adelaide, known as the city of churches, was unlike the others. This city had charm and catered to strollers, rather than motorists. The highlight of their trip here was to visit the hidden hills of the Barossa Valley, Australia's most celebrated wine region. Here the German influence was strong.

Their last but not least day trip was to Brisbane's State Fair, which was most spectacular, as it showed the promise of this new nation. The most skillful event of the day was sheep shearing.

Hundreds of sheep awaited their doom, while human hands sped the cold metal sheers through the thick wool, which left them naked of their beautiful pride, as it fell to the ground in mounds. The shorn sheep were separated to one side, their pink, taut, naked skins stretched over their carcasses. Mutton was a popular meal for the Australian. There was also a woodcutting race, and this brought about as much excitement as the bronco busting rodeo performance.

Mother and Thea went by bus to the Currumbin bird sanctuary. Here they strolled around the lush gardens, which were surrounded by hundreds of wild multicolored lorikeets. These were fed by visitors regularly at 4:00 P.M. The visitors were previously warned not to be afraid of the birds as they flew in from their wild bushland habitat. The sounding of tin plates causing a lot of noise attracted the attention of the lorikeets, which fluttered overhead and perched on heads and shoulders of those standing around. The extreme noise was reminiscent of Hitchcock's film *The Birds*. Thea's final visit was to the koala sanctuary. Here she held for the first time one of Australia's famous tree-dwelling marsupials. They feed exclusively on eucalyptus leaves and buds. She found it to be most timid as she posed for a photograph with it clutching on to her, like a baby. They can be held only by their wrists, or behinds, or else they cry.

The balmy weeks passed into months, and Thea enjoyed every minute of her holiday. Both Mother and Lydia had shown her the best the country had to offer. She even attended the first Australian tour of the famous French-Armenian singer Charles Aznavour.

Thea was adamant about leaving her family, but she felt she couldn't have made a living in this country on her own. She looked upon Australia as a man's country. But she was glad she'd had the opportunity of visiting.

Chapter Forty

Upon returning to Chicago, after living her family's life-style, Thea felt it to be an unacceptable letdown. She missed her mother's infinite counselling, which had taken her back in time, and what a long road she had traveled since then. To retrieve her self-respect in her workaday life was a bore. Within forty-eight hours of her arrival, she flew out to Lexington, Kentucky, to visit her son Marc, whom she hadn't seen in ten years. He was just a baby then, when Jason died, and the child looked upon Thea as a stranger. Marc was aware she was his mother, but it was just a word. He called his grandmother Mom, and Thea wasn't addressed by any name. Between the ages of ten and sixteen, Marc wasn't receptive toward his mother. One time when she called to speak to him on the telephone, she heard him tell his grandmother, "I don't want to talk to her. I don't know her. Tell her not to call me."

Thea never gave up on him. She sent him gifts and cash over the years. It wasn't because of guilt that she did this. She felt he was still hers no matter what. When he turned seventeen he acknowledged his mother for the first time.

Thea was remorseful for not having supplied her son with a more fortunate foundation. Her father probably would turn in his grave, if he knew his grandson had been subjected to such a mother. But if it was any consolation to Thea, her son was surrounded with love from the Travis family. In the past the family had blamed Thea for her negligence as a parent. But as the Travis boys had been degenerate, the heat had lessened on her these ten years later.

Her mother-in-law welcomed Thea. One could only assume that the grievance she may have held once was of no consequence now. Marc was apprehensive when his mother made her sudden appearance. He was cautious at first, but then he grew curious. Thea brought him gifts from Australia. He was particularly interested in the boomerang. Mother and son walked to a field nearby to test it. He threw it as far as his strength would allow, and like most little boys of ten, marveled at the flat curved stick returning to him in full circle.

"Wow, I never seen anything like this before!" he said. This gave Thea the opportunity to hug her little boy. The ice was broken, as he shared his little world of fishing rods, and BB shotgun, and they walked to the river where he fished with other boys his age. Thea sat on the bank for sometime wishing she could take him back to Chicago with her. But she was aware this was not possible. His grandparents had custody of him, and he shouldn't leave his home, the only one he was comfortable in. The life here in Kentucky was his security. Besides Thea had to work, and she still wasn't responsible for her own life, let alone her son's. Thea stayed in Kentucky just long enough to get acquainted with Marc. Then she returned to her job in Chicago.

From here on discontentment set in. Her world had been a product of thought, a creation of the mind. She created her world by these thoughts. So in actual fact she made her own heaven or hell. Nobody owed her a thing, she owed it to herself. She lived precariously, and unless she changed her way of thinking, her life would stay precarious.

She couldn't tolerate Nick or the barber shop much longer. It wasn't enough. Poor Irwin spent more of his life in the hospital and less with her. Maybe she should leave Chicago and try some other city. But she was still running from herself, and she wasn't aware of it as yet. She hadn't achieved a business sense, just a living.

One Sunday afternoon, she received a call from the Michael Reese Hospital. The nurse asked for her by name.

"I regret to inform you Irwin Glass passed away in his sleep early this morning. He spoke often about you, and asked me to notify you immediately, if anything should happen to him. I truly am sorry, Thea."

So am I, thought Thea. Poor dear Irwin had been her only confidant. More the pity that he hadn't provided for her, other than moving her to a condo in Des Plaines, Illinois.

It was Thea's fortieth birthday, and she celebrated by having a few of her friends over for a curry dinner. Her apartment overflowed with guests, booze, and food—a fun time was had by all. Not until the wee hours did the last of the people disperse, leaving her with the cleaning up.

She didn't feel any the worse for having reached this age, in fact she felt rather comfortable with it. She felt in good spirits, in more ways than one, as she sipped on the last of the champagne.

She heard the door buzzer from the main entrance. At first she was reluctant to answer, as it wasn't the hour for callers. But when it persisted, she took the elevator down to the main lobby. True she had consumed more than her full share of champagne, but not enough to be hallucinating. She stood fixated behind the glass door in absolute horror.

"Oh no! How did you find me? I won't let you in, go away."

Luke demanded that she open up immediately.

Intimidated, she did.

"Happy birthday, honeybear, long time no see."

"How did you find me, and as far as I'm concerned the longer the better. I'm sorry, Luke, you are not welcome here."

He smiled sheepishly, "Mother gave me your address, but she said your phone was unlisted because of me, so I couldn't call before coming."

"I swear the price I have to pay, to keep in touch with my son. I told her I wasn't to be bothered by you ever again, and she gives you my address. Now you had better forget it, and not cause me embarrassment."

"Do you have company? I must talk to you, and then I promise I'll leave."

"Unfortunately I know you better than that, Luke."

He followed her into the elevator, as she looked at his dissipation. The years had been rough on him, and he looked a lot older than Thea. He stood pathetically in her living room, as though he were a stranger.

"Hey, bear, you've done okay for yourself. You must have found you a rich sugar daddy."

If only he knew, she thought.

"Yes, I'm doing just fine on my own, and I'm keeping it like that, I have more than one sugar daddy and a good job. If it's money you want, forget it."

"Shame on you, honeybear, I never asked you for money."

"That's right you didn't. You stole from wherever you could, you cleaned out my purses, and even my piggy bank I had with half dollars, you took them all, and filled it with pennies. Get away from me, Luke."

"Bear, we've been through a lot together. After Jason's death, it all went bad for us. I'll always love you, bear."

"Yes you brothers caused me a lot of grief. It's all in my past and I'd like to keep it there, forgotten. You've never loved anybody, you use women. I buried you along time ago. It was a nightmare."

"I wrote your mother in London, and she replied to me from Australia, telling me she wouldn't care to give me your whereabouts, and that she was sorry that Jason and I were ever in your life. So I wandered around until I met Kimberly. She tended bar and provided me with free drinks, so we became friendly, and I married her. She has five children by previous husbands, and drinks more than I do. She knows I love you, and when we make love, I call out your name. So I would appreciate if you would talk to her, and convince her that you do not want me back. She always says I'll return to you, and leave her. I don't love her like I do you, but we are married.''

"Damn! Luke you have a nerve, she has a worse problem than you do, what can I ever say to a woman I don't know? The only way you have a hope in hell, is if you both seek professional help.''

"She won't, but she'll listen to you. She's a smart woman.''

"She couldn't be that smart, to have married you, to outdrink you and have five brats by somebody else. I realized there was little to choose between you and Jason. I deplore alcoholics, both you guys drained me of my energy, and my pride, the little I had. Why don't you take her to Kentucky? You always have to run home to Marmie, so take her with you. Your mom always helps her boys.'' The stereo softly played "Misty" in the background, and Luke took Thea in his arms and shuffled around the floor. He kissed her ear.

"This song will always remind me of the night I sang this to you, Gosh! How I loved you and wanted you so bad.''

Thea pushed him away. "Oh no you don't. Grow up Luke, all that smooth talk is old hat. It won't wash anymore. I'm going to bed, you may sleep on the sofa and leave when the dawn comes up. Please do not bother me, I am extremely tired.'' Time wasn't of any consequence as she slept soundly. She didn't awaken when she felt Luke's warm body around her. Of all the men in her life, he had been the most persuasive, and alert in the mornings. Fully aware of her weakness for making love at this time, he penetrated her. She didn't even open her eyes, as they repeatedly culminated. Only he could arouse her so erotically. Her desperate urgency had surrendered to his needs, and he was victorious one more time.

"I can't fight you, you bastard. We know each other too well.'' She got out of bed, and left it to him. As surely by now he was fatigued enough.

Thea sat in the kitchen with her pot of tea, thinking of ways to get him back with his wife. Now that he had found her again, there was no telling when he would repeatedly land on her doorstep. She had been playing with the idea of going to California. *Now was a good chance to disappear*, she thought. To put a peace bond on him again, didn't stop him, she had already done that in the past.

Thea periodically thought about Howard and Laura's welfare, which her mother kept her informed about from time to time. They were now living on the East Coast someplace. Was it Boston?

"Where is my address book? I'm sure they live in Boston, here it is. Now what time is it there? I could call Howard and enquire about Laura. He can only hang up on me, but I don't think he will. I hope I don't get his wife, she always has to get in on the act. Somehow I feel Laura is not doing as well as she should." Thea dialed the number. The phone was ringing, and Thea was tempted to hang up, but she didn't. Howard's familiar voice answered.

"Hello Howard, it's me your ex-wife. Is Laura all right?"

"Lord, this must be telepathy you're calling now. She's all right I suppose, other than the fact she ran away and married an irreputable chap against our wishes. I am now in the throes of nullifying the marriage."

"Is there anything I can do to help?"

"Well! I would appreciate it if you could take her off my hands, for as long as it takes to be rid of this awful man. But then again, she may not agree to go to you. Do you think you could do that for me?"

"Can I speak to her right now?"

"I'm afraid not. She's terribly stubborn." He snickered as he said, "I wonder who she takes after? Unfortunately Laura is twenty, going on twelve, which makes things even more difficult."

"Well, Howard, I'll leave you my phone number. Please feel free to call after you have spoken to her. I am planning to leave for California, so don't make it long, I'll wait till I hear from you."

As Thea hung up the phone, she discovered Luke standing in the hallway. "What's this about you going to California? Who were you talking to?"

"I was talking to Howard, my daughter is coming to live with me Luke, so you had better disappear."

"I promise I will, if you would just condescend to see Kim."

"And if I refuse?"

"I know you won't, because it will get me off your back."

The snow was knee high, as Thea and Luke ploughed toward uptown Chicago. Thea cringed as they neared his flat. She followed him up the dismal stairway, through the ramshackle abode, as though she were a social worker on a case. Luke promptly disappeared into another room, as Thea awkwardly stood in the front room, which was cluttered with laundry baskets, a baby's crib bed, and shabby furniture that had seen better days. Shortly after, he returned with Kimberly by his side. She had the traces of what might have been an attractive woman at one time, until she had given way to dissipation. She spoke intelligently and wasn't reproachful, as she examined Thea from head to foot.

"Kim, you wished to meet Thea, so here she is."

"A bit rich for your blood, you were aiming high, country boy. I'm sorry you have caught me at a disadvantage, Luke's been gone too long. I reckon you two have been in the sack together. I know my husband well. If he's not home he's in a bar, but he never stays out the night."

Thea was at a loss for words as she watched the pathetic woman wandering around the room with a cigarette hanging out of her mouth.

"Well I've been asked to come here to speak to you. But I can't imagine how I can help, or what I could say that would be of any consolation to the two of you. We do have choices you know, and apparently this is your choice."

"Your damn right, Miss Prissy, with your fur coat and fancy language, I guess you think now he's found you again, he'll leave me. But you're wrong. He's my husband, and I am a damn good lay. He could play us both up the middle, but that's the risk I have to take."

"Kimmie, you're wrong, she doesn't want me. I asked her to come here to tell you, so you wouldn't be threatened anymore."

Thea thought it wise to change the conversation.

"That's a nice watch you have, I have one just like it."

Kim snickered, as she took it off her wrist.

"It's yours, Luke brought it to me as a peace offering, so I'd keep quiet in your presence. I don't want any handouts from you. Next time he visits, be sure he doesn't steal more than a watch." Thea took the watch from the woman, and excused herself, but she had to leave. As she walked down the hallway, Kimberly shouted after her.

"You'll never get him. I'm pregnant with his baby."

Thea turned up her eyes, and said to Luke, "You are a sorry sight."

"Well, husband, I guess she fucked you for the last time. You could never aspire to the likes of her. She left you, and it was my bad luck to find you."

Luke chased after Thea on the street, and got her by the arm.

"Bear I'll see you later, okay?"

"No Luke, you won't! She's right. I am too rich for your blood. You can't afford me. Besides which I couldn't stop at you. Life goes on to bigger, and better things."

As Thea quickened her pace toward a taxi, she shuddered at the thought of having subjected herself to such degeneracy.

A week had past, and Thea was waiting for Howard's call. He finally called late one evening, saying Laura had agreed to visit her estranged mother. Thea had given her notice at work, and was home in the late afternoon. Once more Luke returned on her doorstep. She was furious with him, and told him to get out.

"Bear I've left her. Her husband before me showed up, and I have no place to go."

"What do you think I'm running? Try the YMCA. My daughter cannot find you here, besides I don't want to see your face."

"Listen to me, honeybear. I have a plan. When Laura gets here, we can all go back to Marm's. This way she will meet her brother Marc, wouldn't you like to see two of your children together?"

"You won't stop at anything will you? You have no morals or scruples. Laura and I have to get acquainted; she doesn't have a sound image of me. She is a young woman now, and you will be in the way. How am I supposed to explain you? It won't work. Don't you understand? I want nothing to do with you. You have to get out of my life, once and for all."

After he left, she thought visiting Kentucky wasn't a bad idea. She would take Laura to visit Marc, and take her trip to Los Angeles at a later date.

Chapter Forty-one

Thea anxiously awaited the arrival of Laura at Lexington airport. It had been twelve years since she had seen a child that hadn't said a word to her, in her mother's living room in London.

At last she recognized this vision of beauty get off the plane. She was five feet seven inches tall, slim and graceful, with her flowing auburn hair blowing in the wind on a beautiful sunny day. Her enormous hazel eyes with long lashes, squinted at the sunshine, as she smiled hesitatingly in Thea's direction. She had an extraordinary likeness to the actress Jane Seymour. She was taller than Thea, as she leaned forward to kiss her.

"I wondered if you would recognize me."

"Of course I would. You are my daughter, no matter what."

She suddenly began to cry, and Thea's heart went out to her.

"It seems so strange to meet you as a friend, when you are my mother, and we know so little about each other. You couldn't possibly understand how I feel this moment. I have lived with Daddy all of my life, and he doesn't know me at all. What he is doing now is unthinkable. I love my husband, and I can't visit him in jail, so I've been shipped to you. Don't you think that cruel?"

"Laura my dear, I am in the dark about the details of this man. But who am I to judge? If you father thinks he is not good for you, then you must trust his better judgment. I'm sure you will not stop at this man's attention for you. When I was your age I married Daddy. To this day, I truly don't know why I left him. Heaven knows I've kept company with a slew of reprobates. Not one could have been compared with your father. I was addicted to men like a nymphomaniac. I sure paid in full for my foolishness, but life goes on. At the time it didn't seem foolish, or smart, it just was."

"Well! I hope I don't follow your course of events. Whenever I do something that he disapproves of, he lashes out at me and says, 'You remind me more of your mother daily.' That isn't fair. You were not around when I was growing up. Suppose I never wise up.''

"Eventually we all do my dear, some delay the process because of their little ego trips of stubbornness. You're not the first or the last to get impulsive.''

"Daddy says I've never grown up.''

"Ha! I haven't either. What is grown up anyway, being careful? Well we are not all blessed with such a temperament. Your Aunt Lydia still thinks I'm retarded.''

Mother and daughter both giggled, while getting on the bus together. The bus ride took all day. They finally reached the Travis house at the bottom of the hill. Marc was standing on the porch, astonished at the arrival of both his estranged mother, and half-sister. Laura was nine years his senior, and acknowledged him immediately.

"Hi! Marc, I'm your big sister, I've heard a lot about you.''

Marc on the other hand showed no enthusiasm, he turned around and fled to his room, locking the door behind him.

Mother Travis now joined the two women, excusing her grandson's behavior. He was confused at suddenly being told he had a big sister. No sooner had Thea and Laura got seated in the living room, when Luke appeared through the garage entrance.

"Well! Fancy you being here, and you must be Laura. Your mother has spoken a lot about you to me over the years.'' Laura queried his presence, but kept silent. Thea overlooked him, as she said to herself, "This is every bit his home and I should have known he'd intrude on this visit.''

Marc now curiously opened his door and showed acceptance of Laura, as he gestured her toward their privacy in his room. Although these children were both from incredibly different backgrounds, they felt a kinship with each other. Thea stood behind the closed door and eavesdropped on their conversation.

"What happened to your daddy, Marc?''

"I think he went to heaven. I didn't know him. Who is your daddy?''

"My daddy was our mother's first husband. She left him and married your daddy.''

"Why do you think she did that? And why don't we have the same dad?''

"Because my dad is English, and yours was American.''

"It's all very confusing, I don't understand any of it. She may be

276

our mom, but she wasn't with you, and she wasn't with me, so that doesn't make her a mom at all. My grandma is my mom, and I think Hope is my sister.''

"No silly, she's your aunt. Our mom isn't that old.''

Thea wanted to be included in their quest for knowledge. She needed to share in their disillusionment, but she felt so wretchedly intimidated. Her desire was to go through the closed door and hug the two of them, but how could she do that, having already deprived them of mother in their impressionable years? She'd only fumble, so she had to leave things as they were, unexplained.

The Kentucky life-style was disconcerting for Laura, and she became rebellious toward the family, all of whom were strangers to her. She demanded that Thea send her back to Boston, which was her home. So this was the second time she requested her father immediately. Thea could not abide by her daughter's demands. Their brief reunion had brought about estrangement and frustration to both women. There was little doubt in Thea's mind the whole episode of their meeting would be related to her father in detail. Thea would be held less in his estimation than she already was. Their parting of ways would be indefinite.

This brings Thea back to the start of this story. Luke accompanied her on the Greyhound bus to Indiana. She received the money from her mother at the Western Union office, and they continued on to Chicago. She had got him back to the end of the line, so they were now even. They went their separate ways from the terminal.

A week later Thea took the Santa Fe all the way to Los Angeles.

Chapter Forty-two

It was a very hot afternoon when Thea's train pulled into Los Angeles's Union Station.

She was grateful to be met by her sister-in-law, Hope, and her new-found friends Craig and Dana, all of whom were ''gay.'' Craig was to become her closest friend and confidant in the future. They were all a jovial group as they ushered Thea with her baggage out to the parking lot. Driving through Los Angeles seemed a lot different to any other city in the U.S. The traffic was wild on the freeway, and the palm trees with clustered tufts were comical. Hope had lived here a year, and taught school. She didn't care for the city but her life-style was more favorably tolerated here, than back home in Kentucky. Thea complacently took her residence in the gay ghetto off Hollywood Boulevard. It didn't fit her image of Hollywood, and she was a bit disappointed with her introduction to Tinsel Town.

As the weeks passed, she discovered her friends were not partial to full-time jobs, and living on unemployment seemed to be the trend. Thea's mother provided for her until she obtained a job in a barber shop in Beverly Hills. After six months of a lackadaisical existence she had her furniture shipped from Illinois to her own apartment on Las Palmas Avenue, which also was off the Boulevard.

Thea had worked at the barber shop in Beverly Hills a year. Although it hadn't been as carefree as working with Nick, it was different. She had met interesting clients, and work to her had always been playtime. She lived in the moment, and never planned a future. Her restlessness had set in one more time. Although she had never worked at anything other than beauty and barber shops, she thought if her friend Craig could acquire versatility, why shouldn't she? Being gay, which she wasn't, was advantageous.

One evening as they sat around the kitchen table, Craig was scanning the want ads of the newspaper for himself, when he exclaimed, "Listen to this, Thea, it sounds perfect for you: 'Personable well traveled gentleman of means, retired at age fifty-eight, a writer living in Carmel, is in search of lady in early forties with similar background, willing to travel and be a companion. Call . . .' "

"Oh Craig! You're not serious. That sounds positively kinky."

Craig laughed. "Let's call the number, and find out more. You would make an interesting companion, and he is a man of means. He's a writer, and you love to be on the go."

Craig dialed the number, and Thea was thankful the line was busy. He tried again, as Thea listened in on the extension.

"I'm calling on behalf of my friend, because she doesn't think this ad is for real. But I know if you met her, she'd be your choice."

"I know she's listening into our conversation, so why don't you let her speak for herself, young man?"

"I'd like to know more about this job, and meet you before I involve myself any further."

"So you should, and I do have a list of ladies in front of me, that are equally interested. So I am having interviews for the next couple of weeks at the Beverly Hills Hotel. I can set up an appointment for us to meet if you wish."

"On second thought, I don't think I'm interested, but thanks just the same."

"Well if you wish special consideration, why don't you have lunch with me on Tuesday."

"No thank you, I'm sure one of your other candidates would be a lot more appreciative."

Before Thea had time to complete the sentence, Craig grabbed the phone from her hand, and said. "Her name is Thea Travis and she will be delighted to have lunch with you next Tuesday. I'll give you her phone number, in case there is a change of plan. By the way what is your name, and could she have a description of you?"

"You must be a very good friend, to take such interest in the lady in question. My name is Conrad Schaffer, I'm five eleven, I dress western style, so tell your friend to look for a handsome cowboy at the bar of the hotel. Better yet, you are invited also, so you can satisfy your curiosity on her behalf. I'll be there at noon, good-bye."

After Craig hung up, he laughed hilariously, making Thea furious.

"Ah come on sweet thing, you need something different, I'm sure it will work out to your advantage."

"Bloody hell Craig. He sounds like a twit. He probably has a year round ad in the paper. This city has its share of creeps and crazies. You better check him out. I've never done anything so weird before."

"He sounded like Richard Burton to me. I tell you what? If you don't like him, then I'll work him over."

"Well one doesn't know anymore these days. Since being friends with you, I have found out more about the opposite sex in this country then I have ever experienced in my lifetime. He may have his days for boys, too. Just let me know, okay?"

Thea and Craig were dressed for the occasion as they entered the Beverly Hills Hotel at exactly noon. They hadn't got as far as the lobby, when Craig immediately recognized Conrad Schaffer. He was slim and tall, wore a cowboy hat and shirt, a kerchief around his neck, and drain-pipe jeans that hugged his tight ass. The jingle-jangle spurs on his boots were a riot, as he came forward to introduce himself. Thea amusedly smiled at this character. Was he for real? But then that could have been said of the other personalities around them. "Enchanté Madame," he said.

A cowboy even speaks French, that's a laugh! Thea thought.

Craig shook his hand, as he kissed Thea's. She was going to enjoy this.

"Shall we have a drink before lunch? Or would you rather have lunch right away? Your preference Madame."

Thea felt a challenge was in order. He was too smug for his own good and needed to come down a peg or two. As lunch commenced, Thea discovered he was intelligent. His conversation roused her skepticism. His looks even more so. Craig, however, assumed a prankish "Puck" attitude from *A Midsummer Night's Dream*, who weaved spells and enchantments about these mortals. He was so taken with the unusual hotel ambience, he had forgotten the reason for being here. Conrad's astute conversation distracted Craig completely, so Thea had to keep her wits about her. After lunch was completed, Conrad suggested they all drive out to his home. Craig by now was sure that he could be trusted, so he excused himself, and thought Thea would enjoy the drive there, as she hadn't ever visited Carmel. They said good-bye on the steps of the hotel entrance, and each went their separate ways. Thea and Conrad

280

got into his sports Alfa Romeo, and he gave a performance, expecting flattery, which of course he didn't receive.

"So tell me a little bit about yourself. How long have you been in the U.S.? Did you marry a serviceman?"

"I've been in the country twelve years. I'm still an English citizen. No I didn't marry to come here, my husband was in the navy, and he died. I first visited America when I was fourteen, with my mother and sister. We lived in New York City."

"How long ago were you in England?"

"I visit at least every other year. I've lived in Chicago most of the time, and thought I'd try it here."

He looked askance at her.

"Why did you answer my ad?" he said.

"I didn't! Craig did. He was curious."

"You thought it weird. Do you think I'm weird?"

"I haven't formed my opinion as yet. It's still too early to tell."

"Do you have children or any present commitments?"

"I have had children, none are living with me. I work as a manicurist in a barber shop."

"Do you think I could do with a haircut?"

"I don't think it matters what I think, but yes, you need one badly."

He chuckled. "I like you Thea Travis, you're honest, and you've been around, yet you're very tactful. Are we near where you work?"

"If you go left on the corner of Little Santa Monica it's close by."

He swirled his car, and as he did, Thea informed him he required an appointment for a haircut.

"Oh I trust you, you can give me one."

They arrived at the barber shop, and she introduced him to the owner, Sal. Sal was working on a client, and he smiled at Thea as he shook Conrad's hand. "I'm giving this gent a hair trim, Sal, he needs one badly." She was careful about the length she took off, because he obviously was proud of the shabbiness.

Conrad drove along the beautiful Pacific Coast Highway.

"I'll show you some beautiful coastline, like you've never seen. Thea I'll be straight with you, and I'd like you to be the same with me when I get through. I need a companion like you, as since my wife's death five years ago, I've had difficulties in meeting a woman with a brain. I'd expect you to travel with me, and accompany me wherever I go. I don't work for a living, as I took care of my assets well before

281

retirement set in. I drive to Santa Barbara often, I have a hippie son living there. I enjoy dining in good restaurants. I won't be paying you a salary, but you will always have cash on you. In other words I'd expect all the wifely duties, minus the contract. How does that sound?"

"How long is my probation period to be?"

He laughed! "I hadn't thought of it that way."

"Well I'm sure you expect your ad to pay off. This isn't the first time you've interviewed housefraus. I'm not that naive."

"Let's play it by ear. It's still too early to make demands on each other."

"I think after our visit to your home, you had better drive me home to Hollywood. I feel I don't fit the bill."

He came to an abrupt stop on the highway shoulder, and kissed her on her cheek. "You don't mean that do you? Give it a try. I don't mean to be presumptuous. That's my old air force colonel arrogance."

"Are you a writer? If so, have you published?"

"Not yet I haven't, but I hope to. Why do you ask?"

"Because I'm thinking of writing a novel."

"Good! Maybe we can do it together. Did you know Carmel is a writers' haven?"

"No! I didn't, neither did I expect to stay. I never prepared my overnight bag."

"Oh I'm sure I can provide you with a toothbrush, and pajama top."

"Well I have a job to report to, and an apartment to maintain, I am not in the habit of spending nights away."

"Boy! You drive a hard bargain, lady."

"That's my prerogative. We have nothing in writing." He impatiently stepped on his gas peddle, turning around toward Hollywood. When they had reached the Boulevard, he parked outside the restaurant Musso Frank, which was popular with celebrities. It was early afternoon and he ordered a couple of old-fashioneds as they were seated at a table.

"I come here often for a good bowl of soup. But you may have whatever you desire."

"That sounds good. I leave it to you." After they had finished their soups, he ordered a Dover sole, saying they would have an early supper. He hailed a few characters that passed from time to time, including talking to the "Little Feat" musicians, who were not familiar to Thea.

Thea had been in the company of this Don Juan all day long, and she saw him to be a lonely individual, with a desperate desire to fantasize.

He had been self-sufficient before his middle age. He had a tremendous enthusiasm for the good life, and could afford its pleasures. He also was a drinker! His wife had died of cancer. She had been a beautiful blonde, successful in her own right. They'd had a spoilt son who relied on Daddy, who paid for his decadent life in a commune in Santa Barbara. Conrad wore custommade clothes, most of which were purchased at the popular cowboy shop "Nudeo's." He was in a rut, but would tackle the fast lane if given the opportunity.

They arrived at Thea's apartment.

"This is most colourful and in good taste," he said looking around the flat. He sat himself down on a lazyboy, while Thea placed a glass of Drambue in front of him. She then placed a record on her Grundig Majestic Stereo, and got into comfortable lounge attire. She moved around the living room with grace. He stretched his arm out toward her, from where he sat.

"Do I make you so nervous that you can't stop pacing the floors?"

"Not at all, I'm glad to be back in my surroundings." He got up from the chair and held her close to him.

He cupped her chin in the palm of his hand, which was warm to the touch. "I think you've been living alone too long, my dear."

His grey eyes looked directly into hers. As they came closer, she felt his lips upon hers. They kissed passionately, until he was roused and she willingly reciprocated. Not letting go of each other, they tantalizingly danced to "Moonglow" in a fixed embrace. He nibbled on her earlobe, backing her toward the bedroom, and onto the kingsize bed.

"Thank you for not turning me away. Now I need your sensuous, lithesome flesh around me tonight more than ever." His foreplay was delectable, and his erection most enjoyable. He drove her crazy within seconds. He was an excellent lover, and she hadn't submitted so soon to a man, since being with Robert. They made love all night long, until it became painful for any further eroticism. They were blissfully asleep, when at 9:00 A.M. the telephone disturbed them. Thea jumped! Had she missed work? No, it was Wednesday. It was Craig inquiring after her welfare.

"Just say yes or no. Is he with you?"

"Yes."

"Enjoy! Speak to you later."

Conrad was half awake with a smile on his face.

"That was Craig checking up on you, and you said I was still here."
Thea bounced herself on his chest in her nudity, and rumpled his hair.

"You're so damn smart. Sure he's concerned about me. He's my true friend."

"But he doesn't fuck you, does he?"

"Shit on you! I'm as hungry as a bear, let me fix us a breakfast," she said.

"Not before we take a shower together," he said to her.

"I don't trust you, you'll start being lecherous once more, and we will never get out of here."

Conrad's home was situated on a hilltop surrounded by evergreen trees, and manicured bushes around a green lawn fringed with flower beds. This was a far cry from the ghetto in Hollywood where she had lodged herself for nearly two years.

The interior of his home was packed to capacity, with mementos from Europe, and Southeast Asia. Classical music was piped throughout the house. Conrad was a man of many moods, and Thea feared he required much variety to fulfill his craving appetite. This was often the case when a man went through the Peter Pan syndrome.

Their first weeks were similar to most hyped-up romances. They lived on an eternal merry-go-round, ate lobster and drank Remy Martin every evening. His life wasn't in jeopardy, but hers was, and she knew it. A host of females of all ages and nationalities were still responding to his ad in the Herald. Thea never trusted him, and was sure he interviewed several women while she was at work. He probably had a file of phone numbers in his desk, under lock and key. So to justify her claim, she sold her flat and belongings, gave up her job, and became a twenty-four hour nursemaid, by moving in with him. She never loved him or had that magical attraction she had with Hans and Robert. But at the time he provided the excitement she eternally craved. If things didn't work out as they should, she could always return to Craig. Though he had warned her of the mistake she had made.

The weeks passed rapidly while Conrad planned their days. He golfed once, sometimes twice a week. She rarely accompanied him. He did his grocery shopping at Blandenburg Air Force Base, while she waited in the car. A bowl of Anderson's pea soup was a must each week. All summer they swam at the beach close to his home, and in the evenings he would cook trout and salmon on the outside grill. He was indeed a wine connoisseur, and replenished his stock to full capacity. In the mornings they would stroll by the tourist trap of gift stores, and drive to Santa Barbara for more of the same. Conrad would purchase overseas newspapers and read them thoroughly, checking mostly his investments in Switzerland, which also arrived from time to time in the mail. He chose Thea's clothes commendably as they shopped at the better boutiques. He was a distinctive dresser, and said to her, "I enjoy a well adorned woman beside me when we go out together." She noticed he had few friends, except for a couple of English neighbors, whom Thea was friendly with. Conrad never rushed their time together. They held on tenaciously to their illusions, fearful they would be parted in their sleep. By the time fall came around, they'd made their nights into day. They listened to music as they lay on the rug in the living room, until they were thoroughly absorbed in a cloud of alcohol. They watched the new dawn creep through the windows, and the birds chirp their own delightful sound. They made love recklessly.

One evening Conrad was driving her around the beautiful Carmel hills, when he took a sharp curve leading to the Highlands Inn Hotel. He hadn't informed Thea of his reserving a suite here for the weekend. He was a man of surprises, and so she always accepted them with delight. They walked up the garden stairs with beautiful winter foliage on either side, and to the front desk, where he signed them in. They were shown to a luxurious suite overlooking the rock formation as the waves beat against them. She stood on the balcony taking in this beauty. Not since she was a little girl living at the Mount Lavinnia Hotel in Colombo, had she seen such a vista. He joined her presently as they both absorbed the view all around them.

"Why didn't we bring any clothes, Conrad?"

"I have one bag in the trunk of the car that I packed for us both. I wanted to see your expression when we came up here. Now that I have, the bellhop will deliver our bag."

"You are a rascal! What's next?"

"Dinner and dancing downstairs. I have a special table booked with a view like this."

They took a shower together, and sipped some Harvey's Bristol Cream as they sat on the plush rug in front of the fire in their room.

As he promised they were enjoying a wonderfully prepared dinner by candlelight. Thea hadn't sat in such ambience while living in this country. All the diners had a look of prosperity. She hadn't asked what a night like this cost him. But they were here for two nights and two days, and she was going to enjoy every minute of it. On their second night, Conrad had toasted many a glass of champagne, and Thea went along with it as usual, until he presented her with a gorgeous diamond ring.

"I'm asking you to be my wife, Thea. I think you have earned our year together, and if you can tolerate it further say yes!"

"Oh Conrad, it's beautiful, and I don't know what to say." She wept! But not from excitement, more from confusion. She didn't really want to marry for the third time. She knew if Robert had been free, he would have been her choice. Yet she hadn't enjoyed freedom. She was meant to share with somebody, but it wasn't Conrad. She was aware of her feelings, yet she said yes to him.

"Good, we'll go to Vegas, and then to Britain and Switzerland. We'll call your mother tomorrow and tell her we are coming."

"No! Mummy can't take anymore of my imprudence. It wouldn't be fair to her."

"I'll talk to her my sweet, don't you worry your pretty little head over it."

They married at the Chapel of the Stars on the Vegas strip.

It was January of 1973 and after a week of extraordinary extravagance, they returned to their quiet abode in Carmel.

Conrad had begun to plan their trip to Europe. Thea didn't wish to get a new passport in her new name. There would be too much redtape attached for new papers, besides she had traveled extensively on her present one, which she wished to keep. This disturbed her husband, and it didn't take much to trigger him off.

"We were planning to visit Mexico, why don't we do that instead?"

"Because I have to go to Europe, and I thought we could visit your family on the way."

It turned out that they didn't go anywhere. For this Thea was as much to blame as Conrad. With each relationship in which she trapped herself, she entered a world of separateness. She was as crippled as her mates, with her creations and unconscionable desires. In the years gone by she had frivolously delighted in her escapades. She hadn't ever provided for her middle-aged years. Age was unacceptable, however unavoidable. Conrad lived in fear and dread of getting older. He drank even more than before and started to go out alone. One night he hadn't returned home, so Thea called his son, whom she had as little as possible to do with. The boy was so high on dope, he laughed on the phone.

"Sure Dad's here, we just got through with a ménage à trois scene. You're no fun Thea. Dad's on speed, he's my father."

Craig was at Carmel by 6:30 A.M. to collect Thea bag and baggage, and take her home with him. He didn't say a word as he looked around the house making sure she hadn't forgotten anything.

"I don't intend to make a repeat trip here," he said to her.

Thea never looked back, as she got in his Mustang, and they drove the scenic route to Hollywood.

Her first night back in "gay heaven" the two of them got happily inebriated on Black Russians at the Gaslight Club, a gay bar owned by Craig's lover, Dana. They continued to another called Oil Can Harry's. This was a vast room lined with huge mirrors from ceiling to floor. The disc jockey's music blared on the street outside, as they entered the kaleidoscopic atmosphere.

"Gosh Craig, this place is as wild as the music."

"I thought you'd like it."

They both strutted to Ike and Tina Turner's "Proud Mary," until they left the floor exhausted. They were both hilariously inebriated by now in the wee small hours of the morning, driving down Sunset Strip. Craig took a sharp turn up a long winding hill.

"Where are you going, you nut?"

"Oh you're such a pussy, I must share my hideaway with you."

Getting out of the car, they started to climb toward a grand looking home, belonging to the entertainer Liberace. Thea started to laugh hard.

"I don't believe my eyes, this is truly crazy, us sitting here on the front veranda like a couple of swells."

"Oh he isn't here, and his mother is probably asleep. Nobody will bother us. I come up here often by myself just to look at this view. Isn't it p-r-e-t-t-y?"

"Oh it is Craig, it's beautiful."

They quietly stalked around the property, as they gazed through the windows into the piano player's drawing room. The lights shone brightly on a vast painting on the wall of the smiling entertainer. The room was cluttered with mementos, and the grand piano was surrounded by the famous candelabra, ornate furniture, paintings on a busy wall paper, and a vast crystal chandelier suspended from the ceiling. This dramatic interior with its red plush wall to wall carpet, instantly sobered the intruders, who now collapsed on a swingseat on the front porch. Craig rolled himself a joint, and took a deep breath of his pleasure, as Thea watched the view in front of them.

There wasn't a soul in sight to disturb their innocent frolic. From where they sat, they looked out over Hollywood, with the twinkling lights against the horizon. Daybreak upon them, the electrical splendor started to become obscure, and it surrendered to the early morning smog of the City of Angels.

"You know, Craig. I have a dream that someday I'll return to Tinsel Town victoriously. After all why shouldn't I? I may not be a personality of renown, but I could be a writer, and then my book will be another 'Gone with the Wind.' It will be on the silver screen."

"I wouldn't put that beyond you. You are very special, you bitch. I swear you've had more lives then a cat. You could do anything if only you'd stay away from men for a while!"

"Isn't that the truth? I wonder who I was in my past lives."

"A princess. You still are, except nobody knows it, but me."

Before leaving the hilltop home, Craig balanced Thea upon his shoulders over the back fence, to gaze upon the opulent outdoor swimming pool representing a piano.

"He sure knows how to live right, doesn't he?"

"Well, I did too, and I must admit it's a whole lot nicer."

After this most eventful evening together, Craig deviated one more time before getting home. He drove through the secure gates of Belair to show Thea where the homes were truly beautiful. Not disturbing the silence of the movie mogul residence, they got out of the car and merrily picked flowers in its front gardens and filled the car to full capacity.

"Craig, my love, you may be a flower child, but I only have one vase in my room."

"We'll put them in the bathtub," he said.

They laughed and sang "Hurray for Hollywood" all the way to his house.

A few weeks later Thea left for London to visit her mother.

Chapter Forty-three

It had been seven years since Thea had touched these shores, yet it seemed as if she hadn't ever left them. The jet plane now saluted its wing tip curving toward the landing strip of Heathrow airport.

She wandered around the airport in search of her mother, as she was somewhere in the crowd. Finally she came across Muriel, their dear friend who had lived with Mother for years. They embraced each other, as always.

"Where's Mummy?" Thea asked.

"She was looking at the time schedule for your plane—here she is."

"Mumsie!" Thea cried.

"Baby! I thought you weren't here."

They got settled in a minicab and drove toward North London.

"Where is Lydia? How come she didn't drive you here?"

"Lydia had to go to work, so Muriel accompanied me instead. When did you start wearing glasses, baby?"

"Oh about six years ago. I wear them for reading mostly, but I misplace them, so I keep them on for fear of loosing them. I'll never get used to the wretched things."

Mother and Lydia had now taken their residence in the area of Mill Hill, which was rather more conventional in comparison to Golders Green. Thea couldn't understand how they had settled to live in the damp climate of London, after eight years of Brisbane. Lydia had remarked it was because they were pro-British, and Australia was not. She had divorced her first husband and left him there. Since then she had married a delightful Englishman, and was presently living in a pretty home opposite Mother's. Lydia would never have strayed far from Mother.

Thea strolled around the West End, an area that would never cease to fascinate Thea. It was as cosmopolitan as she was and part of her heritage. California seemed like a dream, and Hollywood degenerate in comparison to the English refinement. Though she was sure there were similar areas in London, either in the East End, or even Chelsea, but she hadn't been exposed to them. Yet she had lived in foreign countries most of her life, and she found London too crowded and congested. Making a living here was terribly difficult in comparison to the U.S. It was the niceties of this country that she missed in others. So she accepted it for what it was, a vacation, and a roundtrip ticket. She intended to return to Chicago within the ninety days.

However after a couple of weeks at home, and her travelers checks diminishing rapidly, she decided once again to get a job closer to home. Her family probed her about the children from time to time, and her indifference toward them, and why had Marc been separated from Fiona and Philip?

"Once and for all, I promised my mother-in-law I would not interfere with their well-being. I cannot vouch for myself, let along three kids. Yes I care, I have guilt, I'm irresponsible, and the chapter is closed."

Mother, who had been a total example of perfection so far as her daughters were concerned, found it difficult to accept her daughter's indifference. They had both offered to give the three children a home and fine education, and it was all Thea's fault for returning back to the U.S.

It was the summer of 1975. The evenings were long and balmy. Thea would get off the bus on the corner of her street after work, and frequent the pub for a couple of hours of relaxation. This was much to her mother's disapproval, as nice girls didn't do that! *Why was her younger daughter always rebellious*? she wondered.

Thea was referred to as "the Yank" by Henry the bartender, who had her pink gin ready as soon as she walked in the door. The usual cronies welcomed Thea each evening, as she propped herself on the high stool alongside of them. They were her devoted audience, as she captivated their attention with her ability for story telling. It hadn't gone unnoticed that Thea was particularly attracted to a handsome gentleman that sat a distance from her, and showed amusement over her animation, and ability to hold the interest of this local inhabitant. His curiosity couldn't resist the temptation any longer.

"You're not really a Yank are you?" he asked her.

"That is Hank's nickname for me. I've lived in the States for sometime now, but I'm here visiting my family. They live up the street," she said with a smile.

He shook her hand, introducing himself as Matthew Furgeson.

"I've been tempted to talk to you before today, but hadn't got up enough courage. If you hadn't smiled in my direction, I would have left here frustrated once more."

"Has anybody ever told you you resemble and speak like Errol Flynn, Matthew Furgeson?"

"Lord no! He was such a handsome bloke and a film star never to be replaced. I would never aspire to such."

"I should hope not, he ended degeneratively."

Thea had noticed he wore a wedding band. But she didn't refer to it.

"Do you live around here?"

"Not too far, but I'm new to the area. My wife and I are separated. We have a teenage son, and they live in the Channel Islands. So I rent a room from a widow lady. I come here sometimes, I like the beer. Most Englishmen have their favorite pub, they enjoy drinking after a day's work, as I'm sure you can appreciate."

"Yes! My mother doesn't approve, because neither she nor my sister frequent pubs unescorted. My sister and her husband do enjoy country pubs, but that's only over the weekend. Mummy frequents them from time to time, when she goes to the country with them. She would never set foot in here as I do."

From the instant Thea met Matthew, she felt comfortable in his company. After her American episodes, he was most refreshing.

He immediately invited her to dinner the following Saturday, and she accepted. He left very suddenly, and she wondered at his disappearance. She knew nothing about him, except that she was to see him here at the pub Saturday evening. Hank knew less, except that he was a quiet one, and rarely talked to anybody. This affair would be unexplainable to her mother, as she had literally picked up a stranger in the pub, and that wasn't cricket! So on the walk home, Thea rationalized a plausible explanation she would give her mother, and would suffer the consequences. Which she did . . . "My dear girl, I don't know about your American conduct, but in this country you should at least invite the man over to your home once, before accepting a dinner invitation. He won't think any the better of you, by being picked up in a public place. If he were a decent man, that is what he would expect of you."

"Well! I'll asked him over, after the dinner date. I don't even know if we are going out on Saturday. He left suddenly without a given time to meet. You don't seem to understand the generation we live in. We are not in India, where everything is cut and dried. You must keep abreast of the times, Mother.''

Matthew apologized for having left her abruptly at their last meeting.

"You see after my wife and I split a year ago, I moved in with this old widow as a handyman around the house. I do her chores and gardening, etc. For this she makes me a dinner each night except over the weekends. I am always on time for supper. So the evening I got so involved here, made me late getting home to her. She knows me to be punctual and has been kind to me. I'm sorry I couldn't phone you. But I'm sure you understand now. I was fearful you may have stood me up this evening, and I'm glad you didn't.''

"You don't have to explain your life to me. We don't even know each other. If you're living with a woman, that's your business. You asked me out. I accepted.''

"Oh no love, it's not what you imply, believe me. I work at a sales job, selling machine tools to big companies. I'm fortunate to have found her at a most distressful time of my life. You are terribly American in your attitude.''

"Call it living alone too long, and bad manners old chap.''

Matthew and Thea dined superbly at the George and Dragon restaurant in Hendon. He conversed with ease in a beautiful flow of the English language, which sounded like poetry. His uncanny resemblance to Howard stunned Thea. Both men were originally from the same part of the country, both had refinement of speech and manners. They dressed meticulously, and wore Aramis cologne. Was it that she couldn't differentiate the two, or did she want to reestablish what she had lost a long time ago?

After dinner neither of them wished to return to their respective homes, so they went for a drive in the country. Matthew stopped the car in an open field, which could have led to complications, but it didn't. He held her hand as he continued to talk.

"Do you find the life-style here drab in comparison to the States?''

"It's different and takes getting used to. I have never been able to adjust here. I'd say I've escaped to the States. My family can't cope with my undisciplined conduct so I live alone, away from them. Yet I get homesick from time to time and return to Mummy for refueling.''

"Are you always so wonderfully honest? I find you terribly uninhibited, which is most refreshing to me.''

"Let's just say I don't beat around the bust, I tell it like it is. I was

292

dreadfully protected in my youth. I married a man similar to you, and never grew into my marriage. The excuse then was I was too young. The second time I married an American because I got pregnant. That was stupidity, and I think I had better stop right there.''

"Oh please, I don't require an explanation. My story isn't any more gratifying to say the least. I married Vera, we were both young, we had an only son, but there wasn't much encouragement on her part. Three years ago my company went under, and I lost my job and my home. I had a nervous breakdown, and Vera had me committed to an asylum. Then I went to my parents who live in the Cotswolds. There I regained my strength and sanity. As you know, the unemployment in this country is rife, so I was forced to return here for work. I haven't felt this good about myself in ages, since meeting you. Time seems to have stopped for me. I hadn't even realized how much before making this admission. I feel you should know the truth about me. And I won't hold it against you if you do not wish to pursue our friendship after tonight.''

"Well Matthew it's a good sign that you can trust someone, which happens to be me, as everybody needs to free themselves of their repression. Humility comes with strength, and I sincerely belief our paths crossed for a purpose, whatever it might be.'' He kissed her gently on her cheek and said thank you.

Mother was still awake when Thea got home, which was past midnight. She looked angry. Thea was so familiar with her various facial expressions. They hadn't ever truly spoken of their differences. Both Mother and Lydia were the voice of authority, and Thea had never questioned them. But what gave them this right? To be reprimanded at forty-five was ludicrous.

"Is this any time to come home on a first date? You have no shame. The men here do not understand impetuosity such as yours, especially the ones that have never left these shores. They are terribly naive in worldly matters. The majority of them don't even make a substantial living. It probably cost him his week's pay to take you to dinner. For God's sake child, wake up.''

"That's all the more reason he should be enlightened, and I'm just the one to do that. Live a little Mum, don't be so judgmental.''

"I realize you require some diversion from your work. Nobody says not to date him, just don't fall in love anymore. It's become a joke, the men that have passed through your hands.''

293

Thea snickered. She knew how to provoke her mother if it came to that.

"So what? If I choose to fall in love that's my business, I'm like the singer Edith Piaf, she couldn't sing unless she had an affair. I can't exist unless I have one. It's wholesome, and didn't hurt so far."

"I wouldn't compare myself with Edith Piaf. She ended a sorry sight."

Ritualistically Mother prepared her chicken curry for Sunday lunch. It almost seemed like the good old days, minus the servants and grandeur of their mansion in India. However the three of them were together once more around a family dinner table. Matthew had been approved of, and he appeared comfortable in their company. As they chatted amicably, Matthew spoke with sincerity.

"Thea is such a delight. I have never met anyone so enthralled by and enthused with life. Maybe between the lot of us we can talk her into staying here where she belongs."

"Unfortunately, Thea doesn't know where that is," said Lydia.

"I'm sure she would, if she felt we were genuinely concerned over her welfare. After all these years abroad, she hasn't found her roots."

"Matthew, my dear man. My sister has wandered because she wanted to. She loathes this country, and would have gone by now, if not for meeting you. She has some weird idea through some miracle or another that she will find her children, and be reunited with them. They are all adults now, and who says they would want that? Thea is a dreamer, as no doubt you will find out in due course."

Matthew winked at Thea across the table from him. They excused themselves from the lunch table and went for a walk around the neighborhood.

"Thea has your sister always spoken so harshly toward you?"

"She does sound kind of brusk, and has always had an authoritative manner. I don't think she's aware of her air of superiority, which Mother has contributed to over the years. Lydia has taken the role of matriarch in our family. Father was rarely home, Mother is a nervous lady. I'm supposedly the rebel, and she conducts traffic. I suppose an onlooker such as yourself, wondered why I kept mute. If I had taken a stand, it would have made it unpleasant for Mummy. Hence Lydia always has the last word, and it will always be that way."

"More the pity. She is truly conventional, where as you're not. I'm sure she couldn't pick up and leave her home at a minute's notice, and make the best of it. That takes initiative. If you were supposedly such a spoilt brat, how come you've been a capable survivor? You shouldn't subject yourself to their intolerance."

"Ah! But they would never find themselves in the predicaments that I do. Never!"

As the weeks passed Matthew visited Thea daily. She had disposed of her roundtrip ninety-day ticket to Chicago, and decided to live at home with her mother. On Saturdays when she was at work, he was off, and he'd spend the glorious sunny afternoons tending her mom's garden. He would feel at peace with nature, as it was therapeutic for him. In the evening when Thea returned from work, they would dine at the Tally-Ho Pub in North Finchley. Little did she know when Howard had first introduced her to this quaint environment in the early fifties that later, she would dine by the same window with another that favored her husband, and be hopelessly in love again.

Matthew planned a weekend in the country alone together. Their reservations were at the delightful Bell Hotel in Market Square in the picturesque town of Aylesbury. The English took pride in their country dwellings. Their room overlooked the Market Square and was situated above the hotel sign "The Bell" which depicted an old world scene from a picture book. They stood by the doorway of the room gazing at the double bed with its crisp ironed sheets. Matthew gently closed the door behind them, and they both jumped onto the bed joyfully.

"Alone at last," they chuckled like kids.

"Oh Matthew! Hold me close, say we'll always be together, I'm so happy, it's frightening."

"Don't be afraid my love, I'll never let you out of my sight, I promise."

Such terms of endearment passed between them, as they wrapped themselves around each other. His lithe strong body was warm and responsive, as hers pulsated with sexual desire. Matthew was overwhelmed by their lovemaking, as he tenderly caressed her hair, and her face, and then kissed her softly as their eyes met.

"Thea you are a prize to be proud of. If anybody had told me that love could be so fantastic, I would have said they were crazy. I thought making love was just a functional project. I never felt such tremendous passion within me before."

"I must admit I have never experienced such magnetic passion and wild spontaneity. It was so beautiful, I wish it could have lasted a little longer.''

She was such a dreamer, and now she had found someone to dream along with her. From her past unethical enthrallment with men, you could I daresay judge her to be temporarily unconscious. She had repeatedly sought this quest for perfect love. If it wasn't agreeably satisfying, she'd get despondent. She was sure now she had met her match, and could never get bored with him.

"You know Matthew, I think I am seeing Britain for the first time with you. As you know I have covered a lot of this country, both with Howard and Steven, but with you it's more enjoyable. You talk to me, and explain things in detail as we drive. We are sharing our adventures together.''

He smiled that beautiful Errol Flynn smile at her.

"Darling you desperately need to have roots. You must come to terms with yourself. It isn't all that bad here, if you would just give it a chance. I'll help you.''

Their initial months were a series of sightseeing trips over the summer weekends. They held hands in Hyde Park as they visited speakers' corner and were entertained by the people from all walks of life as they professed their political differences.

They indulged in several ploughman's lunches, starting at the Nag's Head at St. James: Warm crusty French bread, Stilton cheese, pickled onions, chased with a mug of draft beer. Umm! It was delightful. In the sunny afternoons they fed the ducks on the pond of St. James's park, which in London during summertime, was the prettiest of them all. Evenings they frequented the Brahms and Liszt wine bar, it was forever crowded. The Tally-Ho was their favorite rendevous, where they were so completely absorbed with each other.

"The middle-class English have such suavity in their manner and speech. Does it bother you when I compare incidents here with the States?''

"No, not at all, it intrigues me to see how fortunate you've been to be able to compare the differences. I can't do that.''

One afternoon when Thea returned from work, her mother informed her that she had received a couple of letters from the States. One was from Howard, with photographs enclosed of Laura's second marriage.

"Here are her wedding photos. Isn't she gorgeous? She looks like a movie star. I wonder how long this one will last?'' Howard wrote.

"The man looks comparatively younger than Laura. In this picture she resembles you a lot, the starryeyed expression."

"Mum, I wish you'd refrain from corresponding with Howard. He's aware of the fact his affairs are related back to me, and frankly I don't wish to know anything about them," Thea said.

"Laura is my grandchild. You have deprived me of my others, so I don't intend to give up the only contact I have."

Thea went upstairs to her bedroom and opened the first of two letters which was from Craig.

Dear Thea,
I hope this finds you and your mom well and happy. I hate to be the bearer of bad tidings, however I felt I should inform you of the latest. Luke Travis died in a motel in Kentucky. He was on his way home from Denver, Colorado, to visit his mother and dad. I don't think it was his intention, more of an accident I'd say. Between the booze and the pills, he overdosed. He was dead for a week before they were informed about it. Poor guy was doomed! Please write me soon as you receive this. I think about you often, and wonder when you are coming home. Love you and miss you.

Your friend, Craig

Mother entered Thea's room, and questioned her reaction to the letter she had just finished reading.

"It's from my gay friend, Craig, in Hollywood. Apparently Luke Travis died of an overdose in Kentucky. Poor Mrs. Travis, the men in her family were sure a selfish lot."

"How dreadful! How you got so involved with such decadence, I'll never understand."

"Mother dear, there is a lot you will never understand. It's people that crossed my life, decadent or otherwise."

"Do you ever reveal any of this to Matthew?"

"Yes! I have nothing to hide from him, or anybody for that matter."

"I wouldn't do that. The English are rather conservative, and you should be discreet about your private affairs."

"That's too bad isn't it? If he cares at all about me, he shouldn't be prejudiced. If he can't accept me the way I am, then he had better not plan a future with me."

"Rubbish child! The man is married, there is no question of a future with you."

"He's asked his wife for a divorce, and we plan to marry, Mother. I'm not ashamed of my past, at least I've lived, and I never question people that haven't. Everything we do involves a decision, and every decision we make involves a risk, I think he knows that by now.''

''Well! You have always done as you please, and I do suggest you shouldn't marry Matthew. Neither of you have come to grips with the realities necessary to base a relationship on.''

''Mother dear, once and for all, I have survived the school of hard knocks with no help from anybody. I may have been a spoilt child, but that was a long time ago. Life wasn't handed to me on a silver platter. I've never had a home I could call my own, I've lived like a gypsy out of suitcases. I've broken bread with the best of folks, and scratched shit with the worst while you and Lydia have sat on your high horse and never left your rose gardens.''

Mother walked away from Thea's bedroom to her own.

Thea lay awake for the best part of the night, as her thoughts reflected back to Kentucky and their life-style there.

''God keep Marc safe from harm, let him not experience the erroneous existence of both his father and uncle.''

It was morning already when Muriel brought Thea a cup of hot tea.

''Muriel, you are a lifesaver. You know more of what's going on than any of us. You had your share of happiness and grief, and would never doubt me for a minute. That's why I can talk to you.''

As Thea ran for the double deck bus around the corner, she clutched the other letter in her hand, which she began to read. It was from Robert. He asked how much longer she would be staying in London, and if she planned to return to Illinois. At this point she couldn't answer him.

The beautiful summer was drawing to a close as the fall colors appeared slowly, with shades of brown, and crimson, and golden yellow. Mother's back garden now covered in a carpet of fallen leaves, made more work for Matthew as he diligently pursued his duties. Thea and her mother were watching him from the dining room window.

''Poor Matthew,'' Mother remarked.

''Why *poor* Matthew?'' Thea asked.

''Because the man is obviously deprived of his own home and garden. I'm sure he hasn't as yet accepted his loss, and it may take longer than any of us realize. Next summer my garden will look even more lovely, because of his earnest dedication.''

Thea distracted her mother's concern with a question.

''Do you ever play the piano anymore?''

"You know I don't child. Besides it's terribly out of tune."

"Remember in Calcutta, when I was a little girl, I would turn the pages for you. Play me something, Mum."

Mother attempted a few chords of "When I Grow Too Old to Dream." However she got saddened by it and stopped.

"I played that when I was younger. I never thought the day would come when I'd fade with age. I can't relive the old days. I'm tired, and sometimes I wonder why I am still here, when all my contemporaries have gone on. Living alone is wretched."

"Mum, how can you be so ungrateful? You have us with you, and you're not alone. You've had a wonderful life and you're blessed."

"Thea you worry me so, you always have. Please don't contemplate marriage with Matthew. He isn't in any condition for a commitment. Life isn't dining, movies, and pubs. Matthew has confided in me. He is mentally troubled, and feels he cannot discuss it with you, because you will threaten to leave. Every time you have an altercation, you say your leaving to return to the States. He is in constant fear that one day he will return from work and find you have left him. I'm warning you the man is not well."

"Mum, I'm sure we can iron out our differences on our own. You have worried about me only because you have this need to worry, about something. When you run out of other trivia, you revert back to me. It's not fair. You must stop treating me like a child."

It was Christmas of 1976 and one of the nicest family affairs that Thea could remember. She cooked the turkey with all the trimmings, and the aroma of baked mince pie, and plum pudding wafted through the house. The two sisters decorated a tree, and the family gifts were arranged all around it. They attended midnight mass at the Catholic church, which to Thea was beyond recognition. She had stopped attending before her divorce and was completely out of touch with the English service. For New Year's Eve it was customary for Mother and Lydia to attend the Church supper dance accompanied by a live orchestra. Thea's obsession of the old year out and new year in always saddened her. She reminisced about the happy parties in their Calcutta home, which her father and mother lavishly conducted. On the midnight count Father would burst the pretty balloons connected to the electric fan suspended from the center of the ceiling. The guests triggered the assorted noise makers, and formed a circle in the drawing room to sing "Auld Lang Syne." Everybody kissed and hugged the New Year in. There was such gaiety as they danced to the orchestra, and Father poured umpteen bottles of champagne in crystal glasses. Thea would dance up a storm along with their friends. Such glorious days they were.

Now as they circled around the vast church auditorium, Thea held her mother's hand on the left of her, and Matthew's on the right. Lydia and her husband were across from her, smilingly singing the familiar lyrics. Thea felt a tremendous chill come over her. It was almost as though she wasn't even present in the room. She couldn't hear the music, and the people's rejoicing was silent to her ears. Something was terribly disturbing as Matthew got her immediate attention. He whispered in her mother's ear, as he guided Thea out of the room for fresh air.

"Darling what is the matter? You seem so spacy. I'm taking you for a drive, you'll feel better."

It was a cold crisp evening as they drove along the Finchley road. Some time had passed when she broke the silence.

"I felt my father's presence in that room. His spirit was there, I know it was."

"You hadn't had much to drink, in fact very little. Perhaps you are overtired. You must stop living in the past, my dear. We have each other, and a new beginning. I know you had a close attachment to your dad, but look at it this way. You were fortunate enough to have one. I haven't any memories I'd care to recall, not even a father. I never told you I was a bastard. The man that's married to my mother, came along when I was three years old and gave me his name. You still have a mother that adores you. You're very blessed, Thea."

She slowly turned toward Matthew's distressed expression.

"I'm sorry Matthew, how selfish of me. I love you darling, Happy New Year."

On February 13, 1977, Matthew had dined with the family, as often was the case, except on this day Mother wished to share her treasured photograph albums with him. It took the better part of the evening as Matthew absorbed the Martin history, pictures of Thea from babyhood, to her three marriages, and four children. Their prosperous days on the turf, to their downfall. Their extensive travels over the years, to their final departure from India. Thea excused herself to go in the kitchen and make a pot of tea. She overheard their conversation.

"I daresay Thea has wandered most of her life, and probably it causes her to be unstable. I think she would like to stay here now."

"I fear, Matthew, she is unfamiliar with permanency and may never settle anywhere for a lengthy period."

On February 22, Mother and Thea had decided to take a trip into Stratford-on-Avon. It didn't materialize as when they got to the bus terminal, the buses were full and there weren't any seats available. Mother complained of her legs hurting. Thea got most impatient.

"You find little pleasure in anything we do; everything is such a task for you, you're bound to the house like an invalid."

They took the long trip home on the train in silence. Thea left her mother at the garden gate without so much as a good-bye. She headed for the pub on the corner where she met Matthew. Thea was complaining to him about their unfortunate excursion, when suddenly, Lydia frantically entered the pub and ordered her sister out immediately! This sudden outburst wasn't unusual between the sisters, but Lydia seemed to be upset. Both Matthew and Thea followed her out to the car and they drove hastily toward the Edgware general hospital. Lydia and her husband reached the hospital before Thea and Matthew, who weren't aware of the circumstances. Upon arrival Thea found her sister in tears.

"She's gone, Mummy's gone, she had her one and only heart attack."

"My God!" Thea screamed! "She can't be gone, we were out together this afternoon. She complained about her legs hurting, that was all she went on about."

Matthew tried to console Thea, but she turned him away.

"I got the message on New Year's Eve, it would be our last one together, but you all think I'm crazy."

She wished so much to be compassionate toward her only sister at this time, but she herself was too stunned to show sympathy. Thea got terribly hostile with herself.

"How could she leave me now, without even a warning of some kind? It's not fair, I needed her so much right now. But come to think of it, when did I not need her? She has always been there for me."

Thea's presumptuous behavior hadn't allowed for her mother's sudden death. Her immediate reaction again was to run away from all of them, when in actual fact she was running from herself.

Her poor worrisome mother, who was petrified of being an encumbrance or a liability in a nursing home, had left planet Earth with pride intact. The sudden death of a loved one causes delayed reaction.

Thea's first night with Muriel in the house for company, was one of deep sadness.

"She said she was tired, Muriel."

"Yes child, your mother hadn't been herself for some time now."

Thea browsed around her mother's bedroom. It was as tidy as she had been. Everything was in its place. Thea handled her keepsakes one by one: Old pictures on her night stand of Father and her two daughters, taken in their youth. Her frayed prayer book and worn rosary beads, handled over the years. If there was a heaven, she was certainly on her way there. The lace curtains blew gently in the wind, as Thea gazed through the windows at her beautiful garden. She would not enjoy it as Matthew had promised her. Thea sat on her bed, which she had made hurriedly this morning before they ventured on their doomed trip. Her eyes wandered to her favorite portrait taken of Thea and her three children before they all left for America. She indeed had given her mother considerable grief all of their lives, and they hadn't even parted on good terms. But she was sure she understood, wherever she was now. They had always loved each other, even though Thea misunderstood most of her logic. On February 28, Thea attended her first funeral, that of her mother. Lydia had taken care of the necessary arrangements, as her younger sister was in a state of shock.

Katherine her best friend and a reassuring face from the past was present. Thea was pleased to hug her lovely friend. Their parish priest conducted the last rites, and Mother was cremated and laid in the Hendon Cemetery. Matthew grieved with a heavy heart alongside of Thea. He had held the highest esteem for a grand lady he had known for so short a time. As the days passed, and the sympathy and condolence letters and calls ended, Thea received another two letters from the States. One from her dear friend Valerie, and another from Robert. Lydia put the house up for sale, and Thea had to now make arrangements to leave one way or another. She gave Matthew an ultimatum that he find a flat for them, or else she had to return to Chicago.

"Matthew, I can endure almost any condition, but I don't think you have enough gumption to do your part, so I have little choice but to return to Chicago as soon as possible." He looked at her with tears in his eyes.

"That was inevitable. When your Mother was here, we both had a hold on you. I am not strong enough to do it on my own. You never really adjusted here, and I can't say I blame you one bit."

Thea's last days in Mill Hill were a nightmare. First she had lost her mother, and now she was giving up the man in her life. She never told him of her departure date, as they sat for the last time in the corner pub.

"Thea you treat life with such mockery. What would take a normal person time to decide you do immediately without thought."

"Matthew I've know you two years now, and it took my mother's death for us to act upon our lives. I have no choice in the matter, I have to live somewhere, and it appears it's easier in Chicago, than it is here."

Thea felt utterly remorseful as she arrived at Heathrow airport. She got seated by the window of the TWA aircraft, and in minutes was flying over the Thames river on a dreary evening.

Bye-bye London. No doubt I'll be back someday, she thought.

Chapter Forty-four

Before leaving London, Thea had written and requested her gay friend from the past, Jeremy, to meet her flight at O'Hare airport. It arrived on time as scheduled at 9:00 A.M. the next morning. She had acquired a high temperature while flying over the Atlantic. So when Jeremy discovered his friend looking so utterly distressed, he got her baggage and promptly ushered her to his car.

The first week at his apartment on Lake Shore Drive, she had lost all concept of time and place. He was of course most sympathetic toward her, as this wasn't the woman he once knew. Jeremy felt once she had recuperated, which was fast, there wasn't any point in letting her defeat her purpose for returning back to Chicago. So he immediately secured a job for her in the beauty salon where he worked in Highland Park, Illinois.

Work was the best therapy, besides which she had to take care of herself. However she remained in an apathetic condition. She missed Matthew's daily presence, his constant attention to her, with cups of tea, and most of all she couldn't tolerate sleeping alone. A month had passed when her endurance reached breaking point. She wrote him a long letter, telling him she felt strangely misplaced in the windy city, and if he wished he could write her to the given address. Within the week she received his reply.

He said that he was lost without her, and didn't frequent the neighborhood pub anymore, because their mutual friends enquired about her, and it was more than he could bear. He wished now, that he had shown more initiative and support, when she needed it most. He had let her down. He was planning to leave London and move north to the Cotswold country, where his parents lived. If he could find a flat for them, would she be willing to return and try once more? But she had to be sure, and truly desire this, because these one way flight tickets were rather costly. Their transatlantic calls to each other became more frequent, until finally in her tenth week she departed from O'Hare for London's Heathrow airport.

In Thea's exceptional exuberance she hadn't slept a wink on the plane. She couldn't believe she was returning to Matthew. When she arrived at Heathrow, she scuttled by customs in search of him. She began to panic as her eyes scanned the crowds. Suddenly from behind her, a pair of hands gripped her waist, and circled her around.

"You wouldn't be looking for me by any chance?" She expressed laughter, then tears, as they kissed each other's breath away.

"God! How I've missed you. I'll never let you out of my sight again, you little devil."

"Matthew you've lost a lot of weight!"

"Is that any wonder, after what you've put me through? You want to have a laugh? I left Cheltenham last night after having supper with my mother, and while you were flying over the Atlantic, I was already parked here at the airport. Right up till now, I was in fear of you having changed your mind and not arriving. Only then could I appreciate how your poor mother worried over you."

"Oh ye of little faith, Matthew. I can't believe I'm back here so soon. Living in Chicago without you was a nightmare. Poor Jeremy was glad to see me go."

"By the way does your sister know of your return home?"

"Not yet she doesn't, but she will in due course, as we have to be present at the lawyer's office for the reading of Mummy's will."

"Darling, you will love Gloucestershire. It is the most beautiful countryside you have ever seen. Cheltenham where we will be living, is an inland spa, with fine Georgian buildings, like the postcards I've been sending you. The tree-lined promenade is where the elegant shops are situated, at the head of which stands the Queen's Hotel. We will lunch there tomorrow. It's as regal as its name. The folks here are so polite, a far cry from Londoners. Ever since my arrival here, I've pretended you were beside me."

"Well, you need not do that any longer, because from now on we will be together in everything."

"My family is eagerly waiting to meet you. In fact my sister-in-law is having a party to welcome you here. Both my half-brothers will be present with their wives. I can't wait to show you off to them. By the way you are Mrs. Furgeson to the landlady. I told her you had been on business in the States."

"Oh Matthew, how could you? She'll think I'm some kind of executive, and here I don't even have a job lined up."

The summer of 1977 Cheltenham had proved to be all that Matthew had described, and more. Their Georgian flat faced the beautiful Pitville Park, on the Evesham road. The rich natural beauty of the Cotswold's was exceptional. Each weekend the lovers would drive for miles exploring small towns, and villages, such as the Severn Valley, and the Royal Forest of Dean. Thea's favorite was Tewkesbury, where they relished cream teas in an old-world tea shop.

They frequently took a picnic on Burton-on-the-water and watched the artists painting on their canvasses at Upper and Lower Slaughter. They visited Bibury with its old-world charm, where they caught stream trout for their supper. Hand in hand they climbed Cleeve Hill, from where one got a marvelous view of the Severn Valley. On to Sudley Castle, the home of Catherine of Aragon. There never seemed enough weekends to visit, or enough places to run out of. The season was glorious for fresh strawberry and pea picking. They filled pillowcases full, and took them back to his mother to prepare.

The local pub they frequented was the Royal Oak, to which they rode on horseback. It had been years for Thea, and she enjoyed every minute of it. Twice a month she volunteered her services to a senior citizen disability home. The old people were ever so humble, and grateful for her attention and storytelling, which were a great comfort to them.

On Saturday nights she and Matthew attended the British Legion Club dance, where once again Thea danced the old fox-trot, and quick step, which was a dance of the past, but much enjoyed by both old and younger people here, as was the picnic up the river.

There hadn't been a fault to find, other than a job for her. Matthew worked in a machine tool company, but Thea couldn't find employment of any kind, and Matthew got discouraged over this. He also objected to her attendance at the Baptist church.

"If you were brought up a Catholic, why then have you turned to the Baptist religion?"

"Frankly I think I am in search of something greater than religion per se. Though at this point I can't explain it."

"Well I'm an agnostic, and prayer never helped me none."

"Matthew! How can you expect us to share a life together, without spirituality, or a power far greater than we perceive? We were brought together for a reason, it didn't just happen you know."

"Oh rubbish! I have never heard such utter rot. I've noticed since your mother's death you have gone on a religious binge."

"That's not true. I think I go to church just to be quiet, until they start singing. Than it's like being out here, eternal noise and arguments. I must achieve recognition of self in my own way. Lately Matthew, I seem to be living for and around you. I can't do that. I did with Howard, and now you. You're not to blame, I am. Being religious isn't helpful either, that is why I rebelled in my early life. I'm searching, that is all I know."

"Your conscience must be troubling you, Thea. You never cease to surprise me."

She watched him drift into apathy and said no more. They had lived in Cheltenham for ten months, and Thea managed her part of the finances from her savings left to her by mother. She never visited Lydia in London during this time, as her sister did not approve of her association with Matthew.

He in the meantime had become withdrawn and despondent. She never questioned his strange behavior, when he'd disappear from her for hours at a time. She had always trusted Matthew, as they never held secrets from each other. However one morning she followed his direction from the living room window, he hadn't got in his car as always. About half an hour later she discovered him sitting by the pond in the park under a huge tree watching the ducks. He hadn't changed his position for over an hour. She finally walked home without him seeing her. He was indeed acting most strangely.

His next peculiarity, was the loss of his appetite. He who had always enjoyed her cooking, and going to restaurants, now said he wasn't hungry. She had discovered several of her spices were missing from the rack in the kitchen, only to find they had been thrown in the garbage. She questioned him about it.

"I don't care for that American garbage you put in the food. I did all right before without them," he said.

In her state of utter confusion and embarrassment, she visited his parents on her own, hoping they might understand the situation better than she did.

His folks lived in a pretty little home in the nearby village of Bishop's Cleeve. Thea took a bus to visit them.

"Thea my dear," said his mother, "Our Matthew is not himself. I'm afraid the doctor will assist you a lot better than we can. We hoped his being with you would have made him happy, as he was so excited about your return, and told us you were to be married. But I don't think he will ever be his old self again. He's just getting worse.''

The doctor cautiously observed Thea as she entered his office.

"It's Mr. Furgeson that you have come to see me about, is that right?''

"Yes, Doctor. Have you seen him lately?''

"As a matter of fact I have been seeing him rather often, but he asked me not to mention it to you. However if you are living together, and he is your concern, I feel you should be aware of the circumstances. Have you ever noticed his habitual intake of pills?''

"No, I can't say that I have.''

"This is the first signs of a classic manic-depressive. They get hooked on tranquilizers such as Valium, until their lives depend upon it. Sometimes in the early stages, they are inclined to fantasize in a relationship. When you first met him, over two years ago, he hadn't been fully cured of his illness, so he clung to you. Now it's returned with vengeance.''

"Are you telling me, that our relationship is based on his fantasy?''

"Yes! Matthew has been a sick man for a long time. It's a slow procedure and doesn't always surface for a long time. He would never admit it to himself, or anybody for that matter, because he is not able to. I cannot help him from a medical standpoint, unless he wishes it, and apparently he doesn't. Young lady, he is probably at his worst right now, and I'm afraid your trying to help is only aggravating the situation.''

Thea wept, as she nervously paced the floor and heard the doctor's diagnosis.

"He has confided in me about you, and the loss of your mother. He doesn't feel adequate, or worthy of your attention. You see, Madam, you are up against a severe situation. If you want my honest opinion, I would leave Matthew. He is his own prisoner, and you are aggravating the situation. He did tell me on his last visit, that you meant the whole world to him, but that his impotency and inability to have an erection will eventually drive you away, and he couldn't stand to lose you again.''

"You mean to tell me, I've been oblivious of his malfunction?''

"I wouldn't say oblivious. You shut your eyes to it.''

"So now you are asking me to leave a sinking ship. I love him, Doctor.''

"Do you honestly? This affair can only get worse. His loss of weight, and appetite, his disappearance from you to be on his own. He is living in a shut-in world, which you are not a part of. You don't want that, do you?''

The doctor requested Thea to behave as normally as possible, and not to ever mention she had seen him, as it would kill Matthew's pride.

That afternoon when Matthew had returned from work, he scolded Thea with harsh words for not having prepared supper.

''Let's go to the Promenade for that delicious trout dinner you so enjoy. Then we can take in a movie after that. How does that sound?''

''It costs too much, I'm not that hungry.''

''Don't worry about the cost. I have some money. Besides I think it will do us both good to get out a bit. Let's go love.''

Fall was in the air, and the evening was beautiful as they walked around the town center. Matthew didn't do his supper justice, however he agreed to stand in line for the screening of *New York, New York*. It had always been their habit to hold hands at the movies, now even more so.

''That was entertaining,'' said Matthew as they walked out of the cinema. ''Robert De Niro was aware of Liza Minelli's strength of character, and he had to eventually free her from his inadequacy. Similar to us wouldn't you say?''

''Now what brought that about Matthew?''

''There comes a time when love is not enough. She had left him behind to pursue her career, because she believed in herself. Another similar film was *The Way We Were*. Separation was a means to an end.''

''Don't talk such utter nonsense.''

''Thea, you have always been a survivor. You have an overabundance of self-confidence. The average man can never satisfy your incredible motivation. You don't see yourself as I do. This dream of yours of a complete love and unity, is just an illusion, one cannot live up to such an aspiration. You mark my words, sometime in the future you will grow stronger than you ever dreamed possible for yourself. And you will be alone when you do it.''

Thea had been rejected in bed by Matthew innumerable times. But this night when they returned from the movies he put his arms around her and attempted once more to recapture a fervent love. It was by no means the Matthew Thea ran away with to the Bell Hotel, but at least he had attempted. He cared.

In the morning the alarm sounded as usual for Matthew to go to work. Instead he stumbled toward the dresser drawer for his Valium, and returned to bed covering his head.

"To hell with it, I'm not going to work," he said.

Thea's frustration led her out of the building toward Cleeve Hill, where she'd sit on the hill with her thoughts, sometimes until dusk. She returned at suppertime, to find Matthew hadn't moved from his position in bed.

"Darling are you there? Where did you go?"

"I'm here Matthew. Do you feel any better?"

"Please come in here, I want to talk to you."

Thea sat beside him in bed, she noticed his tearfilled eyes as he spoke.

"Sweetheart, you know I am sick. The doctor can't help me, and Lord knows you have tried. Please return to America before it's too late."

"Hush, don't worry about me. I think we should see another doctor." Thea held onto straws, as Matthew apathetically drifted. He was now on disability, as he wasn't able to work, and they spent the better part of the weeks at doctors' offices. He seemed content to drive around the Cotswold Wild Life Park, holding hands with Thea by the riverside. He'd smile and then get solemn again.

"Have I ever told you, you are an extraordinary woman?"

"I don't believe you have."

"My life would be so empty without you. You have filled these three years with love, life, and most of all, kindness."

They sat themselves down beneath a huge weeping willow tree at the water's edge. Thea leaned on her elbow and said, "This is such a sad but beautiful tree. I guess there is beauty to be seen in sadness, too."

As she spoke Matthew fell asleep. He had little or no resistance these days, and he tired so easily. She leaned across his face and kissed his cool lips.

"Poor poor Matthew, what is tormenting you so? What is causing you such pain? I wish I knew."

When he awoke, it had turned chilly, so they drove to a large, imposing building of famous Cotswold stone, originally constructed as a small coaching Inn. It was called the "Bird in Hand" since it became a major coaching house, and renamed the Cotswold Gateway. After they had dined by a roaring fire, he suggested they spend the night there, in all its old-world charm.

"Can you imagine, how long these buildings have withstood the centuries, and how much longer they will as yet, with their graciousness and distinction," he remarked to her.

Their happy tours around the countryside were coming to a close. Matthew's habitual intake of Valium added to his malnutrition, which in turn caused dreadful malfunctioning. It was painful for Thea to watch his slow suffering. He was literally fading in front of her eyes.

One early morning Thea was awakened by a chill in the air. So she awoke and lit the gas fire, as she covered Matthew with an extra blanket. She felt his face and kissed him gently on his forehead, he was like ice. She got in beside him to give him warmth, and lay her hand across his chest. He was abnormally still. She reached for the light on the night stand.

"Matthew! Matthew!" she called.

There was no response. He had a faint smile on his face, but not a breath in his body. She held him close to her bosom and whispered.

"You promised you would never leave me, I kept my promise, I'm still here."

She rocked him to and fro, to and fro, gazing upon his peaceful face. It was the first time she had seen it so serene. Was he truly at peace? Or was he still awaiting acceptance in his transition? Well at least he was out of his painful body, and maybe now at rest. Or so she hoped for his sake.

Within the year Thea had lost her mother, and Matthew.

There is a bridge between time and eternity;
This bridge is the spirit of man.
Neither day, nor night, nor death, nor sorrow
cross that bridge . . .
To the one that goes over that bridge
The night becomes like day
because
in the world of the spirit
There is no death.

Rabindranath Tagore (Bengali poet)
1861–1941

Chapter Forty-five

Although Thea had this perpetual compulsion within her to find the missing factor in her life, as long as she looked to people and situations, she would fail to find either enduring satisfaction or peace. She inadvertently expected her girlfriend Ferne, a friend of many years, to be supportive. Ferne had sympathized over the loss of Matthew, but did not dwell on the subject. Her friendship for Thea was related in a meaningful way and was based on truth spoken tenderly.

Thea's intuition told her that there was something beyond what she had so far consciously experienced, yet she wasn't ready to respond to it. It was at this period of her life, that she was introduced to her first spiritual book, *Practicing the Presence*, by Joel S. Goldsmith. Thea had lived by "bread alone" all her life, and it was so difficult for her to suddenly comprehend such unfamiliar teachings, as: "You can only feed the tree of life from within; not from without, and that we shall see that the world of supply is within; although it appears visibly in the without. A spiritual God cannot be brought down to a material concept of life." All this was the opposite to what she had been conditioned to. Thea attended "The Infinite Way" tape classes with Ferne, in downtown Chicago. But it appeared to her as a form of occultism (the unknown) and not in the least effective in her daily experiences. Ferne would smile at her friend and say, "You never know when you will be receptive to a new idea. Time is only in the finite world, there is no time in spirituality. Use it as a friend. The teacher will appear when the pupil is ready. There is nothing for us to become, we already are. You will see, I promise you. You will come into awareness, of this I am sure. Sure it's difficult, who said living was easy? Once a person touches a mystical teaching, and has been introduced on the path, there is no returning, there is only progressive unfoldment of consciousness."

Thea was now living in a small apartment in Highwood, Illinois. Of course she would never have admitted that it was of her choosing, that she had placed herself in this town. Her inner unrest and discontentment led her to contact Howard. Several years had past, and she was curious over Laura's welfare. Howard spoke to her in a restrained manner, and said he would write her a letter. Did she expect anything else? Or was it just a past connection she needed in her loneliness?

This was the letter Howard sent.

Thea,

Can't say I was surprised to hear from you. You periodically cycle through memory lane assisted by a few slugs of scotch.

In listening to you, I still find you a complex person, full of contradictions. You may be older, but I doubt if you have matured in any way, just possibly demanding of others and yourself.

However, your main purpose was to ask about Laura. Unfortunately, you are right in this case. There is a great deal of you (the side of you that I am acquainted with) in her. She was divorced for the second time last February. Fortunately her ex-husband's parents live close by and adore their granddaughter, so they babysit while Laura goes to work. We were home in September and found her a changed person; cold, unresponsive, suspicious of all, and getting into trouble. We did what we could for her. Our house was too big for a single working parent, so she moved into a smaller apartment nearby. Laura otherwise is managing, has a good job and loves her daughter. All she wants now is to find herself. At the age of twenty-six she has earned her right, but somehow I doubt if she ever will. Since she has your address, she will get in touch with you, should she have the need to. Our granddaughter is beautiful, long curly black hair, looks like her father, and has a temper like her mother, but very intelligent and loving.

We will be in the States to settle down, as travel and living abroad is not what it used to be. It is a continual strain.

I will now take a few moments, with your indulgence, to relive the past. If time heals, it also scars. I grant you our courtship was beautiful. I looked forward to being with you, and I was proud to be seen with you. They were for me tender, loving, happy times, and our bodies gave us sweet simple pleasures in a young innocent way, hurting no one. However the marriage was a disaster. I offered you my love in every sense, respect, trust, and caring. But starting in Aden, you proceeded to break every rule of consideration, and for this you say you have no regrets. From there on that love slowly converted into one of hanging on to a possession. Others were out to steal you, and you were prepared to be stolen. Therefore my world was threatened.

The night Laura was conceived, I was not sure if it was my seed in you, or someone else's. It, of course, was obvious later that it was mine, that had the desired effect. I will also admit that my subsequent reactions to this threat were adolescent. But I had no experience in those so-called worldly attitudes you wanted to embrace. Which by the way I still firmly believe wrong. Promiscuousness is for animals. Had I not been reduced to the pathetic condition I allowed myself to be driven to, the whole affair would have been terminated much sooner. I realized long ago that I should have had more self-respect. Why accept all that crap? I should have said to hell with you, and walked away. I would have gotten over it sooner and not wasted all those years. You were a part of my life long, long ago, but fortunately my life has been full for a long time now, and I have no need to occasionally reenact past events to fill the void, as you appear to find it necessary to do.

I wish you all the success you are in search of.

Yours at one time,
Howard

After Thea had got finished reading, she assumed Howard was still an angry person. Laura, poor girl, had built a prison for herself, the walls consisting of doubt. She could be in her dream state for a lengthy period, unless she changed her thinking about values. Living in a country so rife with divorce and broken homes, neither of them should be judgmental of Laura.

It was mortifyingly disturbing to watch morning television. The talk shows dominated the single woman's crucial situation. The nationwide epidemic described as the Peter Pan syndrome, had besieged women from all walks of life. It didn't matter if they were executives, housewives, divorcees, or widows—rich, poor, or in between. Women at thirty, and the sensitive ages forty and up, felt utterly disillusioned over men in general. Their accepted affairs with married men were disregarded, and then there was the fear of herpes, and later AIDS, that crushed one's limited prospects.

The ladies in the beauty shop where Thea worked suggested she get interested in evening classes of some shape or form, or that she jog around the sidewalks as they did, or participate in a church group. There were many single groups she could belong to. Ugh! What was happening?

314

Was she to revert to her Girl Scout days, or perhaps better yet attend dances with another woman, or several women? To be picked over as desirable merchandise for the evening? Thanks, but no thanks. Adjustment on the North Shore, and to be surrounded by the *nouveau riche* wasn't exactly her idea of ecstasy.

So she spent her leisure time with Ferne, and began her quest into the unknown, because the usual pleasures were worn out. They'd become faded, and dull. Ferne's explanation was "When you are wholly disconnected, and sincerely desire to change, you will ultimately discover your source. You must want this, and nobody can do it for you. Not all the books you read, or classes you attend. You must veritably become it."

In 1980 Thea was living in an apartment building in Highland Park, Illinois. She used to kid about it to her friends, by saying she was the only one camping out in the affluent Jewish neighborhood.

Her Sunday mornings were spent tuned into TV's channel 32. Before her stood a handsome grey-haired minister, with a twinkle in his eyes, and sincerity in his voice. He was Dr. Robert Schuller, broadcasting from his Garden Grove Community Church, twenty-five miles southwest of Los Angeles. Today it's known as the Crystal Cathedral. His voice boomed in the quiet of her bedroom.

"This is the day the Lord has made. Let us rejoice and be glad in it."

"Nothing is impossible if you believe in yourself," he'd say. His systematic theology of self-esteem, his philosophy of life was similar to that of positive thinkers like Dr. Vincent Peale, and Chicago tycoon W. Clement Stone. Ordinarily Thea rebelled against preacher men praising the Lord and raking in the cash. But religion, too, is a business, and as he tactfully said, "I help you, so you must help me."

When you are not aware of your potentialities, you become fearful, inadequate, and negative, until finally you have become a victim of your circumstances. For most people beginning on the "path" can be a slow process, sometimes one of doubt. To give up one's egoism is almost like streaking down the highway, unless of course one is an exhibitionist. It was a habit she had felt comfortable with. She had to voluntarily guide herself on her transformational journey into the place where she could reweave the tapestry of her life, and to challenge the roots of her true being. Mistakes were nothing to be ashamed of, as she had always perceived. They were growth.

To quote Schuller, "A disappointment is an opportunity turned inside out."

She began with her profession. She couldn't tolerate the boss image, or the personality conflicts of her co-workers in a salon. Over the years she had accumulated a selective clientele, who patronized her weekly services and were loyal to her to the end. This made her work acceptable, as she had a responsibility to herself and the challenge that she required. From the time of her training, she had been of an independent nature. Now that she was older and more experienced, she held herself back for the lack of motivation. Go for it! She now said to herself.

A couple of years had past when she received a lengthy letter from her daughter, Laura, in which she disclosed that her third marriage had ended in divorce. Sure it's easy enough to say, the apple doesn't fall far from the tree. But it wasn't so, Thea couldn't feel the guilt, or take the blame for where her daughter was in consciousness. That was all of her own doing, but nobody wants to hear that, do they? Laura expressed how little she knew about her mother, and would she write? She said it was a pity that they were estranged. She also enquired about her brothers Marc and Philip, and did she have a sister? Thea replied to the best of her ability, giving her Marc's address, which hadn't changed since she had first visited him. Even though he was older, Thea was sure he would like to hear from her. She couldn't help with the other two, as she herself didn't know of their whereabouts. However Fiona, now eighteen, was married and had a baby son. Philip was in the navy, but this she'd heard through the grapevine. About the same time Thea received a letter, with an invitation enclosed from Valerie, to attend her son's wedding later that summer. Thea smiled to herself, as she remembered their children in diapers, in Guantanamo Bay. She had covered a lot of mileage since then, while Valerie had stayed in one town, fortified by her family.

Before attending the wedding in Maryland, Thea flew out to Lexington, Kentucky. Here she was met by her sister-in-law, Hope, who had left Los Angeles some time ago and returned to the hills to teach school. While they drove on a new highway that was brought to Thea's notice, it could have fooled her as she saw little progress in these parts. Thea had always felt that the people here vegetated and could care less about the rest of the world. Some of the younger generation stayed because of their roots, or if they had the nerve and enough sense, they left to improve themselves. But Jason and Luke had an incessant longing to return. It seemed a characteristic trait among Southerners, a profound dedication toward family.

As they approached the little house at the bottom of the hill, Thea searched for the sight of her son Marc. She walked right past him with excitement.

"Where is Marc? Do you know where he is?"

"Standing right in front of you, Mother dear." he smiled.

"Lord! Is it really you? Your so tall and thin, with a mustache, and these long sideburns. What happened to my little boy?"

"I growed. You should come home more often."

"You grew darling, not growed."

He leaned forward to kiss her on the cheek.

"I sure didn't get my height from you did I?"

She laughed! "Nice things come in small packages," she said. She hugged her mother-in-law who always seemed to be on the front porch when she arrived.

"Mother you've shrunk some, since I was here."

"Just got a little rounder I'd say."

Kentucky like most states during summer was green, with wild flowers along the mountains all around. One could almost forgive the deterioration of the nearby surroundings, as the coal trucks tore along the main road. Marc took his mother for a long walk in the woods, and for the first time of their association together, they actually related to each other. At times he observed her with interest, as though she were speaking a foreign language, and at other times he would exclaim "that's cool." Thea never had that generation gap feeling with him, she enjoyed his kind of music, and discovered he could play a guitar. She promised to get him an electric guitar for his twenty-first birthday.

Marc didn't always relate to his surroundings. Considering he had lived here all of his life, he never even discussed coal in his conversation. He spoke of hunting, and fishing, and directed her attention to his new shotgun, and fishing tackle. Thea questioned him from curiosity as to his future in these parts.

"I don't reckon I've given it much thought yet. It will come to me when the time is right."

"Marc, you have a sister, and a younger brother. Are you not curious about their whereabouts?"

"Sure I am. But they live with folks someplace, and I don't know them. I reckon they will find me when they want to."

The two weeks she spent with the Travis family, it seemed to her as if she were relating to them for the first time, on a meaningful level. This had never happened before. All the pent up hostility and contempt she had held for the Travis men had suddenly vanished. This family had only shown her kindness and understanding. She had no right to hold a grudge against them. Her mind had begun to change. The miners were folks that made an honest living at the risk of their lives, and the sweat of their brows. They were presently suffering the decline of what was once a prosperous industry. Thea had underestimated them long enough, because of the lack of knowledge on her part. She felt a sense of sadness when the time came for her to leave. The other times she had visited, she left with a confused ambiguous mind. But this time she felt them reaching out to her to come back sooner. On the other occasions when the time drew near for her departure, Marc would leave the house before she did. The explanation for that was he didn't like good-byes. Because he never knew when she would return. This time he accompanied her to the Lexington airport, and kissed her good-bye. "You come home soon, hear?"

"Expect me for your twenty-first birthday with guitar in hand."

Chapter Forty-six

It had been nine years since Thea and Valerie embraced each other with joy. They were complimentary of each other, and thought the years had been kind to them.

Most wedding preparations were exciting, specially for the young, and Val's second son Michael had just come of age. The out of town guests had already been situated at various lodgings. Thea of course stayed with Valerie and her family. Her first night was spent at the wedding dress rehearsal, after which followed a dinner at the officers' club on the base. The following day the marriage took place in the Lutheran church, after which followed a fair sized reception at the club. The beautiful bride and groom danced to the popular melody of "Evergreen." Thea was placed at the family table, as she watched the young couple all aglow in their finery, not taking their eyes off each other. But that was what young love was all about. It brought back vivid memories of happiness, and youth, and for a fleeting moment Thea saw herself with Howard. She had had this same feeling once upon a time.

Thea moved away from the table and strolled around the vast club room. She stood at the far corner of the room enjoying the beautiful music, when she was startled by a hand from behind on her shoulder.

"It couldn't be all that bad now, could it? This beautiful day of celebration."

"Robert! My goodness, Robert, what are you doing here?"

"Out of sight, out of mind, that's you. I told Valerie to keep it a surprise, and it looks as if she did. I bet you didn't even ask about me?"

"I'm ashamed to say I didn't."

"You're forgiven."

He kissed her on the cheek and directed her toward the dance floor. His sensitive smile before her, he looked even happier than she did. The smile she had never forgotten, and she smiled back. Sometimes a smile could be reassuring when words failed.

319

"Did you ever receive any of my letters?" he asked.

"Yes I did, but life's been so hectic, I couldn't find the words to write."

"Thea my dearest, you could never be at a loss for words. I've been right here all these years, while you've traipsed around the world."

The beautiful melody "How Do You Keep the Music Playing?" caused them to dance cheek to cheek. He whispered in her ear.

"I bet you never thought that we'd be dancing on this floor after all these years."

"To be honest I never did give up on you, but I didn't know where or when? The years have gone so swiftly, yet there seems to be a big gap there, which I can't recall."

"I mentioned in one of my letters to you in London, that I had lost my wife, and was awaiting orders for overseas. It will be my last tour of duty before retirement."

"I didn't get that one. I've been in Chicago a couple of years. So where overseas is it to be?"

"Thea I don't mean to be forward, but can we go to my place and talk? I have so much to tell you, and I need to be alone with you."

"Well! I'm sure Valerie will understand, if I excuse myself earlier than expected."

They were both a little awed, as they sipped on their hot coffee, in his comfortable living room.

"Now tell me about your life in Chicago, and have you got better adjusted since we last met?" he asked.

"Well! I've run away from Illinois innumerable times, and no matter where I go I can't run away from myself. So I decided to stay and learn my lesson. Since the loss of my mother and Matthew, I feel everything we do in life does have a purpose. One has to look beyond appearances. Life is a puzzle, and I make a habit of putting the wrong pieces where they don't fit. Hence I got tired of 'me.' "

"Suppose Matthew hadn't died, would you have married him?"

"That was our intention at the time. But as I see it now, it wouldn't have worked. I never had a sense of values, or a sense of my priorities. So I lost myself in great expectations. The unity of two people should give harmony, I get havoc. One shouldn't fall in love and then form a relationship, it should be in reverse. A mutual need for good qualities. We must not fear the loss of a loved one, or a change of affection. It is natural for affection to change, because they are based on ideas, and our minds are always changing. Our good should not be dependent on a particular relationship, but upon our ability to love. I know the difference between right and wrong, so I must learn to trust it.''

"Do I hear you philosophically inclined?''

"You might say a person who has survived a good marriage, is an excellent candidate for a good marriage. But a person that has failed at it, is a poor candidate. Unless a great deal of mental and emotional revision first takes place. Quite honestly I can't think of marriage until I change.''

Robert came toward her with outstretched arms, and kissed her warmly.

"I detect a lot of bravery on the surface, but what you need is fulfillment in a relationship. I'm sure we both have good stories to relate. I'd say we have both changed since our last meeting. But I don't like living alone, and I'm sure you don't. So at least hear me out before you condemn me.''

"Could I have another cup of coffee before you begin?''

"Of course, are you hungry? I fix a terrific club sandwich.''

"No just some coffee, thanks.''

"Since Francine passed on, life has taken on little change. Of course we were married twenty-nine years. She wasn't always an alcoholic. It began when she discovered she couldn't have children. We had always been good companions, but our sexual drive was limited. I don't have to tell you that, as you discovered that for yourself the night we spent at the motel. There have been others, and she knew it. But we would never have divorced. I think a widower feels the loss of his mate far more than a widow. Women are so much more capable, and structured than men. I deplore the empty home after a day's work. Living with her was difficult at times, but it became a habit. I often wondered how it would feel to live alone. I can't say I like it. I have shared for too long now.''

"I don't like it either, but one can't marry on that account. I've had trial periods of live-ins but that didn't work. Some people are not meant for marriage, and the longer you wait, the harder it becomes. That goes for both men and women.''

"Thea, my final move will be to Guam, in the South Pacific. Why don't you give the matter some thought? Come to me for a holiday. We can play if by ear.''

"You're serious? You're asking me to join you out there?''

"Yes I am. I think we'll welcome the rest of our lives together. If we just give it a try."

Thea and Robert spent a divine long week together, and she almost gave him his answer before she left for Illinois. Their feelings for each other hadn't waned, if anything their relationship had a lot more substance. Robert and Valerie both drove her to the airport, and Thea promised him she would be in touch, but to give her time to make a decision.

Chapter Forty-seven

It was Thanksgiving day in 1983 and Thea appropriately cooked the turkey dinner at her flat in Highland Park, Illinois. She invited her girl-friend Ferne and her daughter, and son-in-law, and Ferne's only baby grandson to share this holiday.

It was 6:00 P.M. and they were about to indulge in the pumpkin pie when the telephone rang. Thea never answered the telephone while eating any meal, as she got distracted from her meal, and more often than most times, she never returned to eat. The phone persisted to ring at fifteen minute intervals.

"Maybe it's your son Marc, or even Robert from Guam," said Ferne.

"No I'm not expecting either of them to call," said Thea.

Finally with impatience Thea answered it. She heard a diminutive voice with a southern accent asking for Thea Travis.

"Who is this?" asked Thea.

"Happy Thanksgiving. This is your daughter, Fiona, calling from Missouri."

"If this is your idea of a joke, I don't appreciate it." Thea hung up the phone, relating the message to Ferne.

"Oh Thea, it is her. I told you she would find you someday. If she calls again, don't hang up, give her a chance to speak."

Exactly half an hour had passed, when the phone rang again. Thea waited a few seconds, preparing how she should handle this.

"Please, please don't hang up on me, I am Fiona. I got your unlisted number from brother Marc. He said you would probably be shocked, but that you would be thrilled to hear from me. I wanted to call you for so long, and today I thought it was time I contacted my real mom."

Thea was so overwhelmed at the exuberance of the little voice from a distance, she burst out crying, losing composure completely, while Ferne relieved her of the telephone.

"Fiona, I'm Mother's girlfriend of many years standing. As you can imagine your mother is unable to talk while we are here, but if you give me your phone number, she will get back to you, as soon as she is able to. I always told your mom, this day would come, but she never believed me. Your mom is one terrific lady, and oh how I've watched her suffer all these years, over your and your little brother's welfare. She has paid fully for her guilt, which she has now learned to overcome. Please be loving to her." On that note Ferne began to weep, and terminated her conversation.

"Hello Fiona, go ahead, I can talk now. Tell me everything, I'll listen," Thea said.

"I'm terribly sorry to have given you this shock. I have wondered so long about you; what you look like, if you were alive, and in this country, and if you cared about Philip and me. I'd like to meet you soon if it's possible."

"Where in Missouri do you live? I heard you were married and had a baby son. Tell me about them."

"My husband's name is Bruce, and my son, Paul, is two years old. Could you come for Christmas?"

"Normally my business wouldn't permit my leaving over the holiday, but this is far from a normal occasion, so I'll be there. The weather isn't good at that time, so the airports don't always function. I'll come by train. It's Poplar Bluff. I presume you have a train station?"

"Of course! But it will be a long ride, and an awkward time of night to arrive. But we'll meet you just the same."

"Fiona, take my address down, and write me a long letter, okay?"

After Thea put the phone down, she was in a state of shock. Ferne and her daughter washed up the dinner dishes.

"I still can't believe after all these years she has found me. I must call Lydia in London, and give her the news. Oh, the time difference, I have to wait until midnight to call her." Thea was too excited to sleep, so she waited till midnight and got her sister on the phone immediately. Lydia got hysterical, and couldn't ask enough questions about her niece. She reminded Thea to show Fiona all the correspondence that relayed between the lawyers over twenty years ago. Did Thea still have the letters? Yes she never did destroy them. The heartbreak she had put her mother through for the custody of her grandchildren that vanished from their lives, and she had been deprived of as a grandparent. This is not to say

324

it was much of a consolation after this length of time, but Fiona had to know she was very much wanted at the time.

On one of Chicago's bitter cold winter afternoons, Thea boarded the Amtrack train a couple of days prior to Christmas. The severe freeze delayed her departure by four hours. The chaotic crowds pushed their way toward the train, which had to accommodate the traffic from the airport which had come to a standstill. Thea couldn't sleep that night, for fear of missing her destination. She kept reminding the porter after St. Louis to inform her of her stop, which was originally to be at 2:00 A.M., now delayed to 6:00 A.M.

"Maybe the children would have given up on her, or maybe they will wait it out." The anxiety was inconceivable! The train finally arrived at Poplar Bluff at 6:30 A.M. The porter placed a footstool on to the iced platform for Thea to alight. "You get off here lady, but the station is ahead of you, you'll have to walk it. Here's your bag, be careful."

"Walk he says. I need a pair of skates." She rigidly stood for fear of taking a step. There wasn't a sign of the welcome she expected. The train moved away from the platform, and Thea noticed a solitary Nissan parked across the tracks. A handsome red-haired man came swiftly to assist her.

"Thea? I'm Bruce your son-in-law." He kissed and embraced her. "Fiona has fallen asleep in the car, she didn't think you'd make it."

"You should have asked about the delay. Then you would have had a good night's sleep."

"Oh Fiona thought she'd be too excited to sleep, wait until she tells you her story of trying to find you."

Thea had formed a concept of a heartwarming reunion between them, but instead Fiona hesitatingly scrutinized her. Thea broke the ice by saying "Well don't you have a kiss for me?"

"Sure. I'm kind of grouchy when I wake up. Specially as it's been such a long night. You are not at all what I expected."

"What did you expect? We do resemble each other don't you think?"

"My step-mom is a lot older than you, and I guess has more of a motherly image, I don't know, you're just not what I expected."

"What does your step-mom think about you finding me?"

"Oh! She knew I'd eventually do that. I knew when I was six years old she wasn't my real mother. I told her so. She kept you a secret all our growing years, Philip said I was crazy to look for you, and he's been spoilt by them, whereas I haven't. I guess she likes boys. What I don't understand is why we were split? Why did the Travises keep Marc and give us away? Don't you think all three of us should have been together? I didn't even know I had another brother. By the way, Bruce and I made a trip to Kentucky, and we met them all. It was Marc I wanted to meet. Maybe you can clear up the gaps in between so I can cope better.''

Thea hadn't prepared herself for this third degree so early in the morning. She hoped it would improve as time went on.

"How did you find me after such ages? I never thought you would. I'd feel a bit like Philip, uneasy of the consequences.''

"I was curious. You read about it in the papers, see it on TV, so why not me? A year ago I was working for the telephone company. I had access to the switchboard, and when I told my story to the girls I work with, we set about checking out the family name. My birth certificate which was given to me by my mom the day Bruce took me away from my home, specified the names Jason and Thea Travis. So I started with that. The doctor that delivered me is still at the Richland hospital, but he couldn't give me the information. So we worked on all the Travises we could find in the Virginia area. Finally it was a mutual friend of theirs that gave me Grandma Travis's number in Kentucky. When I called, I got brother Marc. So that's it!''

"Rather ingenious, I'd say,'' was Thea's reply.

She wasn't about to get her knickers in a twist, or be threatened with a guilty conscience. She had come too far for all that illusion. Bruce drove in the direction of his mother's home, so Thea could meet her and his step-father, and Paul, her new grandson.

His mom, Donna, had invited her part of the family for dinner that evening, to meet the newfound mother, Thea. There must have been at least twenty present. The men were seated at the dinner table while their women waited on them. There wasn't any form of alcohol served at any time. Glasses of iced tea and milk accompanied the meal. Thea stood around awkwardly, wondering where she should seat herself. When the men got through, in a regimental manner, they made room for their chairs to be occupied by their wives. This is when Thea had a plate placed in front of her. The men moved toward the family room, and Donna, the lady of the house, now catered to the women who were probably starved, but polite enough not to admit it. If chastity were absolute, then Thea was in its midst. The community here was Southern Baptist. Their lives were strictly in conjunction with the Bible. The Christian ethnic is centered on going out and converting others to the fold, feeding them, and enclosing them in structured belief.

On Thea's spiritual path, she associated this dogma with poorer countries whose inhabitants are in their first few lifetimes on this earth plane, and structure is just what they need. She incorporated different belief patterns that center on spiritual truth, away from churches and structured form. Everything you see around you, on the material surface is only a reflection of something that exists on the invisible plane. True, revolution is created by a few who see what is "true," and are willing to live according to that truth. To discover what is true demands freedom from tradition, which means freedom from all fears. Thea's early years in a Catholic convent, taught her very little of self. She revolted against the whole tradition of trying like the rest of them. She never initiated or followed a noble example. She was dependent on her mother, sister, and later Howard, all of whom were constantly crushed for fear of freedom of expression, yet she was referred to as the oddball. She was even expelled for this reason. Thea was never influenced by society, and she broke away from its conditioning. She had learned never to depend on a person, because there was bound to be fear on their part. By observing and struggling comes self-knowledge, and in this is the universe, which embraces all the struggles of humanity. So far life had had an astonishing way of taking care of her, because she never tried to be taken care of. She believed death is only the ending of something, and in the dying, there is a renewing. So this was a test in itself to sit among these God fearing folks, and to try not being judgmental. Especially when her daughter insisted that all those who are not "saved" would definitely go to hell! Well! To each his own. Thea's mother had once said, "Religion and politics never solved the issue and the least said the better."

Although Fiona radiated warmth and affection toward her mother, Thea couldn't help but observe her daughter's curiosity about her. Whereas Thea accepted her for what she was, a mystified twenty-one year old, unaware of her actions, with a tremendous zeal for life. Perhaps it was the different circumstances of their backgrounds and cultures that confused Fiona. She had said twice upon meeting, "You're not what I had expected."

In actuality the girl had opened up Pandora's box. After the initial discovery of each other had substantiated itself, Thea produced the private correspondence between her mother and the American lawyers in Chicago, which Thea had kept for nineteen years. Both Fiona and her husband, Bruce, absorbed and digested the sad contents the letters indicated. Fiona wept at her grandmother's despair, and of the unfavorable outcome it implied from both sides of the Atlantic. After she had gotten through reading a dozen or more letters, her comment was. "I could never have tolerated brutality, or lived with a selfish man. I would have long left Jason Travis. But I would never have married him in the first place. To think our future was determined by an alcoholic at the local tavern in Kankakee. What gave them the right to split three younguns apart? If Grandma Travis was in poor health and couldn't cope, what were my aunt's excuses? Philip and I earned our keep working on our step-parent's farm. They weren't the kindest to me, and they spoilt him. It says here in these letters Aunt Lydia wanted us. They had no right to give us away, when we had family that wanted us."

"Yes dear, but one cannot erase the past. You can only heal the pain it has left behind. Besides, forgiveness makes whole both the forgiven, and the forgiver. One learns to transform antipathy into sympathy."

"Well yes, we learn that in church, and I have tried to live my life accordingly, but I find it difficult to accept. It need never have happened."

"When we hold a grievance within our mind, we will always find someone to project it on, and we will be in a state of dis-ease when they appear. The ego will always try to give you a perception and say this is the way life is. The ego's interpretation is never correct. And when we learn to forgive it, we'll find out what life is really about."

Fiona queried her mother again and again, as though she were speaking a foreign language. Which to her it was. *Oh the pity of it all*, thought Thea. *Now that we have found each other after all this time, we have so little to say.*

It wasn't the generation gap, or the peer pressure, Thea just wasn't what she had expected. It was because she was uncertain of who and what, she was and the validity of her beliefs. Fiona had to work on her self awareness first, and free herself of the frustration over her mother being "saved."

After Thea had spent two weeks with her newfound daughter, she continued the platonic relationship on an impersonal basis. Each one of us is unique and individual and must find his own level of consciousness.

Two years after Fiona had found her mother, the energies generated toward the reunion of the siblings. The four children all met for the first time at Thea's apartment in Highland Park, Illinois. Laura, the eldest, flew in from the East, and was met by Marc at O'Hare airport. She was overwhelmed with joy at the sight of him, now a young man. They hugged each other warmly.

Fiona and Bruce drove in from Missouri, accompanied by Philip and his new wife Krystel. The acquiescence of four adult children meeting with spontaneity, amazed Thea, as she observed their acceptance of each other.

"I never imagined having a little sister, I've never had anyone," was Laura's exclamation.

"Leave it to our Mom to be diversified."

They compared their looks in the living room mirror.

"How come I'm so tiny?" said Fiona, "And so much darker, with slant eyes, and high cheekbones. While you're so fair and tall, with enormous hazel eyes, and such long lashes. Are they your own?"

"Of course silly, my dad is tall and he's English. But I think I favor our mom, too. I have her expressions, and her shaped eyes." Bruce clutched her neck from behind.

"You're as tall as I am. It's nice to look you in your pretty eyes."

That didn't go down too well with little sister, who in her pregnant condition was terribly sensitive. She pouted.

"Women will be women, no matter what" was big brother's answer.

Philip was the clown act of the four.

"Want to hear somethin'? I carry your picture in my billfold, to make Krystel jealous. She's always thought you to be my high school prom date. I told her you were my half-sister. She said I didn't have one. See, here she is, and her picture doesn't do her credit. Come here woman, you're gorgeous."

"You're nuts, but you're lovable. You look most like your dad, though I didn't know him."

"Gee! Consider yourself lucky. I didn't either. My dad and mom live in Missouri. They are okay people and I love them." Laura got quiet as she caught Thea's expression.

"I have a mom, too. She resembles my real mom here a lot. She's a good lady, and I love her."

"What about you, big brother?"

"I call our grandma Mom, but this lady here is my mom, and I love her."

"I love you all," was Thea's reply.

329

There was silence. Laura the oldest, didn't realize her mother was just getting acquainted for the first time with all her children. She was cautious of all the attention the others were getting. It was treated like one big party, as they all let their hair down, with rock and roll music, plenty of food, and cases of beer. Thea joined them in the celebration, and quite emotional for what she had conceived for half a lifetime had at last materialized.

Thea had got flashes of insight, and a new way of looking at herself. She had been a victim of her beliefs long enough. She now had the desire to live life to its fullest. She had asked herself why am I the way I am? She was made up of two people. There was the aggressive side of her, which reacted to the senses, this was the personality, and it behaved like a machine. The other part of her was passive, the essence of which was the observer. The passive part waits and sits back, it doesn't surface until later, when she questions herself. Who am I?

The past personalities comprised of her father, mother, and sister were all labeled by her. Her sister was the first born, the older child can feel robbed of her parents' love, by being made to feel the elder and more responsible. Hence she becomes an extrovert or an introvert. The younger child can clutch on to being the younger and the weaker. It's psychological.

Thea had never felt threatened by her sister, she took the role of the parental image. However both girls were equally loved by their parents. Thea behaved negatively, so as to receive the attention she craved. She had her father's personality, and a lust for life. However over a period of years, she had geared herself into a pattern of mistrust of the opposite sex. No matter how men had reacted to her, she feared they would eventually walk out of her life. Subconsciously she attracted them, but because of her uncertainty, she searched for inadequacy in them, and set them up to suit her many moods until she ran them off, or she did the running herself. It was based on her wrong interpretation. Finally when she had got tired of the same stage, and different actors, her passive side emerged and she had the will to succeed. She now centered with her true self, and not the personality. Because of her early misconceptions, she was now aware of consciousness, and was in the process of dismantling her computer machine, and beginning to be the person she truly was.

"I love you, means when I am with you, I'm in touch, with the beautiful capable, and lovable, parts of me."

To quote the following by A. Martin Wuttke:

"As long as we are dependent upon people or circumstances to provide us with personal fulfillment and happiness we will remain disillusioned. True fulfillment lies in the realization of 'the kingdom of God' within our own individual consciousness. Our seeking for this realization has often been compared to a journey home.

"Our lives are a search; a search for happiness, freedom and fulfillment. What we base our success upon varies. Ultimately, when we look past all transitory and erroneous values and accomplishments, we discover that the only true fulfillment lies in our individual relationship with, and awareness of, our Higher Power. To experience this is the purpose of life, the purpose of our existence. We may search, try this or that path, fulfill all our desires, but ultimately all our seeking will be to no avail unless our seeking turns within. The self-limiting concept of personal ego expands to the larger experience of our true Self. The spiritual faculties awaken, perception becomes clear and our thinking more orderly. Outer circumstances unfold to align us with our highest good, fulfilling all our worthwhile needs on time and in abundance. We discover the truth of our Identity; beyond our names and personalities, beyond all seeming separation, we have one common Ground and that is the Reality—the basis of all life and all Being. When we consciously experience and live out of this awareness we function as conscious participants with God's evolutionary intention, fulfilling our soul destiny and living in harmony with all life."

(The above quote is from an article that appeared in the *Truth* journal, which is published by the Center for Spiritual Awareness [C.S.A.], P.O. Box 7, Lakemouth, Georgia. A. Martin Wuttke is presently working as director of Biofeedback and Medilcon Therapy at a northeast Georgia hospital for addictions and eating disorders. He is also director of Northeast Georgia Hospice and president-elect for the Georgia Biofeedback Society. He conducts seminars and lectures regularly on stress management, medilcon, and topics related to purposeful living for various groups and associations around the country. Pamela Constance follows his work closely in relation to C.S.A., where she has found fulfillment over the last few years with Roy Eugene Davis, its founder.)